The Gryphon Generation
Book 3

Colony

By Alexander Bizzell

3

I can't thank you all enough. Here's to all my fans, friends, and Kickstarter backers alike that made book 3 possible.

Hey Trevor Cooley, you're the MVP for helping me through this once again. Without this guy, the book wouldn't be a shining example of what true literature should read like. Im kidding. But Trevor has no reason to be this good of an editor. He helps me through all the stages and points out any inconsistencies in the story. Thanks for putting up with me!

I want to thank every other gryphon author out there as well. I am astounded by the different flavors and varieties they create. Jess. E Owen and Larry Dixon, you all keep on doing what you do best. Thank you for inspiring me.

This stunning cover was done by Cyfrowa "Red-Izak" Izabela once again, and I am constantly honored to have her design my covers.

Book 3 has more works of art than ever before. Many of these pictures were crafted by "Killioma" and the magazine images you find are from "KairiWolfArt"

Cover layout was done by Scott Ford.

Kickstarter backers

Elaq

DUANE EISELE

Christian Largent

Aaron Garrett

onix331

Tiercel

Ricardo S

Cameron Schmitt

Meghan

Shawn Dean

Vale Nagle

Phil Maddox

Birdy the Gryphon

Byron

Adam Gould

A. L. Freeman

Taz

Jay Doran

Andrew Armstrong

Kitt Gryphon

Jere

Willow Mammoth (Magi)

ScaniGryph

moriar

Birdghost

Takel

Hamzah

Skogskisse

Jessie

roscar

Brian John

Ethaes

Gyro Feather and Saewin

Alex Hakenson

AingealWroth

Siren

Tser

Alia

TaranGryphon

J. Park

Ryan

Nivatus

Crissdragon

Kaaryn Wanderski

Purple_Link

Brittany "Obsydian" Vance

Roz Gibson

Baltor

Bryan David Cutshall

Bombird

Tim moore

Fognom

Jessy Smith

Dan

Stinger21

Gawain Doell

Saylor

OnyxtheSnowy

Justin Fortin

Jadehellcat

Gam3rPro64 Justin Johnson

Karl Morini

Leon Jack

un-nain-connue

Stephanie

Megan Jones

Jeremy Drechsel

Teron Gray

Colony

Shade the Raven

Aurigryphon

Michael R. Wells

Reese P

mark grandi

Nicholas Wells

Jedidiah "Kalenai" Davis

James Brackett

Melissa Sumby

Patrick Jesse (Parca)

Val Mumphree

Table of Contents

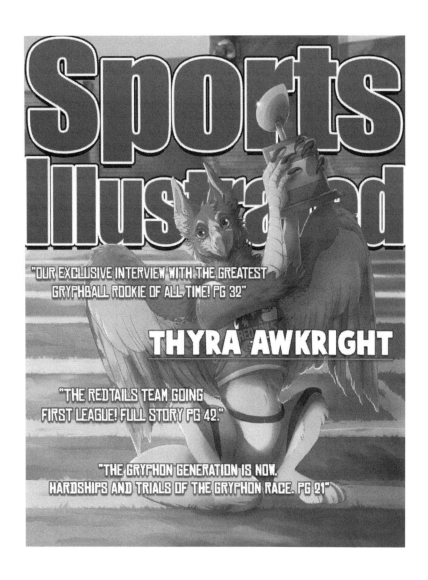

Chapter 1 Through Glass

The muffled sounds of rain battering against the windows drifted through the coffee shop. That soft roar, combined with the sounds of quiet conversation, clicking of keyboards, and the dull thrum of a bean grinder caused Thyra's eartufts to twitch. The rich aroma of fresh roasted coffee was heavy in the air.

Anthony sat across from her in a corner booth, staring out one of the windows, lost in thought. Even though he was essentially Thyra's father and the creator of gryphons as a species, he looked to be just another man dressed for the cold, dreary weather outside. The soft gray light from outside shone on the elderly man's strangely perfect complexion, smooth save for the heavy crow's feet in the corners of his eyes. His short, peppered hair was slicked back and showed no signs of balding.

Thyra cocked her head. It seemed like a dream. This man who was so important in her life, yet so absent, sat nonchalantly across from her. He was the missing puzzle piece in her life, and she desperately wanted to ask one of the thousands of questions stirring in her mind but could not find a way to begin.

As Thyra studied him for a moment, a quiet conversation at a table adjacent to them caught her attention. She heard her name and looked to the couple that were speaking. They were staring in her direction, but as she made eye contact with them, they immediately looked away. Their reaction was irritating, but it was not surprising that people would talk about her. She had become fairly famous in recent weeks, and there were a number of things the couple could be conversing about. It could be gryphball related or have to do with the recent 'murder' of the Gathering's leader, or her supposed relationship with the Sabertooth Slasher.

Thyra chose to ignore them, reaching down to undo the button on her light rain jacket. "They really turned the heat up in here," she said to break the silence.

Anthony seemed to break away from something in his mind and looked back with gleaming green eyes, the same color as Thyra's. "Indeed. Would you like help with your jacket?"

"No thank you. This one is pretty easy to take on and off." She unclipped the two latches on her shoulder blades, letting the jackets wing slits fall open and allowed the garment to slide off. She placed it next to her on the bench.

"It's simply amazing, really. I imagined clothing amongst other common items would be eventually be catered to gryphons, but the magnitude of how far we have come…" Anthony trailed off, again lost in thought.

Thyra opened her beak to question him but saw that his eyes had flickered towards her husband. Johnathen had just turned away from the front counter after thanking a barista and approached the table with a small tray.

"Alright! A latte for Thyra." He handed a wide mug over to his wife. "One for Anthony." Johnathen handed over an identical mug to the older man. "And a black coffee for me." He sat down his cup along with a cinnamon roll.

"Do you really need all that sugar, John?" Thyra jabbed with a slight grin. Johnathen chuckled and placed the empty tray down on a table. He grabbed the cinnamon roll and looked at his wife before taking a big bite. "It'll make you fat," Thyra continued, bringing her mug up to her beak.

"No, it won't. I'm fine with a few sweets. You're just jealous that you can't have any because of your gryphball diet," Johnathen said with his mouth full of the doughy treat.

"I know you're not about to complain about my figure," Thyra said, eying him as she sipped from her latte, messing up the little leaf pattern floating on top. As she sat the mug back down, Johnathen began to grin.

He pointed at her beak and picked up a napkin. "You got a little froth there, hun."

Thyra took the napkin with a huff and returned her gaze to Anthony, who was clearly entertained by the whole interaction. She wiped her beak as Anthony sipped from his mug and cleared his throat.

"I wouldn't have thought that gryphons and humans would live together so peacefully," Anthony commented.

With the mood lightened, Thyra felt more comfortable and it seemed Anthony did too. Her mind began to race once more as the questions began to resurface once more. Now the only question was where to begin?

"Then, what did you think would happen? That they were just going to live on their own or not live at all?" Johnathen inquired, saving Thyra the trouble of asking herself. "What was the goal when you set out to create them?"

Anthony's smile disappeared as he looked down at his cup. It was a heavy question, one that everyone had been asking since the existence of the first gryphon was revealed. People always speculated about the true meaning behind gryphon creation, but Thyra and Johnathen sat across from the person that was essentially the god of gryphon kind in a quaint coffee shop, inside a small town of Georgia.

"Ah, the age-old question we have all been asking ourselves. What is our purpose? What does it all mean?" Anthony took a deep breath and leaned back in the booth. "Some turn towards religion for answers, others turn to science, and the rest of them don't worry themselves with such existential questions."

Johnathen put down his cinnamon bun and cleaned his hands with a napkin. "I'm not asking about us as humans, I'm asking about my wife's kind, the gryphons. Why?" Johnathen's voice remained calm and composed, but what little cheerfulness that had been at the table was cast away as the tension grew.

Anthony remained silent for a moment more, seeming to analyze his response. "Why do we do anything at all? It's because we can. I knew I could successfully create a gryphon, and was able to pull the funding together to do it. The result of decades of research and hard work is sitting next to you today." Anthony stared into Thyra's eyes, not with coldness or calculation, but with warmth and love. "I played god and created something nature did not intend to exist. And yet I don't regret anything."

"Well, I suppose I should thank you for bringing the love of my life here," Johnathen commented. Thyra beak-grinned and pressed her side up against him. Johnathen reached an arm around her. "Still, I'm curious about the funding and the purpose of gryphon creation. I understand about egos and accomplishing personal goals, but others have to believe in those same goals. Last time I checked, there was an estimated ten billion dollars spent on gryphon research in the United States alone before the labs shut down," Johnathen paused for a moment to study Anthony's body language. The elderly man seemed uneasy but not unprepared for such a question. "You had to sell your idea as a product at one point to get funding. Was it for the military?"

"Not at first, but eventually we had no choice," Anthony admitted.

Thyra's eartufts pinned back as she sat back in her seat. It was not easy to hear that her kind had begun as nothing more than a service or a product, and even harder to hear that they had been intended to be sold for killing machines. A killing machine like Anfang.

"So that's where Anfang comes in…" Thyra said softly.

Anthony nodded and sipped from his cup. The rain patter against the windows slowed, and she could now hear the smooth jazz playing across the speakers.

"I'm guessing it wasn't your plan, but when funding was low, you had to sell Anfang to the military," Thyra continued. "And since he was your first prototype and was essentially a failure, it was easier than selling me."

"You sum it up simply, albeit harshly," Anthony responded. "But I assure you, the decision was not easy. I couldn't give you over to them, Thyra. You were perfect, still are," Anthony pointed out, but still Thyra's eartufts remained flat.

She clicked her beak with agitation and shook her head. "But you still sold him off like you owned him. And now look at what he became!" Thyra's voice grew a little at the end, causing curious people to look in their direction. Her hackle feathers were rising, and she had to fight to keep them down. Johnathen ran a hand down the back of her head, earning a sigh from her beak.

"If there had been any other way, I would have taken it," Anthony explained and caught Thyra's eyes. She knew he was not lying. "Everything I've ever done is for you and all of the gryphons everywhere. You are all my children, and I love you just as any father would."

Johnathen shifted uneasily in his seat and cleared his throat. "Back to the main question. How did you get the funding in the first place?"

"Gryphball," Anthony said, turning his attention to Johnathen. "Many of the investors I initially received money from were owners of NFL, NBL, and NBA teams. They were starting to see a decline in profits, and I proposed a new sport for a new species."

"Just like that? You just came up with the sport and told these people they would own stakes in this new sport if you were successful? Seems like a hard sell. Not only making gryphons, but also convincing this new intelligent life to play," Johnathen said. It certainly was a wild jump and Thyra could not believe that billionaires would willingly invest in this man's dream.

"It wasn't easy, but I was able to convince a handful of them to invest. Introducing them to footage of you was helpful," Anthony explained. He paused, looking over to the door as another couple entered the coffee shop. "Now convincing gryphons to play, that's a different story." Anthony sipped from his cup and looked to Thyra once again. "That was something I had to believe would come naturally. Any intelligent life enjoys playing games in some form or another, and with any predatory species, it's engrained in their DNA to chase, fight, and take what they can from others of the same species."

Johnathen was confused by Anthony's explanation, but before he could ask, Anthony continued. "Have you ever been to the beach and thrown a french fry to the seagulls? The one that catches it will instantly fly away, and many others will chase after it. They will fight one another for it until it is gone. That's one example. Hawks will relatively do the same thing. If one hawk comes into another's territory, they will fight and give chase until one surrenders and leaves the area."

"So you hoped we would be groomed to play. You hoped you wouldn't have to force us," Thyra surmised. Anthony nodded and ran his fingers around the mug he held in his hands.

"That was the hope. I was successful with you, and soon after I helped the other labs with their-." He paused. "For lack of a better word, production. It was why I was gone constantly. Unfortunately, while I was helping another lab in Europe, my original lab lost its funding. That was when we decided to speak to the military. They were extremely interested in the research of gryphons. It's why I had to give them Anfang. Soon after, the military took over my original lab, and I quickly made the decision to get you out. I gave you to your foster parents who were two head researchers at the lab. They were of a like mind with me and couldn't continue with their work knowing it would end up torturing gryphons and turning them into killing machines."

Thyra had a tough time absorbing all the information. She stared down at her cup as the hard question came to mind. "Did you continue and help the military?"

It took a moment for Anthony to answer. "I had no other choice. I oversaw Anfang's research and development," Anthony sighed and rubbed his eyes. "I didn't want to, but if I wanted to continue, I had to do what they demanded. I helped make him the monster he is today, but it was for the greater good. The money that came in went to funding the other labs, creating more gryphons, and paying the foster parents for taking care of the gryphons. These new parents had to raise a brand-new species, introduce them into society and home school them. Not a cheap service, I remind you."

Thyra frowned. Part of her was angry with Anthony for letting the military walk all over him. His open admittance of what had been done to Anfang was a bitter pill to swallow, but she knew that Anthony had the best intentions for gryphons in general.

Anthony pushed away his empty mug and folded his hands down on the table in front of him. "Those families raised gryphons as their own children and brought them together to play gryphball. It started small with private tournaments, but once the public caught onto the small games that were happening all over the world, it blew up like wildfire to what you see today."

The gentle jingle of the front door bell rang out as another person walked through. Anthony turned to see who it was, and relaxed. Thyra raised an eye ridge suspiciously, wondering why he was so uptight. She had seen him as calm and composed the entire hour they had been at this coffee shop, but as time went on, Anthony seemed increasingly nervous.

"So, why are you here now?" Thyra asked. Anthony looked up not saying a word. She let out a heavy breath through her nares. "Why did you come to tell me this, decades after I was made? What's changed all the sudden?"

"I can't answer that right now, but plans are in motion for what is to come," Anthony responded and pulled out his cellphone. Thyra grew agitated. She had every right to be confused and upset. Dodging an important question like that was unacceptable. Her wings resettled and she cleared her throat.

"Why?" Thyra asked again, not bothering to stop her hackle feathers from rising. "Why would you keep me, keep us, in the dark for so long?"

Anthony did not answer right away, swiping along the touchscreen device for a minute, and then placed the phone down on the table. He took in a deep breath and exhaled, shaking his head.

"I'll tell you in due time, daughter." Anthony stood up and pulled out his wallet. "I will be in touch," he said and pulled out a hundred-dollar bill to set down on the table.

Johnathen and Thyra slid out from the booth and stood with Anthony. As much as she wanted to, she could not make a scene and try to stop him from leaving. The couple stared back at Anthony awkwardly for a minute, and a smile appeared on his face.

He reached out to shake Johnathen's hand, grasping it firmly. "Pleasure meeting you. Do take care of Thyra."

"Um, a pleasure meeting you too," Johnathen responded.

Anthony reached to Thyra's eartufts and gave them a gentle rub. "Don't worry. You'll see me again soon."

Thyra opened her beak to respond, but Anthony had already turned and began to walk away. Johnathen and Thyra watched as Anthony made his way towards the exit. Two people garbed in black coats and gryphball hats stood as Anthony walked past, following along with him. Thyra noticed one of them took a glance back at her, and she saw the woman's face. She had short blond hair and a thick scar that ran along the left side of her neck up to her earlobe. Thyra's memory flashed as she realized she recognized the woman, but she could not remember from where.

"Thyra?" Johnathen said quietly.

The gryphoness pulled her eyes away and looked up at her husband. "Sorry. I spaced out for a minute."

"Yeah, that was a lot to process. And then he just gets up and leaves?" Johnathen pointed out.

"I don't understand it either." Thyra sighed and looked at the table again. Her eartufts perked up as she saw Anthony's cell phone lying on the table. "John, he left his phone."

Johnathen reached across the table and grabbed it. He looked at it for a second and swiped his finger across the screen. The phone clicked as it unlocked. "Somehow I don't think he left it here on accident. He doesn't even have a password set for it."

He put the phone in his pocket and started to put on his coat. Thyra grabbed her own jacket and sat on her haunches to garb herself. "I think you're right. But what could be on it?" she wondered, working her wings through the openings and buttoning the jacket.

Johnathen walked towards the exit and glanced around to see if anyone else was watching them. There were a few curious eyes, but they could have been just looking at Thyra. That happened more and more lately.

"I don't know. But I think we should look at it closer when we get back home." Johnathen exited first and held the door open for the gryphoness. She strutted out of the café and out into the cold.

The rain shower that had been pummeling the area all day had finally ceased, but the wind still blew steadily. The streetlights' warm orange glow reflected off the wet concrete. The streets were less busy at night then they were in the day in this part of town. People passed them on the sidewalk, seeming to pay them no mind. Thyra and Johnathen walked side by side and watched as cars drove by, splashing in the puddles along the edges of the street.

"I need a stiff drink after that," Johnathen said and turned a corner.

More high-rise buildings lined this road with a multitude of signs hanging off the sides of the structures, advertising business names and restaurants. Cars slowed to a crawl at the stoplights and idled loudly. Loud bass could be heard from one or two of the cars as Johnathen and Thyra stood at the corner, waiting for the crosswalk light to turn.

"There's a liquor store about a block away from Aadhya's apartment," Thyra suggested. The crosswalk light turned green, and they crossed it together. People that passed watched Thyra curiously now, probably wondering why the gryphoness would be walking along the ground instead of flying above.

"Oh, I know. I already stocked up, and got some other groceries," Johnathen replied. "The only thing that was difficult was finding Aadhya's special store to get the tea that she wanted." They walked down the street and turned the last corner. "I couldn't understand anything the people at this store were saying. They had thicker Indian accents than she does. Thankfully, she wrote what she wanted down, and I didn't have to talk to them much."

They approached the apartment building and entered the cramped lobby. It was sparsely decorated with a couple of chairs and some run of the mill paintings that would not be out of place in an Ikea catalogue. Johnathen pressed the elevator button and leaned against the wall.

He crossed his arms and stared up at the ceiling for a moment. "I didn't think I would live in an apartment ever again."

"I know how much you hate apartments," Thyra said, and sat down on her haunches next to him. The elevator hummed and then dinged as the doors opened. They stepped inside and Thyra pressed the correct floor with her foretalon. "I remember you complaining about having to live in so many dorms during college, but this is temporary. Just until we get our feet back on the ground."

The elevator buzzed to life again and began ascending. Johnathen nodded. "I know it is, and I'm really thankful that Aadhya made room for us. I was just thinking out loud is all."

Thyra exited first as the doors opened onto their floor. Her eartufts perked as she heard conversation from down the hall. They approached and saw the door to Aadhya's apartment was cracked. Thyra froze and looked up at Johnathen, "What's that about?"

"I don't know," Johnathen said and took a step ahead of her, taking the lead without thinking. He entered first and looked around the crowded living room. Antonio, Rachel, and Aadhya all sat around the table, sharing drinks. The group of gryphons all paused their conversation to look at the couple.

The small kestrel gryphoness slammed her beer can down and hopped up on the table. "Well? Spill the beans!" Rachel squawked.

Chapter 2 My Monsters Are Real

A cold gust picked up, rustling what leaves remained on the trees. The bitter air caught under Anfang's mangled feathers and shook him to his core. He cursed under his breath and wrapped his leathery wings tightly around his body, desperately trying to shield himself from the unforgiving breeze.

The nights were getting progressively colder and it was becoming hard to sleep. Anfang's crop lurched, squeezing tightly in his abdomen; a painful reminder that it had been days since his last meal. He'd never needed to support himself before. His hunting skills were non-existent, and to his shame, it showed. The only meals he had consumed since beginning his life on the run had been roadkill; meals for buzzards. He was so famished that it did little to hurt what pride he had left.

Anfang's eartufts perked as a car slowly drifted by along the desolate road. He watched from high in a tree, waiting for some critter to run in front of it but nothing came. He was too weak to attempt another catch himself. All of his previous strikes had missed their mark, and ended with him tumbling along the earth. If he could not catch an animal when he was healthy and full, there would be no way to catch one now.

Anfang looked to the sky, wishing in vain to see the familiar shape of a gryphon, of Thyra. The sun was setting, casting a beautiful shade of pink and orange against the scattered clouds, so stunning that Anfang found himself lost in it. He allowed a rare moment of calmness overtake him.

Over the past week, Anfang had realized just how much of life he had missed while locked away in cages; the feeling of the wind under his wings, the smell of fresh air in the forest, sunsets, sunrises, and even the bitter cold. Of course, right now he could do without the cold. Of all the seasons for him to finally be free, it had to be winter.

The more he experienced in the wilderness, the more it opened up his eyes to the cycle of life and death. He had to eat to survive, that much was apparent. Unfortunately, his potential prey were skilled in their own ways.

If he was to survive on his own, he would have to get better at this, but he was afraid that was not going to happen. Rabbits, squirrel, and rodents alike avoided him with admirable speed. No matter how he changed up his angle of attack, they seemed to posses a sixth sense.

"I not die here," Anfang promised himself.

After all, he was a gryphon, a creature with sentience and intelligence way beyond these common mammals he hunted. Yet, the common mammals were besting him. He wondered how a human would do with these conditions. They were all so soft and fragile. Modern life meant comfort and relatively easy living. He doubted an untrained human could make it a week in the wilderness like he had.

Like any untrained and desperate human, Anfang had thought of returning to civilization. It would be the easiest way to find food, but he knew there was not a chance of him getting by without being spotted. His face had been plastered on every newspaper and television screen in the state, if not, the whole country. He considered risking it and making his way to a neighboring town, but knew he did not have the energy for another flight. No, he had to find food and shelter tonight, or risk not waking up tomorrow. Hopefully there was a vacant house nearby, but if it came down to it, he could fake a threatening display to get what he wanted from any humans he came across. After all, they were more afraid of him than he was of them.

He rose from his perch in the tree onto all fours, opened his leathery wings, and glided roughly down to the ground. He landed and fell to his chest, then took in a deep breath, so weak that his wings quivered from the short glide. He took a deep breath and proceeded down the two-lane road, desperate to see a desolate house around the next corner or hill, but as minutes turned to hours, his hope turned into frustration.

The moon rose higher in the sky, and temperatures fell further still. Every breath the beast exhaled turned to vapor in front of him. Malnourished, his shaggy coat of fur and feathers was not enough to shelter him from the bitter cold. He shivered and found himself tripping over his own limbs. His vision began to grow blurry, his heart pumping hard from just walking.

Suddenly, Anfang could not go on any longer. Try as he might, his limbs would not move. He collapsed.

"Is this it . . ?" Anfang said under his breath. Strangely, he felt calm. He accepted death's cold hand outstretching towards him, and closed his eyes. "Thyra…"

He was jolted awake by the loud sound of a car door slamming shut. Anfang opened his eyes and tilted his head to look up at a dark figure approaching him. Bright headlights of a vehicle showed the silhouette of a man standing a few feet away from him.

"Sir? Sir, are you ok?" the voice asked. A light shined at Anfang's face, and then away from him, checking the surroundings. "Are you hurt?"

Anfang could not respond. He did not even bare his fangs at the human. The figure yelled to another man behind him.

"Bob! Bob give me a water bottle out of the truck!" Anfang heard another slam of a door. Next thing Anfang knew, the man was leaning down next him, speaking softly and holding a bottle of water. "Here, take this."

Anfang opened his twisted mouth, the upper portion being a beak and the lower jaw a feline muzzle. The man poured the refreshing water in.

"Jim, back away from him. I think that there is the slasher," the other man said warily.

"So what? He's dyin' Bob. What we supposed to do? Leave him to die?" There was silence between them for a moment as Jim continued to pour more water into Anfang's waiting beak muzzle.

"I...I am what he say," Anfang responded weakly, but Jim did not back away.

"Yeah, I figured so. Just promise not to kill us for helpin' ya, ok?" Jim put the lid back on the empty bottle and handed it to Bob.

Anfang looked up, clearly seeing the man for the first time. Jim was an old man, wrinkled and bald with a gryphball cap on. He wore a pair of blue jean overalls and a thick camouflage jacket. "Anfang promise," he responded and shivered.

Satisfied, Jim nodded and noticed how cold Anfang was. He took off his camouflage jacket to blanket the beast and turned back to his friend. "Pull the truck on over. Just in case someone comes by."

Sighing, Bob got back in the truck and pulled it off on the side of the road. The yellow hazard lights blinked repeatedly as the truck's rear cab light came on. It took a moment for Anfang's eyes to adjust to the new bright light but he could see the two men clearly now, and they could see him.

"Your name's Anfang, right?" Jim asked. Anfang nodded in response. "Can you walk?"

Anfang took a deep breath and moved to lay on his chest. He slowly rose up, sitting on his haunches now. Anfang's head hung low and his limbs trembled. Jim placed a hand on Anfang's back, causing the gryphon to turn his head quickly. Jim pulled his hand back and watched the beast with careful eyes.

"I...sorry," Anfang replied. Being touched was something he was not used to. Physical contact from a human usually resulted in pain.

"It's alright. You're just tired and scared. Here, if you can get in the back of the truck, I'll take ya to the house, get ya fed up, and in a warm bed. How's that sound, Anfang?" Jim proposed.

Anfang's green cat like eyes looked into Jim's gray eyes for a moment. He had no reason to distrust the man, even though his instincts yelled at him. There was not one human out there that had ever helped him. It always ended up with him caged and abused. Unfortunately, he had no choice. If it were not for them, he would be dead on the side of the road in a matter of hours.

"I try…" Anfang said, struggling onto all fours.

Both men stood beside him, placing their hands on his sides to keep him from falling over again. Anfang stood at the tailgate of the truck and placed his foretalons on the back. When he could not make the leap himself, both men helped him into the truck bed. Jim closed the tailgate with a loud clank and opened up the driver's door.

"Just lay down for a couple minutes. We'll be home shortly," Jim said before closing the door behind him.

The truck rumbled to life, and started moving down the road. Anfang made himself as comfortable as he could in the bed. The dizzying movements from sudden braking and going around curves put him in a light-headed state. It was not long until the truck pulled off the main road and onto a gravel driveway. Anfang stood as the vehicle stopped and both men exited the cab.

"You still with us?" Jim asked, opening the tailgate again.

Anfang stood weakly and looked at the house beside him. It was quaint, but still large by human standards. The porch lights shone brightly onto the manicured yard surrounded by decorative flower beds. A well kept residence, as far as he could tell.

"Yes. Still weak," Anfang responded. Both men helped the stout gryphon off the truck bed and onto the ground. They led him onto the front porch and inside the house. The warmth greeted Anfang, giving him a moment of relief from the cold. His feathers and fur ruffled up, absorbing the surrounding heat. Jim led Anfang into the main living room as Bob walked over to the fireplace. A series of clicking noises followed until flames spewed to life.

"Here, sit for a minute, I'll go get ya somethin," Jim said.

Anfang collapsed on the soft carpet in front of the fireplace and let out a loud sigh. His eyes watched the blue and red flames flicker before him as the heat reinvigorated his body. He heard some mumbled conversation in the opposite room. The two men were speaking with a woman he had not met. He could not raise his head to glance back or investigate the source. They spoke for a minute or two, and then he heard the sound of footsteps. Anfang managed to raise his head enough to look back as Jim walked in with a woman in tow.

"Anfang, this is my wife, Debra," Jim said politely.

The gryphon looked at the female human cowering behind Jim. She was smaller than Jim by a good foot or so. Blond hair, blue eyes, and scrawny, she had every right to be afraid. It was not just some stranger resting in their own living room, but a vicious gryphon deemed a killer by local authorities.

Jim kneeled down next to Anfang and placed a bowl of piping hot stew next to his foretalons. He smiled. "Debra just made her famous beef stew this morning. I promise it's the best you've ever had."

Anfang looked at the bowl and grasped it with both gigantic foretalons. He brought it to his beak, and poured the contents into his mouth. He did not stop until the bowl was completely emptied. A euphoric feeling crept through his whole body as his crop was filled, causing his head to buzz.

Anfang set the bowl down and closed his eyes as energy returned to him.

"Well?" Jim asked.

"It good…" Anfang responded. He could not taste what exactly what was in it, all he knew is the stew was substance that he needed. He held his head high and looked to the couple blankly. "Why you help?"

Jim appeared taken back by the question. He scratched his scraggly chin for a moment. "Well, everyone needs help every now and then. They say what goes around comes around." Jim paused. "And it ain't no skin off my bones to bring someone in and give 'em left overs."

"But, I am bad," Anfang responded.

Again, Jim had to consider his response. They knew he was a criminal yet they had brought him into his home. Anfang rose to sit on his haunches, already finding strength from the meal.

"You want to turn me in?" Anfang questioned, his voice rising slightly.

Jim held out his hands and shook his head. "Not at all! We've all made wrong choices in our life. I don't got nothing to gain from turning you in. Relax." He sat down on a brown leather sofa and Debra did the same.

The gryphon turned his chest to them, watching them both for a minute. They seemed nervous, but still calm. Bob came walking in, holding a bowl himself. He read the room and stood for a minute, looking at the two.

"Everything alright in here?" Bob questioned. He was bigger than Jim, and could easily pose a threat. Anfang watched him carefully not saying a word.

"Yeah, just talkin' to this young fella here," Jim replied.

Bob did not completely buy into it, but sat down on a single seat opposite of them. He began eating his stew, watching them. "So what's your whole deal? You're some kind of messed up gryphon and wanna kill people for it?"

Anfang's hackle feathers rose up instantly, his talons digging into the carpet.

"Hey! There will be no disrespect in my house! Got it, Bob?" Jim said sternly, pointing his finger at his friend.

Bob waved his spoon in the air and leaned back in his chair before taking another bite. "Sorry. Just curious is all. All gryphons I ever met seem pretty calm, but…"

"But nothing. If Anfang here wants to explain himself, then he will. Until then, he's a guest in this house and you will treat him as so," Jim stated.

The room fell silent aside from the gentle licks of flames burning behind Anfang. He could feel the tension in the air even with his limited experience in human social interaction.

Bob scraped the bottom of his bowl with the spoon, finishing his meal, and sat the container down on a stool next to him. "This ain't got nothing to do with your meth dealin' cousin, does it, Jim?"

"Don't bring Doug into this conversation," Jim commanded. The tension in the room grew thicker, and Anfang seemed to be ignored for the time being. All the focus was on the two men. "But maybe it does. So what. I'm just a firm believer of second chances. Everyone deserves it."

"Second chance…" Anfang repeated. The group looked over to the gryphon sitting by the fireplace. "Everyone?"

"Everyone. I don't know your whole story, but I'm sure you're a good guy at heart," Jim responded.

Anfang looked down at his talons, unsure. His single eartuft folded back against his head as he thought. "I not sure. I try, but you humans…" He paused. "Humans only want me for bad things. They want to use me."

"What did they use you for, Anfang?" Jim asked curiously. The gryphon shook his head for a moment, trying to clear his thoughts.

"They want weapon. They want control. I give it to them," Anfang responded.

Jim nodded his head and tapped on his wife's thigh. "Hun, you mind grabbing us a couple beers? We're gonna be a minute."

Debra nodded and stood up to walk into the kitchen. Jim took off his gryphball hat and sat it down on the coffee table in front him with a deep breath. He leaned back into the sofa and thought for a moment, then looked back at Anfang.

"There's lots of terrible people in this world, son," Jim began. "But there's also lots of good. Not every man wishes malice towards their neighbor, but in this age, it seems like that's all you hear about. Some men are dealt with a shitty hand, and they have to play with it. All it takes is a push in the right direction and a good hand to make a decent person."

Anfang cocked his head. "A . . . good hand?."

Jim and Bob realized they were speaking foreign to him. "I'm referring to poker, a card game. Do you not know what poker is, son?" Jim asked. Anfang shook his head. "Well, that's not really important. What I'm saying is, not everyone is lucky with what life gives 'em, and sometimes folk gotta do what they gotta do."

Debra walked back in with a couple of cans and passed them around. Anfang accepted one being offered and held it in his foretalons. He watched as all three cracked the tops and drank from them.

Jim looked at him curiously. "It's a beer. You never had one before? Wait, you ain't underage, or at least I don't think so. How does that even work?"

"I not know," Anfang responded.

"Ah hell, not like it matters no how," Jim said and outstretched his hand to point at the tab. It was then Anfang realized the human was missing a couple of fingers on his left hand. "You just pull this here tab up, and it'll open," Jim instructed.

He hooked a talon underneath the tab and pulled up until the can clacked. Anfang's eartuft perked as the can hissed and foam poured out the top. He watched the other humans lift it and pour the liquid into their mouths. He imitated them and swallowed his first taste of beer. The slight fizzy bitterness took him by surprise and he ruffled up what feathers he had on his neck. The group laughed as Anfang shook his head, trying to wrap his mind around the flavor.

"See? Pretty good stuff huh?" Jim proposed.

Anfang looked unsure, but took another swig. It was somewhat refreshing with lots of wheat flavor, like bread, but extremely foreign. "Taste weird… Like bread water."

The room erupted into laughter again. Anfang had rarely seen a human laugh, especially a group of them. A warm fuzzy feeling crept into his chest, one he had not felt in ages. Joy. He was included and felt safe, for once in his life. For some reason, they had brought him into their house, shared their food with him, and made him feel welcome.

"Bread water. I'm gonna start using that for now on!" Bob said and stood. "Hey Jim, you want another can of bread water?"

"Hell yeah brother. Make sure it's ice cold too," Jim replied and finished off his can. Anfang babied his beer; taking small sips and feeling it fizz down the back of his throat. The room fell silent again for a minute. Bob walked back in and handed out another round of beers.

"So, Anfang," Jim cleared his throat to break the silence. He sat on the edge of the sofa. "You look pretty battered and torn up, no offense. I can see you've been through a lot, not just from your appearance, but I can see it in your eyes."

Anfang readjusted his leathery wings and stared into Jim's eyes, seeing a flicker of recognition staring back at him.

"I was in the Vietnam war, way back when. I don't talk about it, but I can always tell when a man has seen true hell. You said they used you as a weapon, and I know what that feels like." Jim held out his left hand and spread out his fingers. Two of them were nothing but nubs. "I got out lucky. A bullet took off a couple of these and struck me in the shoulder, but some of my brothers weren't as lucky. Yet, I don't feel any hate towards the Vietnamese for it."

Anfang sat for a minute, thinking it all over. He did not quite understand what Jim was implying, but he knew what soldiers went through. "It hard not to hate," Anfang replied. "I hate what humans did to me, what Matthew made me do."

"Matthew? You mean that crooked 'priest' that was murdered?" Bob asked from across the room. Anfang nodded his head in response. "And I'm going to assume you're the one that offed him?"

"Yes. I kill. But he the last human I kill. I promised," Anfang said.

"Well he deserved it," Jim chimed in. "He took the good Lord's name and tarnished it in every way possible. We should be thanking you," Jim said.

Anfang blinked in surprise. He had never been thanked for anything in his life and the first thing he was being congratulated for was killing someone else. "No. No thank you. No thank you for kill."

"Some people need to die, Anfang. The people that take advantage of the weak and kill others, they are the ones that need to die," Jim said.

"No!" Anfang's hand clenched, crushed his beer, spilling the rest of it on the carpet. The calm atmosphere between humans and gryphon suddenly left. Bob stood to his feet. Jim raised his hand to stop Bob, sitting still as a stone.

Anfang's protruding fangs ground against the edges of his beak. Deadly feline eyes stared intently at Jim. The single eartuft folded back against his head and hackles rose to attention. "All humans kill. They kill and kill and kill. Who to say who kill and who not kill?"

Jim was taken back by the question. He looked to Bob and nodded, motioning for him to sit back down. "I see your point," Jim said calmly. "No single man should say who dies and who lives. In society, we have courts to judge men for the crimes they commit. Most end up in jail for a long time, but sometimes they are sentenced to death."

Anfang realized the sudden outburst had frightened the group and he began to visibly calm himself. He looked at the crumpled and pierced beer can in his foretalons. "I sorry. I just tired. I try to learn."

"And I say you're doing a good job. But speaking of tired, I'm feeling exhausted myself," Jim responded. Everyone nodded in agreement and stood. "Anfang, you want to follow me? I'll show you to the guest room."

Anfang stood with them and looked to Debra and Bob. "Thank you." It felt odd to thank anybody, but knew it was the polite thing to say. They both wore a smile and nodded, even if it was just a show.

Anfang followed Jim up a set of stairs and down a long hallway. Jim opened up the last door on the end and turned on the light to reveal a small room. The space was restrictive, not even big enough for him to stretch his wings out all the way.

"Sorry about the mess, but we use it for storage mostly," Jim said and moved a couple boxes off of the bed.

Anfang walked over to a dresser decorated with framed pictures. There were a lot of hazy colored photographs of a young man in what looked like army uniforms. "Is this you?"

Jim took a deep breath and sighed as he finished moving the last box. He was clearly winded from just that little physical activity.

"Yeah. And that there was Joe, Jacob, Mitch, and Brian," Jim pointed to each one of their faces as he said their names. "Twenty-second infantry. Joe and Jacob never came home, died in combat, and Brian passed away about five years ago. Mitch and I are the only ones left." He grabbed a blanket lying on a long forgotten chair and flicked it out, creating a cloud of dust.

"Do…do you have bad dreams about it?" Anfang questioned.

"Yeah. The war was decades ago, but . . ." Jim paused for a second, and then returned to his task. "I can't tell you what I had for breakfast yesterday, but in my dreams I still see everything clear as day."

Jim finished making the bed and took a step back. Anfang took up what remaining space there was in the room, and had to move out of the way for Jim to walk by. "Well anyways, I hope you don't have nightmares. Sleep well," Jim said and closed the door behind him.

Anfang stood in the center of the room, finding himself alone once again. For the first time in a long time, he felt safe. He walked over to the light switch and flicked it off. A single wall night light was all he needed to clearly see the room as his eyes adapted to the darkness.

The gryphon hopped up onto the bed, causing the old furniture to squeak and groan under his weight. Anfang circled around and laid on top of the blankets, curling himself up. He took a deep breath of the conditioned air and closed his eyes to drift off into a deep, dreamless sleep.

Chapter 3 It's About To Get Heavy

Thyra and Johnathen entered Aadhya's apartment to find Thyra's gryphon friends sitting around the tiny table in the kitchen, looking at the couple. The three of them took up almost all the space available in the cramped makeshift dining room. The table was littered with bags of chips, beer bottles, a teapot, and a small Bluetooth speaker, which was currently playing an alternative rock station.

Rachel reached to the speaker and pressed it a couple of times, turning the music down. "Well?" she asked, the house cat-sized gryphoness cocking her head in curiosity. Her big black Kestrel eyes looked up at the couple, waiting for a response.

"Well, it was…something," Thyra replied. She felt Johnathen grab the coat from her back. He unclipped the button around her neck and pulled it off to hang it on the coat hanger next to the door.

"I am sure you feel relieved," Aadhya said, her massive form dwarfing the other gryphons in the room.

She sat against the wall on top of her favorite pillow and sipped from the tea mug. The black-feathered 'beard' hanging from the jaw of her beak dipped in the tea, and dripped. She politely picked up a napkin in a giant white-feathered foretalon and dabbed it clean. For the time being, she was free feathered. It was socially acceptable for gryphons to be without clothes around one another, as long as it was not out in public.

"I'm not sure relieved is the right word," Thyra said with a shrug and walked closer to her friends. The gryphons attempted to scoot closely towards one another, now sitting wing to wing.

"He was nice at least," Johnathen added as he took off his overcoat and hung it on the wall. He proceeded into the kitchen as Thyra continued the conversation.

"Yeah, he was nice, but he was just like, shrouded in secrecy the entire time," Thyra said.

"Was he able to answer your questions?" Antonio asked in his Spanish accent as he emptied another bottle of beer. The Harris hawk gryphon looked similar to Thyra, besides a couple details such as the noticeable yellow skin on his face. He wore an extravagant floral shirt that contrasted harshly with the natural browns and chestnut reds of his plumage.

"For the most part, yeah," Thyra responded.

Johnathen walked back into the room and passed a bottle to Thyra. She made quick work of the cap with the jerk of her beak. Johnathen leaned against the support wall between the kitchen and makeshift dinning area, since there was no room to sit.

"Okay, but what did he actually say?" Rachel began. "It's got to be important to you. I mean like, he's your father in a way, right? That's what you were saying when you suddenly left."

Thyra sighed. "I'm sorry about leaving so abruptly, but yes, that man, Anthony, is basically the creator of all gryphons. He's essentially my father, since he used parts of his DNA to make me, and Anfang too." The room fell silent, but for the radio playing quietly in the background.

"Does that mean all of us are connected through his DNA?" Antonio asked.

It was a good question, one that Thyra did not quite have the answer to. They were all created in different labs that spanned thousands of miles between them, but she and Anfang were the first successful experiments. She shrugged her wing shoulders.

"He really didn't go into detail, but the way he made it sound, yeah. Once he was successful with Anfang and I, he was hired to help all over the world, so he oversaw all the labs at one point or another," Thyra stated.

"Can we trust him?" Aadhya asked cautiously. She was right to bring it up. He seemed like a wealthy and powerful man, but he had stayed in the background until now.

"I think so. He doesn't have a reason to lie to me, especially after all these years of no contact," Thyra replied, though she still felt a bit uneasy about it. She had chosen to leave out the bit about Anthony having his own undercover crew with him.

"But why now?" Johnathen chimed in. Everyone turned their heads to look at him leaning against the wall. "I've been thinking about it ever since we left the café. It's the last question Thyra asked him, and we never really got an answer." Johnathen drank from his beer bottle before crossing his arms. He stared up at the popcorn ceiling for a moment. "He said something about having plans, and that he'd tell her in due time, but I have no clue what he meant."

"Johnathen, the phone!" Thyra perked up.

Johnathen smacked his forehead and placed the empty beer bottle down on the bar counter. "I swear my memory gets worse every day. How could I forget?" He reached into his pocket and pulled the phone out. "We're pretty sure he left this behind on purpose. Here, you guys go through it." He handed it over to Thyra and she placed it in the middle of the table. All the curious gryphon eyes were drawn to the screen.

"Here, I've got the smallest and most nimble talons here. I'll start digging into it!" Rachel said and swiped to unlock it. She placed it on the table for the others to see, and started opening up the few apps that were pinned on the screen. "Hmm, there's a passcode app that's apparently unlocked. It has a few random entries with what seems like passwords, but I don't know to what."

"I would deduct the longer passwords with the multiple character placements are for computer logins, or bank accounts," Antonio pointed out. "Although, there are several two digit number codes in a row, along with other four to six digit codes too. Codes to locks, perhaps?" Everybody nodded their head in agreement.

"But why would he hand these over to us?" Johnathen wondered.

The phone clicked and chimed as Rachel swiped through a couple more apps. She opened the navigation app, and saw the previous address entered in.

"Hey, maybe it has something to do with this?" Rachel stated and spread her short talons on the screen to zoom out the map. It showed the lower half of Georgia, with a pin dropped on the coast. "The location says, St. Catherine's Island."

"St Catherine's Island?" Johnathen spoke up. "I've heard of that place."

"What's so special about that island?" Thyra asked.

"Well, for one, it's off limits to the public," Johnathen explained. "But mainly, if I remember right, private foundations used the island to study conservation of endangered species, like the ring-tailed lemur."

"Like gryphons maybe?" Rachel chimed in. "I mean it sounds like to me there could be something that went on there. Like a lab!"

"I mean, I guess it's possible, but not likely," Johnathen responded. "Though people aren't supposed to go there, it's not guarded or anything. People have wandered all over it, and no one has said anything about finding a lab."

"But there's got to be a reason for this. I mean look at the location," Rachel said and pointed at the screen again. "It's put like, almost at the center of the island. There's no telling what's there!"

"I say it warrants looking into," Aadhya agreed. Everyone looked over to the vulture, shocked that she was agreeing with Rachel for once.

"Hell, if Addy agrees with me, then I say I'm onto something!" Rachel said with a proud fluff of her pale and black spotted chest feathers. No one could argue with that.

"I guess if everybody is on board, we could go look. It's only like three hours from here, so we could do it in a day," Thyra said. Everybody agreed.

"I'll drive y'all down as close as I can, but I can't fly to the island myself. And I'm not about to charter a boat to take me somewhere I'm not supposed to be," Johnathen said.

"I do not think that would be necessary. I believe I could carry you a short distance," Aadhya said. Everybody was taken back again. The suggestion was unheard of. Aadhya looked around at the odd stares and looked perplexed. "What? He is not too heavy."

"It is not that we doubt you, Aadhya, but…" Antonio paused, searching for the right words. "Humans riding a gryphon is unheard of for a couple of reasons, mostly because of the implication that if we allow them to ride on us, we are on the same hierarchy as a beast of burden."

"I am not prideful in that respect. Perhaps in a different scenario, I would feel differently, but Johnathen is my friend. My offer still stands, if that is acceptable to Thyra and Johnathen," Aadhya responded and looked to the couple.

"I'm fine with it. You're not hurting my feelings by letting John ride on your back," Thyra said and turned to look back at Johnathen. "What about you, hun?"

"I would be lying if I said I wasn't excited at the idea," Johnathen said with a grin. He stood straight and saluted Aadhya, earning a laugh from everyone. "Johnathen Arkwright, the first gryphon rider! I'll wear it like a badge of honor."

"Ok, ok calm down there, mister 'master of the skies.' I doubt you'd be the absolute first, but you can claim that if you want," Thyra teased. She shook her empty beer bottle above her head. "Be a dear for me, would you?"

Johnathen grabbed the beer bottle from Thyra's talons. "Of course, me lady," he replied mockingly and proceeded into the kitchen.

With everybody in agreement, the focus went back to the cellphone. Rachel tapped on the photo gallery. "Well, there's only like ten photos."

"Hey Addy! You want one of those drinks I made you the other day?" Johnathen called out from the kitchen.

"Oh, yes. That would be splendid," Aadhya responded.

"I didn't know you drank, Addy!" Rachel laughed and bumped wings with the towering vulture. "You know we should go out more often! There's this great bar that I know…"

"It is rare that I do, but the drinks Johnathen has concocted as of late are to my liking." Aadhya pointed back to the phone, pulling the easily distracted Kestrel back on track. "Only ten photos you said?"

"Oh yeah, well, they all look weird," Rachel said, and opened the first picture. "Like, what the hell do you make of this?" She pulled her talons back so everyone could see the image.

"It seems to be a pile of boulders, with several oddly-shaped trees surrounding it," Antonio said.

"Yeah, I can see that, but why have a nature pic on this phone?" Rachel asked.

"Let me finish, please," Antonio said. "What I find peculiar about it is how level and well maintained the grounds are."

Johnathen walked back into the cramped room with a hand full of beers and passed them around before returning to the kitchen.

"Ok, yeah I get your point. Why does a forestry area like that have a manicured lawn?" Rachel replied.

"Perhaps the next photo will help?" Aadhya said. Rachel swiped a talon across the screen. It revealed a photo of a huge metal door, although the lighting was terrible and made it difficult to see much else.

"It's a huge bunker door! Like, big enough to pull vehicles through if you wanted, but maybe it's underground. I mean the first photo was bright and sunny, but this one is all dark," Rachel said. "I betcha this is the lab's entrance that's in the middle of that island."

"That does add up," Thyra commented. They all nodded their heads and Rachel swiped again. This time, it was a photo of a long dark hallway. The passage was barren, with concrete floors and walls painted white.

"You can't tell me this isn't a frickin' lab! The evidence is all right here!" Rachel said excitedly as she scrolled through the remaining photos. "And look! There's also pictures of individual rooms in there. Some are big and some are small. All of them are concrete from floor to ceiling and its dark in there. And, a picture of a wall safe?"

"I bet that's what all those codes are for," Johnathen said as he walked back into the room. He leaned over Thyra and placed a crystal tumbler glass down in front of Aadhya on the table. "You said there was a series of two digit numbers earlier. That's gotta be the codes to that safe."

"If I was not intrigued before, I certainly am now," Aadhya stated. She grabbed the glass and poured the liquor into her beak. Her crest feathers ruffled up as she closed her eyes and trilled. "That is delicious. Thank you, Johnathen,"

"No problem. It's the least I can do for you after you let us stay here," Johnathen mentioned and sipped his drink as well.

"So it's settled! Tomorrow we head out to St. Catherines island," Thyra said.

Rachel sat back on her pillow. "Sweet. I'm excited! Let's see where these breadcrumbs Anthony left take us."

Thyra raised her beer and held it to the center of the table. "To discovery!"

"To discovery," Everyone repeated and clanked their glasses together.

"You found him?" Anthony asked into his phone. He was riding in the back of a vehicle as it traveled down an interstate. He stared outside the dark window, watching the trees and buildings go by. "I wouldn't have thought he would turn up this quickly... Ok. Gather everyone, but do not engage until I am there, understood?...Good. Stand by." He hung up and tossed his phone on the leather seat next to him.

Anthony took a deep breath and folded his hands together. "Amanda?"

The blond woman driving the vehicle gazed back in the rear view mirror. "Yes sir?"

"Looks like you will have your reunion sooner than expected," Anthony said.

A small smile crept on her face as she brought her attention to the road once more. She brushed her short blond hair back revealing a scar on her neck. The bright lights clicked on as she looked for the next exit sign.

"Where to?" she asked politely.

"Round oak," Anthony replied. "I haven't seen him since, well, since last I saw Thyra. Looks like I'm getting a family reunion as well."

A man sitting in the passenger seat typed away at a phone and placed it on a mount to the dashboard.

"Lucky for us," Amanda said as she waited for the navigation to calculate. The voice command came on and she pulled off an exit ramp. "Should I cancel the flight as well?"

"Yes. Just call my pilot in the morning. Tell him that it looks like I'll be staying here for a bit longer," Anthony replied.

"Very well, although, the announcement meeting is in a week, so please keep that in mind," Amanda warned. She waited for the light to turn green and proceeded across the bridge before getting right back onto the interstate heading the opposite direction.

"I am aware," Anthony confirmed and relaxed back into the plush seat. "It might be a little tight, but I'm sure I can pull this off in time."

"Sir, if I may ask," Amanda said as she set the cruise control. "Did you talk to Thyra about the colony?"

"No, the timing isn't right yet. I'm surprised none of the rumors have reached down here," he replied. "I figured everyone on earth would be talking about the rumor, but then again the colony is small and halfway across the world. Besides, America always seems to be in its own bubble."

"Do you think she will accept?" Amanda asked.

"She has to. She's intelligent, and the offer will be appealing. Especially since she just lost her home," Anthony said softly. "I just hope she makes her way to the labs."

"I believe you made the right choice by leading her there, sir." Amanda said reassuringly.

"I hope so. Maybe it will help answer her own questions and give her ground to stand on. Everyone wants to know where they come from, but gryphons actually have physical evidence," Anthony said. "You should have seen her eyes, Amanda. Confused, hurt, troubled, and scared. She may put on a front for everybody else, but I could really see how hard her past must have been. The little innocent gryphlet we knew is all but gone." He sighed and rubbed his tired eyes. "I shouldn't have left her in the dark for so long."

"You had no choice, sir," Amanda replied.

"I know," Anthony said.

"And what of Anfang. You think he will come quietly?" Amanda asked.

Anthony was silent for a minute, considering the options. He shook his head and stared out the window again. "I truly hope he does, but that remains to be seen."

VOGUE

12 POWER FOODS
EVERY GRYPHON SHOULD BE EATING.

GRYPHON FASHION
THE PROGRESS SO FAR.

*"How to match your
plumage to the right dress"*

AADHYA PATEL.
Indian goddess. Renowned gryphball superstar

Chapter 4 Are You Gonna Go My Way?

Anfang awoke, jerking his head to attention. His eyes darted around the unfamiliar room in a panic, but he relaxed as he found everything to be calm. He was not in a cage, nor did he see anyone standing before him ready to capture him.

It took him a moment to find his bearings, his heart still pounding hard in his chest. He was still in the guest room inside the home of his new human friends. It was the same as he remembered it, except for the light pouring in from between the cheap plastic shades. He let out a sigh of relief and uncurled himself, stretching out on the bed. It creaked under his weight. The old flip clock sitting on the nightstand showed eleven am. He had slept more that night than he had in a long time.

A door-shutting closed downstairs jolted him from his groggy stupor. He lifted an eartuft as he heard conversation downstairs. Curious, Anfang stepped off the bed and opened the door. He proceeded down the hallway and carefully down the stairs, talons softly tapping on the hardwood steps. He followed the voices to the kitchen and stopped before turning the corner. He could hear two male voices, but one was unfamiliar and did not possess the southern drawl that his new friends' voices had.

Anfang stepped into the kitchen cautiously and looked at the two men sitting at the kitchen table. Jim sat talking to the other man, but Anfang could not see his face. They were drinking coffee and carrying on in conversation. When Jim caught sight of the gryphon, he went silent, frowned, and looked away. Instantly, Anfang was on edge.

"Good morning, Anfang," the stranger's voice said. "You sleep well?"

Anfang froze in place. His whole body tensed up with his wings starting to spread in defense. The man turned around to look at Anfang with a smile. He felt a chill run up his spine as he stared into the man's green eyes, instantly recognizing them.

"Anthony?! What you do here?!" Anfang yelled and took a step back. He darted his head back and forth, looking for an exit.

Anthony held out his hand calmly and put down his coffee cup. "Anfang, its ok. Calm down, I'm not here to hurt you. I just want wanted to talk is all."

The door opened behind Anfang, causing him to jerk around to see a tall, suited man standing there. The man shut the door behind him, and stood to block the exit, crossing his arms in front of his waist. The only other exit was the kitchen door beside the table, right where Jim and Anthony sat. Feeling threatened and trapped, Anfang hunkered down and bared his curved fangs with a low growl.

Anthony sighed and sat back in his seat. "Please, just hear me out," he pleaded.

"No," Anfang retorted.

"I'm sorry, Anfang. Bob called the police and they…" Jim began.

Anthony held his finger up, silencing Jim. "Please, I don't wish to resort to violence. If I had wanted that, I wouldn't have waited patiently for you to wake up to talk with you. I would have sent an entire team here to contain you, but I didn't. So please, hear me out."

With his options limited, the beast eased up. His great leathered wings folded in, and Anfang took a more relaxed stance, although he was ready to react at a moment's notice. Anthony took that as a sign to continue.

"As our friend Jim here mentioned, I was tipped off by a colleague at the local police department. I don't know why this 'Bob' called the law on you, but I'm glad I am the first to respond. I don't want to see you behind bars, nor in chains any longer. Quite the contrary, I want you to come to the new gryphon colony with me,"

"Gryphon colony?" Anfang shifted his gaze from Anthony to Jim. He ground his fangs against the upper portion of his beak. "I not know this. How do I trust? Jim first human I trust. First time I trust human, and I…" Anfang paused, thinking for the right word.

"You feel betrayed?" Anthony finished.

Anfang snorted through his nares and glanced back at Anthony. "Yes. Betrayed."

"I know you must feel that way, but I'm sure Bob had his reasons. You can see that Jim here has a heavy heart about what is unfolding, but I explained to him that it is for the better. I can take care of you. You can make a new life in the gryphon colony and be happy. I honestly believe it was fate that…"

"Shut up!" Anfang yelled and stomped his foretalon with enough force to break the tile under them.

Both human's eyes opened wide, but only Jim flinched. Anthony reached for his coffee and took another sip from it. When he was finished, he leaned forward and rested his elbows on his knees, folding hands together. Several seconds ticked by, but Anthony did not say a word. He simply stared into Anfang's green eyes, waiting for the gryphon to say something else.

"I not trust you," Anfang said after calming down.

"I understand, but-," Anthony began.

"No. Shut up," Anfang commanded. His body screamed at him to leap out and kill everyone in the room to escape. The only thing stopping him was his promise to Thyra. He had sworn to never kill another person again. He wanted to be a better gryphon and live peacefully. He took a moment to try to put his thoughts together. "Why I trust man that hurt me? Why you come back after long time. Why you here?"

Anthony sat politely, watching Anfang question both the humans and himself. "May I talk?" When Anfang did not respond, he asked, "Do you feel remorse for killing others?"

Anfang looked away from the table and back at the man guarding the door. He took a deep breath. "Yes."

"There is good inside you, Anfang. I believe that because I created you, and a piece of me lives on inside you," Anthony said calmly. "You have the same emotional intelligence any human has. I've been looking for you, because I want to atone for my actions in the past. I want you to be safe, happy, and live a normal life, like other gryphons."

Anfang looked down at the cracked tile under his talons, overcome with confusing emotions. The emotion he knew best was anger and rage, but there was an olive branch being passed to him, perhaps the last one he would ever receive. If he threw it back, that would be the end.

"I try, but humans hurt me. They use me," Anfang said under his breath.

"I know, Anfang. I know. I was wrong all those years ago, but I had no choice. I was the one that signed you over to the military, and I've lived with that painful regret every day, but it's because of your pain that the gryphons live today," Anthony explained.

Anfang's eartuft rose to attention as he met Anthony's eyes. "You…You do this?" The gryphon bared his teeth once more and took a step forward. "You make me this!"

Anthony cursed under his breath, realizing he had picked the wrong words. He motioned to the man who was blocking the front door. "I did. I signed you away. I had to get the funding to continue my research. Without you, the gryphon project would have been canceled."

As Anthony began to explain, the sounds of talons behind Anfang caused the gryphon to break his concentration and look behind him. Another gryphon stepped into the living room. He had great leather wings like Anfang did, but no metal ports on his upper arms. This new gryphon was similar in size, coloration, and appearance to Anfang. The main visual difference between them was that it had a complete beak instead of the half beak muzzle, as well as military grade body armor strapped across the gryphons chest. It did not speak, but simply remained steadfast, ready for action.

"As I said, without you, Thyra and every other gryphon would not exist. I can't stress your importance. You've suffered enough. Now please, hear Joseph and I out," Anthony motioned for the other gryphon to speak. "This is Joseph. He is the lieutenant of the gryphon colony's guard."

Anfang turned his whole body around to face Joseph, his leathery wings still open and body posture poised for a fight. Joseph look unworried, simply staring back at Anfang with similar green eyes, although the glow they gave off was unnatural.

"Anfang, you have heard the proposal. Now, come with us, silently," Joseph said in a low grumble.

Anfang snorted through his nares and shook his head. "I not follow command from other gryphon," he retorted.

Joseph's stone expression turned to a grimace as he took his defensive stand as well. He looked up at Anthony, seeming to ask for permission. Anthony nodded. "Then so be it," he said and leapt at Anfang.

This military gryphon was incredibly fast. Anfang had just enough time to guard his face before he was struck in the scaled arm by Joseph's talons. The force knocked him off balance and sent him into the kitchen wall. His shoulders broke through the plaster with a loud smack. Plates and cups inside the cupboards rattled loudly.

Jim jumped out of his chair and backed into the corner, while Anthony remained seated, watching the two intently. Anfang felt his arm burn from the other gryphon's attack, but he recovered quickly. He screeched and readied himself again before leaping at Joseph.

The opposing gryphon stood on his hind legs, much like a human would, and caught Anfang's attacking foretalon. With a quick spin on his heels, Joseph pivoted and tossed Anfang like a ragdoll out of the kitchen and across the living room. The door crashed open as Anfang spilled out in a tumbling mass of feathers and leathery wings into the yard.

Anfang was shocked by the sudden move. He had never faced another gryphon with such power. He rolled back onto his feet and opened his wings fully. The afternoon sun burned in Anfang's eyes as he looked around. Massive black SUVs surrounded the yard, with a small gathering of people towards the outskirts. Many humans held their phones out, desperate for a picture or a video. Keeping them back were suited men, all looking like the man that was guarding the door. Anfang coughed as he found his breath again, and a surge of energy rose inside him.

Joseph calmly walked through the broken front door on all four feet. "Please, let us not make a spectacle," the gryphon said, making his way down the stairs.

A rare smile crossed Anfang's beak, and he laughed a deep, bellowing noise as he crouched with readiness. "A spectacle? Good. I not fight with gryphon this strong before. Come, make me stop."

Joseph paused in front of Anfang and turned to look at Anthony who now stood on the front porch. Anthony sipped from his coffee and placed it on the handrail. "If violence is the only thing he understands, then proceed. Teach him a lesson, but please, don't break anything he can't heal quickly," Anthony commanded.

Joseph nodded and turned around to face Anfang again, this time, wearing a similar smile on his beak. "With pleasure, sir."

He rose back up on his hindfeet once more, forming his foretalons into fists. He stood sideways, holding his fists out, and crouched slightly. Standing, the gryphon easily towered over any living human.

Confused by the sudden change in personality and stance, Anfang growled and leaped first. Anfang aimed for the throat with his talons, but Joseph was ready.

"Too slow," the well-trained gryphon said under his breath and sidestepped to dodge out of the way. He spun quickly and struck Anfang's face with a wing, blinding him for just a second, but that was all Joseph needed. He continued his fluid movement, spinning his body and raised his hindleg to kick Anfang squarely in the side.

Anfang felt his breath leave him as the thud of force echoed across the yard. The small crowd yelled in excitement as the beast struck the ground. Anfang growled again, this time struggling to recover.

He stood opposite of Joseph, and crouched again, chest heaving as it fought for air. In all his fights, he had never been hit that hard. Every hit from the gryphon's 'fists' felt like shotgun blasts to the chest.

"Are you done?" Joseph questioned and returned down to all fours once more.

"Never," Anfang said breathlessly and spit on the ground. It was painfully obvious this gryphon had been modified just as he had been, created for military use, but improved, drastically improved. Joseph could probably withstand bullets as he could. A talon scratch would be nothing more than a paper cut to him. Even if he were to land a hit, how effective would it be to a gryphon the same as him? Especially since he wasn't fully recovered from his bout with starvation.

Anfang realized his efforts were in vain, but the adrenaline was taking over. He was going to see this to the very end. "You have to drag me away."

Joseph shrugged his wing shoulders and rose back up on his hind feet again. "Then I will drag you by your deformed eartuft. Like a foolish kit."

Anfang saw Joseph stand on his hindpaws once again. The stance was curious, like the old fighting movies he saw. "What is this?" Anfang asked curiously.

"The Eastern humans call it Jeet Kune Do, or Aikido, but it has been altered for us creatures with six limbs. We find it highly effective against any opponent. If you come with me, then I shall..." but Joseph did not have time to finish.

Anfang leaped again. Joseph's eyes narrowed, and he caught Anfang's striking foretalon once again in his. Holding the attacking hand steady, Joseph slid to the side, and twisted his own talon sharply. A loud crack rang out with Anfang's scream of agony as his foretalon twisted at an unnatural angle.

Anfang fell flat on his chest and found Joseph's foretalons on the back of his head. The weight of the opposing gryphon on top of him was crushing him into the earth, and he felt the gryphon could crush his skull with ease.

"I do not like being interrupted!" Joseph yelled loudly, deadly sharp talons digging into the back of Anfang's head.

Anfang's wings flared open and began to flap, desperate to get away. Joseph stepped on one of stretched wings with a hindpaw, pinning it to the ground. Anfang squawked and ground his curved fangs against his beak.

The stronger gryphon hissed and squeezed his talons even harder against the back of Anfang's skull. A trail of blood began to draw down his neck, and drip onto the grass bellow. Joseph leaned his beak down to whisper into the single eartuft. "Yield, or I will break your wing."

"Do it…" Anfang said and struggled against the gryphon.

"So be it…" Joseph raised his head and moved his hindpaw up towards the base of Anfang's wing before beginning to press down. The beast gasped as he felt the bones begin to strain, and he cried out.

"Enough!" Anthony yelled. Joseph's grip slightly relaxed as he looked over to the boss. Anthony walked down the stairs with his hands in his coat pockets. "I think our friend has had enough."

Disappointed, Joseph snorted through his nares. "I thought you said he was better than this. First Class are supposed to be the most refined from what I read."

"He's special. He has great potential, but he's not as trained as you are. Besides, our friend Jim told me they found him half starved," Anthony retorted. The human walked over and crouched next to Anfang, catching his eyes once again. "You're outmatched, outnumbered, and out of options. If you come quietly with us, then I won't have to drug you and transport you in a cage."

The defiant glance Anfang once showed was all but gone. He was defeated, and he knew it.

"Don't you want to learn how to be like Joseph here?" Anthony pressed. "He can show you how to fight. He could train you, and there wouldn't be a gryphon or human out there that you could lose to. You'd never be powerless again. Don't you want that?"

Anfang glanced up and out to the side. He could still see the people standing between the vehicles, and the reflections of their phones against the sun as they recorded everything. He was truly defeated, and yet Anthony still bestowed the olive branch. Anfang began to relax.

"You'll be the most powerful gryphon ever to live. But more importantly, don't you want to live in peace, and have the capability to protect those you love?" Anthony proposed.

"I want...I want to protect Thyra..." Anfang said gently.

Anthony smiled and nodded his head. "I know you do. She will be part of the colony soon enough. That's why I want you there. I want you to protect her, her friends, and all the gryphons that will live there. Can you do that for me?"

"Yes. I will," Anfang replied.

"And I have your word you won't retaliate or run anymore?"

"Anfang promise."

Satisfied, Anthony stood and waved to a female standing nearby. Anfang stared at the blond women for a moment as she nodded back and opened up the rear doors of one SUV.

"Good. Now, if you please. Let's go," Anthony said and began to walk towards the vehicle.

Immediately, the other groups of men began to climb back into their SUVs and start the engines. Joseph stepped off Anfang and dusted himself off with a foretalon, waiting for Anfang to return to his feet.

"After you," Joseph said.

Anfang rose back onto all four feet and jerked as he put pressure on his right foretalon. It was broken, and he had to favor it carefully.

"Don't worry about that. It was a clean break. If you're anything like me, it should heal quickly," Joseph said.

The great beast, now wounded and helpless, looked to the people as they shamelessly recorded the events unfolding. Anfang limped to the SUV and took one last glance back at the house. Jim stood on the porch, clearly shocked by what he just witnessed.

The blond woman smiled as Anfang approached. "Good to see you again, Anfang," She said coyly. Anfang paused before her and looked her over. He noticed the scar running along her neck but did not mention a word to her.

She held the door open for Anfang as he climbed into the rear of the spacious vehicle, quickly followed by Joseph. The door shut with a thump, and the same woman hopped into the front seat. Anthony was sitting next to the driver in the passenger seat, checking his phone.

"Be sure to pay the man for the damages to his home, Amanda," Anthony said.

"I'll make the arrangements, sir," Amanda said and put the vehicle into gear.

The matching black SUVs pulled out before her and led the way down the gravel drive. Anfang glanced over to see Joseph sitting calmly in the seat next to him, staring out the window. It was foreign for him to be in a vehicle. Any other time he had been transported, they had kept him in a cage and in total darkness.

Anfang watched out the window as all the cars turned onto the main road and accelerated down the two-lane road. He continued to glance at the three others in the car, still nervous about his situation. His adrenaline had died down, and now he felt the massive pain starting to build in his broken foretalon, along with the other bruised parts along his body. He closed his eyes and took a deep breath. When he opened them back up, he caught the bright blue eyes of the female driver in the rear-view mirror.

"I'm a little disappointed, Anfang," Amanda said with a fake frown.

Anfang's brows furrowed with curiosity. "That not first time I hear today…" he retorted, clearly not understanding the comment.

Amanda chuckled lightly and put her eyes back on the road. "You've grown a lot. I didn't think I would see you ever again," Amanda commented. When she looked back up in the rear-view mirror, Anfang still looked completely lost. She smiled. "You really don't remember? The last thing you gave me was this beautiful scar."

Anfang's brain began to replay memories, searching for any with her face. He thought he recognized her from somewhere but could not put his talon on it. "I…I not remember. Did . . . when did I do that?"

Debra sighed and shrugged her shoulders. "You didn't mean to. I guess it has been a while. But I'm sad you don't remember your own 'mother.'"

Chapter 5 Sound of Madness

Johnathen took a sip of his energy drink and placed it back in the cup holder. The gentle rumble of the Mustang's V8 rang in Thyra's eardrums as they traveled down the interstate. She turned around to see Rachel sitting comfortably on the back seat while looking at her phone, but Antonio looked cramped. The gryphon's head was forced against the roof of the vehicle while the back of Johnathen's seat pushed tightly against his chest. His feathers stuck out everywhere, looking like a Pomeranian shoved into a tiny box.

"How're you holding up back there?" Thyra asked from her spot in the front seat.

"Oh, I'm doing great!" Rachel replied. "No problem. I rarely get to ride in cars so it's kinda cool! I mean, I'm surprised a car like this has back seats at all, but it's not bad! I feel like I could-."

"Not you! I'm asking Antonio," Thyra interrupted.

"Oh, you mean smooth Spanish boy here?" Rachel laughed and bumped Antonio's side with a wing. "It looks a bit cramped for him, doesn't it? Sometimes it pays to be small. Right, big guy?"

Alex Bizzell

Antonio glanced at Rachel and took a deep breath. Thyra could tell the mixture of cramped spaces and the constantly talking gryphoness was eating at his last nerve. Even the ever-patient gryphon had a limit, it seemed.

"I am managing. Although, I greatly underestimated the size of these seats when I first agreed to this," Antonio commented.

"I can pull over at the next exit if you would rather fly with Aadhya," Johnathen offered. He glanced up out of the sunroof and could see the outline of the vulture in the sky following along.

"I do not believe I could keep pace with you and Aadhya," Antonio admitted as he looked at the speedometer. "But I am fine, really."

Rachel suddenly burst out into laughter and shoved her phone up into Antonio's face. "You've got to see this group of crows taking this gryphons burger! It's hilarious! Look!"

Antonio stared helplessly at Thyra then back at Rachel's phone with a polite fake smile. Thyra held back her laughter and turned back around.

"But I do think pulling over at the next exit for a break sounds good," Thyra mentioned. "Hun?"

Johnathen nodded and signaled to get over. "Sounds good. I'm getting low on my drink, and this old girl is thirsty too," he said, patting the dashboard gently.

"Already? Didn't you just fill up before we left?" Thyra asked.

Johnathen merged over again onto an exit ramp and began to decelerate, shifting down gears. Rachel continued to carry on about something on her phone and Thyra had to push the noise aside in her mind so she could pay attention to her husband's response.

"Hey, when it comes to this girl, it's all about performance and smiles per gallon," Johnathen retorted. Both knew the Mustang was a gas guzzler. "Plus, it's not like we have the Volvo anymore."

Thyra's eartufts folded against her head. The poor car had burned up with the rest of the house. "Yeah. I really loved that wagon. We took a lot of road trips in it. Well, maybe with the insurance check you can get another one," Thyra said hopefully.

"Maybe, but the parking garage next to Aadhya's apartment is expensive," he pointed out.

Johnathen came to a complete stop at the red light and checked the sunroof again, watching Aadhya begin to descend in a lazy spiral. He turned onto the road and began to accelerate again, putting everyone back into their seat. The exhaust roar interrupted Rachel's endless train of thought.

"Oh! We taking a break?" Rachel said eagerly. "I've needed to use the bathroom for a while now, but I didn't want to make John pull off! Plus, I could use a drink and a good stretch of my wings."

"I could use some space myself," Antonio commented.

The car came to a stop next to a gas station pump and Johnathen switched off the ignition. Thyra exited the car and pulled the seat forward, letting Rachel out first. The small gryphoness easily exited the cramped confines, but it took a lot of effort for Antonio to do the same. He grunted and squeezed through the opening, pulling himself out with little grace.

Alex Bizzell

The quaint gas station was mostly empty. Only one car was parked to the side. Johnathen swiped his credit card at the pump and began to refuel the car as Rachel proceeded inside the store. Thyra walked to the edge of the lot and looked up into the sky, watching Aadhya descend quickly. She landed gracefully in the grass and folded in her wings with a deep breath.

"You look like you're having fun up there," Thyra commented as she approached the great vulture.

Aadhya adjusted her loose fitting shirt and shorts before preening at one of her flight feathers. "Yes. It has been some time since I've traveled such a long distance, but my kind are built for this. Lucky for me, the air currents are in my favor."

Aadhya glanced over at Antonio. His colorful button-down shirt was wrinkled and his dark feathers poked out at every crevice. She grinned lightly as he approached.

"Go ahead and laugh," Antonio commented.

Aadhya pointed at the flattened feathers on top of his head. "I assume it was like 'a can of sardines,' as they say?"

"Yes. I knew it would be tight in there, but not that tight," Antonio commented. "And as much as I like Rachel, she is beginning to-."

"Hey Antonio! I gotcha something!" Rachel yelled as she walked over to the group, a plastic bag hanging from her beak.

Antonio tensed up and quickly turned around to see the gryphoness within earshot, but she did not seem to have heard his comment. Rachel placed the bag on the ground and pulled out a water and a pack of mints.

Colony

"Figured you were getting thirsty, and no offense, but I wantcha to eat one of these mints. Your breath smells like dead fish!" Rachel offered them up to Antonio.

Both Thyra and Aadhya had to stifle a laugh again as Antonio thanked her and gratefully took them. Rachel wondered off back to the car, leaving the small group to themselves.

"A dead fish huh? What did you eat before we left? Rotten trout or something?" Thyra teased.

Antonio glared at the two gryphonesses,closed his eyes, and let out a deep sigh. "You are just as bad as her sometimes."

"Y'all ready?" Johnathen interrupted as he approached the group.
"Certainly. How much longer do we have?" Aadhya asked.

Johnathen shrugged and pulled out his smart phone. He flipped through the screen for a minute and showed an image to Aadhya.

"Looks like just under an hour for us. But if you want to take a short cut here…" he said and zoomed in the image for her to see. "You can be there in twenty minutes. We will be next to the beach so it will be simple for you to see us."

"Very well. I will meet you all there," Aadhya commented and stepped away. With a quick run, Aadhya was up in the air and soaring up towards the sky. Johnathen put his phone away and started walking to the car with Thyra and Antonio in tow.

"Thyra, I call shotgun," Antonio said.

"I don't think so," Thyra laughed and opened the car door for him, pointing towards the rear seat where Rachel already sat.

Antonio huffed through his nares and started to squeeze himself into the back again.

"Ow! Antonio! Watch the wings!" Rachel yelled.

"Well if you would direct me this would be much smoother!" Antonio raised his voice. The two of them began to bicker back and forth.

Thyra rubbed her eyes with a talon and sighed. "This is going to be a long trip."

"And, we're here." Johnathen cut the ignition off, silencing the blaring radio. Thyra had turned the music up pretty loud to drown out the bickering between the two in the rear seat.

"Thank god! Get me out of here!" Rachel was the first to say.

"Trust me, I have not enjoyed this any more than you have," Antonio commented back calmly. All four of them exited the Mustang as fast as they could. Johnathen sat on the car's hood and looked up at the sky, searching for Aadhya.

"She's got to be around here somewhere," Johnathen said and checked his phone.

Thyra sat down next to him on the ground and looked around the parking lot. The area bordered a local park. There were picnic benches every several yards at the edges of the lot.

"Hey! That's her," Thyra pointed out gesturing towards the opposite end of the park. "Aadhya!"

What looked like a large white and black blob to Johnathen's eyes was clear as day to Thyra. She grimaced a bit as the blob lifted its head and began to make its way towards them. Johnathen noticed Thyra's discomfort and raised an eyebrow.

"What? Is something wrong?" Johnathen asked. Thyra shook her head and looked away for a second.

"No, it's just a little disgusting. She was eating some rotting carcass over there. I mean it's natural for her kind but, it's still kinda gross," Thyra explained. Aadhya glided over smoothly and set down before them. She looked at the group's expression and cocked her head in question.

"Is something the matter?" Aadhya asked.

"How old was that thing you were eating?" Rachel suddenly spit out. She sniffed through her nares and grimaced before holding them shut with her foretalons. "And I was making fun of how Antonio smelled!"

Aadhya took a step back, folding her eartufts back against her head. "My apologies. I was quite famished after the flight and, as you know, we bearded vultures consume bones as our main source of diet . . . it has been a while since I had fresh bones. I found a deer carcass and it seemed to be only a week old, so…"

"Please, leave out the details. It's ok," Johnathen said, ending the conversation. He withdrew a napkin from his pocket and handed it to Aadhya. "You have a little something on your…um, beard." Aadhya looked away with shame and began cleaning the black-feathered beard hanging from her beak. "Anyways! What's our game plan, Thyra?" Johnathen asked.

"You're asking me?" Thyra questioned and pointed to her chest. "Why me?"

"You are pretty much the leader of this extravaganza, hun," Johnathen replied. "It's up to you."

Thyra thought for a minute and looked up into the evening sky. The sun was beginning its main decent and the darkness would envelope them soon. "Ok. I think Antonio and I should scout first. We will go to the location marked on Anthony's phone and see if we find anything. You three stay behind until we get a clear route and can bring you there under the cover of night. That sound like a plan?"

Everybody seemed surprised she was so assertive after being uncertain just mere moments ago. She blinked. "Is that ok?"

"Y…Yeah! Good! I say let's do that," Rachel responded. "You go ahead! We'll wait here. I've got a couple bags of chips I bought from the gas station that the gang can snack on while we wait!"

With everybody in agreement, Antonio and Thyra walked away from the group. They stretched out their wings and made a quick run before leaping and soaring into the air. The strong winds blowing up off the coast eased their initial ascent, and Thyra looked over the ocean before her. She took a deep breath of the salty seawater air and beat her wings against the currents.

"It's been years since I've smelled the ocean," Thyra commented.

"It reminds me of home," Antonio replied, following Thyra towards the island. She pulled out her phone and checked their location compared to the GPS marker. She memorized her bearings and turned slightly to head in the right direction.

"Did you grow up near the Gulf of Mexico?" Thyra questioned and put her phone away into the pouch hanging from her neck.

"Yes. Cancun, to be exact," Antonio replied.

Colony

"I've been there! Johnathen and I went to a resort in Cancun once. Beautiful place," Thyra said.

"The hotel district is very beautiful, yes. But the rest of the city is poor. I grew up working in resorts as an entertainer. People came from far and wide to see the Mexican gryphon dancer," Antonio said.

"A dancer huh? Well, you'll have to show me some moves sometime!" Thyra laughed and looked back at Antonio who was keeping close to her, dodging her long tail flailing in the wind.

"With enough tequila, you might convince me," Antonio teased and smiled.

She nodded and pulled out her phone again, checking their location. They were near the destination, but all she could see from above the island was a forest of trees, and the ocean in the distance. There was no indication of any clearings for roads, or an easy place to land.

"Ok, we are on top of the marker, but I don't see any landmarks or good places to land. Do you?" Thyra asked as she banked left and began a lazy spiral.

Antonio scanned the area below as they circled around, and then pointed a foretalon towards a small clearing with a rock formation.

"There seems to be a gap there. Perhaps that's the place?" Antonio said. Not having a better idea.

Thyra started a steeper decent with the harris hawk quickly in tow. She slowed her decent right at tree level, and aligned herself. She tucked her wings. "This is going to be tight!"

She fell like a stone in between a small break in the foliage. The ground quickly came to greet her, and she flared her wings open at the last second to back pedal hard, landing on a small grassy patch. Antonio did the same, but overcorrected and fell off the rock he meant to perch on.

"You alright?!" Thyra yelled.

Antonio quickly recovered and stood back on all fours. "Damn rocks are slippery."

"I'll keep that in mind," Thyra replied as she looked around at the sparse clearing. Nothing but trees, grass, and a small hill made of rocks. Thyra pulled out Anthony's phone and scrolled to bring the first picture up. "Does this look like the place?"

Antonio walked up beside her and glanced over. "The foliage and surroundings seem to be similar, but it would be, considering the climate."

Thyra put the phone away into the pouch and began to walk around, looking for any sign of human activity. She jumped on top of one large rock, and almost slipped herself.

"Careful," Antonio said.

"You weren't joking," Thyra said and perched. The small hill descended for a couple feet, and then turned into another small grassy patch. She saw a trail leading to it, a trail meant for vehicles. "Look at that."

Antonio noticed it as well and the both of them glided down to land in the small grass patch. She turned to look up at the hill made of rock and saw a gap between two boulders, just big enough for a person to fit in.

"Maybe this?" Thyra said out loud and approached the gap.

It was tight for her to squeeze through, but she managed. Thyra pulled her phone out and clicked on the light. A sharp reflection shined back at her as she saw a gigantic metal door standing before her. Her feathers stood on end as she felt a tingle flow through her spine.

"Antonio! It's here!" she called out

"You found it?" Antonio asked, poking his head into the gap. His beak fell open as he saw the gigantic bunker door before him as well. "Dios Mío! It does exist."

"I knew it," Thyra said and turned to exit. She squeezed back out of the boulders out into the fading light and sat down on her haunches. "I didn't say it before, but there's something familiar about the salty air, and these trees."

"We should inform the group," Antonio pointed out. She nodded and pulled out her phone.

"On it," Thyra replied and started typing on her phone. "This is pretty exciting. I want to see how Johnathen is after he goes for his first gryphon ride."

"Holy shit!" Johnathen yelled after he hopped off of Aadhya's back. "That was insane! You guys get to experience that all the time! I'm just-." He laughed and stroked his messed up hair. "Just wow."

Aadhya stretched out her wings and tucked them into her side. "He needs to learn how to remain still. It was not easy, to say the least."

"I recorded it too! It was funny to watch him freak out at first. He started yelling and grabbed Aadhya's neck feathers so hard he tore a couple of them out! I even heard Addy curse for the first time ever!" Rachel said.

Johnathen stopped and looked back at Aadhya apologetically. "Yeah, sorry about that, by the way."

The vulture straightened herself up and walked past him. "It was fine. But let us hope the return trip is easier."

Johnathen reached into his heavy coat pockets and pulled out a couple of headlamps. The sun was setting quickly below the horizon, and light was becoming scarce. All the gryphons took their headlamp and strapped it on. With the five of them wearing lights, the entire area was illuminated.

"Well? After you," Johnathen motioned to Thyra. "I'm sure you're eager to get in there."

"Kind of, but-." Thyra looked at the entrance again. "There's a lot going through my mind right now. I'm excited but scared. This could be the place where I was, well, supposedly created."

Johnathen rubbed Thyra's neck and softly scratched her head. "Hey, we are all here. We can do this together."

Thyra ruffled her feathers and took a deep breath. "Ok, let's do this."

Chapter 6 Bad Moon Rising

"Aadhya, give me a talon here," Thyra said as she grabbed the giant handle on the metal door. Aadhya stepped forward and grasped it with both talons.

"Ok, on the count of push...PUSH!" Thyra yelled.

Both gryphons grunted and dug their hindpaws into the dirt as they pushed against the door. The towering metal wall began to slide to the side on its tracks. The wheels supporting the door squealed from years of neglect until both gryphons finally stopped. They breathed heavily and took a step back.

"That should be enough for us to squeeze through."

Johnathen was the first to shimmy through the door. He looked around into the complete black with his headlamp. "I'm just seeing a long concrete hallway."

The other gryphons wedged themselves inside, and with a little more straining, they were able to make the door move just enough for Aadhya. They walked shoulder to shoulder in the vast hallway. The sounds of footsteps and talons reverberated off the concrete walls with every step. Thyra saw what looked like faded lines painted in the concrete with old tire tracks. They walked to the end where they found yet another steel door, this one with a simple handle.

Johnathen pulled the handle and it clicked loudly. "Guess we don't need a key," he said.

The door screeched as he swung it open and peered inside to find a vast room. The group poured inside and looked around. Chairs and desks littered one side of the room and dust floated in the heavy air.

"This must have been the main lobby. I'm guessing like a waiting room for guests and low-level clerical staff," Johnathen observed.

"Guests? For whom?" Aadhya questioned.

Johnathen had to think for a moment as he shined the bright LED light around the room. "My guess is the investors and the like coming in to check progress. See, there's little decorations and fake plants mixed in with the other junk."

"John's right," Thyra said. The group paused and looked over to her. "I came through here a lot when I was brought to visit Anfang. It was crowded in here. People in white lab coats walking around. Well-dressed guys were talking with other people. It's all coming back to me." Thyra paused and glanced over at a door on the right side of the room. There was a simple flowerpot with fake red flowers sitting on a stand next to one of the doors. Thyra pointed a talon at one of the doors on the far side of the room. "I remember the red flowers. His room was down that way, I'm pretty sure."

"Well, it seems as good a place as any," Johnathen said and led the way. He approached the door and gave it a tug, but it would not budge. He frowned and pushed on it instead, but still nothing. "Well, looks like we aren't getting in through this way."

Colony

"I could go through that broken window over there," Rachel said and pointed to a glass pane window that lined one of the walls next to the door. "I'm just small enough to fit."

They looked inside and saw a white room with several stainless-steel workbenches lining one wall. There were old beakers sitting on tables along with microscopes and other lab equipment.

"Looks like some kind of observation lab. Maybe so the visitors could see the work they were doing," Johnathen said as he took off his jacket and wrapped it around his hand. "Stand back a bit," he warned before knocking out a couple shards of broken glass to widen the hole. They crashed to the ground and shattered into hundreds of pieces. Satisfied, Johnathen bent down and held out his hands. "I'll pick you up and drop you in."

Rachel let Johnathen pick her up, much like someone would pick up a small housecat, and dropped her inside. "Y'all sit tight. I'll see if something is barring the door," she commented and ventured deeper into the room. She pushed through another door and disappeared.

A minute passed without any communication. "Rachel? Can you hear us?" Thyra yelled into the broken window. Silence. She took a deep breath and looked to the group with concern etched into her face.

"I am sure Rachel is fine," Aadhya said reassuringly.

The door next to them screeched as it slowly pushed open, and Johnathen rushed to assist. Rachel stood to the side, her feathers covered with dust and smiled as the group walked in.

"Just as we thought. They had these deadbolts on the inside, so that took me a minute. But we are good now!"

77

Rachel explained. "This hallway Ts off down there to a couple more hallways, but I didn't go wondering off."

"I got worried for a minute," Thyra smiled and walked past. "I'll take point."

The group followed Thyra down the corridor, and she turned left at the T. This hallway ended at a door that was wide open. Thyra walked into the smaller room beyond and glanced around, looking at the paintings and other decorations that adorned it.

"This is it.," Thyra said and took a deep breath of the stale air. There was still a pillow-like bed in the corner of the room, and a wooden chest on one wall. She felt a since of clarity finally coming back to something she had seen many times over in her dreams. It seemed out of world, but as she opened his chest and saw the toys inside, it became very real. "I was starting to think this didn't exist.This was Anfang's room."

Johnathen walked up and rubbed her head. "Are you okay?"

"Yeah, it's just, weird," Thyra said and pulled a red ball out of the chest. It had long since deflated, but still felt the same in her talons as she remembered. She placed the ball back in the chest and turned to face out the window, but only saw the flashlight shining back at her.

"The only thing that gets me is that I remember there being a garden outside. But," Thyra reached to tap the glass, and it bent slightly inward. "It was just a television screen. It looked so real," Thyra said.

"Maybe it was because you had never seen the outside," Antonio commented. Thyra nodded her head and looked at one of the talon paintings still hanging limply on the wall.

"It makes me wonder. If that was a lie, what else was?" Thyra walked over to the painting and tore it off the wall. She held it in her talons and looked at the scribbled artwork. She was there when he made this. It was a painting of her. Her memory flashed back to Anfang's smiling beak as he dipped talons into the little cups of paint. The word 'friend' was crudely written down at the bottom. She closed her eyes and took a deep breath. "He painted this for me."

The rest of the group stood back, watching Thyra. "You want to bring it with us?" Johnathen offered. She nodded and Johnathen took it. He rolled it up neatly and tucked it up under his arm.

"So, moving on?" Rachel commented, sounding bored. Everyone besides Thyra glared over at Rachel for her insensitivity. She looked up at the other gryphons in disbelief. "What! There's so much more to explore! Let's go check it out!"

"She's right. Let's go," Thyra replied and walked out the exit.

Aadhya watched Thyra leave and bumped Rachel with a wing. "You need to learn how to keep your beak shut," she warned under her breath.

"What! I'm sorry! I just…" Rachel said, but everyone was walking away. She grumbled and followed the group.

Instead of turning right at the T to head back to the vast entrance room, Thyra continued straight. Another metal door sat slightly agape. Thyra pushed it open with ease and wandered inside. She stood at the entrance and paused, eyes opening wide. There was a massive cage to one side of the room, almost as big as a jail cell. She shined the light around to see several operating tables lining the longer wall and on the far end, a towering glass cylinder with pipes protruding out the top of the device.

"What in the hell?" Johnathen said from behind Thyra.

"I…I don't know," Thyra replied and walked over to the upright glass tank. The rest of the gryphons followed in tow, their lights shining around to look for any clues.

"It looks like something out of a sci-fi movie. Like, alien stuff," Rachel commented.

"Like, an incubation chamber. Made to grow artificial living creatures. Like, me," Thyra paused and ran her talons down the side of the glass. She felt everything connect then and there.

This is where she came from. While the human race wondered what their origin story is, she knew about hers, and she was looking right at it. She felt closure, an odd sense of contentment. What she had been searching for all these years was right before her eyes, yet it did not fill the gap she was searching for.

This human-made machine did not hold all the answers. Only the where and how had been answered, but the why was a mystery. The contents of the incubator were empty, and she could only see her reflection in it.

"Why were we created John?" Thyra asked, scraping her talons down the side of the glass.

"Anthony said Gryphball funded it. He said his reasons were just because he could, but I don't believe that's the full answer. I'm just thankful that he did." Johnathen crouched down and looked into the reflection with her. He smiled. "It was thanks to him that I met the love of my life."

"I'm glad I met you. Its times like this that you give me meaning, and…" Thyra began.

"Hey guys! Look at this!" Rachel yelled from the other side of the room. Thyra clicked her beak with agitation and everyone glanced across the room.

"What?!" Thyra yelled, clearly annoyed.

Rachel opened the gate that attached to the cage and walked inside. She picked up a bone and held it up for everyone to see.

"They had animals in here," Rachel said.

Aadhya took it from her and examined it in her talons. She sniffed it. "A feline, to be specific. A big cat such as a mountain lion. Not gryphon. The skeletal structure lacks the avian variety seen in our own kind."

"You would be the one to know bones," Rachel commented, looking at the bones scattered across the floor. "So, they just like, left these cats in here? Just abandoned this place and left them locked in?"

"It seems to be the case, yes," Aadhya responded. "Certainty cruel, and a terrible way to go, but I see no indication from the remains they were sentient creatures such as us."

"Still, it doesn't make it any better," Thyra stated. "I don't care what their reasons were. You don't just leave a living creature locked up to die." Thyra looked over to the operating tables. "But I don't think they cared much about them anyways. I can only imagine what went on here and how many animals were tortured in the pursuit of making me."

Thyra stood on her hind legs and picked up one of the scattered medical tools on a stainless steel table, a rusted scalpel. "They had one focus. Making gryphons. They didn't care about who or what they hurt." She paused. "All this bloodshed, all this death and pain, for the sake of creating me. Creating us." She hung her head grimly.

"Thyra, you cannot think that way. It was not your doing, nor was it ours," Aadhya added. "You were given the gift of life, as were the rest of us. One cannot continue living with regret with decisions beyond one's control. We can only decide what path to take moving forward."

Thyra remained silent for a moment more before nodding. "You always know the right things to say."

"And speaking of moving on," Rachel interrupted, "How about we see what those pics and numbers on the phone lead us to? I'm sure it's something not as depressing as this shit, no offense."

Rachel saw anger flare up in Thyra's eyes. Rachel frowned and stomped a foretalon on the ground, taking everyone by surprise. "I know this sucks! It all sucks! I don't want to think about what this all means, really, because it's the past. There's no telling how many animals were slaughtered here. We just found a couple kitty skulls and I'm sure there were dozens more! Maybe a couple humans here and there but hell, I don't know! All I know it's not going to do us any good sitting here crying about it! I'm here, we are here, and that's all there is to it. So, let's get a hold of ourselves and get this show on the road!"

Thyra wanted to be angry with Rachel, but she had to admit the small gryphoness she was right. There was no use in wallowing. "Fine, let's go."

The group exited the room and Thyra took one last look back, burning the memory of the dimly lighted room in her brain. She shut the door behind her with a shove and took a deep breath with her face resting against the cold metal door. She never wanted to be in that room again.

A bright light flashed over her from Johnathen's flashlight as he turned around. "Thyra?"

"Yeah, I'm coming," Thyra said and followed them. The group returned to the main entranceway where they began and paused.

"So, where to now?" Rachel asked and stood to the side. Thyra walked out towards the center and pointed at the only other door at the far side of the room.

"Well there's only one more to check, so let's go there," Thyra said. They followed her lead to the opposing side and Johnathen opened the door with ease.

"Looks like this one wasn't bolted shut," Johnathen observed and waived the other gryphons in.

"I wonder why," Thyra asked, following Rachel into the hallway. It was the same as the other corridor and led into a T. This time, one of the doors was forced shut, and not even Aadhya could pull it open.

The group gave up and ventured down to the opposing side, where the door was cracked open. This time the hallway led into a bigger room than before. Cubicles lined the walls with a rather large room on the opposite side.

Johnathen went to one of the cubicles and looked around. "There's only monitors here. The computers are gone."

Thyra walked up to the door on the opposing wall and sat down. It was locked, but there was a keypad mounted on the wall next to the door. Above it was a printed nameplate.

"Anthony Clearwater," Thyra read out loud. The group came over to observe as she pulled out Anthony's phone. "This has to be his office. Maybe it's what these pictures and codes are for."

Alex Bizzell

"You think he wanted you to see what's inside?" Johnathen asked.

Thyra shrugged her wing shoulders and scrolled through the phone. "It's possible. I don't know what he's getting at. I just wish he would tell me." She paused. "John, try 2031."

Johnathen started punching in the numbers on the keypad, and surprising enough, the light started flashing with every number he pushed.

The keypad beeped once Johnathen finished and the door clicked before swinging open. "Well would you imagine that? How is there any electricity here? Everything else is dead."

"Perhaps internal batteries," Antonio commented.

They proceeded into the room. Anthony's office was immaculate without a single thing out of place. His great oak office table sat center to the room with bookshelves lining the three walls. Pictures of Anthony with Thyra and Anfang hung on the walls with smiles on their faces. Thyra walked up to one of the pictures and cocked her head. It was a photo of her and Anthony outdoors, but she did not remember being outside for the beginning of her life.

"Look how cute you were with all that down," Johnathen pointed out as he approached.

Thyra ruffled her feathers and looked up at him. "Oh, shut up," she commented and looked back to the photo. She thought for a minute, "The only thing is, I don't remember being outside as a gryphlet."

"Could have been one of the television screens, like what you saw in Anfang's room," Johnathen suggested.

The other gryphons searched the bookshelves and the rest of the room for anything useful. They went through the desk drawers but found nothing but pens and paper.

"Wasn't there a safe in one of the pics?" Rachel asked loudly after giving up.

Thyra nodded and pulled out Anthony's phone. "Yeah, it looked like…this." She showed the picture to everyone else. They all looked around the dark room with their head-mounted flashlights, observing the screen once more.

"It seems to be on this wall," Antonio pointed at the screen and then the wall with the picture they were looking at. "But the photo is there. Perhaps it is behind it?"

"Let's check," Johnathen said and removed the photo of Thyra and Anthony, revealing a safe embedded in the concrete behind it. "Well there you have it!" He looked at the giant dial before him and started to turn it left and right. "It probably operates like most combination safes. Wasn't there a number we saw in the notes?"

Thyra's eartufts perked up and she started going through the phones screen. "Oh yeah! It was…. Okay, 20, 01, 09, 11."

Johnathen paused and looked at her again. "His code is the year and date of the terrorist attack on the world trade center?"

The gryphons all looked at each other and shrugged.

"What terrorist attack?" Thyra questioned.

Johnathen sighed and started working the dial. "That's a long story, anyways." He turned the dial on the safe back and forth several times and stopped at the last number. He pulled the handle and it clicked open. "I had a dog and his name was BINGO!"

"Damn, John! How did you get it on the first try?" Rachel asked.

"My parents had a gun safe growing up. I figured it probably worked the same way," Johnathen said and opened up the door. He pulled out a stack of thin metal squares and a bundle of feathers wrapped with a rubber band.

"What is that?" Thyra asked. He held out the metal squares and the bundle of feathers.

"Well, it looks like a bundle of feathers, similar to yours," Johnathen pointed out. He held them out for the gryphons to observe.

"They seem like adolescent red tail hawk's feathers," Aadhya said confidently. "Perhaps Thyra and Anfang's young adult feathers?"

"Yeah, yeah a memento for the old man, but what the hell are those thin square things, John?" Rachel interrupted. "It looks like someone 3D printed the save icon."

"These? Well, they are called floppy disks. Or to be exact, diskettes. They are pretty archaic especially with today's standards. We used to use them to store information, mind you they only have like a couple megabytes," Johnathen explained.

"So, those things hold memory?" Rachel asked.

Johnathen nodded. "Yeah and it's pretty cool how they do it. The material in the disc is ferrous, which means it can be magnetized, and the memory is wrote and accessed by using magnets! But you need the right reading device plugged into a desktop computer and pull the information out of it." He closed the safe before putting the disks in his coat pocket.

"That sounds like a pain in the ass! I mean, does anyone even have those?" Rachel commented. Johnathen picked up the framed picture to hang it back on the wall.

"Well, some of the older folk do, and the tech geek collectors," Johnathen said. "You can't count on a digital server to hold all your information. It's a security thing. I mean, we kind of do the same thing now. I have all of Thyra's and my photos backed up to a couple thumb drives and some hard drives in a bank safety deposit box."

"Do you really?" Thyra asked.

"Of course. I don't trust all the digital servers to hold my precious memories. I take comfort in knowing it's all there, no matter what," Johnathen smiled and started walking towards the door. "In a way, it makes me respect Anthony even more. I'm sure he's more old fashioned than I am."

"So, what do we have to do to find out what's on those floppys?" Thyra asked.

"I'll have to go buy another laptop and a floppy adapter, since mine burned up with the rest of the house. But first, let's get out of here, unless you want to continue looking around. Thyra?" Johnathen asked.

Thyra shook her head. "No. I think I've had enough of an emotional roller coaster for the day, and I'm physically tired too," Thyra looked at her phone. "And holy crap, it's almost two am."

"Damn. Well I hope we aren't driving all the way home tonight!" Rachel said. "I don't want to ride with fishbreath for another four hours home in the dead of night! No offense, Antonio," Rachel retorted and walked out towards the room

Antonio looked up towards the rest of the group with a grimace. "Not a word," he said and followed Rachel.

"Yeah, not to worry though. I got us two rooms on the beach just thirty minutes down the road. Well, once we get back to the mainland," Johnathen added.

They exited the room and began their trek down the corridor. The group made their way quickly back through the multitude of doors and out of the main entrance.

Once they were heading down the initial exit of the bunker, Thyra's phone began to ding loudly, but it was not a sound she recognized. They all exited out of the towering bunker door and stopped as Thyra removed Antonio's phone from her pouch first.

When you receive this message, contact me immediately. –Anthony.

"Thyra? What's up?" Johnathen asked. They all gathered around in the pale moonlight in a semicircle.

"It's Anthony," she said.

"You mean on your phone or…" Rachel asked.

"No, on his phone," Thyra responded. She clicked on the phone and held it out on speakerphone for everyone to hear. The dial tone rang loudly even in the open area of the surrounding forest and then clicked before Anthony spoke.

"Did you find what you were looking for?" asked Anthony's voice.

Thyra took a deep breath and spoke up. "Not exactly. I have a lot of questions."

"I figured you would. But, you saw it, didn't you?" Anthony asked again.

Thyra thought for a moment. "Yes. I saw where I was made."

"Good. I wanted you to see your birthplace. If only we could see where we came from, and by we I mean…"

"Yeah, humans. I get that. But why did you leave this phone for me to find all this? Why…"

"Did you find my office?"

Thyra paused and looked to the others. They all nodded with reassurance. "Yeah. We found a…um…floppy drive."

"I'm sure Johnathen knows how to get the information out of it." Anthony said. *"Let me know what you find tomorrow. You and the rest of the team will be receiving a text from Victor tonight about a meeting that will take place at Richard Hopkin's mansion."*

"Richard Hopkin?" Thyra questioned. She had to think of a moment before remembering the name. "You mean that wealthy British guy that owns our gryphball team?"

"That's the one! I have to go for now, as it is very late. You and the rest of your friends should get some rest, but I look forward to tomorrow. Goodnight, Thyra."

The phone beeped, ending the call. Thyra sighed and put the phone away in her pouch. "What do you think that was all about?"

"I don't know, but it looks like we got a big fancy dinner coming up tomorrow!" Rachel exclaimed. "Let's go to the hotel and get some rest."

"That is a good plan. I am exhausted," Aadhya added in.

"I hate to be the bearer of bad news-. Actually, wait I love it. Remember, you still have to fly John to his car!" Rachel laughed and took off into the skies. Aadhya watched her leave and looked to the others with tired eyes.

"Must I?" Aadhya asked. Antonio and Thyra shrugged.

"It's not like we can carry him. Besides, you're the one that volunteered," Thyra pointed out with a slight grin.

"Sorry," Johnathen said apologetically.

Aadhya sighed and lowered her chest to the ground with a wing outstretched. "Fine. Get on, damnit."

Chapter 7 Hometown

Anfang sat on a hotel bed, staring out of the balcony doors. The sun was barely peeking over the horizon, gracing the small city below in a warm orange glow. He had not slept much that night, and could feel the effects of sleeplessness dulling his thoughts.

Debra, the woman with the scar, had talked to him well into the night. She called herself his mother, but that was only because she had been his caretaker for most of his younger life, up until the time he was transferred to the military research facility. She had showed him photos of himself during those times, and he looked so happy. It was an eerie feeling to him, seeing himself smiling and playing without a care in the world. Debra was nice, for the most part, but it was a reminder that even the kind ones had betrayed him in some way or another.

Debra had also explained the scar on her neck. She said that he had given her that scar, but not intentionally. Apparently, he had lashed out in fear when she administered a shot in one of the ports on his arms. He did not remember hurting her, but he still felt a tinge of guilt knowing he had left a permanent mark on her.

Colony

The squeaking of box springs in the bed next to Anfang's jolted him away from his thoughts. Joseph rolled over in his sleep and grunted, curling one of his wings over his head. The military gryphon had not said much last night besides asking an occasional question.

For whatever reason, he and Debra had left Anfang to his own devices. He could have escaped off the balcony at any time through the night, but then again where would he have gone? Perhaps that was why they gave him free will, for the time being.

"Good to see you're still here," Joseph said and slowly sat up on his bed. "It saves me the headache of having to track you down, again." He yawned and hopped up off his bed. Anfang glanced away to stare out the balcony door again. "Not a morning gryph, huh? Well, you'll learn soon enough."

Joseph stretched his foretalons and hindlegs before disappearing into the bathroom. Anfang could hear the shower cut on and the sound of a toilet flushing.

Anfang hopped off of the bed and walked over to the urban camouflage duffle bag that was sitting next to the television. He unzipped it and checked the door again, listening to the sound of water droplets change when Joseph walked into the shower. He had at least a couple of minutes to check out Joseph's things.

Inside were fresh pairs of clothes, nothing but neutral polos, cargo shorts, and a second set of 'shoes' for his four feet. The front gloves were thick with padding, and had hard inserts where his 'knuckles' would be. He dug through the rest, until his talons connected metal. Carefully, he pulled a handgun out and observed the weapon. It was currently in a heavy-duty plastic holster. It was not his first time handling a weapon, but the first when he was trying to be careful with one.

"Why?" Anfang questioned out loud. He pulled the weapon free from the holster and held it by the grip. The weapon's grip was modified to fit a gryphons foretalon as was the trigger. There was a long narrow guard that ran the length of the barrel, perhaps to shield the gryphon user from getting their talons caught in the slide. For someone that bragged about his talon to hand combat, or talon-to-talon, what use would Joseph have for a human firearm?

Anfang carefully re-holstered the weapon and placed it back inside. He was careful to arrange the clothing back to as it was, and zipped the duffel bag closed. With that investigation done, he turned his attention to the military bulletproof vest hanging on the coat hanger. The plating looked relatively the same to a human's vest, except for the straps that connected it to the gryphon user. There were several pouches on the front of the vest and Anfang began inspecting them.

Inside one of the pouches was a photo of Joseph, another gryphon, and a small gryphlet all together on the beach, beaks wide with a smile. The other adult gryphon seemed to be a female Redtail, from her coloration, and the gryphlet was the same species. Anfang carefully placed the photo back into the vest pouch and searched the others. He found a wallet with a military-issued ID inside. "Joseph Joestar. Lieutenant General," Anfang read, but the country it was issued to did not make sense.

"Twenty eighth, EU," Anfang read out loud. He placed the wallet back into the pouch and searched the last pocket, finding Joseph's smart phone. The background was whatever stock photo the maker used, and naturally, the phone was locked with a passcode.

The shower cut off, startling Anfang. He quickly placed the phone back and carefully walked over to the balcony door. He grabbed the handle and slid it open to step outside. A cold breeze picked up under his patchy feathers and caused them to ruffle slightly.

The bathroom door opened behind them, but Anfang did not glance back. He heard Joseph shuffle around for a minute, perhaps putting on clothes.

"Here, try these on," Joseph said and tossed something onto the bed.

Anfang turned to look at the polo and cargo shorts. He raised an eye ridge. "You want me to wear those?"

Joseph pulled out his handgun and set it aside, digging around in the bag.

"Yeah. For one, I'm tired of seeing your balls. And two, you'll stick out like a sore thumb around these parts," Joseph said. "Then again, put it on after you shower. You smell like a rotting fleabag. I left some feather shampoo in there too. So, please, scrub deep."

Anfang sat speechless for a moment and Joseph looked up from his duffelbag. "What?"

Anfang remained silent and walked past Joseph into the bathroom. He looked at the shower and cocked his head. "How I make work?" Anfang asked.

Joseph groaned, shoving past Anfang in the cramped restroom to reach over and turn the showerhead on. "First off, its 'how do I make it work?' Or in normal people speak, 'hey, how do you turn the shower on?' You know, like that. You're not Igor, goddamn it. Learn how to talk." He shoved past Anfang to get out of the bathroom. "Second, there's that big nob on the wall." Joseph pointed with a talon. "You turn it towards the red to make it hotter, and towards the blue to make it colder." Joseph said slowly, mimicking Anfang's simple speech. "Got it?"

Anfang remained silent, feathers rising out of irritation.

"Oh for the love of god, please tell me you know your goddamn colors!"

"I know red and blue!" Anfang turned and shouted.

Joseph held out a talon in defense with a grin. "I'm just fuckin with you man!" He sighed and shut the door. "I don't get paid enough for this bullshit."

Anfang snorted out through his nares and looked at the water spraying from the showerhead. In the past, the only cleansing he had received had come from a high-pressure water hose aimed at him inside his cage. That, and the rain itself. The water hose had never been pleasant, and he nearly drowned multiple times.

So naturally, he was slightly afraid of how it would feel, but all the fear left him as he felt the first spray of warm water across his feathers. Anfang closed his eyes, and sighed, finding the sensation to actually be relaxing. He wanted to spend forever under the cascade of water, but knew it would be short-lived. He began to scrub the shampoo into his feathers, and watched as sticks, dirt, and other debris were washed into the drain beneath him. Joseph was right. He was filthy.

A knock came at the door. "Quit jerkin around in there! You about done?" Joseph yelled.

Anfang grumbled and turned on the knob, but the water did not turn off. He cursed as the water became scalding hot. He quickly turned it the opposite direction until it shut off completely.

"Yes! Done," Anfang responded.

He grabbed a towel and started to dry himself off. The mirror was completely fogged over but he used his towel to wipe it down. He barely recognized himself. He could not remember the last time he looked into a mirror and observed himself. His feathers were duller than he remembered, even freshly washed, and his green eyes had a darker tint to them.

He was aging. Mortality became very real to him, and he realized that he was older than most gryphons, maybe even all the gryphons. Joseph had said something about First Class, but he did not know what it truly meant. Was he older than Joseph? And if so, by how much? The door opened up and Joseph sat there on his haunches, watching.

"Have fun?" He asked.

"It felt…nice," Anfang responded.

Joseph nodded and pointed at the counter. "Good. Believe me, everybody will be thankful for that. Also, there's mouthwash there. Take a swig of that, rinse it around, and spit it out. Don't swallow it!"

Anfang looked at the container of blue liquid and opened the top. He poured some in his lower muzzle, and held it for a second. Immediately, the liquid began to burn on his tongue and he spat it out with a couple of coughs.

Joseph laughed and shook his head. "Okay, that should do. Get dressed, we need to meet the rest of the group in the lobby."

Anfang walked into the bedroom and started to put on the clothes. He pulled the shirt over his head and pulled his wings through the slots awkwardly.

Joseph rubbed his eyes. "It's like watching a platypus slip into a wetsuit." He waited patiently as Anfang struggled with his pants for a good minute and groaned when Anfang collapsed on his back. "I swear I'm chaperoning a gryphlet."

Once Anfang was finally dressed and Joseph had collected all his things, Joseph handed him the gryphball hat. "It's not that much of a disguise. We can't do anything about your god-awful face. So, keep your beak, muzzle, whatever the hell thing you have, down."

"Can you not make fun of me for one minute?" Anfang asked sternly.

"So the beast can speak his mind! And so well put too." He paused and acted like he was thinking for a moment. Joseph shook his head. "But, no, I don't think I can." With that, Joseph opened the hotel room door with his duffel bag slung over his shoulder. "I'm just hoping nobody will recognize you. After all, your ugly face was all over the news."

Anfang growled. "Stop making fun, or…"

"Or what? You going to try to kick my ass again? Well go ahead, asshole. I'll teach you another lesson," Joseph replied sternly. He looked over to Anfang, who immediately glanced away. "That's what I thought." Joseph approached the elevator and pressed the down button. "And try not to smile so people don't see your fangs," he said as the doors opened to the elevator. They both walked onto the lift with a human couple lugging suitcases with them. "Not like that's hard to do."

They exited the elevator without so much as a greeting to the humans in the lobby. Anfang looked back at one of the humans. He was standing with his wife, whispering to her as she dialed something on her phone. Anfang did not think too much on it and proceeded into the main lobby. There were about a dozen people all sitting around at tables, enjoying their free continental breakfast. Joseph pointed out Anthony and Debra sitting together, enjoying their coffee.

Anthony raised his head up and waved the gryphons over. "How did you all sleep?"

"Very well. Thank you sir," Joseph replied and continued to the breakfast bar. Anthony nodded and looked to Anfang,

"Not sleep good," Anfang responded.

"Well that's a shame," Anthony said politely. "Go ahead and grab something to eat. We have some time to burn before the meeting at the mansion."

Anfang cocked his head. "Meeting at mansion?"

Anthony nodded and sipped from his coffee. "Yes. It's a very important announcement for all members of the Redtails Gryphball Team. Thyra will be in attendance as well."

The mention of Thyra caused Anfang to perk up to attention. "Thyra will be there?"

"Yes! She doesn't know you'll be there yet, but I'm sure it will be a welcomed reunion," Anthony smiled and glanced over at the television. His smile faded as he watched the news playing. "Debra, look."

There was a home-shot video of both Joseph and Anfang fighting in the front yard.

*"This viral video went over one million views overnight. We cannot confirm if it is indeed the Saber Tooth Slasher seen here, but the resemblance is uncanny. The whereabouts of the Slasher are still unknown after his last attack on the gryphball stadium three weeks ago. This video, shot by user ChevySucks69, said in the comments 'Look at these gryphs beat the **** out of each other! I think one of them is the Slasher, but they all loaded up and disappeared after this fight.' The user is located just northeast of Macon, in Round Oak."*

Anthony put down his coffee cup and looked around the room. Everybody was glancing at them nonchalantly. "Debra, how long has that video been on social media?"

Debra pulled out her cellphone and began typing furiously. Joseph came back carrying a plate stacked high with sugary pancakes. He sat the plate down and looked over at Anthony's concerned face.

"Sir?" Joseph asked. Anthony pointed at the television screen, causing the gryphon to turn and watch the video play over and over. "Godamnit. I knew we should have confiscated their phones."

"By force? Right now we have not broken any laws besides aiding a wanted gryphon. I didn't want to add assault and robbery to that list," Anthony commented.

"Sir, it looks like the video was uploaded ten hours ago at ten PM," Debra replied.

"Seems this has gotten away from us," Anthony said, and rose from his seat.

Joseph's eartufts perked up and Anfang turned his head to follow the gryphon's eyes towards the entrance. "Sirens. They are getting closer."

"I don't hear them yet so we may have just enough time," Anthony said and grabbed his suitcase. "Let's go."

"Looks like we're skipping breakfast," Joseph said with a disappointed sigh, looking down at his syrup slathered cakes. He pushed his plate away, picked up his duffle bag, and followed behind the group. Anfang left with them, noticing that the people they passed were whispering to one another.

An elderly security guard walked out from behind the front counter and blocked the main entrance door. He held out one trembling hand and placed the other on a holster at his belt. "Stop!"

Anthony looked over the frail man and tried to reason with him. "Sir, I know what you think you're doing is noble, but step aside."

The guard pulled out a taser and pointed it at him. "On your knees!" The old man yelled, voice cracking.

Joseph stepped forward and rose up on his hind legs, towering over the man. The fear in the security man's eyes told Joseph all he needed to know. "Lower the stun gun," he commanded and took a step forward.

The gun popped as the officer pulled the trigger, sending out trail of wire, which struck Joseph square in the chest. The gun clicked loudly as it sent high voltage through the wires, causing Joseph to buckle slightly and return to all four feet. Anfang rushed around Joseph and tackled the old officer, bringing him to the ground with ease.

"Stop! Don't hurt the man!" Anthony yelled.

Anfang had pinned the man to the ground, talons around his throat. Embarrassed, he looked over to Anthony, and pulled his talons away.

Joseph grabbed the wires and pulled the barbs out of his chest with a curse. "That still hurts like a bitch."

Anfang looked down at the frightened security officer. Without a weapon, the old man could not hurt so much as a fly, yet, just seconds ago, his talons were wrapped around the man's throat. He could have easily killed him. Anfang felt the guilt rising in his chest. He had to be more careful and keep his emotions in check.

The group turned to see a small gathering of people, watching the action, some raising smart phones.

"Just what we needed," Anthony said and proceeded out the main door.

Anfang followed behind the group and saw multiple police vehicles pulling into the parking lot, sirens blaring. A shiver shot down his back, causing wings to twitch. He had the impulse to run once again. It would be easy to fly away and leave the others behind. After all, he did not completely trust Joseph and Anthony. Why should he have to fight for them?

"Sir, get to the car," Joseph said sternly. Anthony and Debra rushed to the vehicle as two cop cars came to a stop in the parking lot. As Joseph walked out into the parking lot to face the officers, he looked back expectedly at Anfang.

The weight of his choices came down heavy, fight or flight. Anfang found himself walking to stand next to Joseph, his mind made up. He would stick with them. After all, he had plenty of chances to leave through the night, but could not find the will to flee. No, he was done running.

"Anfang, don't kill anyone," the gryphon said and poised himself to strike.

"I promised not to kill," Anfang responded and copied Joseph's stance.

"Hey, almost a complete sentence," Joseph stated and watched as two officers exited each vehicle. "Quick, concise strikes."

The officers knelt down behind their doors, handguns drawn. "Get on the ground!"

"You take the two on the left," Joseph said calmly to Anfang.

"I said! Get on the fu…" Suddenly Joseph lunged forward, and Anfang followed his lead. Bullet fire rang out as the officers discharged their firearms.

Anfang moved quickly to get out of the direct line of fire, and circled around to the side. He stayed low, but still felt the familiar pain as a round hit him in his side. Anfang tackled one of the officers against their vehicle and heard a loud crunch of metal bending against the human's body. The officer gasped and collapsed on the ground.

The opposing officer leaned over the car and emptied his clip at Anfang. The gryphon quickly ducked behind the vehicle and waited until he heard the gun click a final time. Anfang leaped on top of the squad car, his weight denting in the roof. The fear in the officer's eyes was like a drug to him. He could feel the pleasant endorphins fill his brain with a primal hunting instinct, and his beak curved into a grin. "Useless…"

The officer dropped his clip and frantically pulled out another. Anfang swiped at the officers hand, cutting it to the bone with his talons. The man yelled and dropped his weapon to clutch his bleeding hand. He stumbled back into the other squad car and grimaced. Anfang looked over to Joseph who had just dispatched the last threat with a quick jab to the head.

"You think you stop us?" Anfang said and hopped off of the car. "Useless, useless, useless." He approached the officer, and spread his wings out to look even more threatening.

"Please don't kill me!" The officer pleaded.

"Enough!" Joseph commanded. "We have to leave before backup arrives. Whatever backup is in this redneck town." Joseph dropped the clip and racked the slide of the handgun he held in his talons. He crushed the polymer grip with ease, rendering the weapon useless, and tossed it to the side.

Anfang stood on his hindfeet, planting a foretalon against the window next to the officer's head. The man was younger than the others, clearly a rookie, and scared to no end.

"I have a wife! And a daughter! P...please!" the cop begged, cowering under the towering beast. Anfang could see tears in the officer's eyes and chuckled with delight.

"I not kill you...Sad...I want to kill you, but I promise not to," Anfang said and caressed the officers face with a talon. He was feeding into his older instincts, and it felt good, really good.

Anfang stopped and his expression changed to regret once again. He was still struggling with his need for bloodlust, and it took him over like a fire burning inside. The promise to Thyra still rang true in his mind, he would not kill any human ever again, but it did not mean he could not have some fun with it all. "It hard not to...I want to taste flesh. Taste blood. But I won't..."

"Anfang! Now!" Joseph yelled and opened up the door to the Cadillac SUV.

Anfang sighed and patted the rookie's face. "That fun. Maybe play again soon," he commented and returned to all four feet before trotting away. The young officer fell to the ground, clutching his hand, and wept. Anfang climbed up into the SUV and closed the door behind him.

Debra quickly turned the SUV around and sped past the parked cop cars. They hit the main road, and she punched it. The great v8 engine roared loudly as Debra sped away from the scene. Anfang watched as Joseph picked a crunched bullet out of his chest and tossed it to the ground. He hissed and grabbed a rag to wipe up the small amount of blood leaking from the wound. "Goddamn it that stings. I hate

.45s," Joseph said. He glanced over to Anfang, and saw the smile still on his crooked beakmuzzle.

"You really enjoyed that, didn't you?" Joseph asked, raising an eye ridge.

Anfang trilled happily and glanced back to Joseph. "Yes. I love the thrill. I not kill again, but it fun to fight."

Joseph chuckled and nodded, looking down at his wound. "I think we'll make a guard out of you yet."

Chapter 8 The Outsider

Thyra stepped out of Johnathen's Mach-1 and looked up at the familiar mansion. She tied this house with good memories, and she hoped that tonight would be the same. Here she had experienced one of the best nights of her life. The night she had officially become a gryphball player. The mansion looked even larger in the evening light than it did last time in the dark. A little good news right now would surely lift her spirits.

Rachel hopped out from behind the front seat and stood next to Thyra. "Holy shit! This place is huge!" she commented while she smoothed down her burnt orange dress and readjusted the straps going over her tiny shoulders.

Johnathen shut the door behind him and put his hands on his hips. "Is it just me or did it get bigger?"

Thyra laughed and shut her door as well. She looked around the oversized parking lot, seeing an arrangement of high-end luxury cars and exotics. "I was thinking the same thing. You think all of these are his?"

"Probably. At least the most expensive ones. I doubt any of your gryphball teammates drive McLaren's and Ferrari's," Johnathen commented as the group walked towards the massive entrance. "No offense, but even if you could drive something like that, I know you couldn't afford it." He paused as he saw a sports bike. He admired the lowered bike with its café-style handlebars, extended rear trailing arm, and modified foot pegs. "But who the hell rides this BMW RR?"

"Oh! That's Nathanial's," Rachel replied. Both Johnathen and Thyra glanced down at Rachel with a curious look.

"Gryphons ride motorcycles?" Johnathen asked with surprise.

"Yeah! It took him a while to find a bike that fit his form. He had to spend a ton of money getting custom made gear and get all those mods done to the bike so he can properly ride it," Rachel explained.

Johnathen and Thyra both locked eyes for a second, clearly entertained. Thyra looked back down at Rachel with a grin. "And how do you know all of that?"

Rachel realized she had messed up and ruffled her feathers, looking away from the two as she came up with a quick lie. "I…I've just heard him brag about it to other guys! That's all!"

"Sure, you have. So, tell the truth, have you ridden on it with him?" Thyra asked, rolling her eyes.

"No! Why would I ride with that dweeb?!" Rachel shouted and padded away from the group.

Once Rachel was out of earshot Johnathen asked Thyra, "Why doesn't she just admit it already? Didn't you say the whole team basically knows she's dating him?"

Thyra shrugged and proceeded up the front porch steps. "I don't know. Young love is complicated."

Colony

One of the massive wooden entrance doors opened slowly and a butler stood before them. "Ah, Mr. and Mrs. Awkright, pleasure to meet your acquaintance once more, " he said and stepped to the side, motioning them in. "And Miss…"

"Jones," Rachel said and stepped inside first.

"Welcome, Miss Jones," the butler intoned.

Upon entering, the sound of stringed instruments filled the vast entranceway, echoing off the marble floors. A group of humans and several of Thyra's gryphon teammates stood together in the living room to their right.

"May I take your coat?" the butler offered to Thyra.

"Please," Thyra responded and sat on her haunches. She let the butler remove her coat, revealing a simple t-shirt and jeans underneath. Johnathen took off his blazer and handed it to the man as a server walked up to them with a tray of drinks.

"Champagne?" the server asked.

"Absolutely," Johnathen responded and took a glass.

The server bent down and offered one to Thyra. She took one and thanked him before he went to make another round of the guests. Thyra stood in the entranceway and sipped from the glass.

"If I knew it was going to be this formal, I would have overnighted you a dress," Johnathen commented.

"I don't think we could find one for me that quick anyways. You know how much measuring we had to do for the other dresses that burned in the fire," Thyra replied and walked into the living room.

There was an open bar set up on the far end of the room where a group of servers stood patiently waiting on requests. A small band quietly played classical instruments next to the bar for everyone to enjoy. Cocktail tables were evenly spaced at the center of the room. There was a dozen or so humans she did not recognize standing at the tables, conversing amongst themselves. It was a lot to take in.

Rachel walked straight up to Nathanial who stood at one corner of the room talking with the two corvid gryphon twins. He clearly had not known how fancy it was going to be either. He wore a simple button down with jeans. Thyra saw Nathanial smile and look over Rachel as she approached. Then Nathanial's eyes met Thyra's and the smile disappeared.

"Looks like he's still acting like there's nothing going on either," Thyra pointed out.

"Yeah, I saw that too. Watch this," Johnathen commented. He sipped from his champagne flute and adjusted his suit jacket, then walked over to the table. "Nathanial! What's up man?"

Nathanial glanced up at Johnathen and shrugged his wing shoulders. "Just seeing what the hell all this is," he replied, trying to look cool and looked over at Thyra. "You know anything?"

"Clearly not. I'm the one rocking a t-shirt at a tuxedo ball," Thyra responded.

The corvid twins both waved politely, and the group waved back. They must have had a better idea what to expect because they looked the exact same, sporting identical run of the mill tuxedos.

"So, Nathanial, Rachel was telling me you ride that BMW RR out there. That has to be fast as shit!" Johnathen said, breaking the ice. Thyra saw a twinkle in Nathanial's grey eyes as he suddenly became interested.

"Yeah, you could say that. It kicks anything's ass. I doubt even those Ferrari out there could keep up with me," Nathanial said with a self-confident puffing of his chest feathers.

"I betcha I could take you in my 69' Mach 1." Johnathen grinned and drank the rest of the champagne. Immediately another server approached Johnathen to take the empty glass and offered another.

Nathanial huffed from his nares and made eye contact with Johnathen. "You think that ancient and outdated 351 Windsor could keep up with the fine German engineering in my bike?"

"Oh no, no," Johnathen replied smugly. "Except for the fact that it has the 428 Cobra Jet."

"No shit? With the ram air?" Nathanial asked, suddenly interested.

"With. And it's all original," Johnathen sipped from his glass. "I guess it's possible you could wipe the floor with me, but I doubt it. It would be fun to find out, though."

"Hell, where did you get something like that!" Nathanial asked excitedly.

Thyra zoned out as Johnathen started talking about how he got the car, a story she'd heard dozens of times now. She looked around the room and saw Coach Victor walking in through the front entrance. The massive gryphon refused the butler's request and made eye contact with her. Victor's long gray crest feathers rose as he walked with dignity into the main room. He surely knew how to make a scene and every human in the room glanced over to see him. Several humans broke their conversation to approach the gryphon and shake a foretalon. Victor put on a smile and shook their hands, carrying on with them.

Thyra looked past the main entrance room and could see a small group of humans walking down the stairs. She recognized the first one, Richard, the host himself, but the other one was surprising to her. It was Anthony. He had mentioned the meeting tonight, but she hadn't expected him to actually attend. Thyra watched the group descend the stairs and turn the corner into the opposing room and thought to go after them. She wanted to run across the room and see if it was really Anthony or just her mind playing tricks on her.

"...Isn't that right, Thyra?" Johnathen asked. Thyra paused and collected her thoughts. She turned back to attention and looked up at Johnathen before smiling.

"Yeah! That's right," Thyra said, not knowing what she was agreeing to.

Nathanial laughed and waved a talon off dismissively. "Oh bullshit! I don't believe that for a minute! Thyra? A mechanic?" Nathanial chuckled and finished his drink. The waiter quickly took the empty glass and offered another. "No, I don't want any more of that shit. What kind of gin do you have?"

"Hey John, I'm going to the bathroom," Thyra said.

"Have fun," Johnathen commented. Thyra placed her drink down on the table, returning to all fours and turned to head out of the room.

"I'll come with you!" Rachel exclaimed and followed. Thyra paused and let the gryphoness catch up with her. "Those guys were boring me to death anyways."

"Yeah, I like cars but sometimes it does get old," Thyra said absently and entered the main entrance area. She looked down the long hallway between the staircases and saw Richard close the door behind him but did not catch a glance at the other members of the group.

"Excuse me! Where's the bathroom?" Rachel asked the butler. He pointed her in the right direction, and she began to walk away. She paused and looked back at Thyra. "You coming?"

"Yeah, in a minute. You go ahead," Thyra said.

Rachel shrugged and wandered off, leaving Thyra alone. Thyra proceeded down the long hallway, between the suits of armor, and approached the door. She pressed her head up to the wooden door and closed her eyes, trying to listen to the conversation.

"I'll have the paperwork ready for those that accept the proposal within two or three days." The voice was Richard's, she assumed by the accent. *"And all I need from you is your signature on these documents. I shall cover the initial cost of relocations, flights, first year's housing, and having the paperwork drawn up. After that, they are your responsibility."*

The next voice sounded like Anthony, but she could not be sure. *"Very good. I have confidence that the colony will be self-sustaining and profitable within the year. Especially when the gryphball stadium is completed come new years."*

"Gryphball stadium? Relocation? What does that mean?" Thyra wondered. She heard footsteps behind her and turned to see the butler standing there, hands behind his back.

"Mrs. Awkright, I'm afraid that is a private affair. If you would, please return to the entertainment room," the butler said and stepped to the side.

She made an apologetic smile and walked past him to the main entertainment room. Her mind was racing with thoughts of what they could mean. What were they planning and why was Anthony involved? Maybe she would find out soon enough.

The small gathering of gryphons had almost doubled in her time away. Aadhya and Antonio had both arrived along with several others of the gryphball team. Victor sat at a cocktail table on his haunches, conversing with Jason. Thyra walked up beside her husband and sat down, grabbing her glass once again.

"Well there you are, featherbutt," Johnathen replied and rubbed the top of her head. His cheeks were slightly flushed from the alcohol. He chuckled and took another swig of his mixed drink. "Rachel came back a while ago and I was wondering if I had to go track you down."

"I was really gone that long?" Thyra asked. It had not seemed like a lot of time, but the house was gigantic, and she had listened to the conversation for a while.

"Yeah, just a little longer than usual. You feeling alright?" Johnathen asked.

"Not as good as you, apparently. Looks like I'm driving us home tonight," Thyra responded. Johnathen killed the rest of his drink and sat it down on the table.

"Uh-oh. Well, it's been a while since you drove the mustang, and I put the original seat brackets back in a couple months back. So, you won't be able to reach the pedals," Johnathen admitted.

"Sober up then," Thyra said.

The waiter came up and grabbed his glass but Johnathen interrupted him. "Water, please."

"But there's something else," Thyra said and tugged at his suit jacket. Johnathen followed her lead to an empty table and leaned on it with her. "Anthony is here," Thyra said.

Immediately, Johnathen perked up. He looked around. "What? When did he get here?"

Thyra shrugged her shoulders and glanced back at the main entrance. "I don't know, but I followed them to the study down the hall. I could barely hear their conversation, but I listened enough to get a couple sentences. They were talking about relocation, and a new gryphball stadium, and paperwork. But then the butler saw me and asked me to leave."

Johnathen scratched his chin and thought for a moment. "You think maybe someone else is buying the Redtails team? This big party has something to do with that?"

"That's what I was thinking, but with Anthony involved, I don't think it's that simple," Thyra responded.

The live band stopped playing and everyone began to clap gently. Thyra and Johnathen both looked up to the stage as Richard walked out. "I guess we're about to find out."

"Thank you! Thank you," Richard began and looked around the room with a smile. "I hope everyone is enjoying the party! This is a momentous occasion for many of us, and I'm excited to have everyone here," Richard said and held out his glass. "But first, let us make a round of applause to the Redtails for their best season ever!"

The humans in attendance turned to face them, clapping and smiling. Thyra felt a slight ruffle of her feathers and waved back. It felt good to be complimented.

"I imagined this would be our year. With all the new players, and Coach Victor's determination, I knew we were destined to win!" Richard said, not mentioning the explosion and controversy at the final game. "But, that's not the only reason I have invited you all here tonight. We have a big announcement to make. Years of planning and preparation have made it to this moment. And with that, I'm going to hand it off to Dr. Anthony Clearwater. Anthony?"

The round of applause started all over again as Anthony took the stage. Thyra looked over to her group of friends and saw the shock in their eyes as he waved to all in attendance.

"Thank you very much! For those that haven't heard of me, I mastered in social sciences and bioengineering. I went to Harvard for over a decade and lived in Europe most of my life after that. I have kept my studies and name out of the spotlight. For years, I was the lead scientist in labs all across the world, the labs that would later produce the first gryphon kind. In fact, there was a time when people called me the father of gryphons."

He paused for a minute as many of the guests began to whisper to themselves. Anthony cleared his throat and drank from his champagne glass, "I suppose it's a fitting title, but one that I don't enjoy, simply because I didn't do it alone. It took hundreds of other highly intelligent and talented individuals to create what you see before you today."

Anthony looked around the room at all the confused and shocked faces. "You may be wondering why I am just now coming to light and putting my name out there. Well, those reasons are my own. I've never felt I deserved the praise, the money, the awards, and what have you, but that's beside the point. I'm coming to you all today with a very special announcement. Something that has been a dream of mine since the first gryphon was ever created,"

Anthony paused and stared directly at Thyra. He took a deep breath and seemed instantly calmer as he looked at her. "A place for the gryphons to call their very own. A utopia. A city catered especially for them, where they can live out their lives in peace, fall in love, have children, and grow old just like the rest of us. A place where gryphon kind can own their own property, open businesses, and do as humans can without all the red tape.

"But most importantly, I wanted a city that would show the world that gryphon kind is good and kind, extraordinary, and talented." Anthony began to pace the stage, reading the crowd as they began to catch on. "I have negotiated with the European Nations and acquired a plot of land in Austria to start not just a city, but a new country that has the ideal infrastructure to accommodate gryphons, produce and manufacture gryphon specific everyday commodities. And a gryphball stadium that will host next season's First League Gryphball Championship."

A shocked round of applause followed from those in attendance and even some of the gryphons began to clap their talons together.

Anthony smiled, as he seemed to be winning over the crowd and the gryphons themselves. "I have to be honest; I was very nervous you all would laugh me off stage!" The audience chuckled with him as Anthony finished off his champagne flute. "But you see what I'm getting at. Along with this announcement, I wish to make you an offer. Though we have the groundwork taken care of, we are looking for additional funding. You can be one of the first investors to take part of this amazing gryphon colony. Imagine the possibilities! What we could create together! Imagine the revenue! All for the greater gryphon good. I hope you all can help me make this dream become a reality. Thank you," Anthony finished, and the room erupted with a round of applause.

"A gryphon country?" Thyra said out loud to Johnathen. He proceeded to clap and leaned down to hear her.

"It looks that way," Johnathen said as Richard took the stage again.

Richard clapped along with the audience until they went silent again. "Wow what a speech! I hope he won over your hearts, and checkbooks." He paused for the slight laughter in the crowd. "But please, enjoy the drinks and the music. We have a Q and A in the second parlor for those that wish to donate to the cause, and opportunities for potential investors. So please! Go talk to my associate and I when you feel free to do so, but in the meantime, I would like to invite all the team members and their party to the dining room for a discussion. Thank you all for coming tonight and feel free to stay as long as you would like!"

The live band began another piece as conversation filled the great room. The gryphons all gathered with beaks agape in surprise. Rachel was the first to find words. "Can you believe this? A colony just for us?"

"I don't know what that means really, but he mentioned a gryphball stadium as well," Thyra replied.

Jason walked up to the group. "Did you know anything about this, Coach?"

"No, I am just as surprised as you all are," Victor responded, shock evident in his eyes.

Richard approached the group and put his hands together. "Here's the stars of the hour!" All the gryphons began to ask questions at once, and he held out his hand for them to pause. "I'm sure you all have questions and concerns, but please, hold them until the meeting is finished. We have prepared something in the dining room, so please follow me."

With that, Richard turned away. The large group of gryphons and Johnathen followed behind Richard. They moved through the crowd as they walked through the room and through a separate door.

"What do you think about all this?" Rachel asked Thyra.

"I don't know, but let's just hear him out," Thyra responded.

The hallway opened up into a great banquet hall, the one where she dined before, albeit with a much smaller group. The gargantuan dining table was every bit as big as she remembered it, but all the chairs had been moved away, and in their place were large pillows meant for gryphons to sit on.

Every gryphon took their place at the table and found a stack of papers before them. Thyra grabbed the stack before her and started reading the headline, but before she could read the first sentence, a door opened on the far side of the room.

Thyra lifted her head and watched with wide eyes as Anthony and a very familiar gryphon entered. The room fell completely silent as the group stood at the head of the table, and Thyra's eyes met the gryphon's.

It was Anfang.

Chapter 9 With Arms Wide Open

Thyra's eyes did not leave Anfang's. She stared at him, and he seemed to give her an apologetic look. Yet, he seemed happy to see her. She felt like she was having an out of worldly; almost dream-like experience. The gryphon she had tossed away, her oldest friend, was there in the same room. The same gryphon that had murdered so many people was in a suit inside a mansion, seeming as if nothing had ever happened.

"All the details are in these pamphlets. Legal mumbo jumbo and all that. Feel free to read all of it over in due time, but for now take a look at section B..." Richard began.

Thyra tuned the team owner's voice out as she stared at Anfang, and he stared back at her. The once wild and uncivilized gryphon was sitting at the head of the table, calm, poised. He seemed excited, but steadfast. One would even say he looked business-like. There was discipline and etiquette in his posture. Thyra looked to her friends and could tell they were just as surprised as she was.

"Richard, why don't you tell everyone exactly what you are asking of them?" Johnathen asked. He had evidently seen enough of the document to decipher their intentions, but it seemed the others were lost. Johnathen was not the only one growing tired of Richard's long and drawn out explanation. "Also why are Anfang and Anthony a part of this?"

Anthony and Anfang shifted on their feet as they were addressed, but before they could speak, Richard held his hand up. "In due time, my man. We need to talk about the proposal first. I thought you of all people would understand, considering your occupation."

"Oh, I understand, sir," Johnathen said, a lawyerly tone entering his voice. "But, I think these fine gryphons deserve to hear you come right out with it,"

"You're asking us to be part of this, right?" Braden, one of the corvid gryphons asked. "The gryphon colony, the new team, everything?"

"Bravo! They always said ravens were the smartest. Ahem, no offense to the others." The other gryphon eyes glared at Richard as he laughed awkwardly, readjusting his tie. "Apologies, I was simply making a joke to lighten the mood."

Richard paused, looking over to Anthony and once he received a nod, continued, "To put it simply, we are proposing a permanent relocation of the Redtails to this new gryphon colony where you will be provided housing, relocation arrangements, daily transportation, legal fees, and a very substantial paycheck. All we require you to do is continue playing gryphball at the new stadium in next season's European Gryphball League."

Rachel put down the stack of papers and grabbed her drink. "Jesus, that's a lot of zeros! I'm in." Thyra gave her a shocked look and the small gryphoness shrugged. "What? It's a lot of money. And we get free everything with it. Yeah sure it's kind of fishy with your old friends up there and I don't know everything about what's going on, but it's a no brainer!"

"Well, that was easy enough!" Richard replied. "I know it's a big decision but as Rachel here pointed out, you will be grossly compensated. With a show of talons, who all is on board?"

The majority of the gryphons raised their talons to his question. Richard smiled and looked around the room. "As for those of you on the fence, please, ask your questions."

Thyra put it bluntly. "You're asking us to leave our hometown behind, everything we have known and put our trust in you, a scientist with an unknown past, and a mass murderer," Thrya said. Anfang and Anthony both frowned.

"And I will not go if Thyra will not," Aadhya said confidently.

Anthony sighed and crossed his hands on the table. "Thyra, I understood that your teammates don't know me, but you do. I thought I would have your trust by now."

"You think so? Really?" Thyra clenched her talons and looked down at the papers on the desk. "After leaving me in the dark for all these years, you suddenly appeared just a couple days ago, talk to me briefly, and all the sudden you want me to trust you?"

Richard licked his lips in concern. "Thyra, think of what you would do for history! Your team would represent the first gryphons in this new country that belongs to your kind. You could make history, and a lot of money!" He paused when she did not reply and looked around the room. "The others are interested. Don't you want to be with your team? I mean, why would you want to stay here? What have the people of this state done for you besides show you prejudice, put you down, and burn your house down?"

"Thyra, he's right," Johnathen said. Thyra's eyes widened as she looked up to her husband. His eyes were pleading as he reached to grab her talons. "We don't have anything left here. All we have is each other, and the gryphball team." He sighed and shook his head. "Wouldn't it be nice to start over?"

"But this is your hometown, John. Your job is here. Your life is here," Thyra replied, lost with thought.

"Home is wherever you are," Johnathen replied.

Thyra blinked and chuckled lightly. "You're really going to make a sappy remark like that right now?"

"It's true," Johnathen said with a smile.

"Thyra, I promise to help. I promise to do better," Anfang suddenly spoke up.

Thyra looked over to Anfang as he sat straight, his eartuft perked as he made eye contact. He seemed pleading and honest. She wanted to believe him, but she could not forget how he had been the night of the fire, a killer, enslaved by his instincts despite knowing he wanted to change.

"Ahem, for those that don't know, Thyra and Anfang have history with each other all linking back to Anthony who…" Richard began.

"We all know," came Victor's low booming voice. Everyone turned to look at the great gryphon as he took a stand at the opposite head of the table. "We are a team, a family. Thyra's past is only a mere example of the baggage we all carry, but we carry it together. There are no secrets between us." He looked around the room, his tall gray crest feathers rising at attention. "We could spend hours at this table debating the pros and cons. We could go on about the skeletons in our closets, but we need to decide here and now if we will continue to go forward together. As for me, I will not agree to this proposal until every one of my family is on board."

The room remained silent as Victor finished his speech. Everyone turned their attention to Thyra.

Sweat had broken out on Richard's forehead. He cleared his throat. "And you should see the housing! It's gorgeous! The neighborhood we have for you is set up in such a way that it looks like tree houses high up in the mountains. Uh, I'd usually have a powerpoint presentation, but this all came together so fast . . . I'll show you on my laptop."

"I have a question," Nathanial said. "What about my motorcycle, and other personal belongings?"

"My friend, with the money you will receive, you will be able to buy ten motorcycles without batting an eye," Richard replied.

"I don't give a shit. I love that bike. I'm not going if I can't bring it," Nathanial said.

"I'm not going unless my Mustang goes too. It's irreplaceable to me," Johnathen added in. Nathanial looked over to Johnathen with a grin.

"Really?" Thyra whispered, looking back judgingly at Johnathen. "All that talk about home is where you are and family stuff?"

Richard let out an exasperated laugh. "Fine! We shall supply a shipping container for those with belongings too big to bring in their luggage. Tell you what, three shipping containers for all your affections. Things that can't be bought with the gigantic paycheck you'll be receiving," Sighing, he held out his hands. "Anything else? Or are we all good here?"

"Of course, I will have to read over these documents fully before I sign anything," Johnathen said.

"My man, I assure you my legal department is one of the best. Everything you find is iron clad and-." Richard began.

"There's a typo on page three..." One of the corvid twins mentioned and pointed at the paper.

"Bloody hell," Richard replied. "Again, ravens! Am I right?" He cleared his throat. "Anyways, please sign these documents and get them back to me as soon as possible. By tomorrow at least. I have arranged a private plane to leave in five days, and I hope to see everyone on it. If any of you don't have your passports current let me know so we can get replacements expedited."

"Five days?" Thyra repeated.

"Yes, five days. I believe that should be plenty of time to get your affairs in order," Richard replied.

"But why so soon?" Thyra questioned.

"Because I will be announcing the new country to the world tomorrow evening," Anthony added in. "And I want to show the EU what we have in store for the country. A gryphball team moving in will bring a lot of good press."

"And that's the only reason?" Thyra questioned again. She could tell there was more to this deadline that he was leading on. Anthony simply looked back at Thyra without a word.

"If that's all, then this meeting is adjourned!" Richard exclaimed. "Again, it's imperative to get these signed documents to me within the next twenty-four hours if possible. The hard deadline is forty-eight. In the meantime, feel free to get back to the party! Celebrate! Relax!"

Many of the gryphons picked up their pens and began to scribble away at the pages. Other members of the team stood up from the table and exited the room, laughing and chirping with one another. Thyra and her immediate friends were more hesitant. Victor walked up to Thyra and placed his massive talons on her shoulder, giving it a gentle pat.

"I think you will make the right decision," Victor said before taking his leave, papers tucked under his arm. Moments later, the room was empty besides the friends, Anthony, Anfang, and Richard. They sat silently for a minute, exchanging an occasional glance.

"Richard, if you would, please give us some privacy," Anthony mentioned.

Richard cleared his throat and stood from his chair. "Oh, of course," he said before exiting the room.

Thyra looked to her friends and back at Anthony sternly. "Before I sign anything, I want you to spit it out. All of it."

"Woops, well there goes my ace in the hole. I already signed," Rachel admitted. "Sorry! Nobody told me we were still doing the whole negotiating thing!"

Thyra, Aadhya, and Antonio sighed and shook their heads.

"What did I tell you before? Read the room," Aadhya pointed out.

"Is this about what you saw in the labs?" Anthony asked and sat back in his chair. "I assume you all found what you were looking for."

"Actually, I have more questions than answers now," Thyra replied. "But let's address the elephant in the room first. What is Anfang doing here?"

"He's part of the deal too. I want him to be part of the colony," Anthony said. "I brought him here tonight because I wanted everyone to see that he's a changed gryphon."

"I want to change, Thyra. I want to do better," Anfang added in and looked down at the desk. "I sad when I leave you. I sad from what I did. All of it," Anfang closed his eyes, his single eartuft lying flat against his head. "Anthony says I can help. I can become strong. I want to live free…with friends, with family."

Anfang looked up at Thyra again. His eyes seemed livelier than she had ever seen them, as if he was thinking clearer than he ever had. It was like any instance of animalistic tendency was gone from his thoughts.

"I found him before the police could. He was, let's say, stubborn at first; much like how you're acting now," Anthony said. Thyra glared at him, but it seemed to have no effect. "But I showed him what I mean to accomplish, and the only way I can do it is with all of gryphon kind united. I can give him purpose and care for him, care for all of you."

"And how are you going to do that? How do I know you aren't going to use him like Matthew did?" Thyra asked sternly.

Anthony sighed and shook his head. "Thyra, I'm disappointed you would even think to compare me to that horrible human being," he said, his expression sad as he folded his hands together. "I know you've been hurt by the way people have treated you. I'd understand if your trust in humans was gone. But, I'm your father. His father. In a very real way, you all come from a piece of me. Now why would I try to hurt you? Please, trust me."

Thyra looked away and closed her eyes, trying to regain her thoughts.

Johnathen placed his hand on Thyra's back. "Let's go talk in private, hun."

Thyra nodded and stood up to walk with Johnathen out of the room. She could hear her friends asking Anthony questions as they left the room.

"I think this is a great opportunity for us," Johnathen said.

"How can we know he's not lying to us?" Thyra asked.

Johnathen sighed and kneeled down to face Thyra head on. "I don't think a man would go through all of this for a lie. Not only that, he's not the only one running this show. It seems to me this has to be a collaboration from hundreds, if not thousands, of wealthy and powerful individuals."

"That's supposed to make me feel better?" she asked.

"If nothing else, they are obligated to stick by the contract," Johnathen mentioned. Thyra looked away and he took a deep breath. "There's nothing left for us here. Our house is gone, our reputations are tarnished, and when the gryphball team leaves, we won't have anything."

"Your job is here. What about the other friends we made? Like Isabell, Saul, Carl, and Keith. Don't tell me you're forgetting your best friend," Thyra responded. She perked her eartufts as she heard laughing from the dining room, only slightly drowned out by the smooth classical music echoing through the mansion.

"I can get a job anywhere. Anthony seems determined on bringing you. Maybe he is really doing all of this for you and Anfang," Johnathen said.

"You're always so positive," Thyra chuffed. Her mood began to lift as she thought about the positives this would all bring. The only reason she had not signed away was because of Anthony and Anfang's involvement, but maybe they were there to help.

Johnathen smiled and rubbed her feathery cheeks. "I have to be. It's my job as a husband." He leaned in and kissed Thyra's beak before standing back up. "So, what do you say?"

"Ok, I'll sign, but only if you want to," Thyra said.

"I wouldn't be trying to convince you if I didn't think it was the right thing to do," Johnathen smiled and walked to the door. He opened it for her.

The group became silent as Thyra walked back in. She held her head high now, eartufts raised with proudness.

"Have you made your decision?" Anthony asked.

"Ok," Thyra said, looking at her teammates.

"Ok?" Anthony responded. "Your'e in?"

She turned back to Anthony. "If everyone else is, then who am I to stand in the way? We're in this together, But on three conditions," Thyra said and sat down at the table again. Anfang's beak curved into a half smile as his eyes lit up.

"Anything. Ask away." Anthony picked up his pen and prepared to write.

"I want to bring my friend Isabell with me," Thyra said. The group seemed confused by the request of demanding someone else coming with them, but Thyra quickly answered their question. "Isabell doesn't have any family here. She's broken, hurt, and without purpose. I think you can give her a job and let her live free. She's had a hard enough life in the past and I want her to have a better future, like all of us will," Thyra finished. Anthony thought for a minute and scribbled something down on the paper before him.

"I believe I can arrange something for that, but it will have to be her decision. I will go talk to her personally and see if she accepts the request," Anthony said. "What else?"

"Anfang lives with us. I want to watch over him," Thyra said, looking over to Anfang. He looked surprised, but quite happy with her decision.

"Thyra, I assure you that…" Anthony started.

"No. That's a demand," Thyra said. Johnathen gave Thyra a worried glance but she ignored him. "He's basically my brother and I feel you will be too busy to watch over him like I can."

"He's not technically your brother." Anthony took a deep breath and rubbed his eyes. He looked over to the waiter standing in the corner and waved him over. "Bring me the best whisky you have. And make it a double."

"I didn't know you drank," Thyra said.

"Oh, I didn't drink much in the past, but tonight I'm throwing caution to the wind," Anthony said. "And what your demanding on top of all this is…Difficult, to say the least," Anthony said exhaustedly.

"Yeah and those are still my terms. But I'm not done," Thyra said.

Anthony watched the waiter come back with his drink. He held out his finger for Thyra to pause, and quickly disposed of the brown liquor. He placed the crystal glass down on the glass and began to cough. The old man pulled out a handkerchief and coughed into it several times.

Once Anthony regained himself, he picked up his pen once more and underlined a couple words. "And your last demand?"

"I want my own personal tailor," Thyra said.

Anthony looked up from his paper and paused. He suddenly burst out into laughter and placed the pen back down. "Ok. That one is easy. Richard already arranged for a personal tailor for the team. He said he couldn't have his gryphon stars going out in t-shirts and jeans."

"Damn. I should have asked for something else," Thyra said.

"I promise you will have everything you've ever wanted and then some. But the time for negotiation is over. I've gone far and beyond for you and your friends." Anthony motioned with his hand. "Now, please, sign the papers."

Thyra picked up the pen and looked down at the paperwork. She flipped over the pages, glancing over some of the words.

"Thyra, we are here with you," Aadhya said and picked up her pen.

"And me as well," Antonio clicked the top of his and turned the papers over.

Rachel sat with a frown. "Oooohhh. Ok. I get it now. We were going to do it together and I screwed up." Aadhya gave Rachel a patient smile and nudged her with a great wing.

As Thyra signed her life away, the fear and worry that she felt deep in her heart lifted. When she was done, she found herself sighing with relief. She was going to be with her family. No matter where they would go and what obstacles would befall them, she was going to be fine. With her friends and her husband, she could conquer the world.

Chapter 10 No One Gets Left Behind

Isabell stared up at the ceiling fan slowly spinning above her. The morning sun shone through the blinds and reflected off the eggshell white walls of her cramped hospital room. The small gryphoness sighed and sat up in her bed, leaning up against the many pillows on the backboard. She looked to her right to see her mangled dark purple wing still wrapped in a cast. It ached and itched but she could not do anything about it. She looked down at the digital clock sitting on a nightstand. It was eight A.M. Sunday the twenty first.

Isabell had lost track of how long she had been in the hospital now. It seemed this would be her permanent home. She should have been sent home after the first week, but the doctors had been adamant about her staying longer. They were curious about how she would recover and wanted to do tests.

Macon's hospital had very few gryphons and every time one was admitted, the staff studied them constantly. Insurance representatives had assured her that the treatment would be compensated, so long as she stayed and willingly participated in medical tests.

Being in this small, sparsely decorated room brought back memories of the labs, memories she did not enjoy. Unlike Thyra and the other gryphons Isabell knew, she was from a third world country. The labs in Africa had been poorly underfunded and the treatment she received showed it. Some of the labs staff were very kind to her and tried to make her as comfortable as they could, but most treated her no better than a lab rat. Memories of long sleepless nights in cramped cages, pain of probes being shoved under her skin, and maggot infested meats came flashing back to memory.

She closed her purple eyes and took a deep breath. "At least the food here is better," Isabell said out loud to herself. The meals she had to choke down growing up in the lab could barely be passed as livestock rations. Hell, she would bet the cows ate better than she did during those times.

Isabell's crop squeezed and rumbled reminding her that it was breakfast time. The nurses had offered her all the meals in bed if she so desired, but ever since she had been able to get up and out, she had refused them. Isabell slowly rose out of the bed and walked down the little foam staircase that was attached to the side of her bed. The staircase was manufactured to be sold to human owners of small dogs, but it worked well for her too. She was careful to keep her casted wing tucked in close to her side.

All the furniture was made for humans, which made using anything difficult for a gryphon her size. They had placed a step stool in front of the sink to easily allow Isabell access to the sink and mirror.

Isabell stood on her hind legs, looking into the mirror. Her feathers were ruffled, but still shined the brilliant iridescent dark purple they always had. She had been worried they would lose some of their vibrancy from lack of sunbathing and normal preening, but at least she still had her looks, despite everything else.

Isabell opened her long and slender black beak to peer inside, checking for abnormalities. Satisfied, she grabbed the container of mouthwash and poured a healthy amount of the liquid into her beak. The fluid stung as she sloshed it around and then spit it out. The minty clean feeling afterword was worth the stinging, and the doctors appreciated the cleanliness when they were giving routine inspections.

"Sunday. It's the Sabbath," Isabell reminded herself. She was not religious at all, nor could she understand the humans' infatuation with God, but it did mean the chefs pulled out all the stops for breakfast and dinner.

With a little pep in her step, Isabell made her way to the door and leaned on her hind legs to pull the lever back. The door to the hallway opened up, and her little eartufts perked up to hear the sounds of ringing phones. She continued down the hallway and passed the nurses' station.

"Well good morning ma'am. You're up and at em' early," one of the male nurses said. The nurse scooted his rolling chair to the entryway of his desk and leaned over, folding his hands in his lap.

"Yeah, didn't sleep worth a shit. Plus, I remembered it's Sunday so that means pancakes and bacon. What about you, Steve?" Isabell questioned. "I thought you worked nightshift this week?"

Another male nurse turned around the corner and started to make his way towards them. Steve quickly grabbed a clipboard and handed it to the man without so much as a word. "Yeah, Jacob called out sick today, probably will be sick all week. So, it looks like sixteen hour shifts for a while." He grabbed his coffee mug and sipped loudly from it, making an ugly grimaced face.

Isabell looked up at the dark-skinned man and could see the circles under his eyes, as well as a slight redness around his brown irises. "Damn, well don't work yourself to death. I still need you to bring me medication and fluff my pillows."

Steve chuckled and shook his head. "Always with the language. Well, I'll try not to. These doctors are persistent with their orders on what to do with you. If I didn't know any better, they were all trying to get their greedy hands on every strand of DNA you possess."

"Yeah no kidding. I'm about tired of it. And you can tell that asshole doctor of yours if he orders one more thing shoved up my-."

"Steve? Where is the paperwork for 202?" asked a female nurse who was approaching the counter, cutting Isabell off.

Steve rolled his office chair back to his computer. He dug through the pile of clipboards and paperwork for a moment before handing her the right documents. He then turned his attention back to Isabell and grabbed his mug once more. "You were saying?"

The petite gryphoness ruffled her feathers, sending a couple plumes into the air. She huffed through her nares and shook her head. "Nothing. Well I'm going to go grab some breakfast, want me to nab you something?"

Steve thought for a minute and looked down at his coffee cup. He gave her a teasing smile. "Well, if you could bring me back a decent cup of Joe, that would be swell."

"Yeah, let me get right on that. I'll hobble on two legs and carefully carry up some hot coffee," Isabell replied sarcastically.

"Hey, you offered!" Steve laughed and turned back to his computer.

Isabell waved him off with her good wing and proceeded down the hallway. She had learned early on that it was best to walk close to the walls to avoid being tripped over. Sometimes people did not pay attention where they were going, distracted by clipboards or their smart phones. The last thing she needed was another broken bone from someone's carelessness.

Isabell stood on her hind paws and pressed the down arrow on the elevator controls. A pair of metal doors flung open on the far end of the hallway with a loud crash. Isabell tensed instantly and looked to see a group of doctors rushing a bed on wheels down the corridor.

"Out of the way!" One of the nurses shouted. Everyone, including Isabell, pressed tightly against the wall as they pushed the bed quickly past her. Isabell could not see too well since the bed sat up high, but she saw one of them running behind the patient's head, squeezing a large bulb to supply oxygen. As the group turned the corner, she saw the injured man's hand fall off the side of the gurney, covered in blood.

Blood. She looked down at her miniscule talons as her vision faltered. She could see his eyes again, the eyes of a corvid gryphon. His brown eyes were glazed over, cold and dead, his body surrounded by a pool of deep red blood on the white concrete floor. Masked people shouted orders all around in a flurry of chaos as one man sat in the corner, clutching his bleeding arm.

The scene played out again in her mind in slow motion. The bleeding gryphon had gone insane and retaliated against a group of scientists. He had lashed out and sliced open one human's arm shortly after being released from his cage. The guard had drawn his weapon and open fired on the gryphon.

Her ears had rung loudly as she watched the corvid hit the ground and take his final breath. She had not blamed the gryphon for lashing out. He was scared and confused, just like the rest of them were, but the memory of watching his final moments still burned in her mind.

The elevator dinged, bringing her out of her own thoughts. The doors opened and she stepped inside with a couple of other nurses. One of them smiled at her. "Hey Isabell, how you feeling today?"

"Same as yesterday, good," she responded, trying to shake the traumatic memories from her mind.

"Ground level?" The nurse questioned. Isabell nodded. The nurse reached over and pressed the button as the elevator door closed. The pair of nurses turned back to one another, blabbering on about something to do with the weather.

The door opened once more, and Isabell made her exit. She turned the corner and looked at the grand entrance room that was mostly empty. A human couple sat together on one of the couches at the far side, comforting each other. Most likely the injured man's family. Her eartufts folded back against her skull. She couldn't help but feel sorry for them, though there was nothing she could do.

As Isabell continued, the aroma of sweet pancakes and salty fatty bacon filled the air. The cafeteria was mostly empty. She watched a couple bus boys wander from table to table, spraying them down and collecting the left over dishes. The hot bar buffet was all but cleaned out. Isabell sighed, thinking that she was too late for breakfast. A double door swung open as a clean-shaven middle-aged man came walking out, carrying an empty serving dish.

"Ah, Just in time, little'n! I was about to do my final cleaning for lunch prep," the chef said. He placed the tray down on the counter and leaned over it, looking over at

Isabell. His sleeves were pulled up, revealing multiple faded tattoos on his forearms. "Was wonderin' when ya would show up."

"Better late than never, I guess. Please tell me you still have some pancake batter and bacon?" Isabell asked hopefully.

"For you? Of course!" the chef said and ducked behind the counter. Isabell approached the bar and stood on her hindpaws, placing foretalons on top. The chef stood back up with a small tray of uncooked bacon and a serving bowl of batter. "You like your bacon floppy, right?"

"Yes please!" Isabell said happily.

The chef nodded and threw the strips of meat on the flat top grill. The bacon instantly began to sizzle loudly as the grease built up around them. He then poured out the thick batter to make silver-dollar-sized cakes. "So, how are things? That wing healin' up alright?"

"As far as I know. It's been in this stupid cast for what feels like forever now. I should have it off tomorrow and start to do physical therapy," she responded.

The chef nodded and took out a spatula. He ran it around the outside of the forming pancake and quickly flipped it. "That's good, but I've gotta to admit, it's a bit strange they kept ya here for so long over somethin' like a broken bone." He checked the other bite-sized circles and started to quickly flip them over. "Usually they just set bones, cast em up, and send folks on home." He withdrew a plate and staked the cooked cakes on top of one another. "I don't know. Maybe they just like your charmin' personality so much."

"Oh, go eat a dick, Chef," Isabell retorted.

The chef laughed and scooped up the bacon, placing it on the plate as well. "You better be nice to me or I'll stop making exceptions like this." He turned and placed the plate down on the countertop.

The cheeky gryphoness simply smirked and pulled the plate towards her with a free foretalon. "Thanks again," She said happily.

"Any time, Honey." He smiled and pointed at a table over by the side. "You know where the syrup and toppings are."

Isabell grabbed the plate with her beak and hopped down to all fours once more. She approached the toppings table and set the plate down. She grabbed the syrup and added a hefty serving of the thick sugary substance to her pancakes. Licking her beak, she then grabbed a can of whipped cream out of the ice bucket. She had to use both foretalons to operate the nozzle, and created a mountain of white cream on top.

"You want some pancakes with all that sugar?" A voice came from behind her. Isabell turned to see an elderly man standing behind her.

He wore a button down shirt underneath his black jacket. His peppered gray hair was smoothed back, and his bright green eyes shone in the light. Isabell snorted through her nares and grabbed the plate with her beak. The man approached and reached out a hand to offer his help.

"I'm only kidding! Here, let me help you with that," he said.

Isabell refused, holding her head high and continuing to a table near the window. She placed the plate down on the table and hopped up in the seat.

Alex Bizzell

"I don't need help from an old geezer like you," she said and picked up one of the medallion-sized pancakes. "Especially smart ass geezers." Isabell tossed the sweet cake in her beak and swallowed it whole. Her talons dripped with the syrup clinging to them.

The man stood beside the table and let out a regretful breath. "It seems we got off on the wrong foot. May I?" He asked politely and gestured to the chair across from her.

Isabell thought for a second and looked him over. He genuinely seemed interested in talking with her and looked apologetic for his comment earlier. She sighed and held a palm up to motion to the chair.

The old man took off his jacket and hung it on the seats back before sitting down. "My name is Anthony and you must be Isabell."

"Congratulations, Sherlock. It's not like I'm the only violet-backed starling gryphoness in all of Georgia," Isabell retorted sarcastically. She picked up a piece of floppy bacon and ripped off a chunk, throwing manors out the window.

Anthony shrugged. "That is true, but your colorations are only found in male violet backed starlings, so I was a little confused at first."

Isabell chomped down the last piece of bacon and wiped off her talon with a paper towel, not sure whether she should be offended by that remark. "Your point?"

Anthony sat silent for a minute, looking perplexed. Isabell raised an eye ridge watching him closely and then he seemed to understand. "Oh! Well, my apologies, Miss Isabell." He cleared his throat and folded his hands on the table. "Anyways, I didn't come here to discuss matters of gender identification. I came here today to offer you something splendid."

140

Colony

"Something splendid? Like what? Can't you see I'm already having a 'splendid' time right now? Well, I was until you interrupted my quiet Sunday brunch," Isabell readjusted her good wing and grabbed another pancake.

The old man frowned a bit and closed his eyes, taking a deep breath. She was getting under his skin already. Good, she thought. Maybe he would just get up and leave her alone.

"I was warned you may be difficult to deal with," Anthony said gently.

"Warned by who?" Isabell asked.

"It's by whom. And the answer to whom is Thyra," Anthony replied.

Isabell laughed and pushed the empty plate away. "What the shit! You should have started with that. Don't just walk up to strangers, make fun of their eating choices and then offer them some shit. A good start would have been something like, hey, I'm a friend of Thyra's! You know, like a sensible normal person would be."

She visibly relaxed now and leaned back into the chair a bit as her crop started working on its breakfast. She was feeling pleasantly buzzed from the sensation of being full, and this made her more tolerant of his company. "I thought you were another reporter trying to get something out of me."

"Right. Well, I'll remember that for next time," Anthony said. "Continuing on, I have a proposal for you."

Isabell cocked her head. "Yeah, like what you said earlier, what is it?"

"There is a colony of gryphons we would like to relocate you to. You see, Thyra's entire gryphball team will be moving to this colony, and seeing how you two are close,

141

I would like to make you the same offer." He inclined his head. "Actually, to be honest, Thyra demanded it."

Isabell's eyes widened. "You weren't kidding. That is a big proposal. Shit, a whole colony huh? I mean I've read about one or two small towns having half and half, but I've never heard of a whole colony made up of entirely gryphons."

"It is true," Anthony said. "The details were just recently made public."

Isabell sat for a second and then narrowed her eyes, distrust building up inside. "Wait, why isn't Thyra here?"

"Currently they are packing to leave. You see, their plane leaves tomorrow," Anthony responded.

"Well, how come she hasn't sent me a text or anything?" Isabell asked, still not buying into it.

"I had all of their phones turned off, for the time being. It's a complicated affair that I do not want members of the press getting a hold of," Anthony said.

Isabell leaned her head back, relaxing slightly. "And you're telling me that everyone I've come to know is going? Well, besides my human friends."

"There are still details to be worked out since the colony is exclusive to gryphon kind, Mr. Clearwater being an exception. While there are a handful of humans that work in the city, they do not live within its borders," Anthony mentioned. "It's not so much as they aren't allowed to, it's something that was decided by the gryphons and humans have come to respect that. I'm actually part of the City Government Committee, and I highly recommended that course of action."

"Hmph! Doesn't sound half bad. And I assume all of this is free, right?" Isabell asked.

"Of course. I would not come to you making this proposal if I expected you to pay. On the contrary, you will be compensated. For now, you will be the Redtails PR representative."

Isabell sat for a second and looked out the window. There were a couple people sitting outside in wheelchairs, watching the falling leaves blow in the wind. "What's the catch?" When he did not respond right away, Isabell turned her focus to him. "What's. The. Catch?"

"Catch? Why would there be a…"

"Don't play me like a fool. Nothing in this world is free," Isabell said. "Even if Thyra demanded I come, and trust me, I do think that's pretty sweet of her, there still has to be a use for me. A PR rep? You kidding me?" Isabell almost laughed at herself. "Yeah, since I'm so good with people and kind and respectful, I'll just be the best PR rep. I don't know what use there is for an alcoholic, chain smoking, crippled asshole of a songbird."

"Well . . ." Anthony was a little shocked by her response and had to really think this through. Isabell raised one of her pierced eye ridges with question. "I'm sure there is some talent you possess. I believe we can find you a perfect fit in this new city. After all, there will be endless possibilities for a gryphon to thrive. Think of it as a sandbox, as you will."

He withdrew paperwork from his coat pocket and placed it down on the table. "Now, keep in mind, we had to go through a lot in order to draw up the paperwork for you this suddenly, so—."

"Shut the hell up and hand me a pen," Isabell demanded, holding a tiny foretalon out. Anthony quickly pulled a pen out and placed it in her grasp. "I don't really know who you are but screw it. What else do I have to lose?"

"Well that was much easier than anticipated," Anthony mentioned and watched her finish the signatures. He picked up the paperwork and placed it back into his jacket. "May I ask why?"

"Because I don't have a goddamn thing to my name anymore. And if you're lying to me or hurt Thyra in any way, I'll be there to tear your throat out," Isabell threatened. Anthony looked surprised by her response but did not seem frightened.

That bothered her. "If you think my broken wing is bad, you should have seen the other human," She placed her talons on the table and rose up to meet Anthony's face. "They had to ID his body by his dental records," Isabell squinted her purple eyes. "So do not fuck with me or my friends. Got it?"

"Loud and clear," Anthony said. Isabell sat back down in her chair and nodded her head, satisfied.

"So, when does the party begin?"

Chapter 11 Who I Am Hates Who I've Been

"It's not ideal, but I don't think it will be a problem," Joseph mentioned as he checked his vest.

The SUV came to a stop outside a security gate and Debra rolled down the window. Before them was a small airport with one long jet-black runway that extended off further than he could see at the moment. Enormous hangars decorated both sides of the runway with some of their doors open to reveal the private jets parked inside.

Anfang found the evening sunshine reflecting off the sloped metal roofs blinding. He hid his head behind the passenger seat and watched Debra as she showed the guard her credentials. Soon enough, the gate opened.

Anthony's voice replied across the Bluetooth speakers. "It shouldn't be, but I still have my concerns. All the arrangements are in order for your arrival. You and the others will be picked up at the airport. Anfang will go with the gryphball team, and you two will come back to the office."

"I happy for this," Anfang mentioned. He sat back in his seat as the car accelerated and looked out the windows to see the different airplanes in their hangers. "I live with Thyra, but I train every day with Joseph."

"It's not what we had in mind," Anthony said irritably. "There are only a couple dozen gryphons that are in training and we wanted you to live with them. You will be a part of the city's guard, and we don't have time to waste. We have plenty of room in the military housing on the site. I want you to socialize with other gryphons, study daily, learn the laws of the country, learn discipline, and become stronger. You need to be trained and out protecting the citizens as soon as possible." His voice lowered to a mutter. "I wanted to keep a close watch on your progress, Anfang."

"Sir, I will ensure you get a full report twice a day and make sure he is punctual," Joseph promised.

"I have no doubt that you will," Anthony replied. "And we are trusting Anfang will hold up his end. As I said, the situation is not ideal, but as long as you do what you are told, we won't have a problem."

"I promise to be good. I promise to change," Anfang reassured them. "I hate old me."

"Good. Well, it's very late here so I'm going to get some sleep. Have a safe flight," Anthony said before the speakers clicked.

Debra's phone beeped and the soft rock resumed on the radio station. The car came to a stop outside one of the hangars, and Debra climbed out first with briefcase in hand. She walked out of sight for a moment and came back to wave the two gryphons in.

Anfang exited the vehicle with Joseph and stepped foot inside the enormous hangar. The polished concrete shined like a mirror surface. Exotic cars and furniture decorated the far end of the room. At the very center, however, was a pure white private jet, easily big enough to hold the whole gryphball team and maybe more. The human-made flying machine mesmerized Anfang. He had seen pictures of them but had never been this close to one.

"I'm guessing you've never flown in an airplane," Joseph said, taking notice of Anfang's expression.

"No," Anfang responded. He glanced over to see a man and woman walk out of an open door in the side of the hanger. Both were dressed in white button-down jackets with pins decorating their breast pocket. Fancy black hats adorned their heads.

"Are we on schedule?" Debra asked the pilot and her copilot.

"Yes, ma'am. Everything is ready for your departure when your party arrives. Take off is planned for three hours from now and the estimated time of arrival in Innsbruck is 13:30 local time," the female pilot said.

"Very good. I expect everyone to be here soon," Debra said and turned to walk towards the well decorated living room section of the hanger. Anfang followed Debra's lead and glanced at the pilots as he walked by, but they did not seem to be interested in the gryphons. Debra walked up to the dry bar and poured herself a drink.

"Might as well make yourselves comfortable," she said and sat down on one of the plush leather couches.

Anfang walked over to an area rug and sat down while Joseph poured himself a drink. He watched several other men begin to unload suitcases from the SUV.

"Anfang, when we arrive, we will have to go through immigration and show your passport," Debra said. Anfang lifted his single eartuft curiously and turned to face her. She blinked at him. "Do you know what that is?"

"No. What is a passport?" Anfang asked.

Debra unlatched her briefcase and pulled out a stack of little blue books. She sorted through them, opening each one, and handed the correct passport over to Anfang. He opened the blue book and saw a picture of himself, along with all kinds of information listed on the page.

"It's your identification. In this case it means you are allowed to go to different countries. It was easy enough to forge one for you since you technically don't exist," Debra explained.

Anfang looked at his picture again. He remembered Debra making him stand still and taking pictures of him earlier that week. It had been weird letting someone take a picture of him, but even more odd seeing the picture actually in front of him. It relieved him in a way he could not describe, even if it was a fake. He felt like he was somebody now. He was not a ghost any longer.

"Surname…Clearwater…Given name… Anfang Charles?" Anfang repeated. Debra smiled and sipped from her crystal glass.

"Very good! I'm glad to see you haven't forgotten how to read. You know, I was the one that taught you," Debra said. "Surname means your last name, which is Clearwater, your given name is first and middle name which is Anfang and Charles. So you are Anfang Charles Clearwater. Make sense?"

Anfang nodded at her explanation and pointed at the passport. "I hear you call Anthony 'Mister Clearwater.' My name Clearwater too?" Anfang asked.

"Yes. That's his last name, and Charles was my father's name. On paper, you are Anthony's adopted son,"

Debra said and finished off the rest of glass. "He insisted on it actually."

Joseph rolled his eyes and pulled his phone out of a pouch. Debra leaned over and gently caressed Anfang's eartuft. The sensation was indescribable. He could feel a tingle work its way down his spine and caused his tail to twitch. A gentle rumble came from his chest, causing Debra to chuckle.

"Don't soften him up, Debra," Joseph said, sprawling out on the opposite couch with his drink.

"Oh, shut your beak. He's been through enough and deserves some affection," Debra said and turned back to Anfang. "But as I was saying, we will have to go through immigration. Now we are really hoping the news about your past crimes hasn't reached Austria and they won't recognize you. There will be one officer checking these passports once we arrive. If things go to plan, the officer may just collect them, look over them, and that's it, but sometimes they walk through the aircraft and ask individuals questions."

Debra set the glass down and faced Anfang. "There's other information on that booklet, like your birthday, place of birth, and so on. I need you to memorize that and commit it to memory," Debra said. "Like right here, it says you were born in Georgia, USA, so he may ask 'What part of Georgia are you from?' and you'll say Atlanta," Debra saw confusion on his face. "Here, let's try some role play."

"Role play?" Anfang asked.

"Yeah! I'll act like the officer and ask you questions. Hand me the passport," Debra said and grabbed the blue book. She opened it up and put on a stern expression, getting into character. She puffed up her chest and broadened her shoulders, flipping through the passport. "Evening, Mr.

Clearwater. Where are you coming from?" Debra said in a low voice.

"I…Georgia," Anfang stumbled. Debra raised an eyebrow and continued flipping through the passport.

"What part?" Debra asked in character.

"Atlanta. I come from Atlanta," Anfang replied.

"Oh really? How is it over there? I hear Atlanta is huge!" Debra exclaimed. Anfang opened his beak and went wide-eyed, not knowing how to respond. Debra chuckled and leaned it, cupping her mouth with a hand. "Say something like, 'It's crazy! And the traffic is awful!'"

"It…It's crazy. And the traffic is awful," Anfang stumbled on the expression, repeating the phrase back like a mindless baritone cockatoo.

"And smile!" Debra commanded. Anfang blinked and tried to curve the ends of his beak into a grin but ended up gaping his beak to show the protruding fangs awkwardly. Debra laughed loudly and shook her hand. "We will have to work on that."

"God damnit, Deb. He's not a child," Joseph said and finished his drink.

"One more negative peep out of your beak and I'll pluck out those pretty red tail feathers of yours for my hat," Debra threatened. Joseph snorted through his nares and stood off the couch to walk over to the bar. She held out her glass and rattled the ice cubes around in it, getting Joseph's attention. Reluctantly, Joseph grabbed her glass and refilled it as well.

Anfang turned his attention towards the hangar's entrance and watched as a SUV began to pull up. Debra rose up out of her seat and straightened her suit jacket as a couple gryphons began to exit the vehicle. Anfang remembered the great harpy eagle gryphon and the chatty caracara gryphon, but not the golden eagle that was with the party. Anfang followed Debra to greet them as Joseph hung back, finishing pouring the drinks.

"I figured the coach would be the first to arrive," Debra commented and extended her hand to the harpy eagle. He sat before her, sitting as tall as she was standing, and offered a single talon for her to shake.

"Debra, was it?" Victor asked.

"Yes. I'm Anthony's assistant. We chatted briefly after the meeting. I wanted to introduce myself to everyone else that night, but I wasn't able to." Debra smiled.

Victor looked around the room, choosing to ignore Anfang at the moment. "I see Anthony is not here."

"Yes. He had a very big meeting with the EU to sign all the official paperwork for the colony. As of last night, Greifsburg is now officially the 28th country in the EU." Debra said. Victor could not help but chuckle at the mention of the name.

"How original. He has named it 'Gryphon Castle' in German," Victor said.

"Yes. He took a vote, actually. We figured it would be bold and on the nose," Debra replied. "I hope you are ready for your new life, Victor."

"It wasn't a hard decision. If my team is on board, so am I," Victor said with confidence. He glanced over to Anfang, now suddenly interested in the beast. "And I see he will be joining us on the flight?"

"Yes. I'm not sure if you were informed. Thyra had a small list of requests once everyone else left. Anfang living under the same roof as her was one of them. He will be living in the team complex with you all for the time being," Debra began.

Victor raised an eye ridge. He turned to watch multiple men begin to retrieve suitcases from the SUV. "I was not aware we would all be living together."

"Temporarily, yes. It was in the amended documentation," Debra said. "The gryphball team as a whole will be living under the same roof for a period of time until construction of your housing is built. I assure you, the resort that we have provided for you will be more than sufficient."

"I understand that, but, him as well?" Victor said.

"Thyra demanded it," Debra said.

"Is problem?" Anfang said in concern.

Victor looked into Anfang's eyes and read him for a second. "If you don't cause trouble, then no." Victor mentioned. The golden eagle and caracara walked up to sit next down to victor, all of them facing Anfang.

The golden eagle gryphon stuck out his foretalon. "We've met before! It was under different circumstances, as in you were trying to tear us limb from limb, but I'm Jason!" Anfang reached forward and grasped talons together in a firm handshake. "Let's hope we can get off on the right talon this time."

Anfang remembered the golden eagle on the field, challenging him and trying to defend Thyra, but he showed no hatred in his eyes. "I not that gryphon now," Anfang said and released his grip.

"Let's hope so." Jason grinned and patted Anfang on the shoulder before walking past him. "Hey! Be careful with that suitcase!" he yelled at one of the baggage men and wandered off.

The caracara gryphon stared up at Anfang and huffed through his nares before standing up. He nudged Anfang slightly as he passed without saying a word to him. Anfang squinted and turned to watch Nathanial walk off. He had an urge to turn around and rip the stuck up gryphons tail feathers out.

"That's Nathanial," Victor said to Anfang. "Don't pay him any attention. He's difficult with everyone. But I'm sure you will have plenty of time to get to know everyone, seeing how we will be living together," he added, taking in a deep breath.

"Why don't you make yourself comfortable while we wait for everyone else, Coach," Debra offered.

Victor inclined his head and departed, making his way over to join Joseph by the couches and bar. Two more SUVs pulled into the hanger. Two male corvid gryphons along with a peregrine and osprey exited the vehicle.

Debra pointed to the two black gryphons first. "You might remember them from the other night, the twins, Brandon and Braden. I don't know which one is which, but they both seem pleasant enough." They both waved politely as they walked back to join Victor in the back of the room.

"The osprey is Viola, and the peregrine is Priscilla, a married female pair. I didn't get to talk with them at the party. They apparently left early, but from what I've heard, they are incredibly skilled, and kind as can be," Debra put on a smile and waved to the two. The peregrine waved back with a smile, but the osprey hid behind her mate, refusing to make eye contact. Priscilla laughed and wrapped a wing around Viola, tugging her in and whispering something to her. They walked wingshoulder to wingshoulder towards the back and mingled with the growing group. "And cute as a button, if I say so myself."

"Debra, you think everyone hate me?" Anfang asked, watching the group of gryphons converse between themselves. They all shared smiles, hugs, and preens between them. He wanted to have that. He wanted to be seen as a normal gryphon and get along with others.

"Hate is a strong word. Do they fear you? Most likely," Debra placed her hand on Anfang's head, rubbing his single eartuft again. "But everyone can change their opinion. You'll have to show them that you've changed. It'll take some time for you to build a relationship with them, just like with any other person or gryphon. You just have a bigger hurdle."

He sighed and nodded his head. "I try."

Another SUV pulled into the airplane hangar and stopped. His mood lifted as he saw Thyra and her friends climb out of the SUV. Johnathen followed after the gryphons, carrying a backpack on his back. Thyra made eye contact with him and Anfang felt his heart sing. His eartuft stood straight, but he did his best to keep his body composed.

The band grew nearer and Anfang had to push down his excitement. "Thyra!"

"Anfang." Thyra paused and collected her thoughts. "I've been thinking of what to say to you these past few days. It's difficult, I-."

Rachel interrupted. "Man, I gotta ask, what is with those big metal circles on your shoulders? Like, they look like ports or something. Like cyberpunk stuff! It's been bugging me ever since I saw you! I mean what are those for?"

Anfang raised his head up and blinked with confusion.

"God damnit, Rachel," Johnathen commented and reached down to pick up the cat sized gryphoness. She screeched angrily and desperately tried to escape Johnathen's grasp, flailing limbs every which way.

"What! I mean, we all have to be thinking the same thing! I just wanted to know!" Rachel exclaimed as Johnathen carried her off under his arm. Thyra rubbed her eyes and sighed.

"I have told her time and time again," Aadhya commented and sat down next to Thyra. She looked over to Antonio as he sat on the opposite side of Thyra, shaking his head.

"I'm not sitting next to her on the plane," Antonio stated. "I'll fly myself across the Atlantic before I do that."

"Th-they said it called access ports," Anfang said hesitantly. The other gryphons perked their eartufts, and it was obvious that they were just as interested as Rachel. "They tried to put needles in me, but needles break. Not work. They make the ports and put it in me. They said easy to get blood. Easy to give medicine," Anfang explained.

Thyra opened her beak to ask more questions, but changed her mind. There was clearly something else on her mind. "Anfang, as I was saying, it's difficult to see you. We've had some really bad experiences together, and it's hard to forget that."

"I want to start new. I be better," Anfang assured.

"I know, but it's still hard to forget everything. All the bloodshed, the fighting at the stadium, you in my burning house holding Matthew's dead body in the air like a ragdoll," Thyra paused and took a deep breath. Aadhya extended a wing and wrapped it around Thyra to comfort her. She looked down at her gloved talons on the shimmering concrete floor. "All I'm saying is its going to take some time for me to trust you again, and I'm probably going to seem distant to you."

"Distant?" Anfang asked curiously.

"Um, like far away, up here," Thyra said and pointed to her head. "Emotionally distant. But despite that, I need you to know that I still care for you like a brother." She looked up into his eyes again. "It's why I want you to live with me, with us. I believe there's still good in you, but I want to keep a close eye on you."

Anfang nodded even though he did not quite understand what she meant. Emotions and social structures were still a difficult concept to grasp. What he had done in the past had been completely natural to him, but as time went on, he could see the implications of his actions. She was still hurt, and he could see a slight tinge of fear in her eyes. He understood that. Usually, fear in others' eyes fueled him, but all he could feel now was remorse.

"I . . . care for you, Thyra," Anfang said back.

Antonio adjusted himself on all fours and cleared his throat. "I am going to go check on the others," he said awkwardly before taking his leave.

The three remaining gryphons stood together silently, not knowing what to say next. Bright Halogen lights above their heads suddenly clicked on as the sun began to set. The fixtures buzzed loudly as they warmed up, casting an artificial white light to brighten up the hanger.

Debra approached cautiously and saw they were finished speaking. "Now that everyone is here, we can depart in thirty minutes."

Thyra looked around the room and back at Debra, disappointedly. "Everyone is here? What about my friend, Isabell? I thought she was coming with us."

"Oh! I forgot to mention. She has accepted the offer and signed the paperwork but will not be departing on this flight with us. Instead, she will be on a commercial flight next week," Debra explained. "Last minute change but don't worry. She's coming."

"I wish you all would let us have our cellphones back so I could talk to her," Thyra mentioned.

"Sorry, but it was per Anthony's orders. Isabell will not be far behind us. A couple days, at most," Debra responded.

"Ok, good. I was worried for a minute," Thyra said. Debra smiled and turned away to head to the plane. Thyra cleared her throat and motioned with her talon to the airplane. "I guess we should take our seats." She focused her eyes on Anfang. "Have you ever flown?"

Anfang shook his head. "No. I not see plane before. You?"

"Nope. And to be honest, I'm kinda excited," Thyra mentioned with a slight smile. Aadhya followed them over to the airplane as the group began to line up.

"I call shotgun!" Rachel yelled from halfway across the hanger, running on all fours to the stairs leading into the aircraft.

"Rachel! There is no shotgun!" Thyra yelled out, but it fell on deaf ears.

Rachel jumped up the stairs and glanced inside. "Holy shit! This thing is nice! I've never flown before, well like, on an airplane, but it's nothing like what you see in the pictures!" She laughed and disappeared into the cabin.

157

Anfang and Thyra hung at the back of the group, letting the other gryphons enter first. He could hear the little gryphon's shrill voice arguing with other human voices towards the front of the plane.

The enormous turbines on the side of the aircraft began to spool up. They were quiet at first, but within a minute, the sound was defining to Anfang. Even at idle, the high-pitched whining they made hurt his head. He flattened his eartuft to the top of his head.

Debra tapped on Anfang's shoulder and leaned in towards his head. "Don't worry! That's just the engines getting warmed up."

Anfang nodded and climbed up the stairs after Thyra. The interior was as plush and exotic as he imagined it to be. Everything was foreign about the airplane, down to the ceiling and windows. All the gryphons sat in their seats, talking excitedly with one another.

Debra and Joseph were the last to board the plane. One of the pilots exited the cockpit, motioning Rachel out of it. She cursed and went to the back of the plane before picking out a seat. The copilot closed the cabin door and rotated a large lever to lock it in place.

Immediately, the sound of the engines was muffled, and Anfang could hear his own thoughts again. He followed Thyra and sat in the opposing seat, facing her and Johnathen.

Debra sat next to Anfang and buckled her seat belt with a relieved sigh. She patted her thighs and smiled. "And away we go!"

The intercom buzzed as the pilot and copilot checked across the speaker. "Good evening ladies and gentlemen, and, um, gryphons. This is your pilot, Andrea speaking. Today we will be embarking to Innsbruck, Austria. Estimated flight time is nine hours and twenty minutes. Skies look to be clear throughout the trip. Current temperature at destination is a brisk 26 degrees Fahrenheit. We will taxi within the next 10 minutes after our final checks and be on our way soon."

The radio clicked as the pilot hung up the radio.

Debra leaned her large leather seat back slightly and folded her hands together. "Well, it looks like we have some time to get to know each other. So, who wants to start?"

Chapter 12 Nothin' But A Good Time

"Have you ever seen anything like this?" Rachel yelled, looking out the window of the plane.

Thyra felt the whole plane rock as the landing gear extended. She looked out the window to see a pure white landscape below. The Alps were close in view with the city directly below them. Even while flying high, she swore she could reach out and touch the rocky mountain faces. There was a definite tree line along the mountain ridges that patched the sides and down into the valley. The plane banked hard, turning Thyra's crop slightly. She closed her eyes and pushed down the feeling of sickness.

"It's just like those fairy tale village pictures, isn't it?" Rachel smiled and looked over to Thyra in the seats across the plane. "You alright?"

"Yeah, just a little nauseous," Thyra complained.

Johnathen rubbed his hand along the top of her head to comfort her. "Did that medicine already wear off?"

Thyra nodded as the plane started descending quicker. She had decided flying on an airplane was not her style. She looked around the cabin and saw many other green-faced gryphons. Apparently, she was not the only one having trouble adjusting to plane flight. Anfang was too busy looking out the window with wonder to notice the discomfort of the other gryphons.

She tried to settle her crop and glanced outside, seeing the ground coming into view rather quickly. She held her breath as the plane's wheels touched down, and the whole cabin bounced hard. The wheels screeched and the turbines roared loudly, causing the plane to decelerate quickly. She was glad she had on her seatbelt or she would have ended up on the floor.

The speakers beeped and the radio clicked on accompanied by the pilot's voice. "Welcome to Innsbruck, Austria. I hope everyone had a pleasant flight. We are currently in route to the main gate and the radio tower has requested that we remain inside until the border patrol agent is present. Thank you."

Debra unfastened her seatbelt and stood to reach up into the overhead bins and pull out a briefcase. "Alright everyone, I'm going to be passing out passports for those that have never been through customs." She paused and looked around the cabin. "Which I assume is everyone. Anyways, it's easy. All you will do is hand the agent your passport, they will look it over, and perhaps ask you some simple questions."

Debra walked around the cabin to hand out the passports. Every gryphon took their own and opened it to look inside. The plane came to a stop as Debra sat back down in her seat to hand Thyra's over. "Once we are done with the customs agent, there will be cars waiting for us at the gate. Your baggage will be taken care of, so just proceed to the vehicles. We are all going to the same place first."

The copilot walked out of the cockpit and opened up the cabin door. Immediately, an icy gust of cold air ripped through the cabin, making all the gryphons fluff up their feathers.

A blond-haired man stepped into the cabin and brushed the snow off his puffy black jacket. "Welcome to Austria," the agent said in a rough accent. He looked around the cabin. "You are the gryphball team, yes?"

"Well duh, I mean who else-," Rachel began and was quickly silenced as Aadhya nudged her with a wing.

The agent raised his eyebrow at her and held out his hand. "Single file. Papers please." Debra was the first to walk up and hand him her passport. "I assume you are the leader?" he asked.

"In a way," Debra stated. "We are all heading straight to Greifsburg. These are the new residents."

He flipped through the passport and handed it back. "I see! It has been interesting watching the new city be built. Do any of them speak German?"

"Sadly not! But they will learn eventually," Debra said.

"Very good! Greifsburg may be its own country, but it is still in Austria!" The agent laughed and stepped aside to let her off the plane.

Victor was the next to approach and handed the agent his passport. He looked it over without much interest and handed the book back. More gryphons proceeded, going through the motions, until Anfang approached.

"What have we here?" The agent questioned and took Anfang's passport. He looked it over for a moment and did a double take on the picture versus Anfang's appearance. "I have not seen gryphon such as you."

Thyra felt her heart skip a beat and held her breath. Anfang was a different gryphon to anyone's eyes, but with enough clothing, he looked like a hybrid of sorts. Thyra walked up behind Anfang and waited patiently.

"I, I old gryphon," Anfang responded on the spot. The officer flipped through his passport and leaned down slightly to get a better look at him.

"An old breed? With wings like dragon, face of lion and eagle? Interesting," the officer began. Thyra swallowed hard but waited to see if Anfang could get himself out of this situation. "So, old gryphon, where were you born?"

"Atlanta. Not born, made," Anfang said confidently.

The officer nodded and held open the main page. "I see. When were you made?"

"November seventieth, 2011," Anfang responded. "But you know that. It is there."

Thyra's eartufts laid flat. Anfang was actually talking confidently with another human but she did not expect him to be testy. The officer looked back at him sternly as if to reprehend his smart-ass comeback but smiled instead.

"I was curious is all. I have not seen a gryphon such as you, or as old. Must make you one of the firsts, yes?" The officer asked. The remaining gryphons in the cabin stared on in awe at the realization that this was probably true.

Anfang nodded his beak and took the passport back as it was offered to him. "Not one of. The first."

The officer stood back up and stepped to the side with a show of his hand. "My! The first gryphon? A pleasure to have you here, Mr. Clearwater. I hope you have a pleasant life, and may we meet again," he exclaimed.

Thyra let out a loud sigh of relief. For a minute, she was thinking the officer had recognized Anfang from a news report from Macon. With how connected the world was nowadays, she had no way of knowing.

The rest of the border checks went by without a hitch, and Thyra proceeded down the stairs. She squinted her eyes as an icy breeze blew into her face, taking her breath away. A thin blanket of snow lay across the ground in front of her, with the great Alps towering above. It was like there was a wall around her, holding her in, but instead of feeling trapped, she found herself mesmerized by the sight.

She had never felt smaller in comparison to the world, but at the same time, she felt like she could conquer it. All she could think about was trying to fly to the top of the mountains. If it was possible, it would be one of the first things she would try.

"I should have unpacked my damn jacket!" Rachel cursed. Thyra turned to see Rachel walking down the stairs; feathers ruffled out to the point of looking more like a ball than a gryphon. Aadhya remained steadfast, unaffected by the cold breeze. Rachel scowled up at her. "And what's with you?"

"My kind is built for this weather," Aadhya commented. She looked comfortable even with a thin layer of clothing on. Her white and peppered black feathers blended in with the snowy landscape perfectly. Without the clothing, it would have been easy for her to visually disappear into the backdrop.

"Well good for you!" Rachel said and rushed past Thyra towards one of the Mercedes SUVs.

A group of people were taking baggage from the airplane and bringing them to the cars. Gryphons and humans piled into the square-bodied Mercedes vehicles and Rachel pushed one of the corvids aside to jump into the car.

"You alright?" Johnathen asked as he walked up behind Thyra.

She nodded and walked towards the line of cars. The snow crunched under her weight and sent a cold shiver up her legs. "Yeah! It's beautiful even if it is freaking cold."

Johnathen laughed and opened up one of the large doors, letting her in first. "Just a little bit. It's a big difference from Georgia winter. Us southerners aren't built for this weather."

Thyra climbed into the backseat and Johnathen entered after her. He shut the door with a loud thud and Thyra ruffled her feathers. She leaned in to rest against Johnathen and he wrapped an arm around her neck, holding her in close as she shivered gently.

"I guess one of the first things we will need to get is some proper winter gear. Our light jackets don't do shit for this weather," Johnathen commented.

"We can do that tomorrow," Debra said from the driver's seat. Anfang hopped into the front seat next to her. She put the SUV in drive and followed the other trucks out of the airport.

Thyra looked out the window and watched the foreign houses pass by as they proceeded down the small streets of the city. The structures looked ancient and outdated, but well-kept. It was a striking difference compared to the buildings around Georgia. People walked up and down the city streets covered in snow, and everywhere she looked there were towering mountains framing the background.

"Where exactly is Greifsburg?" Thyra asked.

"About twenty five kilometers due southeast of Innsbruck," Debra began. "It was a small town that was known for its ski resorts and even hosted the winter Olympics decades ago." Debra paused at a red light and looked into the rear view mirror. Thyra thought for a minute and Debra could tell she was confused. "The Olympics were a competition between the best athletes across the world. It was a pretty big deal back in the day. Anyways, the town was almost completely ruined by an avalanche, and Austria decided to not rebuild it."

The town quickly disappeared after they passed over a frozen river and proceeded onto the Autobahn. "So that's when Anthony, along with a lot of other wealthy investors, went before the EU and offered to buy the land to create a new country for gryphons. It took some convincing and years of red tape, but it's now officially its own sovereign country," Debra explained as she cruised up to speed.

Thyra watched the non-deciduous trees fly by at an incredible speed. It was snowing and yet she had never been in a vehicle moving this fast. The locals seemed used to it. Even at the rate they were traveling, other cars still passed them. "I wonder what the Austrian citizens think of it all?"

"Some are against it, to be expected. As you know, Germans are very keen on tradition, especially in areas like this, but the land has the perfect infrastructure for growth and expansion," Debra replied.

"Well, we are here now, whether they like it or not," Johnathen chimed in. "But don't worry, Thyra. I don't think we'll run into anything like the Gathering's way of thinking. Drom what I've read the Germans and Austrians are more open-minded." He smiled. "Plus, I'm excited to learn German. It's a pretty cool language."

"It new start for us," Anfang added in agreement.

Thyra looked to the beast calmly sitting in the passenger seat. He was staring out the window, lost in thought. She could only imagine what was going on in his head. She knew he was intelligent, even if he could not express it clearly.

He sighed. "No more hide. No more run. No more kill."

Debra glanced over to Anfang and back at the road. "I sure hope so."

The vehicles began to exit off the Autobahn in the middle of a steep hill. Debra followed after them onto a small two-lane road that winded in between thick patches of trees that opened into fields again. In Georgia, the forests seem to go on forever outside the city, but here things were broken up by open fields.

Thyra saw a big brand new sign on the side of the road that simply read 'Republic of Greifsburg' with an insignia of a gryphon in flight printed on it.

"And now we are officially in the country," Debra said.

Thyra had expected a big border checkpoint that they would have to stop at. She thought the different countries had more separation to them, but it was nothing but a sign. It was as if she was crossing a state line and nothing more. Still, it did not affect the way she felt. This was the place she would live in for the foreseeable future.

"So, how do the laws work as far as citizenship and travel?" Johnathen asked curiously. Of course, he would think of the implications and logistics of it all, Thyra thought to herself.

"You're a part of the EU, plain and simple," Debra responded. "Now as far as your law degree goes in this country, I'm not sure how that works, but it's something we can figure out in time. We are still ironing out the little things."

The SUVs slowed down to a crawl as they entered town. Construction equipment littered the streets. The weather had abated. Gryphons and humans worked together running the equipment in the sunlight.

Some of the original structures remained, keeping the charm of the old Austrian city alive, but Thyra could see other buildings that were no more than rubble. Thyra watched as one gryphon picked up a load of stone in his talons and took to the air, handing them off to a worker on the next level up.

"I've never seen anything like this," Thyra commented.

"Humans and gryphons working together to build a town. It's really something, isn't it?" Johnathen added in.

"That's what we want to see. All of us working together for the greater good," Debra said as she navigated the small city streets.

They pulled away from the compact area and turned up a backroad. The SUV's engine rumbled as they climbed up a steep hill away from the center of town. At the base of one of the hills, Thyra saw a large building in the distance that seemed untouched by the avalanche. The convoy came to a stop outside the building and parked in the makeshift lot outside.

"Well, welcome to your new home, for now," Debra said, pointing at the hotel-style building. "It was an old ski resort, but feels more along the lines of a grand scale bed and breakfast. It has fifteen rooms, a pretty spacious common room, and a kitchen big enough to feed everyone with ease."

Thyra opened the car door and stepped out into the snow. She took a deep breath of the crisp air and shivered. The grand building was in the shape of a giant rectangle made of mostly wood with a sharply-angled roof hanging off both sides. Thyra's eyes were drawn to a picture of a gryphon painted into the white brick on one side of the building.

Debra noticed her looking at the insignia and chuckled. "That was a little addition I did myself."

"You make that?" Anfang asked as he exited the vehicle.

"I thought it was cute," Debra commented and opened up the tailgate of the truck.

Other gryphons pilled out of the other vehicles, gasping and talking amongst themselves as they looked around. Johnathen tapped on Thyra's shoulder and pointed down the hillside to the vast valley that lay before them. Thyra turned to see the breathtaking view of the small country of Greifsburg, the grand city of Innsbruck, and the massive Alps that framed it all in. This would be a view she would see for years to come, and something she would never tire of.

"Is that the gryphball stadium?" Johnathen asked. He pointed to one of the fields littered with construction equipment and a leveled piece of land. Thyra could make the outline of the concrete base in the snow and thousands of pallets of material surrounding it.

"Exactly. It's going to be the biggest gryphball stadium in the world. We are estimating just over a hundred thousand seating capacity," Debra said.

"Jesus. Well if you want a way to boost economy quick, that's one way to do it," Johnathen replied and went to grab luggage from the back of the SUV. Thyra heard someone running her way and turned to see Rachel rushing her way.

"Thyra! This place is huge!" Rachel exclaimed. She tried to stop but ending up sliding right past her on the icy road surface. Thyra laughed as Rachel crashed into a snowbank and disappeared for a second. The kestrel popped out of the snow and gasped.

"You alright?" Thyra asked with a laugh.

Rachel shook the excess snow off her feathers and clothes before carefully walking up beside Thyra. "Yeah! All I need is some hot chocolate and a nice schnitzel! Maybe we can learn how to ski! I mean, is their even skis for gryphons? Has a gryphon ever skied? I don't know but I wanna try! I'll be the first combo gryphball and skiing star in the world!" She puffed up her chest and ruffled her feathers.

Thyra brushed some of the snow off the top of the tiny gryphon's head and smiled. "How about we just start with the hot chocolate."

171

Chapter 13 The Red

"I just want to thank everyone for being here today," Victor said as he stood at the head of the cramped dining room.

Gryphons sat wingshoulder to wingshoulder around various tables, all looking towards their coach. Empty plates sat towards the center of every table in the room. The dim dining room lights illuminated the area in a burnt orange.

The harpy eagle leaned against the glass double doors that led to the outside patio and held up his beer. "I know it's been a long couple of days, and it will take time getting used to living together, but I think we will do fine," Victor assured them.

Thyra concurred, even in the cramped former ski resort lodgings, there was plentiful space for the team and the others that were joined with them. The sun had set hours ago, yet it was still early into the night. Thyra looked out the glass doors behind Victor, watching a full moon rising over the towering mountains in the background. Even in the dining room, she could see the splendor of the towering bluffs in the close distance.

Her crop buzzed pleasantly from a hefty meal of schnitzel and spaetzle with fresh red potatoes. The savory taste lingered on her tongue, only being washed away slowly with every gulp of wheat banana flavored hefeweizen.

"We have become a family in this short time," Victor said, holding his slender long mug in one foretalon and standing at the edge of the room. "Sure, we knew one another well enough before this, but I believe in time, we will grow as a household too." He sipped from his mug. "It will take some getting used to, what with some others living amongst us." The great grey harpy locked eyes with Anfang who was sitting next to Thyra. "But I believe the experience will make us stronger yet. The more we unite, the better we will be." Victor raised his glass for all to see. The gryphons and humans in the room raised their glass with him in a toast. "To our future together!"

The rest of the group chanted the same phrase back before clinging glasses together and drinking. Thyra smiled to the rest of the gryphons and to Johnathen sitting next to her, but Anfang glanced away from Thyra. Her eartufts fell flat as the room erupted in conversation once again. Despite being surrounded with gryphons, Anfang looked so alone. His eyes drifted down to his half-eaten plate, seemingly lost in thought.

As Thyra looked around the room, she caught her teammates looking in their direction, motioning to Anfang and talking quietly amongst themselves. She tried to push the lingering thoughts away and bumped Anfang with a wingshoulder.

"Saving room for dessert?" Thyra joked with him, but Anfang only glanced over at her. The half-smile on her beak disappeared as she saw the hurt in his eyes. "You've barely touched your food. Are you ok?"

The beast looked around the room and shook his head. "Stomach hurt. Not hungry," Anfang replied before getting up from his seat. Conversations started to quiet down as he stood and walked out of the room, up a small set of stairs into what used to be a lobby. That's when she started to hear the whispers grow louder.

"You think he will kill us in our sleep?" Thyra heard Viola ask her mate, Priscilla. What Priscilla said next, Thyra could not know. Her voice was too soft to make out from the opposing table.

"I don't know what the hell Victor is doing allowing that freak live with us," Came Nathanial's voice next, loud enough for Thyra to hear it across the room. She waited for Rachel to reprimand him for saying it, but it looked like she agreed with him. She whispered something back that Thyra could not make out.

"…and under the same roof as us? I thought this place was for our team. Not for harboring a fugitive. I mean, I had to fight him on a gryphball field in front of a live TV audience!" Jason the golden eagle said to Victor. Thyra perked her eartufts, straining to hear Victor's response.

"Thyra? You ok?" Johnathen's voice cut in, breaking her concentration. She put on a mask for her husband, turning to him with a smile.

"Yeah! I'm just a little out of it. I think it's the jetlag," Thyra replied. She was not completely lying. She really did feel out of it, but it was more than jetlag. Johnathen eyed her suspiciously and finished off his liter glass of beer. She held out a foretalon palm up. "What?"

"You think after ten years of marriage you can fool me?" he said with a chuckle. His speech was slightly slurred, his nose and cheeks displaying a rosy red from the alcohol. "What's really up?"

Thyra sighed, knowing she was exposed. "It's just Anfang. I'm worried,"

"Oh, don't worry about him!" Johnathen exclaimed and wrapped an arm around Thyra's neck. "He's safer than he's ever been. Come on, let's just enjoy the company and the dessert, whenever it comes out!"

As if on command, Antonio walked down the small steps from the lobby, sporting a dirty chef's apron, his expression stern. "For your information, my marbled Tres Leches Cake takes hours to prepare, even with the right ingredients. I had to make do with what I could find in the market. It wasn't easy getting the shopkeepers to understand what I needed. A little difficult to translate Spanish ingredients into German language."

Upon their arrival in the country, it had quickly come to attention that a chef would be needed to feed the team and their guests. Antonio stepped up, much to everyone's surprise. As far as Thyra could remember, Antonio never talked about being a cook. But not only was he passionate about cooking, he had once been a chef for a resort back in Mexico. Rachel even confirmed his credibility with a quick google search and found Antonio on the front page of a cooking magazine.

"And I know we are going to love it! Take all the time you need," Johnathen responded rather quickly, trying not to insult the strung-out chef. "Might I add, your schnitzel was a delight! The best one I've ever had actually."

Antonio's slightly ruffled feathers seemed to lay flat as he relaxed. Thyra had never seen him even the slightest bit upset, but when it came to cooking, apparently it meant more to him than gryphball.

"It was my first attempt, if I am honest. I am glad you enjoyed it," Antonio replied with a slight smile.

Johnathen nodded and pointed to his empty plate. "You can tell I enjoyed it!"

Antonio picked up their dirty plates. "Thank you. The cake should be ready in twenty minutes." He walked away to the next table, carrying the plates on his half extended wings with dexterity to be admired.

Thyra could not help but think about Anfang and what he must be feeling, or where he went. Johnathen and Aadhya, who had been sitting next to him all this time, began to talk amongst themselves. Surprisingly, Aadhya was also drinking hefeweizen.

"Hun, I have to run to the bathroom," Thyra mentioned quickly.

Johnathen broke from his stumbling conversation for just a moment. "Have fun! And remember, it's a water closet! We're in Europe now," He laughed and turned back to Aadhya.

Thyra walked out of the dining room quietly. She passed the old reception desk and moved up the stairs to the second floor. Doors and paintings decorated both sides of the hallway. An odd picture of a large chicken being hugged by a woman really stuck out from the rest, but she guessed it could be a normal decoration for this part of the world.

She proceeded down the hallway and found the second door to the right cracked open. It was the room she and Johnathen shared with Anfang. They hadn't actually spent much time in the room. Besides sleeping and the initial unpacking, they had been spending most of their time around the old resort. One reason was that the room was small.

The space was cramped for two people, let alone two gryphons and a human. Two twin-sized beds were permanently affixed longways on the right side of the room, creating one long bed that they could sleep foot to foot or head to head if they felt like it. Anfang's bed was a rollaway bed stationed in the middle of the room, making moving around difficult. They had all been assured this was temporary, but for how long was unknown.

The balcony door was cracked open, creating a cold draft in the room. She opened the sliding door the rest of the way to see the balcony was empty but heard the slight scuffle of talons along tile above her. Thyra looked onto the roof and saw the figure of a gryphon in the moonlight. "Anfang?" She called out loud. The figure turned to her but then looked away.

Thyra leaped up from the balcony onto the roof and proceeded over to Anfang, sitting next to him on the peak of the steep rooftop. The gryphoness ruffled her feathers in the bitter cold and let out a long breath, watching the steam cloud form in the air. She stared out over the distance, eyes adjusting to the dim white glow of the moon on the mountain side. Thyra sat with him, looking over the mountain ridges and the snow that reflected off the mountain ranges.

"I not belong here," Anfang said bleakly, breaking the silence. "I not belong anywhere. I am a freak. A murderer. I not deserve peace." His voice was hollow, as if a ghost were speaking through him.

"Anfang, this is an opportunity to restart. You were manipulated before. What you did wasn't you, you…" Thyra began.

"But I enjoyed it, Thyra," Anfang interrupted. "I liked killing and It felt good. I felt powerful doing it." Thyra would have complemented his use of words if the subject were not so serious. "I belong in prison, but Anthony thinks I should be guard in this place. I want to protect you and other gryphons, but I fear I want to kill again," Anfang said, staring at the black sky. "How long I go before I kill?"

It took a while for Thyra to answer, considering what Anfang was feeling. "I don't think you will kill again."

Anfang's single eartuft folded against his skull as he looked towards her. "How can you be so sure?"

Thyra looked away, considering his question. "Because you love me, and you want the greater good for gryphon kind," Thyra responded with confidence looking into his glowing green eyes. "I think you'll honor our agreement, and you will become the protector that we need. You're strong, Anfang. And I believe you have a good heart.

"I'm not saying it will be easy. You have a bad reputation to say the least, but I think in time, we will all look up to you," Thyra added, motioning to wrap a wing around him. Anfang embraced her, leaning against her side. "Hell, everyone looks up to me and all I do is play gryphball."

"Yes, but you not murder like I am," Anfang said.

Thyra sighed and felt his leathery wing wrap around her as well. "You have a chance to change that. There are only a talonfull of others that know your past here. You can prove yourself, and be the gryphon you were meant to be,"

Anfang thought for a moment, leaning into the warmth of Thyra's feathers. "What am I meant to be?"

It was a hard question for Thyra to answer. Anfang was as much a gryphon as anyone, yet he had been abused and redesigned to be nothing more than a military weapon. It was hard to think about what good could come of that. She had to play into his basic instinct; to protect her.

"A guardian. If not for anyone else, but for me," Thyra said. "I see you as my brother, and a brother's role is to protect their younger sister, right?"

"I not know, but I will try for you," Anfang replied and leaned in to preen the hackle feathers of her neck. The action was a friendly one between gryphons, yet it felt awkward between her and Anfang. She might claim they were siblings, but Thyra could not help the strange feeling that he felt more than that.

"Thyra! Are you up there?" Came a high pitch screech that could not be mistaken for Rachel. Immediately, Thyra brought her wing back to tuck it against her side.

"Yeah! Just up here with Anfang," Thyra replied, settling her feathers.

"What the hell y'all doing up there? Antonio just brought out his Mexican cake, and he's wondering where y'all are!" Rachel yelled from the balcony.

Thyra could not help but chuckle and rose to all fours. "We will be down in a minute!"

Her response must have satisfied Rachel as she heard no response from the small Kestrel. Thyra turned to Anfang and held out a foretalon, wanting him to stand up with her. Anfang grabbed her talon and stood.

"Just put on a good show for now. I promise it will be easier in due time," Thyra told him. Her words seemed to hit home as a new energy sparked in Anfang's glowing green eyes. Both gryphons glided off of the rooftop and down on the patio.

"Thyra…" Anfang interrupted before she walked into the bedroom. She stopped and turned to him. "Thank you."

Thyra smiled and closed the door behind them. He could have flown off that rooftop at any time and permanently disappeared into the darkness, but he chose to remain steadfast. Whether he was staying for her, or his own personal gain, she would never know.

Thyra proceeded down the stairs and back into the main dining room with Anfang in tow, thinking of the other gryphons and how they talked about him. She had to address their issues right then and now if Anfang was to be accepted amongst them. With a new vigor, Thyra walked down the small steps of stairs and to the same place coach Victor had just stood.

The conversations between the tables of gryphons grew to a halt as both entered the room again. She looked to the group, cleared her throat, and stood tall to address the team. "I have something to say to everyone," Thyra began, watching as conversations died and forks were placed down. "I want you all to know, Anfang is my friend, my brother, and he will be a part of us from here on out and it's time you accept that."

Some gryphons looked between themselves, doubting Thyra. Even her own husband's brow furrowed worriedly. It was a tough subject to bring to attention in the midst of everything going well, but she had to bite the head off the snake as soon as possible, or risk it poisoning the group.

"He deserves a second chance, like any of us," Thyra declared, looking over the group. "We all come from different backgrounds. Some of us worse than others, but Anfang was abused, neglected, and manipulated. He regrets his actions in the past, but we know he had no choice."

She looked at every gryphon in the room. She locked eyes with her friends, and could not tell how they were taking her speech. Her body trembled; worry about rejection creeping into her mind. But it was too late to back down. She had to follow through.

"He is one of us," she pressed. "A gryphon that needs a new beginning. That's what we have all been given. If he never again acts anything like he has in the past, can we all agree to forgive him?"

The room was silent for a time being before Aadhya stood before them. "I can. I believe he is honestly a good gryphon, one we can trust."

Her statement alone caused many gryphons to stand in agreement. If the bearded vulture of reason could agree, then it was law. Most were on board, rising to believe what Thyra was preaching, but some were reluctant.

Nathanial rose from his seat with a grimace. "How can you be so sure? I've seen the videos of him killing and he's smiling the whole time. You're going to stand there and tell me he's sorry for it, but I don't believe a damn word! I know that euphoric pleasure. It's the same when I win a gryphball match! You can stand there and claim brotherhood and other shit, but I know what he was feeling at that time, he was happy doing it!"

Many gryphons suddenly started to talk amongst themselves. Thyra's eyes widened. She looked over to Rachel who was sitting next to him, but she remained silent. The one time she needed Rachel to open her loud beak and she was choosing to remain silent for her lover's sake? Thyra ground her beak and prepared herself for a shouting match, but suddenly, Anfang stood before her to address the crowd.

"It is true. I liked what I did. I killed others, and enjoyed it," Anfang began, looking at every gryphon in the room. "But I regret what I did. I acted as a beast. I was not aware of what I did was wrong." Anfang's eyes moved down to his talons silently. "I not stand wanting you to forgive me now, but I want hope. I need hope."

Anfang looked around to the other gryphons, feathers and eartuft flat against his head. Anyone looking into his eyes could read them like an open book. He was hurt and he sincerely meant what he was trying to express with his limited vocabulary. "I make promise to Thyra . . . to everyone. I not kill again."

His words must have hit home with Nathanial as he did not debate him. His accuser sat back down in his seat, somewhat reluctantly, but he seemed satisfied with Anfang's response.

"As you all may not know," Thyra added. "Anfang has been chosen to become a protector here in Greifsburg. Tomorrow, as we start our gryphball training, he will start his. I know we can depend on him to look over us. I just ask for patience. If you can't find it in yourselves to trust him, trust me."

Clapping suddenly echoed from the far end of the room. Everyone turned to see Anthony standing at the entrance, wearing a broad smile across his face. "It seems I arrived just in time for a good speech," he said and walked down into the dining room. He turned his attention to Antonio. "I was just stopping by to see if I was too late for Antonio's famous cooking!"

"I do have extra, if you would like," Antonio offered.

"Well of course! If you don't mind," Anthony said in response.

Antonio disappeared into the kitchen while Anthony sat in the only empty seat at the far side of the room, right next to Johnathen and Aadhya. No one spoke, leaving Anthony curious. "Oh, don't stop on my behalf! Please, finish," he offered.

"Well, I was just reassuring everyone that Anfang is a changed gryphon, and how he's been selected for a protector role," Thyra explained.

"Yes! And let me add to that," Anthony began. "I handpicked Anfang along with a hand...ahem talonfull of other gryphons." He sat back calmly in the booth and crossed one leg over his thigh, pointing at Anfang in particular. "I understand that it may take time for you all to adjust to this, but I think you all will see why I chose him in a few short months. After all, the safety of Greifsburg is of the utmost priority!"

Antonio brought out a plate full of food balanced on his wingshoulder and carrying a tall glass of beer in a foretalon. "And would you look at that! This looks exquisite, my dear gryphon." Anthony exclaimed as Antonio set the table for him. He wasted no time cutting into his schnitzel. "I hope everyone is on board with my decisions. Even if there is little you can do about them," he added with a stern look. He received a round of silent stares and suddenly cracked a smile. "I'm kidding! Greifsburg is a democracy."

Anthony delicately prepared his first bite and chewed it slowly, making a loud exaggerated sigh. "That is incredible, Antonio! Thank you," he complimented before looking around at everyone's dessert laid before them. "Please! Don't let me hold you all up. Go ahead! Enjoy your dessert."

The gryphons all turned towards their dishes and normal conversation slowly began to resume. Thyra and Anfang approached their table and sat down, still slightly lost in what just happened.

"You're welcome," Anthony said looking across the table.

Thyra cocked her head. She did not need to be saved by 'father,' not now, not ever. "Excuse me?"

Anthony looked a tad lost as he continued with his meal. "I must have walked in at an awkward time. I just wanted to check up on everyone, but it seems in just a short couple days, this house has fallen into disarray."

"I believe everyone has been handling the change naturally, given the circumstances," Johnathen chimed in, his voice still somewhat slurred.

"The circumstances? And how do you define that, my inebriated friend?" Anthony retorted with another motion of his fork.

Thyra was confused by his sudden change of demeanor. First, Anthony walks in with a friendly attitude, and then suddenly attacks Johnathen for his choice of words.

Johnathen laughed and motioned across the room with his beer. "What do you expect? You put more than a dozen gryphons in the same house halfway across the world and expect it to be Full House in here immediately? You couldn't expect that from humans, let alone gryphons."

Thyra took issue with that one. She gave him the same look she had been giving Anthony. "Hun, what do you mean by that?" She could not see Anthony's little smirk out of the corner of his mouth as he took another bite.

Johnathen realized his mistake almost immediately sat his beer down. "I just, I mean…"

"No, go ahead, finish up your thought, Hun," Thyra paused for the last hun, really letting it sink in.

"I am also curious what he means," Aadhya asked, now reading into the situation. Johnathen looked over to Anthony, who simply shrugged his shoulders and worked at his food, leaving Johnathen alone to explain himself.

Johnathen laughed nervously and pointed at Nathanial. "I mean, come on babe, you know most gryphons are... hotheads! They're more than ready to start fights!"

"Oh, I see. Hotheads. Would you describe them as animals? Would you say I'm an animal?!" Thyra questioned, raising her tone. Her nerves were still frazzled from trying to defend Anfang, and it showed. Even the rest of the table knew not to intervene and everyone present fell silent. Johnathen was on the chopping block.

"Thyra! No, no that's not what I meant! I..." Johnathen tried to explain.

"What, Anfang is a hothead animal too? He can't be trusted? We all can't live together? Is that what you're saying?" Thyra asked angrily, drawing in the attention of other tables.

Johnathen sighed and held his hands up, noticing the quieting silence around them despite his drunken state. "Hun, I didn't mean it like that. Please just..."

"No!" Thyra yelled this time, silencing everyone still talking. She stood up from the table. "Find somewhere else to sleep tonight," she said hastily and left. Johnathen quickly got up from his seat, following behind her.

"Thyra, please! Featherbutt, please," Johnathen pleaded as he walked to her.

She had let everything bottle inside her for too long. Maybe it was the stress of it all, and maybe he did not mean what he said, but she could not help it. Thyra turned around and stomped her foot. "What!"

Johnathen froze in place, and then got down on one knee to look at her eye level. "You know that I love you. I love gryphons and I would never think differently of you versus my own kind. Of all people you know that, right?"

Thyra looked away for a moment, and her eartufts collapsed against the sides of her head. She leaned into his shoulder and cried. Johnathen simply wrapped an arm around her and held her close.

"I'm sorry. I overreacted. It's just…a lot," Thyra choked out.

Johnathen slowly stood and placed a hand on her head, leading her towards the bedroom. "It's ok. I'm exhausted too. Let's get some sleep."

Chapter 14 Bloodfeather

"What about this place? It's pretty cool! And look at all the gryphon mannequins in the window!" Rachel exclaimed, not even pausing before rushing into the open shop.

Thyra readjusted the straps of her full backpack before following the small gryphoness inside. Johnathen, Aadhya, and Antonio all followed into the warmth of the clothing store, shaking the snow from themselves at the entrance. The coats that they wore did a decent job at keeping them warm, but they were in desperate need of hardier gear.

The outfitter store was one of many that decorated the somewhat lively downtown center of Greifsburg. They had passed at least two bars, one of them being a discotheque, several small grocery stores, and a handful of clothing outlets. This particular outlet specialized in winter gear made especially for gryphons. Thyra walked over to an eye-catching jacket that complimented her feathers and sat down, running her talons across the smooth sleek surface.

"Do you like that?" Johnathen asked, walking up behind her.

"It's nice, and looks pretty warm," she replied nonchalantly.

Johnathen sighed, hearing the tone in her voice. He looked around and saw the other three gryphons were out of hearing range. "Honey, I'm sorry about last night, I-."

"It's alright, John. Let's just drop it. You were drunk, I was tipsy and exhausted and dealing with a lot. It's ok," Thyra replied, but something still ate at her. He might not have meant what he said, but the way he referred to her species still hurt like a pinfeather. Johnathen leaned in to kiss her cere and took the jacket off the hanger.

"Why don't you go try it on? Let's see how it looks on you. I like the red," he said with a gentle smile. "Matches your gorgeous tail fan."

Thyra could not help but smile at that. He was right, it did match almost perfectly. Just then, a Northern Harrier gryphoness wearing a nametag approached the two with a smile on her beak.

"Hello! I see that you like this coat, yes?" the harrier gryphoness asked in a thick Bavarian accent.

Thyra read her nametag. "Yes! Gretah, am I saying that right?"

Gretta chuckled and shook her head. "It is close! Gret-Tah! No matter. Would you like to try on?" she asked once again, making her way over to the cashier's desk towards the middle of the room.

"Yeah, that would be great. But I have to ask, do you own this shop yourself?" Thyra questioned.

Gretta nodded her beak and grabbed the key for the changing room. "Yes! It was good opportunity! I much enjoy this past week. Lots of gryphons come here. Is like a dream. My mother made clothing for me growing up. I try to do the same and sell online for many years. Mr. Clearwater came to me with business, and I could not be more….ah… what is the word? Excited!" Gretta smiled and handed the keys over.

"You made all of these?" Thyra questioned as she walked with the other gryphoness towards the changing rooms. She shrugged her wing shoulders.

"In one way or another, yes! I . . . design. Much too much work for one gryphon. I have employees that make them now."

"It's incredible that you've done all of this," Thyra complimented. She knew the city was filled with gryphons' talents from far and wide, but the scale of it was mind blowing. Gretta opened one of the dressing rooms and motioned for her inside.

"Thank you! I try," Gretta said and closed the door.

Thyra removed her ill-fitting coat and hung it up. She was wearing a baggy t shirt underneath and quickly tossed on the new coat, fitting her wings through the ample slits in the back. The red coat fit like it was made especially for her. She had been worried about the sizing, but it seemed Gretta's design was perfect for her.

"How does it fit?" Gretta asked from behind the door.

Thyra walked out and tested the mobility of her wings. "Perfect! How do you size these? I mean we are all extremely different."

"We not so different as you think. Coats are easiest. As I have seen, there are five sizes in total, ranging from your friend there," Gretta paused to point at Rachel who was exploring the tiny jackets in the back. "To your other enormous friend there." Gretta pointed to Aadhya, who had surprisingly little options for her. "You are, as I say, mittlere."

189

Thyra nodded her head. "That makes sense. It looks like you have it down to a science almost!"

"You can say this! It comes with experience, but some gryphons are different. Longer, wider, and other variations. Some require, ah, Änderung," Gretta mentioned, searching for the right word.

"Alterations?" Thyra filled in the blank.

"Yes! Alterations. But it seems you do not require this," Gretta said motioning towards the jacket.

Johnathen whistled as he walked over. "I love it. That jacket looks good on you. But let's be honest. Just about anything does."

"I think it does too, and I'm already burning up." Thyra mentioned and worked at the buttons across her chest. "Also I'm glad you use buttons instead of zippers. Can't tell you how many feathers I've caught in zippers."

"They work well, yes," Gretta said just as Rachel ran up with a little green jacket slung over her shoulder.

"Hey! Can I try this on? I think it's my size! You have a lot of jackets and other stuff here, but I really like this one. I'll totally buy it if it fits me!" Rachel's enthusiasm threw Gretta off balance. She held a foretalon up, stopping Rachel.

"Much too fast, little one. Yes, take the dressing room," Gretta said, watching the Kestrel all but run into the small room. "Is she always like this?"

Thyra could not help but grin and nod.

Antonio walked up beside the group, carrying a multicolored jacket made of dark reds to bright blues. "I also need some help. Is this the thickest jacket you have? I have been freezing ever since arriving. My kind is not built for this weather."

Gretta shook her head and started to talk to Antonio, leading him over to the same area Thyra had been in.

"Here, I'll take your jacket to the counter," Johnathen said and reached down to help Thyra, but she refused.

"No, I'll pay for it and wear it out," Thyra said, turning away from him.

Johnathen sighed and shook his head. "I said I'm sorry."

"It's not about that, John," Thyra lied sternly. "They gave me a budget for clothing, remember? And you're out of a job. I'm the one making the money now," She let that last point sting a little and glanced up to Johnathen, watching his reaction. He must have received her intention. He held up his hand and stood back up straight.

"Alright, have it your way," Johnathen said before walking away, heading over to see how Aadhya was doing.

Thyra closed her eyes and let herself calm down. She did not know why she was acting this way, or why she was letting her anger manifest itself so sternly. He was only trying to be a good husband.

Thyra thought about Anfang again, and how he must be doing during his first day of training. She had heard him get up that morning and wished him good luck before he flew off the balcony. She looked over to see another red jacket that looked similar to hers, and it looked to be his size too. Maybe she would pick one up for him too.

"Whatcha think, Thyra?" Rachel exclaimed and posed, clearly proud of her new outfit. She had even chosen the right ski pants to go with it.

Thyra smiled. "I think all you need is some skis and poles."

"Again!" Joseph yelled as Anfang tumbled through the snow.

Anfang stood up and rubbed his cheek, the previous hit had been stronger than the rest Joseph had dealt all day. He shook the excess snow off his bare feathers.

"You need to learn how to balance on your hindfeet more. If you depend entirely on all four legs, you'll go down every time," Joseph said, taking his stand once more.

Anfang looked around the area, locking eyes with several of the gryphons standing in a circle around them, observing their bout. The wind picked up, blowing cool air under his feathers. Every labored breath turned to vapor before his eyes. Joseph stood wide on his hindlegs, one talon extended forward. His side was turned to Anfang with one leathery wing extended for balance. Anfang mimicked the stance with significantly less grace.

"Ready?" Joseph questioned. Anfang nodded in response.

Joseph leapt forward on both feet, beating his wings once to gain ground. Anfang struggled to watch as his vision filled quickly with the body of his opposer. Joseph struck out with a curled foretalon, aiming to hit Anfang again, but he managed to dodge the initial punch. He fell off balance on his hindfeet and Joseph quickly took advantage of that.

Joseph fell to his foretalons, turned on them, and kicked Anfang squarely in the chest with both hindpaws. A loud sickening cracking of bones filled the area. Anfang gasped as all breath left his body and he found himself sliding along the snow on his back. His vision blurred as he stared up at the sky, fighting for breath. He knew at least a couple of his ribs were momentarily broken and it was enough to hold him to the ground for the time being.

"Get up," Joseph commanded.

Anfang hissed and rolled over to his legs again, green eyes squinting as pain filled his mind.

"Cadets! Where did Anfang make his mistake?" Joseph called out to the group watching him. Anfang's chest heaved, and felt the pain subside to something more manageable. One of the younger looking gryphons raised his yellow talons. "Goshawk. What is your name?" Joseph questioned.

"Holger, sir!" the goshawk said, his autumn red eyes practically piercing through the falling snow. Joseph made the motion for him to continue. "Anfang was successful at dodging the initial attack, but quickly lost balance due to his stance. His wing did not adjust to his moving weight."

Joseph cracked a smile and nodded. "Very good!" By this time, Anfang had regained his breath and walked within striking distance of Joseph. Anfang's pupils had narrowed into slits as his hunting instinct was taking over. Rage was filling him. "Anfang, take a deep breath, and return to your stance," Joseph commanded, watching his reaction. "Contain yourself. Use that rage, but don't lose control."

Anfang realized he was allowing himself to become fueled by anger, and he knew it would only end badly. The beast took a deep breath of the bitter cold air and let it clear his mind.

"You need to be fluid, like water," Joseph added. "If you're not calm, your actions will be rigid and easy to read."

Joseph readied himself as Anfang did the same, resuming the stance. With a nod, Joseph advanced again on two legs, keeping his leathery wings outstretched to not only maintain his balance, but create more distraction for Anfang. He feinted a right hook with his foretalons. Anfang reacted, moving his left foretalon to block but the right wing came in to strike Anfang across the face. His vision blurred for only a second before he saw Joseph spin like a top. His paw connected with Anfang's beak.

Anfang hit the ground hard, earning a round of applause from the surrounding group. Anfang pulled his beak from the snow and regained himself, feeling his blood boil once again. This time, it was too much to contain. His vision turned red, and every muscle on his body tightened. Joseph turned towards the group once again, leaving his back exposed to Anfang.

"Holger! Your observation?" Joseph asked once again. Before Holger had the opportunity to answer, Anfang screeched loudly and seized the small opportunity he had. He leapt like a feral lion; talons outstretched towards his teacher's throat.

Joseph seemed to expect exactly this. He turned and caught Anfang's outstretched foretalons in his own. Joseph used Anfang's own momentum against him, and twisted to throw Anfang over his shoulders, slamming the bigger gryphon on his back. Before Anfang could even blink, Joseph was on top of him, holding the beast by his throat with all his weight.

"Calm yourself," Joseph sternly demanded.

Anfang struggled for a minute, and found himself calm, thin slitted pupils turning more round with cognition.

"There we go. Your power is impressive, you just need to learn how to contain it," Joseph commented, letting go of Anfang's throat. He turned to the rest of the group and waved them off. "Alright, lessons over. Everyone hit the showers. You're dismissed."

At once, the small group of cadet gryphons all turned and headed back inside the building behind them, leaving the two gryphons alone. Joseph walked towards the edge of the arena and grabbed his body armor off a hook attached to the building. "You lost control again."

Anfang slowly brought himself onto all fours, shaking the snow from his bare cream and almond brown feathers. "Yes. But I better than I was." He walked towards the entrance of the building.

"Anfang, small improvements aren't enough. If I would have let one of the other gryphons spar with you today, you would have killed them," Joseph said firmlyy. "They're not made like us. They aren't engineered to stop bullets and heal broken bones almost instantly. If I would have hit one of them like I did to you, I would put them in the hospital. Do you understand that?" He put on his uniform, throwing a heavy jacket over the top.

It was a hard concept to grasp for Anfang. He had known how weak humans were, but had only recently come to understand how frail other gryphons were in comparison to him. It was a huge reason he had been selected to protect them. "I . . . understand."

Joseph sighed and walked past him to hold the entrance door open for Anfang. "You don't have to pull your punches with me, but first you have to land one," he taunted. The beast almost smiled, baring one of his curved fangs for him to see. Joseph let out a small laugh and followed after

Alex Bizzell

Anfang. "God, you're ugly. How do you even eat with those ridiculous teeth?"

"The same as you," Anfang responded.

They walked past the other gryphons in the locker room. Each one stopped and saluted the two of them with a wing. Anfang looked to each gryphon, still curious why they not only saluted Joseph but him as well.

Once in the hallway, they headed towards Joseph's personal office. Joseph entered first and made his way behind the stylish new desk. The room itself was barren. Only a few photo frames decorated the desk along with a name plate that read 'Sergeant Joseph Joestar.'

Joseph grabbed a bottle off of a nearby bookshelf and sat down on a large pillow behind the desk, withdrawing two crystal glasses. He poured a hefty amount for himself and Anfang, sliding a glass across the desk.

Anfang was confused by the sudden hospitality but thought it rude to deny the offer. He knew at least that much of human culture. "Why do the gryphons make that motion?" he questioned, making a saluting gesture.

Joseph swirled the clear liquor around in his glass and took a deep breath of it with his nares. "Saluting? Goddamn, you really are a moron." He emptied the contents of his glass in a smooth motion.

Anfang blinked and sniffed curiously at his glass. It smelled of peppermint and spice, making his eyeridges raise with curiosity. Joseph watched him with interest. Anfang returned the glance before tossing the drink back. He immediately started coughing loudly.

Joseph screeched with laughter as Anfang sat the glass down on the table, coughing and shivering as intense

196

burning filled his throat. He burped and shivered, all feathers standing on end. "What is this?"

"Schnapps! It's a fantastic German liquor. You don't like it?" Joseph grinned and poured himself another drink. Anfang pushed his glass away, still slightly coughing.

"It taste like the mouth wash," Anfang said. Joseph shook his head and grinned.

"It's not that bad. Unfortunately, our bodies process the alcohol too quickly. It's hard to maintain a buzz, and almost impossible to get drunk," Joseph said, quickly swinging back another shot. "And as good as this shit is, it's pretty low alcohol content."

Anfang doubted that because as soon as the burning left his throat, he could feel the effects of the alcohol. His head buzzed slightly, giving his body a pleasant numbness. But it only lasted for half a minute before it was gone again. "Oh."

Joseph refilled his glass a third time and held it in his talons, this time turning his attention to Anfang. "I didn't bring you in here to talk about alcohol and get chummy with your ass," Joseph began, his tone becoming serious. "I want to continue our earlier conversation because I expect more from you.; These cadets know about us. They know what we really are, and they look up to us because in their eyes, were indestructible." He took another swig from his glass, then sighed and placed the tumbler back down, closing his eyes as he finally got a buzz.

"They will look up to you, and I want you to behave like a role model. That shit that you pulled out there is not acceptable. They might have seen a desperate attempt at a last shot, but I know what it was, a killing blow. If it were anyone else, you would have let your bloodlust get the best of you and we would have a dead body on our hands. So, get your shit together, you got it?"

Anfang had to look away from Joseph's green eyes. He knew that the gryphon was right. He had let himself go after the last hit and he regretted it. He had thought it would be easier to change, but put into a fighting situation, it came back, an instinct he still could not control. Everything Thyra's teammate said the previous night came back to his mind. He was still a killer at heart, and it would take a long time to curve his bloodlust.

Joseph cleared his throat, causing Anfang to look back at him. "Understood?"

"Yes. I will not let it happen again," Anfang said.

Joseph swirled around his glass, staring at Anfang with doubt. He took his shot and placed the glass down on the desk. "I think it will. Listen, I want you to communicate with me next time. I can help talk you out of it. You're not the only one with a dark past and blood under your talons. I know what you're going through."

Joseph was finally beginning to level with him. Anfang held his breath, waiting for the sergeant to continue, but he did not. He turned his head to stare at a photo on his desk. He poured himself yet another drink. "That's all for the day. Now get your ugly ass out of my office."

Anfang wanted to press the conversation further but nodded and left. He closed the door behind him and stared up at the ceiling. *What has Joseph gone through?* Anfang thought to himself. Maybe Joseph would tell him more another time.

Anfang made his way out the building and into the cold. He took to the sky. The sun was beginning to set over the towering mountain ranges in the distance. The snow had stopped for now, leaving the air currents smooth and easy to navigate. He watched a car pass down the street, blaring heavy techno music. He opened his wings and took to the sky, sights set on home. He wanted to talk to Thyra more than anything and hoped she would hear what he had to say. He didn't feel quite as alone knowing that there was another gryphon much like him.

Chapter 15 Emperor's New Clothes

Anthony leaned back in his chair, listening as another gryphon in the room gave his two cents. Along with himself and Debra, there were eight gryphons gathered around the large wooden table that made up the meeting room. While construction around the town continued Greifsburg's town hall was nothing more than an old, repurposed post office. Anthony had great plans for his own town hall, but they would have to wait for construction. Just as the Redtails team had to make do with their lodging.

This meeting was their first official meeting as a sovereign nation, and there were many specifics that needed to be hashed out. Some specifics needed attention now, while others could wait the weeks or months it would take to get to them. Right now, the pressing matter was border control. Anthony had made it the utmost priority, but as to why, no gryphon knew.

"Mayor Anthony?" the red kite gryphon asked. She tapped her pen on the table and clicked her beak. Anthony snapped back to attention, returning to his natural smile.

"Ah yes, Anna. Sorry, I drifted off for a minute," Anthony admitted. He chuckled apologetically and rubbed the crow's feet at the edges of his eyes. "I didn't get much sleep last night."

Anna cleared her throat and pointed down at the paper. "I was asking about page 12 section 2. It says here that every human will have to be documented and accounted for as they enter and leave the city. My first question is exactly how do you plan on doing this, and second is why? Do we even have the resources for that kind of tight control over our border?" she asked, raising a white eye ridge. Her ivory eyes stared at him intently, waiting for his answer.

"We can and we will. There are only two roads in and out of the city, and I highly doubt we are going to have any humans come wandering in from the surrounding mountains. All we need is eight gryphons in total stationed at these two roads to check ID's and enter their information into the database, twenty-four seven," Anthony waved his hand as if the request were child's play. "I don't have to remind you the follies of humankind. I worked too hard to create this country for gryphons to only have a handful of rotten apples spoil the bunch. Not to say I don't trust my own kind, but . . . What am I saying? Really I don't," Anthony paused once more and looked over to Joseph, wanting him to weigh in. "General?"

Joseph cleared his throat and readjusted his leathery wings. He turned his green eyes towards Anna and gave her an assuring nod. "I agree with the mayor whole-heartedly. I took this position with a promise to protect our gryphon citizens from any harm. No offense to Mayor and Deputy Mayor, but I do not trust a human as far as I can throw them. It will be no problem assigning eight gryphons for this reason. I have over twenty candidates right now. All look promising for protection work."

Anna thought for a moment and turned to her laptop sitting before her. She typed something in and looked it over.

"I have allowed the yearly budget to account for exactly twenty-four protectors. What is not in the budget is the cost of the facilities that will need to be built at either end of the border."

"If I may," another gryphon spoke up on the far end of the table.

Everyone turned to look at the great horned owl gryphon that sat still as a tree. His rather large eartufts stood straight, showing his calm demeanor and his vibrant yellow eyes had turned their attention to Anna. Anthony motioned for him to continue.

"I have reassessed several of the buildings since our last meeting and it seems the damage is not as extensive as I once believed. I could easily calculate a new number that would be in favor for these unforeseen expenses," the owl said.

"I trust that you could, Elijah, thank you," Anthony replied. "While we are on the subject, is the construction of the gryphball stadium and the Redtails housing still on schedule?"

Elijah picked up his glasses from the table and balanced them on the cere of his beak, turning to the computer screen in front of him. "Construction of the gryphball stadium is well underway, and actually ahead of schedule. The contractors I hired say the additional support from the gryphons has had a considerable positive effect." The owl scrolled through some pages. "However, as far as the completion of the Redtail's housing is concerned, I have unfortunate news."

Anthony frowned and leaned up on the desk, folding his hands together. Elijah looked up from his computer, expression unchanging as he explained, "The ground under the original placement of the structures has proven to be unstable, and unpredictable. A new location will be necessary."

"That's unacceptable," Anthony said sternly. The sudden change in his tone was noticed by everyone. Even Elijah's long eartufts folded back slightly.

"Mayor, the decision was not easy. Upon beginning the preparation to the grounds, it was discovered that…"

"I don't care how much it costs. That's where I want their housing," Anthony demanded, his stern tone unchanging.

Anna interrupted, trying to talk reason into Anthony. "Mayor, I highly recommend that we…" He quickly turned to stare at the red kite gryphoness, and her beak clamped shut.

"I do not care. Make it happen, Elijah," Anthony said one last time before leaning back in his seat.

The great horned owl reluctantly nodded his small beak and began typing away on his laptop. "Very well, Sir."

Anthony began to cough suddenly and pulled out his handkerchief. Several of the gryphons turned their attention towards him as the coughing did not stop for a solid minute. Debra seemed concerned but said nothing. Once he stopped, he put away his handkerchief and cleared his throat.

The room fell silent once again, save for the clicking of keyboards as the gryphons filled out their own personal notes. Anthony folded his hands together and stared at the blank white walls around the meeting room.

"Susan?" Anthony called out, looking over at the well-dressed turkey vulture to his right. She perked up, the golden hoop ring that ran through her nares dangling in the light.

"Yes Mayor!" she said excitedly. The way she presented her form with decorations and a unique fashion sense was second to none. However, some found her featherless and fleshy face to be grotesque, resembling the skin of a red hairless cat.

"Have any gryphon artists moved into town yet?" Anthony asked curiously, turning his attention back to the bare walls. Susan scrolled through her laptops screen, thinking out loud.

"Let's see, I approved business licenses last week for two more boutiques, and a brewery, interestingly enough! He was an amusing older Kite that grew up in Bavaria and learned from a local…"

"Any artists? Artisans?" Anthony asked again.

Susan cleared her throat and looked back at her computer again. "A third restaurant titled 'Flavor town,' and, oh yes! Humphry! He's a common redtail painter that applied for a license. Doesn't plan on opening a shop for a while, but he applied for one just in case he decides to sell his paintings."

"Very good. Get in contact with him and tell him the Mayor is interested in commissioning him. I need some paintings for city hall. These walls are much too barren for my taste," Anthony replied. Susan nodded and typed away at the keyboard. He looked around the room and saw that the group was all concentrating on their own work. He checked his silver watch and cleared his throat. "Does anyone have anything else?"

The group of gryphons looked up from their computers, shaking their heads. Anthony nodded and stood, with Debra and Joseph quickly following his lead.

"Good work, everyone. I'll see you all tomorrow morning," Anthony said before taking his leave.

Once outside the room, Anthony paused and leaned against a wall, struggling to stand for a moment. "Sir," Debra asked, but Anthony waved her off. He stood upright and straightened his suit jacket. Joseph walked up beside Anthony, standing almost eye to eye with him.

"I think that was the right decision regarding the border," Joseph confirmed as they walked down the hallway.

Anthony nodded as they approached the front door. "I knew that you would, given your past experiences with my kind." He grabbed his long black jacket from the coat hanger and threw it on, waiting for Joseph to put on his. "I want to do everything I can to make sure the gryphons of my country never experience what you or Anfang went through."

Joseph sat on his haunches, buttoning up his green overcoat. "And they never will, as long as I breathe," he added sternly.

Johnathen waved to another gryphon as he passed them on the tight cobblestone streets. The gryphon seemed surprised to see a human but smiled and nodded his beak as he passed. The gryphon continued his conversation with the gryphoness he was with but Johnathen could not help but hear the mention of the word 'human' just out of earshot. It was a different world, he realized. He was now the minority in this town.

Yesterday, the sun had come out and melted much of the snow from rooftops and other hard surfaces, but today was all white once again. Snow drifted down, blanketing everything in a layer of white fluff. He had some time to kill as all the gryphons in the house were out at practice.

Thyra had given him the usual kiss on the cheek before she left, but there was something still eating at him. He knew he had made a stupid comment, categorizing the gryphons negatively as a species. Hell, it was true! Gryphons were easily more emotionally unstable than humans. Gryphons were two thoughts away from reverting to feral instincts at any time. They were quickly angered, always showing their emotions through their eartufts and feathers.

He shook his head and placed his gloved hands inside his brown coat pockets. He should not have those kinds of thoughts, not after being with Thyra for so long. It was little seeds of negativity like that which could grow into weeds of speciesism.

Yet another reason to beat himself up. He sighed. Usually, he would have a job or another form of work to distract himself with. Now, he was alone and lost to his own thoughts.

"At least the scenery is beautiful," Johnathen said out loud to himself. Everywhere he looked, the gorgeous swiss chalet style and timber framing architecture struck out at him. It was other worldly, like he was living in an old fairy tale village. The towering white capped mountains beyond only added a captivating frame to the whole picture. He could not wait until it was spring.

Johnathen shivered, the thoughts of warmth reminding him just how ridiculously cold it was outside. He looked down at his smart watch, showing negative ten degrees Celsius, whatever that meant.

He walked by a construction site and paused to watch a handful of gryphons moving around the building. Some were flying shingles up to those on the roof while others helped erect wooden support beams. He even saw a pair of gryphons operating a Genie boom lift.

His lawyer brain immediately tuned into the legalities of having a quadruped gryphon operating a human piece of machinery. It would never be allowed in the states. The necessary permits that needed issued to allow gryphons on a construction crew would be extensive, but it seemed like a normal thing here. Needless to say, he was captivated.

As Johnathen continued, he came across a little shop with "Lenny's Electronics" written on the window. Curious and searching for a reprieve from the cold, Johnathen entered. A small bell above the door rang as he stood on the entrance mat and kicked the snow off his boots. A pygmy falcon peeked its head over the edge of the counter and perked its ears.

"Oh! A human! Welcome, welcome!" the little falcon said with a smile. He hopped up on a large platform to bring his waist above the counter. He was wearing a simple shirt with the logo of a flacon holding wires on the breast pocket. "What can I do ya for?" He had a strange English accent.

Johnathen looked around the shop, observing the wall of various televisions, gaming consoles, computers, and cellphones. The shop was cramped, but it seemed all well organized and clean. The new age electronics were strange to see in a place with wooden slat walls.

"I'm just looking around, honestly. I just moved here with my wife, and…" Johnathen began, but saw the falcon's black eyes grow wide.

"Moved here you say? With your wife? I thought only gryphons could live here!" There was a slight panic in his voice.

Johnathen held out a hand and shook his head. "That's true! But my wife is a gryphoness and plays for the Redtails gryphball team." It took a second for the falcon to process all the information before his eartufts perked up.

"So, wait. You're THE Johnathen Awkright?!" the pygmy falcon asked, clearly excited. He hopped up on the glass counter, black tail twitching behind them and a big smile on his beak.

Johnathen looked at him confused. "Yes?"

The falcon squawked happily and extended a gloved foretalon for him to shake. Johnathen grabbed it and immediately the falcon began to shake his hand with both foretalons quickly. *What was it with falcon gryphons being so energetic and twitchy?* he thought to himself.

"Wow! Big fan! I've read all about you and your work in America!" The falcon exclaimed. He cleared his throat and stepped down off the counter, back to his platform. "Where are my manners! Names Lenny, Lenny Kravitz."

Johnathen raised an eyebrow and opened his mouth to say something but thought differently. "Um, nice to meet you, Lenny, but how do you know about me?"

Lenny quickly withdrew his cellphone from one of his many pockets and scrolled through it with the other foretalon. "You're the lawyer that initially proposed the bill for gryphon rights. The right to marry, the right to own property-. Basically, you made us equal to humans as far as the American government is concerned! And all while having a smokin-hot redtail at your side," he added with a laugh.

"She plays a hell of a game of gryphball! That's what brings us here," Johnathen said.

"But what about you? Going to start up a firm here for us or something like that?" Lenny asked.

Johnathen really had not thought about what the future would be as far as his career. Lenny did make a good point, he could start a new firm in Greifsburg to help Anthony and the others.

"You know, I just might," Johnathen responded.

The pygmy falcon placed the cellphone on the counter and rotated it for Johnathen to see. The video he was showing was the time when Thyra had made her speech during her confrontation with The Gathering.

"This is when I found out about you all. I have to admit, the only reason I know so much was through looking at pics of Thyra," Lenny grinned.

"Uh. thanks?" was the only response Johnathen could muster up. The bird was talking much too fast and the situation was extremely odd, to say the least.

Lenny looked up at Johnathen, finally realizing he had flustered the human. Lenny cleared his throat and put his phone away in his pocket. He forced his feathers to a more natural position.

"Ahem! What I mean to say is, I appreciate your contribution to gryphon society and Thyra is an incredible gryphball player with a heart of gold," he finished, holding significantly more poise than before.

"Well, I appreciate it. I wanted to marry Thyra, and being a lawyer, I thought I would put my privileged position to good use for all of gryphon kind," Johnathen said. He thought back to Lenny's previous comment and added a playful grin.. "But mainly because I wanted those sweet red tailfeathers."

The pygmy falcon busted out in laughter and slammed his talons on the glass countertop. "I knew that was the motive! You bloody dog!" Lenny reached across the counter to lightly punch Johnathen in the shoulder. "Anyways, you just come in here to chat it up with the locals or are you shopping around?"

Lenny motioned around the room. "I mean, I've got all the latest and greatest tech you could want for your new place! I compare and beat the best prices you can find anywhere!" he said in a rehearsed radio tone. "And I also carry some other older junk because I'm a nerd for the ancient tech you humans used in the past."

Johnathen thought back to the stack of floppy drives he had brought over. The same floppies they had found in the old laboratories inside Anthony's safe. "Old tech? Like floppy drive readers? For 3.5 inch diskettes?"

Lenny's black eyes widened as he smiled, feathers fluffing up excitedly once again. "You bet I do! I love those old machines!" He hopped off the platform and walked under a section of the counter, quickly padding towards the back of the shop. "Follow me!"

Johnathen walked with the gryphon. Old tube televisions, first gen gaming consoles, and an arrangement of various ancient computers sat neatly in a display case. To his left were several work benches cluttered with torn apart machines and a wall of working tools.

"Looks like you know your stuff," Johnathen complimented.

"As I said, I'm infatuated with human tech. Hell, I'm the result of it. So naturally I have some sort of respect for where it came from," Lenny explained. He reached into one of the many pockets on his pants and pulled out a set of keys.

"My old friends tell me that's why I don't have a hen," he said before unlocking the glass case. He reached in to grab one of the floppy drive readers carefully in his foretalons and looked it over with admiration. "This beauty is a Commodore 1541, the best read write drivers for 3.5 floppies on the market during its time. This baby could-."

"How much?" Johnathen interrupted.

Lenny sighed, clearly a little upset not being able to share his knowledge. He stroked over the metal body of the reader and thought for a minute. "A hundred and twenty euros," he said. "I rebuilt this girl from scratch after I found her in a junkyard of old computer parts. She's a labor of love."

"Done," Johnathen said with a smile. Lenny looked up at Johnathen towering over him and perked his eartufts, tail twitching happily.

"Splendid!" Lenny said, handing the drive over to Johnathen to carry. Lenny closed the display and headed back towards the counter. "Anything else I can interest you in?"

Johnathen looked over to the wall of PC's and pointed at the most expensive one. "If I buy that, will you give me a discount on the the drive?"

Lenny laughed and nodded his small beak. "That bad girl is five grand! Talon-built it myself. It outperforms anything else out there, guaranteed. Hell, I'll give you this floppy drive for free at that point."

Johnathen reached into his pocket and pulled out his wallet. "You take American Express?"

Chapter 16 Short Skirt, Long Jacket

Thyra pulled the faux fur hood of her jacket up over her head and shivered. She cupped the hot coffee mug in her foretalons, watching the steam rise up into the early morning light. The sky was completely clear as the sun peeked over one of the towering mountains in the background.

Bright white fresh snow from yesterday's storm reflected the orange light like a mirror, making it a little hard to see. She shivered and readjusted her hood to let her eartufts slip through the slits at the top. It was more comfortable but left the eartufts exposed to the elements.

The small town down the hill was motionless and silent, save for the chirping of songbirds in the early morning. She could see the city of Innsbruck in the far distance with her binocular-like vision. Few cars traveled down its streets as the humans went about their business.

The sliding door behind Thyra opened, causing her to glance behind her. Anfang stepped out on the balcony and took a deep breath. His green eyes glowed in the morning sunshine. She smiled and moved over to the far pillow in the corner, offering him the other.

"Good morning, Anfang," she said.

Anfang slid the door closed behind him and reached down to finish buttoning up his brand new jacket, a price tag dangling from one of the buttons. "Morning," he said and sat down on the pillow next to her.

She sipped from her coffee mug as she looked over the matching red jacket that she had picked up for him. "That looks good on you. Seems like it fits pretty well,"

Anfang ran his foretalons across the sleek surface of his jacket. "Yes. It feels, odd, but warm. I not used to wear clothes."

"Well, you better get used to it. This is modern society and we can't have you running around free feathered." Thyra chuckled and placed her coffee mug down on the small table in front of her. "You want a cup?" she asked, reaching towards the steaming metal pot.

Anfang considered it for a minute. She could tell he was thinking about the implications of refusing a drink. He was quickly adapting to social behavior. "Yes. Thank you."

She grabbed a clean cup from the table and poured him a cup before handing it over to Anfang. He took it from her somewhat awkwardly and held it in his foretalons as if the mug was going to bite him.

"It has a handle on its side. Hold it like this." She showed him, holding it with ease in one talon. Anfang did the same and Thyra nodded. "And when you drink it, you have to pour it into the bottom of your beak. That's what that little spicket lip is for," Thyra pointed to the curve on the cup, like what is found on a water pitcher. "It's simple for humans to sip from a regular mug, but I found these cups at one of the stores yesterday. It makes drinking from it easier for gryphons. You'll get used to it."

Anfang looked down at the black liquid and brought it to his beak, carefully sniffing it. His feathers ruffled slightly from the intense aroma, and he gently poured it into his beak. Anfang jerked as some of the hot liquid poured over his coat and he made a grimaced face. Thyra laughed gently and took the cup as it was offered back.

"It taste bad!" Anfang exclaimed, using a sleeve to wipe off his beak.

"Maybe you'll like it with cream and sugar, like I do," Thyra said and poured an unhealthy amount of sugar into the cup along with a generous splash of cream from a metal container. She gave it a quick stir with a small spoon and handed it back to him. "Careful, try it again. Smoothly pour it."

Anfang sniffed at the mug again and poured the contents into his beak. This time he did not spill any, and he did not grimace. Quite the opposite. Anfang raised his eye ridges and almost smiled. "This is very good," Anfang complimented.

Thyra smiled and nodded. "I thought so. I mean we are practically the same, so it's not really a surprise."

The two gryphons were silent for a couple minutes, slowly watching the sun rise higher into the sky. There was a calmness between them as they sat together, enjoying the early morning. Thyra could tell Anfang was relaxed and happy, something rare for him. For a moment, all the stress of this new life melted away. She was with her brother and her husband, who was sound asleep in the room. All she could ever want was before her and it was simple things like enjoying a cup of coffee with them every morning that she could look forward to for the rest of her life.

Anfang tilted back the rest of the coffee and held his mug out to Thyra. "Can I have another?" he asked politely.

Thyra was a bit surprised, wondering where he learned to ask like that. She took the mug from him and started to pour another. "First off, it's 'May I have another cup, please?' and second of all, only one more. It's probably the first time you've had caffeine and I don't want you to get too jittery," Thyra said. Anfang tilted his head slightly, confused as to what she meant. "Caffeine and sugar will make you feel like your full of energy, but you'll crash later. It will make you feel a little buzzed, almost like your brain is lightheaded. You feel that?"

"Yes. I like it," Anfang said. She made his cup and handed It over to him. Anfang quickly took it and began to empty it in his beak, causing Thyra to smack his side with a wing.

"Hey! Not so fast! You're supposed to enjoy it. Don't just hork it down!"

He pinned his eartuft back apologetically and slowed himself. "Sorry."

Thyra rolled her eyes. "It's like taking care of a gryphlet," she said under her breath.

The door behind them slid open once again and Johnathen walked out wearing his jacket and a pair of jeans. With the two gryphons occupying almost all of the space of the back deck, he squeezed himself into a chair at the opposite corner. "Morning hun, and Anfang," Johnathen said and yawned.

"You sleep well?" She asked, in their normal morning tone. She poured him his own cup and offered it to Anfang. He looked confused again.

Anfang's eyes widened as a little lightbulb went off in his head. He quickly grabbed the cup with a free foretalon and handed it over to Johnathen, who seemed a bit surprised by the action. Johnathen looked at her curiously, and she simply smiled. Anfang was learning how to be part of a civilization, a family, slowly but surely.

"Y…yeah. Slept well enough. The mattress is really firm, which is ok, but kind of miss having a big mattress to snuggle up with you," he admitted.

"Well aren't you adorable," Thyra said and sipped her coffee with a grin.

"What is snuggle?" Anfang asked curiously. Both Johnathen and Thyra went silent for a minute.

"This coffee is fantastic, Thyra," Johnathen said, changing the subject. "It has a really nice citrus-like acidity and a little fruity back end to it. I can get used to this."

Thyra shook her head and leaned over to Anfang. "See, he likes his coffee black. He thinks he can taste other stuff in the coffee and considers himself a 'connoisseur,' but I think he's a liar. All I get out of black coffee is bitterness," she said, earning a frown from Johnathen. Anfang blinked and looked over to Johnathen before observing his now light colored liquid.

"He likes the stuff before you added the sugar?" Anfang questioned. "How?"

Anfang's comment caused Thyra to bust out in laughter. Johnathen waved them off and stared out over the landscape, taking another sip. "Y'all are just jealous of my fine-tuned palate."

Thya's eartufts perked up as she heard tires crunching snow underneath them. She looked down the long driveway to see a black G Wagon Mercedes ascend the hill in front of the resort building.

"Who is that?" Johnathen wondered.

The Mercedes stopped and the rear door opened. A tiny violet-backed starling gryphoness stepped out of the vehicle into the snow and looked around. She was dressed in a thick black coat that matched her coloration, and a short purple skirt with leggings.

"Isabell!" Thyra shouted from the balcony.

Immediately, the small iridescent purple gryphoness looked up and smiled, causing Thyra to jump up. She placed her coffee cup down and leaped over the railing. She glided down and landed a few feet in front of Isabell. She ran up to the gryphoness to scoop her up in a tight hug. Isabell laughed and threw her lithe limbs around Thyra, embracing her friend.

"I'm so glad to see you!" Thyra exclaimed.

"I am too! I have to say, the proposal to move was a bit shocking, but I don't have much anyways. Everything I own fits in a single suitcase," Isabell explained as Thyra let the gryphoness down on all fours once again. She shivered and looked around at the snow covered land. "Plus, I've never seen Austria before. Figured if all my friends were here, then I might as well."

Thyra smiled and leaned in to preen along her neck, causing the gryphoness to ruffle her feathers. "Are you staying here with us?" She watched the human driver walk towards the rear of the vehicle and open up the back hatch.

"Apparently so. At first, your...um...'dad' told me you requested me by name, which is a little weird but I'm glad that you did," Isabell admitted, kicking away some snow from her talons. "He offered me some tickets and we talked for a while about what I could do. As much as I appreciate the offer, I need some sort of reason to be here. So, it looks like I'm the Redtails PR rep," Isabell explained.

Alex Bizzell

Thyra's eyes widened as she explained the job to her. "Really! That's awesome! I didn't know we would be famous enough to need PR reps."

Isabell nodded and watched as the human withdrew her single luggage bag. "I'm sure you and the other gryphons are the talk of the town. Whether it be negative or positive is what I'm supposed to figure out. And then see if I can't regulate it." Isabell offered to grab her bag. The well-dressed human refused politely and carried the suitcase towards the front door. "Anyways, let's talk inside. It's cold as hell out here."

Once inside the lobby, Isabell found herself a nice couch to splay out on with a loud sigh. She looked up at the clock on the wall and thought for a minute. "Damn, I've been awake for like thirty hours at this point," Isabell said. "And the food on the plane was terrible."

The well-dressed human simply put Isabell's suitcase near the front desk, nodded to the group, and left without a single word.

"They didn't fly you first class?" Thyra asked, making herself comfortable on the couch opposing her in the homey lobby. "The food should be pretty good."

"Yeah, but it was just really heavy with salt and other human preservatives," Isabell explained.

Just then, Antonio came wondering around the corner wearing an apron and flicked his eartufts to attention. "Isabell! What a surprise." Antonio had only met her once in the hospital but remembered her clearly.

"Good to see you too," Isabell said. "You're Antonio and you play with Thyra, right?"

"That is correct. The whole team lives here for the time being," Antonio explained. "And Anfang as well," he

218

added, looking towards the staircase as Johnathen and Anfang walked down into the lobby.

Isabell turned to look at the beast and frowned. The last time she saw him face-to-face, he had been covered with blood from murdering a human in the hospital. Thyra felt the tension grow in the air as the two looked at one another.

"Isabell! How was the flight?" Johnathen said, breaking the ice.

Anfang sat with his single eartuft folded back and avoided Isabell's eyes.

"It was ok. First time I've flown without being locked in a dark cage," Isabell looked from Anfang back to Johnathen. She harshly addressed the elephant in the room. "So, we are just suddenly cool with this, huh?"

Everyone fell silent. Antonio cleared his throat and turned back to head into the kitchen. "I need to go check on the oven," he said, excusing himself from the room.

Isabell, despite the uncomfortable subject she had brought up, looked as calm as could be. "I'm going to take everyone's silence as a yes. I guess forgive and forget. After all, it was just a couple humans."

Thyra wasn't sure if she was being sarcastic or not. She could tell the comment made Johnathen uneasy as well. "Anfang is a changed gryphon. Besides, we are all starting over here. It's an opportunity to push the reset on life," Thyra stated.

Isabell seemed to weigh Thyra's words for a minute but simply shrugged her wingshoulders. "Sounds good to me. I'll forget about it. Anyways, you have any beer around here? I'm parched."

Anfang stood up quickly. "I will get you some," he said, much to Isabell's surprise. The huge gryphon disappeared into the kitchen for a moment and walked back with an opened bottle.

"Thanks. Yeah, I know it's supposed to be early for drinking, but when you've been awake for a couple days, it doesn't matter now does it?" Isabell poured the contents into her beak. "So, what do you all do all day? I saw the construction around town and the beginning of the gryphball stadium."

"Nothing much for me," Johnathen said, sitting next to Thyra on the sofa. "Anthony was mentioning something about getting me books on European Union law. There's a lot of groundwork to lay down when it comes with setting up a law office in a new country, let alone a gryphon country . . ."

Isabell yawned as Johnathen carried on, seeming uninterested in what he had to say. Her eyes moved to Thyra.

"And I've been training with the team every day," Thyra said. "It looks like our stadium won't be ready until the season starts up in January, but there's a small gym in town we have been using. And we use a field nearby for matches and drills."

Isabell nodded and sipped from her beer while looking over to Anfang. "What about you? Pillaging villages and raping women?" Her tone deaf joke made Thyra uneasy, and she watched Anfang brush off the insult. He was learning how to control his anger more and more every day.

"I train to become city guard," Anfang replied.

Isabell almost choked on her beer and began to laugh. "A guard huh? Like what, some sort of police duty?"

"Yes," Anfang answered.

"I suppose he doesn't know what irony is, does he?" Isabell asked the couple.

"I think it's a fitting job for him and I know he will excel at it," Johnathen stated, giving Anfang a confident nod.

Thyra was glad that Johnathen was trying his best to connect with Anfang. Thyra looked up at the clock on the wall. She could hear the footsteps of other gryphons on the floor above as they all began to wake. "Speaking of training, I should go get ready," she said, hoping off of the couch. She walked over to Isabell and preened her gently on the neck. "You behave today, ok?"

"Me? Behave? Yeah, that's not going to happen," Isabell retorted slyly. Anfang stood up and took his leave, following Thyra up the stairs.

"And I guess that leaves you and I unsupervised," Isabell said, turning her attention to Johnathen.

"I guess so," Johnathen said and made himself comfortable on the couch. "So they have you working as the teams PR rep, huh?"

"For now," Isabell said.

"Does they really need one?" Johnathen replied skeptically.

"Think about it for a minute. The whole team just moved into a brand new gryphon-only city without paying a dime and having everything handed to them on a silver platter," Isabell began. "From what I read; this town was a wreck when it was purchased a couple years back. There's been a lot of work going on here. You think those other gryphons just moved right in and were pampered to? No, they've been busting their tailfeathers day in and day out. Probably had to pay for everything themselves trying to get this country established. You think these rich, spoiled and spoon-fed gryphons are going to be well liked around town?"

221

"I guess I never thought about that," Johnathen responded. "But Thyra and her friends aren't like that. They've worked hard for…"

"You think the gryphon residents know that? And what about the local Austrian humans? You think they are happy about a huge plot of land being sold off as a different country and populated by gryphons? This is a country in which tradition thrives and families remain here for generations."

Johnathen opened his mouth to respond but was quickly cut off as she continued. "Think about this building. It was probably a family-owned resort for decades. I would guess the sons and daughters of that family aren't too keen on having it sold off and populated by gryphons," she pointed out and finished off the rest of the beer bottle.

Johnathen rubbed his scraggly chin and shook his head, impressed by her observations. "I get your point."

"Exactly. It's my job to think about these sort of things, do some recon, and build up a good rep for the rest of the team," she hopped off the couch and stretched out her legs, much like a cat would.

"Looks like someone's done their homework," Johnathen said.

"Someone had to. You all have these rose-colored glasses on right now, but sooner or later everyone will face the music. I just have to figure out what beat we have to dance to."

Chapter 17 Fake It

Anthony slammed the car door shut and adjusted his long overcoat to combat the cold breeze. He looked up at the towering hill that stood before him, populated by construction equipment and busy gryphons going about their business. Debra approached from the driver's side of the vehicle and stood next to him, looking at the work around the foundations of the Redtail team's housings.

"As you can see, construction has resumed at your request," Debra stated. "But we are still getting some resistance."

"I see. I assume he is the CM?" Anthony asked, motioning with his head at a gryphon garbed in thick winter clothing and a reflective vest. The gryphon was walking towards them, a concerned look on his face.

"Yes. He's the one that suggested we find an alternative location for the houses," Debra confirmed. Anthony nodded and put on a smile as the white-faced gryphon approached.

"You must be Mayor Clearwater! A pleasure to meet you," the CM said in a rough German accent. The gryphon, who stood to about Anthony's chest, reached a foretalon out to shake Anthony's gloved hand.

"And you must be Lucas. Pleasure is all mine," Anthony said and followed the gryphon to a portable trailer sitting off to the side. They walked up the small set of metal stairs and into the cramped building. A space heater was running, and the heat was a welcoming gift. The snow quickly began melting off his jacket.

"Can I get you anything? Water? Seltzer? Schnapps?" Lucas asked, making his way to his desk at the far end of the small room.

"No, thank you," Anthony sat down in a cheap plastic chair across from the desk as Debra sat in the chair next to him. He began taking off his gloves. "I won't be long. I just want to know why you recommended we move locations."

Lucas poured himself some water from a jug and sat on his pillow behind the desk. Layers of papers pilled upon one another decorated the desk, with a laptop sitting off to the side. He cleared his throat. "We made a discovery about the grounds that raised a red flag."

"That is what I was told. What discoveries did you make?" Anthony asked, folding his hands.

Lucas seemed apologetic. "We used our ground penetrating radar to evaluate the condition of the surface before beginning our work and found what looks to be a large cavernous space underneath the area where you wish to build. Therefore, we are not entirely sure the ground is stable enough for a neighborhood of this weight."

Anthony pretended to be confused. "Like a cave underneath the surface? In this area?"

Lucas nodded and began to dig through the stack of papers until he found the right one. He slid it over on the desk and pointed at the fuzzy black and white image. "What you see here are the layers of sediment. You can see sections of rock and crust here and there, as to be expected in this mountainous area, but what is curious is this." The gryphon pointed at a large black square at the bottom of the image with his talon.

Anthony looked over to Debra and grunted. He paid close attention to Lucas' response to his next question. "What do you think it is?"

"Not completely sure. It could be caused by a natural underground spring or river, but it is much larger than any I have seen," Lucas shrugged his wing shoulders. "It just means the ground could be unstable. This is why I haven't been comfortable continuing to build, but it seems you are very set on this location." Lucas brought the glass to his beak and sipped from it.

Anthony nodded and slid the paper back to him. "I understand you are just doing your job, but I love the view and I want to continue with construction. Just reinforce it where needed."

Lucas nodded and reached into his coat pocket, bringing out a pack of lucky strike cigarettes. " I expected you would say that. I will agree the view is beautiful. Although, the additional groundwork that is needed will be costly. That is why I halted construction until a decision was reached."

Lucas put a cigarette in his beak. He offered the pack to Anthony and Debra, who both shook their heads. He flicked his lighter and puffed, sending a plume of smoke out inside the cramped trailer.

"Who else knows about this?" Anthony asked.

Lucas held his smoke in between two talons and flicked the ash into an empty cup. He shook his head. "Just the technician who runs the GPR and myself."

Anthony nodded and grabbed his gloves off the desk. "Good. I would prefer to keep it that way, please."

Lucas seemed curious as to why but nodded his beak. "No problem. After all, it is your money. Is there anything else you want to discuss?"

Anthony stood and Debra followed his lead. "That is all. Thank you for your work so far and let me know directly if anything else pops up," Anthony said, reaching into his coat pocket to pull out a business card.

Lucas took it and gave Anthony one handshake. "I will. Have a good day."

Anthony walked out into the cold with Debra in tow. He descended the stairs and looked up at the hill once again. Loud construction equipment beeped and rumbled as they cleared the land, prepping it for the new buildings. Gryphons screeched commands at one another from the hillside that could be heard over the rumble of diesel engines.

"I thought the GPR machines only read up to four meters deep," Anthony said to Debra as he watched the commotion.

"Apparently his equipment is more advanced, Sir," Debra responded.

Anthony pulled out his cellphone and began to type a message. "We need to keep an eye on Lucas and figure out who his technician is." He walked back towards the car. "I don't need them talking about their discoveries to others."

Anthony opened the passenger door and climbed inside. Debra entered the driver's side and started up the car, turning on the heat. Anthony's cell phone dinged, and he pulled the device out to check the return message.

"So far, nothing on his social media," Anthony said. They drove down the snow-covered street, heading back into town. "He knows more than he's leading on. He knows it's not a cavern formed by some natural spring or river, but he won't come out and say it. Even the untrained eye can see those images depicted solid concrete construction underneath."

Debra was silent for a moment as she drove down the decedent snow covered road. Finally she asked, "And what if he decides to reveal this information?"

Anthony took a deep breath and leaned back into the plush leather seats. It was a weighty decision. He grimaced. "As much as I would hate to do so, we would have to silence him." The thought of disposing one of his own creations sickened him to the core, even more so than giving the command to eliminate another human. "I just hope it doesn't come down to that."

Johnathen watched the LED lights begin to glow inside the computer case as the device hummed to life. This new PC was a little too flashy for his tastes, but it seemed to be the style that went along with high end computers these days. The computer booted up without a hitch and displayed the desktop screen. He plugged in the floppy drive reader and inserted one of the diskettes, then glanced around behind him.

There was not a desk to speak of in the confined quarters except for a tiny breakfast table sitting near the windows. He grabbed his wireless keyboard and mouse before sitting down on the bed across from the television hanging on the wall. This would have to make do for the time being.

The computer recognized a text file document on the floppy disk. He took a breath and opened the file, watching as the computer decrypted the text and displayed it on the screen.

Project alpha, series A-ZZZ.

Series A, unsuccessful. Test subject deceased after 12 hours.

Series B, unsuccessful. Test subject deceased after 4 hours.

The list continued much the same for several pages with minimal variation to the text. Johnathen thought back to the large feline skeleton they found in the labs and could not help but think about how many others there must have been in the trials. He was beginning to understand why Thyra had felt guilty for being created. There had to have hundreds of trials and bodies tossed aside before any successful tests. He skimmed through the rest of the initial text until the descriptions began to show promise.

Series BRA, moderate success. Test subject shows excess shedding of fur and feather pins have been observed protruding through the skin. Subject deceased after 7 days, 12 hours.

Johnathen could not imagine the sounds of pain from the subjects. He knew how irritable Thyra was when she was molting her feathers, but to imagine a living creature transforming and growing feathers for the first time . . . it made his skin crawl. He scrolled a couple of more pages down.

Series GQA, promising success. Day 24. Test subject has a mixture of avian and feline resemblances. Beak and face are malformed. Wings resemble fleshy stubs protruding through the back. Subject expresses constant pain. Cannot consume food unassisted. Morphine and nutrients have been administered every 2 hours. Subject seems to be somewhat aware of surroundings and vocalizes its needs.

Day 62. Subject has vocalized one coherent word, Pain. Subject expresses itself, leading me to believe it is sentient. Morphine and nutrients continue to be necessary via IV.

Day 70. Subject deceased due to heart failure.

Johnathen sat back and rubbed his eyes. He took a deep breath and stared up at the white popcorn ceiling. "Why did Anthony want me to find these files?"

All he could see for pages and pages was nothing but suffering. Did Anthony even care about these initial test subjects? Or did Anthony want him to realize the difficulty he went through in order to create Thyra and gryphon kind as a whole? He knew it had to be frustrating at the very least, even for someone with no heart, but he imagined with each failure, Anthony had a piece of his soul taken away from him.

Johnathen scrolled down to the end of the data on the first floppy disk.

Colony

Series HAA, first successful artificial birth. Subject grew within the incubation egg with phenomenal results. Subject hatched after 22 days, displaying almost perfect gryphon attributes.

"Incubation egg?" Johnathen questioned himself. He thought back to the gigantic broken glass tubes that were stationed around one room they had found inside the labs. They had to be some sort of growth chambers, simulating an egg. He read on.

Day 32, subject has begun to vocalize regularly and eats nutrient paste that simulates regurgitated food from avian parents.

Day 50, subject has doubled in size. It shows no signs of pain, although the wings continue to remain as stumps and the face is deformed. She, as determined by our ornithologist, has begun to repeat simple words such as food, water, and happy.

Day 62, she displays sentience found in children at 10 months. Tests have shown that she can identify different foods and now has a preference, that preference being Pasta. She likes pasta more than anything and asks for it by name. Her eyes have changed to green, as mine are, and have a human like recognition. She seems to recognize me and smile when I come to visit.

Day 68, Subject called me papa. I don't know who taught her this, but she has picked up on it. This one shows promise.

Day 70, deceased due to heart failure.
End of file.

Again, Johnathen had to sit back and rub his eyes. It was all very clinical, but he could not imagine the kind of anger, frustration, and sadness Anthony must have gone through during these trials. That last subject could easily have been Thyra. He thought about his wife, her smile, the kindness in her eyes, and then imagined her dead on the floor.

The door creaked open and Johnathen sat up in his bed, frantically moving the mouse to minimize the window.

Isabell stood in the doorway, free-feathered and chuffed. "You know, if you're going to look at porn you should at least close the door."

Johnathen opened his mouth to protest but thought differently. Honestly, it would be futile with her. "What are you doing up?" he asked, changing the subject.

"Well, I can't lay around and sleep all day. I'll never get used to this time change if I do that. And I'm bored. So, I'm going to go take a shower and you're going to take me into town," Isabell said, watching him expectantly.

Johnathen thought about giving her a witty remark back like 'why don't you fly yourself,' or 'take your small feather butt into town then,' but looked at her scarred wing and thought better of it.

"Alright, I'll go get ready too. I need to go to the grocery store anyways. Antonio made a list for tonight's dinner." He saw the cheeky gryphoness smile as he instantly agreed to her demands but knew that she was just playing around. Even if he would have declined, she would not be angry with him.

"Perfect. I'll be right out," she said and turned to head back down the hallway.

Colony

Johnathen locked his computer with a short keystroke. He did not know what other information would show on the other floppy drives, but he wanted to keep it hidden from anyone outside the immediate circle.

He quickly changed and headed downstairs into the common room, then sat back into one of the large couches and flipped on the television while he waited for Isabell. The news was on, but he knew very little German. What little he did understand was quickly lost to him due to the local accent. His phone dinged which confused him slightly. He had just recently received his new smart phone and only a handful of people had his number. He unlocked the phone and saw it was a message from Antonio.

Do not forget the asparagus. Also, Thyra said bring her more coffee.

Johnathen snorted. It felt odd to be the errand boy for a team full of gryphons, but he did not really mind it.

"You ready?" Isabell said as she walked down the stairs. She was wearing a black leather jacket with long jeans. Her crest feathers were still damp.

Johnathen stood and grabbed his jacket from the coat hanger near the main entrance door. "Yeah, but you're going to freeze in that. We need to get you some thicker clothes." He put on his puffy green jacket and grabbing the single pair of car keys hanging up on the peg by the door.

"Worry about yourself," Isabell said and opened the door.

Johnathen shrugged and followed her into the snow. They walked a short distance to the Mercedes wagon sitting outside and both climbed inside. Johnathen started up the vehicle and rubbed his hands together. He shivered and exhaled, watching the vapor cloud fog up the windshield.

233

"So, what were you really looking at up there?" Isabell prodded.

"Just some emails from friends back home," Johnathan quickly lied. He turned on the seat warmers and glanced over to Isabell. She was staring at him and he could see in her purple eyes that she did not believe a word of it.

"Alright then, keep your secrets. It's none of my business." Isabell sat back into the plush leather seat which seemed to almost swallow her. She could not see over the dash unless she stood on her hindlegs. Johnathen thought it best to drop the conversation and proceeded down the snow-covered driveway.

Being a southern man, he was not used to driving in the snow, and it showed. Even with the vehicle's multitude of advantages, he didn't dare drive faster than a crawl. He carefully drove down the slope and continued on one of the main roads. "Maybe after we get some groceries, we can go get you some new winter gear. There's this gryphon-owned shop that makes all kinds of…"

"I'm fine," Isabell quickly cut him off.

Johnathen shut his mouth and concentrated on driving down the small snow-covered roads without sliding off. He wondered why Isabell always had to put up a tough front. She was clearly cold in her inadequate clothing but would never admit it. It had to be hard for her. She was not one for handouts, yet she was living in a different country, living in a house, and provided an allowance all for free.

"Well how about we grab a bite and a beer beforehand? There's a pretty cool bar I saw the other day and haven't tried it yet," Johnathen offered. He knew she would not be one to decline a beer, after all. He glanced over at her to see a little twinkle in her eyes as she seemed to act nonchalant about the offer.

"Yeah, I could go for a bite," Isabell responded.

Johnathen had to stifle a smile and nodded. It did not take long for them to approach the edge of downtown, or what would eventually be called downtown. He had to slow the vehicle down to a crawl inside the busy streets of the small city. Gryphons wandered around on foot on the city streets going from store to store. Some continued their work on almost completed buildings, laying bricks and carrying lumber.

Isabell perched her foretalons on the dash of the vehicle and looked up, observing the gryphons flying overhead. "It really is a gryphon country, isn't it?"

"I figured you would have seen this on your way here," Johnathen said as he parallel parked the vehicle along the streets. One good thing about living in a gryphon city was there was plentiful parking. Actually, there was not another vehicle on the road. His car's presence was strange enough that gryphons turned to see who was driving.

"I did but it was early in the morning before the sun was even up. I guess there's not many owl gryphons here," Isabell commented. Johnathen shut off the car and thought about the comment for a second.

"You mean like, literally or..." Johnathen asked, but Isabell opened the door and stepped out.

He followed her the short distance to the bars entrance. The sign 'Shooters' on the window depicted a log comprised of billiard balls and a pool stick. He held the door open for Isabell and went in behind her.

The interior of the bar was modern and freshly renovated. The smell of new paint and carpet hung heavily in the air. A few tables decorated the entrance with a great pool hall towards the rear where a small group of gryphons played. The pool tables were modified, being significantly shorter than the average human tables but the same 'competition' length.

Johnathen listened to the smooth eighties rock and recognized Deep Purple playing on the speakers. The bar sat to the left of the area with a black feathered raven gryphon standing at the tap system, pouring a beverage. The raven's feathers gleamed a night blue in the dim light as a professional-looking apron swayed around his chest while he moved.

The raven perked his ears as the two stepped in and turned to look at his guest. "Ah! Moin, Moin! Vie gehts?" he asked in a heavily accented German.

"Gut, und Sie?" Johnathen replied.

"Gut! Nimm einen Tisch," the corvid responded before turning his attention back to the beers, pouring each one carefully and letting them settle.

Johnathen led Isabell over to a small table at the corner of the seating area. The gryphons playing billiards seem to pay them no mind as they continued their game. Isabell sat down on a pillow behind the table. Johnathen glanced around, looking for a chair.

"Die menschlichen Stühle sind da," the raven called out while pointing his talon.

Johnathen understood the gist of what he said and turned to see a single chair against the wall. "Danke," Johnathen responded and grabbed the chair before returning to the table.

"Where did you learn how to speak German?" Isabell asked

"That's about as much as I know. I only understood Stüle, which means chair," Johnathen admitted, glad that he had at least learned a few important words. Within a minute, the raven quickly approached and sat on his haunches before them wearing a big smile.

"So! Was Möchten Sie trinken?" He asked politely.

Johnathen paused and cleared his throat. "Ich… beer," Johnathen said, his knowledge of German now exhausted.

The corvid grinned and chuckled slightly. "You were doing good! You say, 'Ich nehme ein Bier, bitte' now," the corvid said, putting his talon hands on his hips.

"Ich nehmen ein…"

"No. It is not ICK NehMEN. It is ECHHH nehme. Neighma. Once more," the corvid commanded. Johnathen, eager to learn, cleared his throat and repeated it correctly, much to the corvid's enjoyment. "Very good, human! You need a little practice. I assume you are American, yes?"

"Yeah. How could you tell so quickly?" Johnathen asked.

The corvid simply cackled and waved a talon dismissively, "I know these things. Anyways, I am called Kai! Owner of Shooters." Kai ruffled his feathers slightly, dim light reflected off his long black beak that wore a constant friendly smirk. "I assume the beautiful lady wants a beer as well?" he asked, looking over to Isabell.

"Please, and a menu. I'm starving," Isabell said. Kai nodded and left as quickly as he came.

"It looks like we are the outsiders here now," Isabell said and glanced up at Johnathen. "You, even more so."

Johnathen considered her comment. He had earlier realized he was now the minority, but it was more than just the fact that he was human. There was a multitude of gryphon ethnicities in this town. "Yeah, it looks like I'm the odd one out."

Isabell brought out a pack of cigarettes from her jacket pocket. "How does it feel to be on the other side of the fence?" she asked almost sarcastically. She pulled a cigarette out and placed one in her beak, lighting it with a quick strike of a lighter.

"Well, I really don't know," Johnathen admitted.

Isabell dragged a hit and puffed out a plume of smoke into the air. She flicked the ash into the tray at the center of the table and raised an eye ridge. "You don't know?"

Johnathen simply shrugged.

"So, you don't feel the least bit out of place? Like, everywhere you go you're not really accepted, no matter how much others seem to greet you. You just feel completely at home?" Isabell asked.

Johnathen had to weigh her words. He knew what she was getting at. There was a part of him that felt he was not accepted by the gryphons, no matter how they presented themselves to him. He would always be 'the human' no matter where he went, even when other humans began to visit the country. In fact, he was one of only three humans allowed to live inside the country at the moment.

"Actually no," Johnathen admitted. "This is new for me. But I guess I feel like I'm an outsider even though I'm accepted."

Kai came back with two tall glasses of beer on top a tray balanced on his wing shoulder along with a menu in his beak. He quickly placed them down and clapped his foretalons together.

"Prost! Let me know when you want to order. I recommend the doner kebab pizza. Es schmeckt gut!" Kai said with a chef's kiss.

"You know, that sounds amazing. Go ahead and bring us one," Johnathen said. Kai nodded and quickly left the table. Johnathen picked up his liter-sized beer and sipped it gently, savoring the wheaty smooth flavor.

Isabell did the same, except she downed half the glass in a single motion. "So, you were saying?" she said, wiping the foam off her beak with her good wing.

Johnathen sighed and leaned back into his chair. "I think I get your point. I feel out of place, but not to the extent you all have experienced."

Isabell dragged her cigarette and pointed at him directly. "You just said you all, implying gryphon kind," Isabell said. Johnathen held his beer and thought about it for minute. She gave him a stern look. "Exactly. You recognized that we are a completely different species than you."

"Hey. Why are you targeting me all the sudden?" Johnathen expressed, feeling backed into a corner.

"I'm not. I'm just trying to get you to think. You know now what it feels like to be a 'you all.' But, it's that thought process that gives people like The Gathering a podium," Isabell said calmly and puffed on her cigarette once again.

"It's not the same," Johnathen said, frustrated.

"It's not? Please, elaborate," Isabell motioned with her foretalons.

Johnathen looked away, watching the gryphons continue their billiard game. She had a point. Any form of thinking they were different from one another was unwarranted. They should be viewed as the same.

"Listen. All I know is I supported a cause for a small redneck town and now look at me," Isabell motioned to her maimed wing. "I may never be able to fly again. You know what that's like? You know what it means to be given the gift of flight and have it taken away from you?"

Both were silent for a minute as Isabell downed most of her beer. She put out her cigarette in the tray and sighed. "Of course, you don't. You're not a gryphon."

"It's like never allowing me to drive again," Johnathen suggested.

Isabell nodded. "I guess that's as close as you can come. It's like having your precious mustang destroyed and told you can never drive anything again."

Johnathen sighed and took a long sip of his beer. He did not plan on this impromptu lunch hangout to be so heavy, especially with everything that was going on in his head. "Look, I'm sorry for what happened to you. I…"

"I don't need your goddamn sentiment," Isabell kept her voice calm, yet the hackle feathers raised. "It's not your fault for what happened, and I'm not upset with you. It's humanity as a whole. Sure, it could be related to social structures and how people are brought up, but I've dealt with enough speciesism to last several gryphons' lifetimes. I want to dissolve this issue."

Johnathen eased back into his seat, forcing his expression to be relaxed even as his mind raced. He wanted to shout out how he was nothing like the rest of those humans, but some part of him told him to remain calm. After all, Thyra had almost accused him of the same way of thinking just days ago. He took a deep breath.

"What's your point?" Johnathen asked.

Isabell looked across the table and brought out her cigarette pack once again. He looked at the pack for a second, and seeming to read his mind, she offered one. Even with the thought of Thyra's wrath, he took one and lit it up. It had been so long since he had a smoke. He let the nicotine wash through him in a pleasant numbness that calmed his mind.

"My point being, you don't completely understand and you're the best human I've ever met. Maybe it's because you're married to a gryphon, a gryphon that's my best friend," Isabell paused, finishing lighting her own cigarette. "But the rest of the humans just pretend to accept us. It's why we have a whole colony now."

"I really don't think that's the case," Johnathen argued, dragging another hit. Thyra was certainly going to smell the smoke on his scraggly beard no matter how many times he washed it.

"Oh, really now, mister everything is great?" Isabell said. "So, you think this gryphon-only country is just going to thrive all by itself without any intervention? Everything is just going to be hunky dory and have a Disney style ending, huh?"

Johnathen frowned at her and began to grow angry. All he wanted was a day of his new version of normalcy. He thought about shouting at her to calm down and how she was overthinking everything, but a part of him realized she was right. He had rose-colored glasses on. There was something brewing on the horizon, but he did not know how or when it would happen. He dragged his cigarette once more and immediately put it out, feeling sick to his stomach.

"No. You're right," Johnathen said in a low tone. "This can only be paradise for so long. But how do we preserve it?"

Isabell nodded as she saw she had gotten point across and readjusted her aching wings. "I don't know yet. We have to play the game like the rest of them. But we also have to keep our eyes open for what's coming," Isabell said before looking up as Kai carried over a large pizza pan.

"Coming in hot!" Kai exclaimed and roughly tossed the pizza on the table with a laugh. "So! Gutten Appetite! Can I get you anything else?"

"Just a refill, and he's got the tab," Isabell motioned to Johnathen. He sighed and pulled out his American express card.

Kai frowned and shook his head. "Sorry, I do not take this, only euros at the moment."

Johnathen's eyes widened as he looked at Isabell, who simply shrugged her wing shoulders while biting into a piece of pizza.

"Um, do you take IOUs?"

Chapter 18 Hey Man Nice Shot

Anfang took a deep breath and lined up the sights on his Glock pistol. He stood on three feet and pulled the trigger roughly with his remaining foretalon, ringing out a couple shots across the range, all of them missing the target. Joseph sighed and walked up behind Anfang to slap each shoulder.

"Keep your shoulders in, lean forward, bend your forearm slightly, and squeeze the trigger. Don't just pull it," Joseph instructed. "Keep a firm hold, but don't crush it. With your strength, you can easily crush the plastic frames."

Anfang readjusted his stance and did as he was told. He lined up the sights and fired off a few shots. This time all of them hit the target, but nowhere near center. The Glock's slide locked back and Anfang dropped the magazine before reaching into the pouch on his vest to pull out another. He fed a live magazine into the weapon and released the slide, chambering a new round.

"Breathe normally," Joseph said.

Anfang calmed himself and concentrated on the target as he fired again. All his shot hit the mark.

"Good, now you just have to do that all the time," Joseph complimented with a half-smile. "Holster your weapon."

Anfang struggled to put his weapon away on his vest and looked back to Joseph while the sounds of gunfire filled the air. Other gryphons around him were firing down range, practicing themselves.

"I still not know why I need this," Anfang said.

"Because, dipshit, as indestructible as you think we are, we can still be killed," Joseph said and walked over to another gryphon, slapping one of their hindlegs to adjust their stance. "You want to protect everyone else, right? It's not like you can close a gap of thirty yards on a target as quickly as you can draw your weapon and dispose of them," he added, continuing down the line. Anfang followed along, occasionally stopping to readjust the vest on his chest.

"I promise Thyra that I won't kill," Anfang said.

Joseph laughed and stopped at a table filled with ammo boxes. He thought for a minute and picked up a clipboard, scribbling some things down on some papers. "Yeah, I remember that bullshit you keep spouting." He looked up from his clipboard, waiting for a response. "Really? Never kill anyone again? You, of all living creatures, never killing another human being, even if it meant for the greater good?" Joseph placed the papers down on the table.

Anfang was confused. Killing for any kind of good was still wrong. He had convinced himself of that after murdering the leader of The Gathering. He had been so sure it was right at the time, but Thyra had made it loud and clear that his actions were wrong.

"There not good reason to kill," Anfang said under his breath.

The comment made Joseph laugh even louder. Anfang frowned and bared his fangs slightly. Joseph took notice of Anfang's apparent anger and clapped his foretalons together. "Oh! You're suddenly a pacifist! So tell me, Sabertooth Slasher, if it comes down to killing horrible humans to protect Thyra and the other gryphons, you won't do that?"

Anfang glanced away from Joseph, realizing that he was right. He was willing to kill every human in the world to protect Thyra. He'd even give up his own life if it came down to it. Joseph knew very well the killer instinct that rose up within Anfang.

"That's what I thought," Joseph expressed. He looked around to the rest of the trainee gryphons and yelled, "Cease fire!"

Immediately, all the gryphons holstered their weapons and sat on their haunches. Joseph walked behind them all, feathers ruffled with pride. "Anfang here has expressed his displeasure with firearms and the intent to kill! He has forgotten the reason we are here. He thinks he can keep these citizens safe with kind words and a rough talon every now and then," Joseph began, walking back and forth. Anfang ground his beak, staring Joseph straight in the eyes.

"Who here wants to remind Anfang of how cruel the world can be?" Joseph asked loudly, looking among the cadets.

Several seconds went by with no answer. "No one? Not a single soul?" Everyone was silent. "Hmph," Joseph said and stripped his body armor from his chest.

Everyone watched with interest as Joseph walked onto the range. He approached one of the targets and ran his talons along it.

"Anfang, step onto the range," he commanded.

Anfang narrowed his eyes as every gryphon trainee turned to stare at him. He perked his single eartuft and walked onto the range, a great distance away from Joseph.

"I want you to draw your weapon and shoot me," Joseph commanded, readjusting his leathery wings. Anfang clenched his fangs against his upper beak and shook his head.

"No," Anfang responded.

"No?" Joseph said, raising his voice. "You will do as your told! Now draw your weapon and shoot to kill!" Joseph screeched. Anfang looked away, watching the wide eyes of the various gryphons standing in attendance. Still, Anfang refused to draw his weapon. "I knew you would be useless. I don't know what Anthony sees in a stupid, gutless, loveless failed experiment such as you. A spineless gryphon like you could never protect Thyra. You'll never earn her love. How could anyone love an ugly beast like you? No wonder she married a filthy human. She was probably so disgusted with you that…"

Joseph did not have time to finish as Anfang screeched and drew out his pistol. A shot rang out, whirling past Joseph's head by inches. Joseph laughed and began to sprint towards Anfang, only changing direction as he saw Anfang pull the trigger. Snow kicked up from the rounds spraying across the ground as Joseph quickly closed ground.

Anfang tossed his weapon aside as the slide locked back into place and sprinted to meet his opposer. The two collided hard and fell to the ground. A flurry of feathers, limbs, and snow flew into the air. Anfang retreated with a quick reaction, narrowly avoiding a swift kick to the chest.

Joseph rose from the ground and wiped his face with a wing, looking down at the blood in the snow. "You actually landed a hit!" He laughed and began to circle around Anfang.

"Look at you! Finally, able to draw blood from me! Are you in control? Or is it just that beastly instinct inside driving you?"

"No, I control me," Anfang responded, his green eyes narrowed into thin cat-like slits. He could feel his heart beating in his chest, and his vision blurred at the edges, yet he remained focused. The other time she had felt this high, he had practically blacked out. This time, he was in control. He was aware.

"Good. Come on then," Joseph assumed his ready stance, rising on his hind paws and balancing with his wings.

Anfang darted forward, first feinting from left to right and faked a left strike. Joseph moved to block the fake left strike with his foretalons but quickly found one of Anfang's hind legs spinning to kick him squarely in the jaw.

Joseph spun and hit the ground hard, earning a round of talon claps from the audience. Anfang quickly regained his posture, watching as Joseph rose with a semi shocked look. The shock quickly turned into a smile as he laughed again.

Anfang cocked his head, confused by the sudden change of mood. One instant, he felt threatened and ready to kill his opposer, but now Joseph seemed pleased.

"Very good! That's what I wanted to see," Joseph complimented and spit out a glob of blood into the white snow. He turned to address the rest of the gryphons. "And that's it for the day! you're dismissed."

The gryphons in attendance left with minimal chatting between themselves and poured into the large building. Joseph walked past Anfang to grab the pistol out of the snow and held it by the muzzle offering it back to Anfang.

"You dropped something," Joseph commented.

Anfang reached out and retrieved his firearm before holstering it. He looked up into Joseph's eyes, and was surprised to see that they were pleased. "What was that?"

"That was you being in control. And you hitting harder than I've ever been hit in my life," Joseph complimented, rubbing his cheek. "That hit would've been enough to knock out anyone else."

The compliments felt good to Anfang, and he roused his chest feathers in pride. It was an odd feeling for him, but one that he instinctively enjoyed. Joseph read into his body language and huffed through his nares.

"Don't get a hard on. You still have a long way to go." He walked past Anfang towards the building. "But I'm beginning to understand why Anthony says First Class is something to be feared."

Anfang followed along as they walked to the building. "What is First Class and why you say it again?"

Joseph sighed and opened up the door, motioning for Anfang to step inside. "In due time, Anfang."

"Thyra!" Rachel exclaimed, gliding down to match Thyra's pace.

The wind whipped past Thyra's face as another cold gust blasted her feathers. The gryphon had to adjust her wings for balance to keep from crashing into Aadhya, who flew effortlessly a few feet off her right.

"Yeah?" Thyra called back.

Rachel glided in between the two gryphons and pointed to her smartphone. "Did you see that Beast and Man is playing in Greifsburg for the New Year's party?"

Thyra had never heard that name. "One, don't fly and play with your phone at the same time! Two, who is Beast and Man?" she questioned, beating her wings hard against the air current. Rachel's lower beak hung open in disbelief. Thyra looked over at Aadhya and Antonio and they shrugged their shoulders.

"What! You mean to tell me none of you all have heard of Beast and Man?" Rachel exclaimed.

Thyra adjusted her flight, now slowing herself as the resort house came into sight. "No. I don't think any of us have."

Rachel huffed through her nares and followed the group to land on the soft snow in front of the house. The other gryphons from the team followed closely in behind.

"Well! It's only the best and first gryphon band on the planet! The singer is a nightingale gryphoness and the drummer is this cockatoo gryphon," Rachel began to explain as the group walked into the house. Thyra shook herself free from snow and sat to remove her coat. "The other two are humans, that's why the band is called Beast and Man! They've been touring all of Europe for the past year and I've always wanted to see them live! I don't know why they are coming to our small town, but we have to go see them!"

"I'm sure all of us are going to be at the New Years party. It's not like Victor is going to make us practice on the holiday," Thyra said.

She stepped inside the shared living room as the rest of the team followed in her footsteps. They hung their coats up around the entranceway, a seemingly endless mass of feathers and fur piling into the house. Many of the gryphons went up the stairs to shower, while the rest made themselves comfortable in the living room to wait their turn. There was not enough hot water for all of them at once, after all.

"And that's what I was saying!" Isabell exclaimed, pointing to her phone.

Thyra turned around the corner to see Johnathen and Isabell on one of the couches, looking at their phones as the television played as background noise.

"Well it looks like you two are getting along just fine," Thyra said. Isabell looked up at Thyra and gave a quick wave before pointing back down at her phone.

"Hey, hun," Johnathen said absently, looking at Isabell's cellphone.

"Look. The translation is rough, but it's saying exactly what I was talking about. There's a movement of anti-gryphon activists going on in Innsbruck. They aren't happy about us being here at all," Isabell explained.

Thyra's eartufts folded back. Already, that sense of dread she had felt from time-to-time in her hometown was creeping back to her. At least there was a border this time, and she was surrounded by gryphons.

"What are you two talking about?" Thyra asked. Aadhya walked in behind her with Rachel quickly in tow.

"It's nothing. Just a couple of angered kids on the internet," Johnathen assured her. He stood from the couch and walked over with a smile. He leaned down to kiss her on the cere before scrunching his nose and chuckling. "God, you stink."

"Sorry, we can't all be housewives and sit around eating bon bons all day," Thyra retorted.

"Yeah no shit! We've been busting our tailfeathers! Victor had us running intense drills all day." Rachel sat on her haunches and pulled of her practice uniform shirt, tossing it over to the side with a loud sigh. Her feathers were disheveled and matted down. "And guess what! You have to do all our laundry!" Rachel laughed as Johnathen made a fake gagging motion.

"Don't remind me," Johnathen said and walked past the group. "I'll be right back. You all want some water?" The group nodded and he disappeared into the kitchen.

Rachel tossed her shorts at the bundle of cloths and jumped up on the couch next to Isabell. The violet gryphoness squinted her eyes and moved away. Rachel scowled. "What!"

"You stink too, go take a shower," Isabell said.

"Well I would love to! But they are all packed right now. You know how it is! You've been here for a week. We all have to take turns!" Rachel said, pointing towards the ceiling. The sounds of gryphon footsteps and water splashing along the ground echoed in the room.

Isabell sighed and put her phone away in a leather jacket pocket. "I know, but I guess I'm always in my room or out with John when you all got back." She went to the sliding glass door and opened it. A cold gust of wind blew in, making Rachel shiver. Isabell stepped outside and closed the door behind her, bringing out a pack of cigarettes and lighting one up as she stared into the distance.

Johnathen came back in the room with a couple glasses of water and frowned at seeing Rachel's dirty uniform thrown into the corner. "Damnit! Come on! At least take them to the laundry room!"

Rachel groaned sarcastically and leapt off the couch. "You sound like my mom! Fine! Yes ma'am." She gathered her clothes before disappearing down the hallway.

Johnathen took a deep breath and closed his eyes, calming himself. "I swear sometimes I just want to pick her up and strangle her," he muttered as he handed out the water glasses. Aadhya sat on a large pillow next to the couch while Johnathen and Thyra settled on the sofa.

"She's a talonfull sometimes, but we love her," Thyra said, stretching out on the couch. Johnathen relaxed and rubbed behind Thyra's ears, earning a small trill from her beak. She looked around, watching as the occasional gryphon walked from downstairs to take their favorite spots around the living room. "Have you seen Anfang today?"

"Nope. He left around the same time all you all did, as he always does. He's usually home around now, but I wouldn't worry. Maybe he's enjoying himself for once," Johnathen explained and pulled out his cellphone again. He began scrolling through social media as Thyra peeked at the screen.

"I hope so. But what was Isabell talking about?" Thyra questioned.

Johnathen shrugged and locked his phone. "You remember what I told you last week about our little lunch date?" he asked and Thyra nodded. "Well, she's been doing some more digging, and it looks like she may be onto something. As in there are some groups that really don't like this new country."

"If I may," Aadhya chimed in and sipped her water. Her calm voice was still loud enough to carry over the ever-growing noise in the room. "I believe Isabell is correct in her assumptions. Throughout history, humans have valued one thing more than anything else, land." Her eyes were on the television where a British newscaster talked about what else was happening in the world, mainly relating to the disputes around the UK and Scotland.

"Even now, humans argue over where their borders lie. Then you throw in the aspect of homelands, traditions, and ancestry with a new 'invasive' species and it only becomes more complicated," Aadhya finished and sipped from her glass again, some of her black beard feathers dipping into the cup. She realized her mistake and quickly dried off the beard with her shirt.

"You make a lot of good points, Aadhya. But I don't think we have enough concrete evidence that we should worry," Johnathen said. "Not yet."

"Yeah, let's not worry until there's packs of humans rolling in on the city, guns blazing," Isabell said, slowly shutting the door behind her. They had been so wrapped up in the conversation that none of them had noticed Isabell walking back in. "It's easy to just deny, sit back, and relax with a 'don't worry guys, it will all be fine' attitude."

"You're right. I should be more aware," Johnathen responded flatly. "After all, I was part of The Gathering in the earlier years of my life. It felt like the right place to be, because of my upbringing, and the city loved them. They brought unity to the community. I didn't realize how wrong they were until I met Thyra," Johnathen thought out loud. He looked over to Isabell and seemed to think back. "I remember the terrible things you went through, but I didn't live through them, so I'm even trying to compare with them. I…"

"Drop it. I'm trying to make a point," Isabell walked over to the coffee table and picked up her water. She took a sip and placed herself on another pillow next to Aadhya. "What I'm saying is, we may be hearing just arguments and whispers now, but It was whispers like this that led to lynchings and witch hunts in America. You'll be surprised by how much a toxic idealism can grow and evolve on any media platform, but on social media websites like we have nowadays? Even worse."

No one spoke for a several seconds. Then the silence of the room was interrupted as other teammates descended down the stairs, and the sounds of others complaining about cold showers from upstairs. Aadhya was the first one to clear her throat and place the empty glass down on the coffee table.

"What I believe our friend Isabell is communicating is, we should be aware of everything, no matter how small it may seem," Aadhya summed it up.

"How do you do that?" Isabell asked, much to Aadhya's confusion. Isabell almost seemed to smile and look over the vulture. "I mean like read into our bullshit and know exactly how to diffuse a situation with your smooth Indian enchantress voice?" Aadhya opened her beak to speak but found herself stumbling for words. Instead, a light blush appeared on her beak. "Oh! Don't tell me this little starling has your tongue!" Isabell said, clearly flirting. "And you don't smell anywhere near as bad as Rachel did, in fact..."

"Johnathen! Please tell me you picked up Chives and scallions!" came Antonio's voice as he hastily walked into the room. He was already dressed in his black slacks and apron.

Johnathen slapped his own forehead. "Shit! I'm sorry! I forgot!" he apologized, much to Antonio's consternation. He stood quickly and stumbled towards the door looking for his keys. "I'll go back to the store right now!"

"Well! Ándale-ándale!!" Antonio shouted and clapped his foretalons together.

Johnathen scrambled to get his coat and other things together as the Spanish chef followed the human out of the room, shouting in unintelligible gibberish. Thyra and the others could not help but laugh at Johnathen's situation as he was ushered out of the house.

Chapter 19 Them Bones

"It would have been better if Johnathen brought me self-rising flower instead," Antonio complained as he cut into his meal with a knife. He finished the last bite with a satisfied smile. "But that's ok, I still forgive you."

Johnathen folded the napkin on his empty plate, pushing it towards the center of the table. "Look, German is hard enough without using cooking terms! I asked several times if that was self-rising flower at the grocery store with the best translation I could, and I was assured that-."

"It's ok, hun. We all know you tried your best," Thyra quickly cut in. She gestured around the room at the other gryphons enjoying their meal despite the miniscule screw up. "And everyone enjoys your cooking, Antonio." Aadhya nodded in agreement, sitting at the opposite end of the small table.

"I like it," Anfang said quietly, sitting next to Thyra.

Antonio huffed through his nares and shook his head. "It is still missing the extra flavor that I was looking for," Antonio complained, glancing over at Johnathen. The human sighed and sat back in his seat with beer glass in hand.

"I don't care what it's missing. It's still better than anything John has cooked in his life," Thyra said with a cheeky grin, earning a frown from her husband.

Antonio could not help but laugh at that and the tension left the conversation. Even Aadhya broke character with a slight chuckle and sipped from her water glass.

Thyra watched the other Redtails members chat amongst themselves. Rachel sat with Nathanial rather closely, seeming to eat up every word he was saying to her. Their relationship had blossomed tenfold in the short time since everyone had arrived. It seemed they no longer cared who saw their apparent love for one another.

Thyra had to admit it was cute, to say the least. They were made for each other. What was different was how close Coach Victor and Jason were to one another. They had always seemed to have had a warm relationship since the beginning, but now they were always together no matter where they went. She could not help but think it was growing into something more.

Victor cleared his throat and clanged his glass with a foretalon, silencing everyone. The great harpy eagle walked towards the center of the room and addressed them all with his striking gray eyes.

"Redtails, what a fantastic month it has been for us all. Admittedly, we haven't trained enough for my liking, but I have a really good feeling about the upcoming season," Victor paused to take a drink of his beverage. He looked over to Anthony, Debra, and Joseph sitting at a corner table by themselves. "And really, it's all thanks to Anthony. We would not be here without his hard work and dedication. So, let's hear a round of talons for Anthony!"

Alex Bizzell

Claps filled the small dining room as all the gryphons joined in. Anthony wiped his mouth with a napkin and stood, waving to everyone politely.

"And on top of that, I believe Anthony as a special gift for us today," Victor added, stepping to the side and allowing the human space.

Anthony nodded and slicked back his short peppered gray hair before proceeding to stand next to Victor. "That's right! I have very good news for everyone. I am pleased to announce the Redtails stadium construction is going well. In fact, we estimate completion two weeks before the first game in January." He smiled, taking in a small round of applause from the gryphons and walked over to a small box at the corner of the room. "And with that announcement comes new jerseys and logos!"

Anthony pulled a jersey out of one of the boxes. Immediately, Thyra noticed their forest green was gone in place for navy blue. The Redtails logo had changed, and the Nation Gryphball League emblem had been replaced by the European Gryphball League logo.

"We commissioned the new logo with a local gryphoness designer, Olivia," Anthony explained and held up the first Jersey for all to see. "We felt a redesign was necessary for the Redtails seeing how you're now in the European First League," Anthony said, looking at the back of the first Jersey and quickly throwing it over to Jason. "So! Thoughts and opinions?"

Isabell was the first to chime in. "I think it is a brilliant revision."

The entire room looked over at the small violet gryphoness who was sitting next to Aadhya at Thyra's table. She placed her drink down and stood on her hindlegs so that

258

everyone could see her. "With the team representing Greifsburg and becoming a new entry to the First League and European League, I feel a refreshing image is a welcomed change."

Anthony smiled over at her. "For all that don't know Isabell, she is a friend of Thyra's and I have personally brought her on as the team's PR representative as well as the social media consult."

Isabell nodded and cleared her small throat. "Thank you, Anthony. I know many of you, and I am more than happy to be here. I hope you will welcome me and trust me to the full extent to represent the team in a positive manner."

"I feel she will do an excellent job with your image," Anthony added and looked around the room. "As for further announcements, I am sure you heard Beast and Man will be playing at our New Year's party?"

Anthony paused for the nodding gryphon beaks. "Believe me, getting them was not easy! But I feel it is a just reward for every gryphon in the country. I want everyone to have an excellent New Year and celebrate what I think will be the most important year for gryphon kind this world has ever seen." He smiled and raised his beer mug into the air. The gryphons followed his example and raised their glasses with him. "To gryphon kind!"

"To gryphon kind!" Everyone chanted and drank together.

"And lets here it for the Chef. Even after hard days of gryphball practice, he still comes home to cook for all you lazy featherbutts!" Anthony laughed. The whole room burst into squawks of laughter before a round of applause erupted once more. Thyra could swear she saw Antonio's nares blush a slight red. "Some of the best cooking I've ever had! Am I right?"

The room of gryphons nodded their beaks.

"Speaking of that! What's for dessert, chef?" Rachel called out.

Antonio finished his gulp of beer and stood from his seat. "Nothing today, as I had no time to prepare dessert, but there are ice cream sandwiches in the freezer, if you wish." Most of the gryphons began to make their way towards the kitchen.

Thyra settled down in her seat and leaned into Johnathen. "Hey, I know we give you a hard time but you know we love you, right?

"Of course I do. I wish I could be more help than just errand boy," Johnathen admitted.

"I could use a sous chef," Antonio said with a slight grin.

Johnathen laughed and finished the rest of his beer. "Seeing as how Thyra always complains about my cooking, I could use a couple pointers!"

"Not always!" Thyra responded with a soft wing slap across his chest.

Rachel approached and leaped up on the counter and chattered excitedly, her speech slightly slurring into gryphoness screeches. "Hey! So, a bunch of us are planning on going to Shooters for karaoke! I mean, we have a couple days off from practice." She gestured to Anfang, "And I think he has some days off too, so how about we all go burn off some steam and have a good night out!"

Johnathen was the first to pipe up. "You just want us to go because you know I'll drive your lazy ass to the bar."

"Oh screw you! We can fly if we want!" Rachel screeched. "But . . ."

"But it's cold!" Johnathen finished. He held his fists up to his eyes like he was crying fake tears. "Aw, are the poor gryphons too lazy and afraid of the cold to go to a bar?"

"You know what!" Rachel began.

Johnathen held up a hand to interrupt her. "I'm just kidding with you. I don't mind driving."

"I could use a night of the karaoke," Aadhya chimed in, much to everyone's surprise. Rachel laughed and clapped her foretalons together.

"Hell! If even the pure one agrees, then let's do it! Come on, loser, grab your jacket," Rachel exclaimed and jumped off the table.

Everyone stood up in agreement and Johnathen looked over to Thyra questionably.

"Looks like your DD tonight, hun," Thyra said with a smile.

"Anfang! Aadhya! Fold in your wings! I can't see out my rearview mirror!" Johnathen exclaimed as he navigated down the snow-covered roads. He was following Anthony's vehicle in front of him closely and had to continuously move a wing or tail feather away from his vision. Rachel laughed and bumped the human's shoulder with a foretalon as she rested on the center consol.

"Like you need to see what's behind you! What, you worried about? someone riding your bumper?" Rachel exclaimed and adjusted as the SUV turned another corner.

The Mercedes G Wagon was packed full with six gryphons. Wings, tailfeathers, and laughter filled what was a spacious cabin. Despite Johnathen's frayed nerves, it was a relatively short drive down to the bar and it seemed to pass in an instant.

Before Thyra knew it, they were pulling up to the crowded bar. Gryphons stood outside chatting and smoking with one another. They watched curiously as the vehicles pulled up. The doors flew open and the gryphball team exited the SUV's. Johnathen held the door open politely as the team poured into the bar.

Local gryphons filled the booths and tables, all turning to watch the team walk in followed by the two humans. Kai looked across the bar top as he poured several beers and called out to them.

"Why, it's the Redtails! Have a seat anywhere!" the raven gryphon shouted over the loud music and terrible singing. Kai stopped pouring beer for a moment as he noticed Anthony walking in with them. He ran over quickly to lean across the counter and shook Anthony's hand. "And a pleasure to see you again, Mayor!"

At the far end of the room, past the packed billiard tables, sat a small stage with a microphone. There was an owl gryphon on stage, sitting on her haunches and holding the microphone, singing along with the music. It was a German song Thyra did not recognize, but most of the bar was singing along with the main chorus. The energy was incredibly contagious and already Thyra felt welcomed with the number of smiles and nods in her direction, although some few glanced their way with a blank expression.

Thyra and the entire team found a group of tables towards one of the corners and began to sit down around them. Thyra sat next to Johnathen, Rachel, Nathanial, Isabell,

Aadhya and Anfang, while the rest of the team took other seats.

A round of applause sounded out as the owl gryphoness finished her song and Kai rushed past them, carrying a tray of big liter sized beer glasses balanced on a wing shoulder.

"I will be quick!" Kai called out.

Everyone began to get themselves comfortable, taking off their snow jackets and talking amongst each other. Anfang looked around at the other gryphons nervously. Thyra could tell he felt very out of place in such a crowded place and she had to reach across to rub his wing.

"It's ok. No one knows you here. I promise," Thyra reassured him.

He seemed to relax only slightly but felt comforted by her presence. Thyra looked around, watching a few other gryphons walk from table to table, wearing the same black apron as Kai did. She had never seen so many others of her own kind in one place at the same time.

"This is incredible!" Rachel exclaimed, looking around herself. "I feel that same energy high as I do when at a gryphball stadium. Do you feel it too, hun?" She asked, leaning up against Nathanial. He smiled and leaned down to preen along the top of her head, glancing up at the others.

"Finally, you two show some public affection," Thyra said cheekily. Nathanial's eartufts laid down flat.

"Oh, shove it up your tailfeathers, Thyra," Rachel retorted, earning a laugh.

Johnathen quickly wrapped his arm around his wife's neck. "Oh, leave them alone," he said playfully.

Kai approached the large group. He tucked the tray underneath a wing and sat on his haunches. "Welcome! It is good to meet all of you! And good to see some of you again! I am Kai, owner of the Shooters! Can I get you beers to start off with?"

"Absolutely. Bring us all a round of hefeweizen, and I have the tab for tonight," Anthony said. Kai nodded and was quickly off before anyone else had anything to say.

"Well, thank you sir!" Johnathen was the first to comment.

Anthony waved him off as if it were no big deal and proceeded to talk with Coach Victor who sat directly across from him. Thyra watched the two converse with interest. It was obvious they were discussing something important. It was hard for her to read gryphon beaks, but she could make out a couple words from Anthony such as training and worry.

Thyra turned her attention to Kai as he walked towards the stage to approach the DJ who sat off to the side at his own booth. The small pygmy falcon leaned in to hear what Kai said.

"Hey, I know that gryphon! That's Lenny. He's the one that owns the electronics shop I bought that computer from. Remember?" Johnathen said, getting Thyra's attention with a gentle nudge.

"Oh yea! You were saying how much he was like Rachel," Thyra responded. Rachel perked her eartufts at the mention of her name and looked to Thyra.

"Are you talking shit about me again?" Rachel asked.

Thyra laughed and shook her head. "No. He was just saying how that little falcon has the same energy you do. John is convinced all small gryphons have an insane amount of energy."

"Every one of them besides me," Isabell chimed in, puffing on her cigarette. The smoke blew directly up in Aadhya face, and she quickly pulled her head back to avoid it. "Sorry, Addy girl."

"It is perfectly fine. I am used to it by now," Aadhya responded with a slight frown.

A team of gryphoness waiters rushed over carrying rounds of beer for everyone. The group grabbed their mugs and held them up together.

"To the Redtails!" Anthony cheered and the gryphons cheered with him.

The music was turned down and Lenny picked up the microphone. "Alllllright! Everyone! We have some special guests in the house tonight!"

Everyone stopped talking amongst themselves for a minute and turned their attention towards the front stage. The sound of billiard balls clinging against one another remained, along with the gentle bump of bass from some electronic music song.

"We have our very own Redtails team with us tonight! They represent our country of Greifsburg in the upcoming European Gryphball League. So let's have a round of applause for them!" Lenny said and clapping erupted in the room. Thyra sat back in her pillow and waved awkwardly along with the rest of her teammates. "We know they are some damn good gryphball players, but can they sing?!"

Thyra felt dread sink into her chest as she knew she was about to be singled out. She would rather play a game by herself then sing in front of a room full of complete strangers.

"Well? Any volunteers?" Lenny asked.

The group all looked to one another, debating on who should go first, but Aadhya was the first to stand . Another round of clapping ensued as the white-feathered bearded vulture gryphoness walked towards the stage.

"I wasn't expecting that for damn sure," Isabell said, dragging on her cigarette once again.

"Neither was I, but sometimes it's the quiet ones that surprise ya," Nathanial added.

Thyra had heard Aadhya hum and sing on occasion in the shower, but never thought anything of it.

"I bet you it's probably going to be some boring song or something really slow," Nathanial said and drank from his huge, dimpled beer mug.

"I bet ya ten euros it's something badass," Rachel said with a chuckle. Everyone had to laugh at that and shake their heads. "Alright fine! Fifty euros each."

"What is bet?" Anfang asked curiously, still clearly confused by everything that was going on.

"It's like a fun game where we all put money down to see who believes they are right," Thyra tried to explain. Johnathen opened his mouth like he was going to correct her but shrugged as her explanation was somewhat accurate.

Aadhya leaned over Lenny's makeshift desk and made a song selection.

"Deal," Thyra said before Aadhya stood on the stage, calmly holding the microphone.

The music started heavy and suddenly Aadhya screamed into the microphone repeatedly. Everyone froze solid. The chorus came on and Johnathen started laughing uncontrollably along with most of the team clapping and banging the table. Thyra stared blankly across the table at Rachel and Antonio, who all wore the same shocked expressions.

"Is she really singing Them Bones?!" Johnathen exclaimed. "She sounds just like William DuVall!"

"Jesus. And she's a bearded vulture, so it's pretty on character," Nathanial added. "She just gained a couple badass points from me."

"Y'all owe me fifty euros each," Rachel spoke as the song ended.

Everyone squawked and clapped for Aadhya as she carried herself down off the stage, feathers ruffled up with pride. Multiple team members got out of their seat to high five Aadhya as she passed by to take her seat.

"Where in the hell did you learn that?" Johnathen asked as the vulture sat down with a smug expression, a look Thyra had only seen her wear once in her life.

"I was somewhat rebellious in my early years in India. I enjoy the early turn of century music more than anything and learned to mimic voices of the classic singers," Aadhya said, lifting the mug to her beak and draining almost half of the golden liquid.

"What a performance!" Lenny exclaimed across the microphone. "I knew she was one hell of a player on the field, but I didn't expect her to be a grunge rocker as well! Then again, with how fierce she looks, I'm honestly not surprised!" He pointed towards the group once again. "Any more takers from the gryphball team! One more and we will go back to normal rotation."

Pricilla and Viola were the next ones to stand up. Thyra watched the two gryphoness couple walk towards the stage and begin to talk with Lenny. At the same time, Anthony stood and walked up to her.

"Thyra, have you ever played nine ball?" Anthony asked.

Alex Bizzell

She seemed taken aback and shook her head no. He smiled and motioned for her to follow him. Thyra looked to Johnathen and he gave her an encouraging nod. She followed Anthony to an empty billiard table. The elderly human began to remove the extra balls from the table and arrange the remaining ones into a triangle pattern.

"So the object of the game is to knock the ball into the pockets in numerical order using a cue like this one," Anthony explained, grabbing a pool cue and chalking it with experienced repetition.

Thyra followed his lead, grabbing one cue and chalking it as well. He offered the table to her and watched as she haphazardly attempted to line the end up with the white ball. Anthony walked up behind her and leaned down on one knee to guide her.

"Pull the stick up towards your under arm. There you go. Look down the edge of the stick, line it up. Very good. Pull back and follow through."

Thyra hit the cue ball dead center and sent it hard into the others. A pleasant clang rang out in the room as they began to bounce across the table.

Anthony clapped his hands together. "Very good!" He grabbed his beer to take a sip and watched the two gryphonesses begin to sing 'I'm A Believer' roughly, causing him to grimace. "But not that. I think Aadhya was much better."

"I think she surprised us all," Thyra responded.

This whole interaction was a little weird to her, but she didn't know what to read into it. She could tell by Anthony's body language that he wanted to talk about something else, yet he acted nonchalant. There was always more to him than met the eye. He played off his position as

Mayor like he was some sort of easygoing good guy, but he was apparently stressed. There was a reason why he had pulled her to the side, even if others saw it as some kind of father and daughter bonding time.

Anthony had to lean down on one knee to line his shot because of the modified gryphon billiard tables, yet he was able to easily sink the number one ball. He lined it up perfectly with the two and sank that one as well. Anthony stood and chalked his cue once more.

"So, how is Anfang doing?" he asked, walking around the table. There it was, the question she knew was on the front of his brain.

"He's good. He's adapting alright, given the circumstances," Thyra confirmed.

Anthony nodded and leaned down again, cursing playfully as he missed the third object ball. "That's good. I always worry about him."

Thyra thought about what he was getting at as she walked around the table. She had observed enough to know what to do next. She lined up the stick awkwardly and attempted to hit the ball, only striking the white orb a glancing blow, sending it flying off in the opposite direction.

Anthony quickly grabbed the cue ball and placed it back where it was. "Try again. Just breathe and pull the stick back carefully, then strike center at the ball. Practice the move a couple times before making contact."

Thyra attempted once again, practicing her motions several times before making her strike, this time sending the object ball into the third billiard ball and hitting it firmly.

Anthony smiled. "There you go. You're getting the hang of it."

"What do you plan on doing with Anfang?" Thyra questioned. It was the most apparent question on her brain and one she wanted addressed.

Anthony stood silently, chalking his cue. "I wanted him to be part of the community, but I realize he's always been a violent individual. So, I want to aim that violence and destructive attitude towards something good. If he can learn how to control himself, I think he will make a great guardian. Someone we can trust on if things go south." He made a sour face as the gryphonesses on stage hit a terrible screeching note, then shook his head and lined up another shot, easily sinking the third object ball. "Not that I want things to go south, but as the mayor, and your father, I have to have contingency plans. I need to look out for you all."

Anthony lined up the fourth ball and easily placed it into a corner pocket. He also had a perfect shot for the fifth but missed it, almost on purpose.

"You've said that before. A guardian . . . So, a bodyguard?" Thyra questioned.

Anthony nodded and stepped back from the table. "Exactly. He needs an outlet, and he really cares about you as well as the other gryphons. It was what he and the others were designed to do anyway."

Thyra paused as she was lining up her next shot and sat up straight, looking at him with an inquisitive look. "Him and the others? What are you talking about? What was Anfang designed to do?"

Anthony looked confused for a second and thought as he sipped his beer. "Have you all not read the documents I let you find?"

Thyra thought for minute and looked over to Johnathen. She knew he had recently acquired the PC with the floppy drive readers but had not talked to her about anything he read yet. She shook her head.

"No. Not yet, but why all the secrecy about this? Why can't you just tell me what's going on?" Thyra stepped away from the table, the game forgotten.

"Thyra! You've been called to the stage! Come on and get up here!" Came Lenny's voice across the loudspeaker.

Thyra's feathers stood on end and she looked over to her table with a panicked expression. Everyone smiled and cheered her on, pointing towards the stage. Even Johnathen laughed and motioned for her to go towards the mic.

"It looks like your needed. Come on, I remember you singing to some of those classic hits I played to you in the labs. You must know at least one! They aren't going to accept no as an answer now," Anthony exclaimed and sat down in a bench seat at the billiards table.

Thyra's mind spun with indecision but the cheering brought up a newfound self confidence in herself. It was almost the same way she felt before beginning a gryphball game. She could do this.

"Ok fine. But this conversation isn't over," she warned Anthony.

He brushed her off with grin and gestured towards the stage. "And it never will be. Now go ahead and sing your heart out."

Chapter 20 One Step Closer

A loud whistle echoed out in the vast field. Thyra perked her eartufts and quickly banked midflight to avoid an attack from Nathanial. "Hey! Coach blew the whistle! End of play!" She screeched at the slowing caracara behind her. Nathanial quickly turned on wing to glide in gently with her.

"I didn't hear it until the last second! Don't get your underfluffs in a knot," Nathanial chuffed.

Rachel quickly zoomed in next to them at the blink of an eye and batted at Nathanial's side with her tail. "You're lucky you didn't hit her! Coach would have your tailfeathers above his mantel for that."

The three gryphons alighted beside one another smoothly as the rest of the air team followed in suit. Thyra tossed the gryphball over to Victor and he caught it one handed in his gigantic foretalon.

Thyra took in deep breaths of the crisp cool air, forcing her heart rate to slow. She was pleased to find that she could now control it easier than ever.

Victor waited patiently as the ground team made their way over to gather around the coach. "What the hell was that?" he asked calmly, but his tone of voice set everyone's eartufts flat against their head. They were in for a scolding. "I feel like I'm watching a bunch of gryphlets fight over a shiny toy!" Victor yelled and slammed the gryphball down into the thin layer of snow, sending it flying off towards the small gym behind him. Victor turned his dark eyes towards the bearded vulture. "Aadhya! Where was your defense for Thyra?"

"I misinterpreted the play, sir," Aadhya said calmly, not a single hackle feather out of place. Her snow white feathers seemed to bleed into the background.

"I don't want excuses! Your job as rear air guard is to defend the carrier!" Victor yelled. Nathanial chuckled with amusement, thinking he was out of the woods and earned a glare of his own. "And you, cocky caracara!"

Nathanial's small grin disappeared in an instant. He sat up to attention, watching the harpy eagles great crest rising with agitation. "You were entirely out of line! What was that blitz? If you were to take the ball, you had no backup that far on the attackers' side. You want to know why?" Victor asked, eyes narrowing.

"Because.... Um..." Nathanial stuttered.

"Because you didn't follow the play that Jason instructed!" Victor screamed, mantling his wings slightly. The group cowered, and Thyra even saw Aadhya's eyes wince. Usually the coach was more reserved with his tailfeather chewings, but it seemed they were all playing unusually terrible that day. Thyra had not thought it was that bad, but then again, she was not the coach.

"Vic! I think that we were just a little out of line man. I mean, it's really cold out here and the wind is irregular, and we've all got a lot on our..." Rachel started to rant on until Victor turned towards her. His eyes squinted slightly and a loud rumble emanated from his chest. Rachel immediately shut her beak.

"Fifty laps," Victor began. Thyra let out a sigh of relief. That was not so… "On talon," he continued. Ok, that was a bit worse. "With thirty percent weight," Victor finished. Thyra gulped hard and looked at a couple of her teammates defeated expressions. "Except Antonio. You followed the play to the letter," Victor complimented.

Everyone glared at Antonio, but he did not seem to acknowledge them. He was clearly glad he would not have to run with them. "Thank you, coach," Antonio said.

"You're dismissed. Go ahead and get dinner started," Victor commanded. Antonio nodded and gave a somewhat apologetic look towards Thyra before taking quickly to the skies. Victor shot his cold stare back to the others, clearly waiting.

When no one budged an inch, Victor slammed a talon into the snow and flicked out his wings. "You want sixty laps? Go!" He screamed.

Everyone scattered like cockroaches, all running towards the equipment shed. The gryphons lined up and entered the shed one at a time, grabbing their assigned weight harnesses.

"What the hell is wrong with coach?" Rachel asked Thyra under her breath. "This is a little excessive for some small mistakes."

Thyra had to agree. The coach seemed on edge the past couple of practices. It seemed she was not the only one having difficulty adjusting to the new life. They all might look fine on the outside, but everyone was dealing with their personal issues. Still, it did not give the Coach any right to take it out on the team.

"Yeah. I think he's just stressed, like all of us. Maybe-." Thyra began.

"I implore you two to keep your beaks shut for once," Aadhya said in a serious low tone. She was clearly not amused by their arrangement either. Being the largest gryphoness, she had to bear the most weight.

"Let's go, let's go, let's go!" Victor yelled from afar, clapping his foretalons together. As some gryphons scrambled to put on their equipment, the finished teammates took off into a light jog around the field. Thyra groaned as she clipped the last latch on and adjusted its weight.

"I'm going to be feeling this for a week," Thyra said to no one in particular. She dashed after Aadhya, watching the snow kick off from her gloved hindpaws. "I think Rachel is right," Thyra said over the sounds of their talons crunching over the snow with each galloping stride. Her chest began to heave as blood surged through her body. She found herself tiring quickly with the weight, and it was not even halfway into the first lap.

"Conserve your breath," Aadhya suggested before quickening her pace. She left Thyra in a snow trail just as quickly as Thyra had approached. With her longer gait, she could easily outpace any gryphon on the team.

Thyra dropped the line of thought and concentrated on her efforts. Every stride and gallop drummed in her eartufts as she found her steady pace. The world seemed to melt away, as did the question to their punishment. In a way, Thyra enjoyed running. Sure, she and every other gryphon would rather fly any day, but it was more labor intensive to run. It filled her body with pleasant endorphins like a slow IV drip, instead of a sudden rush moments before a tackle.

Thyra passed Victor again and again. The coach sat steady as a rock, watching the gryphons with Jason closely at his side. They talked between themselves and motioned towards several gryphons, perhaps discussing tactics and future exercises.

While she jogged, she could think more clearly than she had in recent weeks. Her eyes drifted across the snowy field up to the towering mountains in the distance. She began to think about her new country as a whole. There seemed to be many elements at play, more so than the typical moving pains that normal people experience. She realized the future of Greifsburg somewhat relied on the Redtails' success as a team. If they were not successful, they would not bring in as much tourism to the country. Without the income, the country would lose its funding, or so she speculated.

"This sucks!" Rachel suddenly yelled breathlessly from beside Thyra.

"Victor is hard on us because we are the future," Thyra said through loud gasps of air. Rachel blinked, confused as to her meaning. Thyra gasped again and swallowed hard. "We are more than a gryphball team to him, we have a responsibility to the people."

"You mean like…" Rachel huffed and struggled to keep up with Thyra. She quickly remembered the Kestrel's disadvantage and slowed her pace. "This is more than a game now?"

"To him, yeah. And we need to realize it too," Thyra said, glancing down at Rachel. "We need to train harder than ever to be the best."

The Kestrel's exhausted expression sparked with a new energy. "That's what I like to hear!" Rachel yelled and suddenly sprinted ahead of Thyra.

She blinked with surprise and laughed through hard gasps. "Oh, no you don't!" Thyra called out after her and proceeded in chase.

As they passed Victor once more, she saw him smile.

"The Gryphon invasion has begun. The small country of Greifsburg has more than tripled in population over the third quarter and grows bigger by day. With the gryphball stadium coming near completion late December, it seems the population will only grow. Greifsburg is the smallest country in the European union at only fifty square kilometers, but the locals cannot help but wonder what will happen when the population pushes past capacity.

"Already, many locals are angered at having a large plot of their ancestor's homeland sold off by the EU to this new influx of gryphons but it seems tensions will rise higher as more of this new species continue to move into the country. Many have shown their warranted worry that Innsbruck will soon become overwhelmed with the overflow of gryphon inhabitants."

Johnathen switched off the news and searched for the right input on the television. He reached behind his PC and plugged in the HDMI cord. "Just need to put this in here," he said before stepping back and watched the desktop appear on the television. He turned to look at the band of gryphons sitting on the living room couches and gestured at the screen. "Well there we go. All set up."

"It's about time," Rachel said, readjusting the ice bag on her thighs. She made herself comfortable on the couch next to Aadhya, Antonio and Thyra.

Alex Bizzell

The sun had set long ago. Currently, they were the only ones in the cozy living room. The main source of light was from an old corner lamp putting out its yellow dim ambiance. The unnatural white glow of the television reflected off the surrounding windows of the living room as snow fell smoothly down to the ground. The house, usually buzzing with activity, was silent for the time being until the sliding door opened behind them as Isabell stepped inside, flicking her cigarette butt into the yard.

"It only took like two minutes! The longest part was carrying all this shit downstairs, no thanks to you all," Johnathen complained. The gryphons shrugged.

"And what am I supposed to do? Balance the computer on my back like a pack mule and walk down the stairs?" Thyra pointed out. Johnathen held his finger out like he was going to suggest something, but she interrupted him. "Yeah, that's what I thought. And don't think about bragging how walking on two legs is better."

"Anyways!" Johnathen exclaimed and plopped down on the couch between the curious gryphons. He clicked a couple icons and brought up a text file before looking over at Isabell. "Are we sure she could be included?"

"And who am I going to tell? I don't know any of the other gryphons, plus I'm you all's PR rep. I need to be informed of everything," Isabell pointed out. She did have a good point. Isabell might have been towing the company line lately, but she was not the kiss and tell type of gryphoness to begin with.

"Fair enough," Johnathen said with a sigh. "I'm sure Thyra has already caught you up on everything?"

"Yeah. Anthony left you the cell phone, led you to the old labs, you found the floppy drives, whatever those are, and you discovered some old logs about the first failed experiments," Isabell recapped with a sigh. "I don't see how any of this shit is relevant."

"It is relevant because it is how we all began," Aadhya said. "Anthony was the original creator of gryphons as a whole, and this may give us insight on what it all means."

"In a way, I'm jealous. Humans as a whole will always wonder where we started and what not, but here we are in a living room, looking at a text file with exact data on your origins!" Johnathen exclaimed excitedly, but his excitement was only met with a stare of gryphon eyes.

He sgrugged and clicked his wireless mouse a couple times before the floppy reader booted up. It hummed to life and clicked several times, reading the drive until a wall of text appeared on the screen.

"Ok. So, I mentioned to a couple of you that the content of most of the disks are similar. Text about experiment ABC, how they acted, how they performed, all to end with the subject's death. It's depressing really," Johnathen said before looking over to Thyra. "I mean I can't help but think that any one of these experiments could have been you."

"Spare us the sappy shit and get on with it," Isabell interrupted, causing Johnathen to frown and huff through his nose.

"Whatever. After Thyra's talk with Anthony the other night, I really began to skim through the files. He mentioned something about 'First Class' and asked why we haven't read anything on it yet. It seems he wants us to discover it on our own, I guess for the sake of not having to repeat himself several times, or he just enjoys toying with us. I don't know," Johnathen thought out loud as he scrolled through the walls of text. He stopped as the text changed and the words 'Experiment Anfang First Class' came across the screen.

"This is where it begins to get interesting. Everything before this, hundreds of misshapen, sickly, and varying levels of sentient 'gryphons', have died. But this is where he renames the experiments as actual names instead of a letter designation."

Johnathen paused and grabbed his mixed drink off the coffee table. He had to take a big gulp of the alcohol to settle his nerves. The other gryphons did the same. Despite their comfy surroundings, this was a hefty subject and the implications of it all weighed heavy on their consciousness.

"I can't imagine what Anthony went through," Thyra added in.

"My thoughts exactly. I don't see how he smiles like he does. Maybe it's because he was ultimately successful and sees you all walking around with your beaks held high," Johnathen speculated.

"Anyways," Isabell said.

"Anyways, it gets interesting," Johnathen pulled up the page and let everyone read it themselves.

Day 22, Anfang, as he has been aptly named, shows more promise than the previous experiments. Although many parts of his body are malformed, he demonstrates good cognition, his vitals are normal, and he seems to be aware of his surroundings.

Day 24. Anfang demonstrates intelligence similar to that found in 16 month human toddlers. He asks for various foods by their color alone. Vitals continue to be normal.

Day 26. Vitals are normal. He sleeps irregularly and cries when hungry. He continues to eat whole foods without problem, despite his malformed beak and muzzle combination.

Day 27. Upon closer inspection of his oral health, I have observed fangs beginning to protrude through the lower portion of his muzzle. A unique abnormality.

"The rest of the pages continue like this for a while," Johnathen said and skimmed some more.

Day 100. Anfang is now the longest living gryphon we have had. He continues to grow steadily and recognizes different objects by name.

Day 122. Anfang can now be considered the first successful gryphon. The next gryphon has been incubated based on his DNA and continues to grow within the test chamber. The military has been extremely pleased with my success so far and have demanded I turn him over to them for project First Class.

Day 185. Thyra has now been introduced to Anfang. They seem to interact much the same human babies do. They enjoy one another's company and learn from each other.

Day 192. Depending on various testing, the military will use Anfang as a baseline for soldiers which will provide the funding I need for future expansion. The decision of our team did not come easily, as we knew what tortures awaited Anfang, but based on his resilience and ability to adapt, we have turned him over to the military. His baseline DNA will be used as a concept template for future members of the First Class.

Day 202. I was informed that project First Class is well underway. Anfang is now 'bullet proof' up to anti-tank rounds. They have determined his initial strength being ten times that of the common black bear. I refuse to read the experiments they have set to find out their data as I am not emotionally prepared for that. I know, as a scientist, I must separate my personal feelings from the implications, yet I cannot help but view the gryphons as my personal children. I cannot think of the pain he has gone through.

Day 210. I have now stepped aside as head scientist of the First Class Division. Instead, I will devote my resources to the gryphon labs across the world. I was promised by the military that as the First Class will contain my personal DNA, I am still in control of their use, if I so wish. Because of our initial contract, they had no other choice but to offer me this and I accepted. More than 10,000 incubation chambers of the enhanced first class gryphons have been moved to –Redacted- And await my personal input.

-END OF LINE-

Everyone was speechless as they tried to digest the information.

"Did you get the gist of that?" Johnathen asked finally. There was a long pause as gryphons looked to one another before Aadhya placed her tea down on the table.

"Anthony has amassed a sleeping army of seemingly indestructible gryphons that remain to be awaken," Antonio summed up. Everyone nodded, reluctantly agreeing with him. "And what does that mean for us? What does he plan on doing with them, and where is the army sleeping?"

"I think they are here," Thyra chimed in. "Why else would he choose this place in Austria for a new gryphon colony if it wasn't for a stronghold?"

"Why have we not seen them?" Aadhya added, asking yet another question on everyone's mind.

"Maybe because they are still sleeping, or being trained in secret, but what are they going to be used for?" Isabell wondered. The group was silent for another long moment as the cursor blinked across the screen. "Is that the final entry?"

"Yeah, that's it. I don't have any other information," Johnathen confirmed. "But he wanted us to find this. He wants us to know what he has at his disposal. We've all seen firsthand what Anfang can do. Can you imagine what ten thousand improved versions of him are capable of?"

"It could lead to war," Antonio suggested to everyone's surprise. "A gryphon is undetectable by modern radar, and untraceable by missile guidance systems. Then you take one that is impervious to ninety percent of munitions, and you have a threat that the world has never faced. A threat no one is prepared for."

It was true. A modern soldier could not go toe-to-toe with that kind of gryphon and hope to win, no matter the circumstance. Military fighter jets could outrun gryphons, but none could move like they could.

"What? Is Anthony working towards world dominance with gryphons?" Rachel scoffed. "Is he some kind of James Bond super villain?" she let out a mocking laugh. "I mean, he has the face for it. Just look at him!"

Thyra shook her head, thinking about Anthony and what he stood for. "I don't think that's his plan. I'm not exactly sure what he wants and what he intends out of all this, but I know it's for the greater good of gryphon kind."

"Well, I'm just glad I'm on this side," Johnathen jokingly said, trying to break the serious atmosphere. "Even if it is the annihilation of all humans! I mean we are terrible, right?!" He laughed nervously, but no one else joined him.

"Does this make Anfang some sort of sleeper agent? Like what Americans feared in the cold war?" Isabell asked.

Thyra somewhat remembered her American history and the implications behind what that meant. She shook her head. "I don't think so. I think this is Anthony providing us a military to defend us past what we can see. It's... comforting, in a way. Even if I don't fully understand it."

The room was quiet again as everyone thought about all the information. There was a lot to digest, and nobody knew if they should feel one way or another about it. They were together and safe for the moment, but how long would that last? There were social implications, gryphball, and daily life to consider in this new country. The last thing they all needed was the idea they might be part of some sort of military movement.

"Um, does anyone need another drink?" Rachel asked awkwardly as she hopped off the couch.

"Yeah, I think we could all use another one," Thyra confirmed.

Chapter 21 The Hand That Feeds

Johnathen parked on the sidewalk right in front of the blockade set up in the middle of the street. Thyra and the rest of the band exited the vehicle and gasped with excitement. Christmas time had come to Greifsburg.

There were lights strung from one building to the next, crisscrossing one another across the road. Little Christmas trees and wooden fences surrounded groups of tables set in the middle of the road. Gryphons laughed and talked amongst themselves while others stood in line at the small wagons parked at various places.

Thyra took in a deep breath, smelling the heavy scents of cooking bratwurst, various spices, and sweets in the air. "I've seen pictures of German Christmas markets, but I've never imagined they'd smell like this," she commented before Rachel full-on sprinted towards the center of the market. She watched Rachel run over to Nathanial, Victor, and Jason who were sitting at a table next to one of the beautifully decorated wooden carts.

"At least we do not need to babysit her tonight," Aadhya commented.

Thyra adjusted the heavy jacket wrapped around her body and followed Johnathen into the market's entrance. "We can relax at last!"

Johnathen pointed to Anthony who was waving them over with a big smile. Joseph and Debra were sitting next to him at a small table, the human woman shivering in multiple layers of jackets. Thyra's joy and excitement turned into slight dread. She usually was excited to see Anthony, but since their discovery nights ago, she did not know how to react to it.

Anfang wandered over to one of the wooden carts, curiously watching as a gryphon attendant stirred a large metal bowl over an open fire. Thyra noticed Anfang had disappeared and quickly approached his backside. She yanked gently at his jacket.

"Hey, don't just walk off," Thyra said.

"What is he making?" Anfang asked, beak clearly watering. Thyra motioned for him to follow her and walked over to join the group.

"Bavarian Nuts. We will get some in a minute," Thyra said.

"It seems you still have to do some babysitting," Antonio commented. Thyra gave him an un-amused look in return.

"So glad you all could join us!" Anthony exclaimed and scooted over at the table, making room for the new guests. The group took their places on the long wooden bench.

Johnathen shook Anthony's hand and sat next to him. "Wouldn't miss it! So, this is going to go on all week?"

"Absolutely! Actually, it will be going on until New Years, and I'm sure you all have heard who I have front lining the New Year's band?" Anthony asked, bringing a steaming coffee mug up to his mouth to sip from it.

"We heard. You announced it the other night," Johnathen commented. "I don't know how you got Beast and Man to play for us, but I think it's going to be one hell of a show."

"If it's going to be this cold, then I won't be here for it," Joseph complained, clutching his own mug.

"You are our head of security, or did you forget?" Anthony replied, much to Josephs distain.

"No, of course I didn't forget," Joseph said and looked over to Anfang who was now sitting next to him. "But, it will be Anfang's first official day on the job, and I'm planning to let him take charge. I'm sure he'll be ready, won't you?"

"I will be ready," Anfang said, still slightly distracted by all the activity around him.

"Well, I'm excited for it!" Thyra exclaimed, trying to break the ice. Yet, as she looked at Anthony, she could not shake that feeling she had since the day she met him. There were questions boiling in her mind that she wanted to ask but knew this was not the time or place for it.

"What are you drinking?" Antonio asked, his voice tinged with curiosity as he watched the three of them drink repeatedly from their mugs. Thyra was curious about that as well. The same spice whose smell hung so thickly in the air was coming from their cups.

"This is Glühwein! It is basically hot wine with spices and a shot of hot rum. Here, let's get you some! John, do you mind helping?" Anthony asked as he stood up.

"Not at all," Johnathen responded and followed the old man.

Many of the wandering gryphons moved out of the human's way respectfully. Anthony even leaned down to a couple to shake their foretalons. The group remaining at the table sat silent, listening to the chirps and gentle music all around them.

Thyra stood and cleared her throat. "Well, Anfang wanted some of those Bavarian nuts, so you guys want any too?"

Anfang's single eartuft perked up as he quickly stood.

"I'm fine myself, thanks," Joseph responded.

"I had some when we first arrived, but I appreciate the offer, Thyra," Debra said with a smile.

"I am curious about how they make them, so I will accompany you," Antonio said and stood to follow.

Thyra cocked her head as Aadhya remained seated, curiously watching a group of gryphon's talk. "Addy?"

"Oh, I will take some. Thank you," Aadhya replied but did not make a motion to stand. Thyra nodded and walked over to stand in the line in front of the cart. Already, the smell of cinnamon, sugar, and cooked pecans was overwhelming. She looked over to Anfang who was beginning to drool once again.

"Should we talk to Anthony tonight about what we discovered?" Antonio asked quietly while Anfang was distracted. They had agreed collectively that he should not know the information. Thyra stepped forward as the line moved. Gryphons laughed and walked past them, carrying paper sacks full of steaming treats.

"If I can get him alone, I'll discuss it with him. He seems to pull me aside quite frequently," Thyra said and peeked across the short line.

They watched as the gryphon worker poured a bag of pecans into the large metal bowl and added a few ingredients to it before quickly tossing them around with a wooden spoon. Again, the aroma hit her nares like a bag of bricks. Her crop churned with hunger.

"But all that can wait. I'm just excited to partake in the festivities and enjoy all these flavors," Thyra added with a light chuckle.

"And I am glad I do not have to cook tonight," Antonio said. "As much I enjoy it, the recent practices have me exhausted. I needed a night off."

"You cook good," Anfang suddenly said, surprising both Thyra and Antonio. The large gryphon had turned to face him with his attempt of a smile. How long had he been listening to their conversation? "It best food I taste. Thank you." Antonio thanked him honestly before the beast turned his attention back to the moving line.

Soon they were front and center. Anfang and Antonio moved to the side to watch the cook make up the fresh batch of candied pecans Thyra had ordered for the group. She pulled her wallet out from the front coat pocket and handed the hawk gryphoness a twenty-euro bill, telling her to keep the rest.

They waited impatiently as the cook poured the freshly cooked nuts into individual bags and handed them to the hungry gryphons. They all quickly left the line, and Anfang paused to throw a talonfull of them into his beak. His feathers ruffled as he let out a satisfied sigh. Thyra tried hers as well, her eyes widening as a symphony of nutty flavor, cinnamon and sugar rejoiced on her taste buds.

"Ok, this is the best thing I've ever tasted!" Thyra exclaimed, much to everyone else's agreement. They made their way to the table, seeing that Johnathen and Anthony had already made it back.

"Just in time! Here you are," Anthony exclaimed and passed around the mugs. Thyra took one from Anthony and looked at the side, seeing the images of gryphons in flight and Christmas trees engraved on the side.

"Thank you, and here's some hot steaming nuts," Thyra said with a grin, handing the bags around while everyone giggled like grade school students.

She sipped her first drink and immediately every feather stood on end. Her eartufts perked as she tasted the alcoholic spice flowing down her throat. The warm drink sat heavy in her crop, thawing her body against the cold.

"You weren't kidding. This is incredible," she moaned.

"And these treats are just the beginning! There are several other carts selling all kinds of baked goods and sweet treats," Anthony explained. The old man had a wide smile on his face. "I am so proud of the gryphons adapting the traditions of humans and throwing their own twist into it. Never would I have thought to see my own creations altering themselves to establish their own customs."

Thyra looked down at the red liquid in her mug, lost in thought. "Anthony, have we exceeded your expectations?"

"Well of course!" The old man exclaimed. "When we started the experiments, it was nothing but a 'what if,' as rude as that sounds. But as you know, I had greater plans for you all. I have always wanted to see this world flourish with a different sentient species besides humans. I honestly believe there are too many of us, and not enough variety."

Anthony grabbed a handful of pecans and chewed on them. He chuckled as he watched another group of gryphons chat amongst themselves. "Sure, humans come in many shapes, forms, colors, and backgrounds, but no matter where you go, we are all basically the same. I wanted something different to break the mold, but never in my wildest dreams would I have thought it would grow to be to this extent."

"I've asked this before, but what was your ultimate goal?" Johnathen asked curiously.

Anthony laughed and looked at the gryphons before him. "Honestly, I wanted a new element to add to the table. I wanted my name in the history books. I wanted gryphons to be the new evolution of human species," Anthony said. This took them by surprise, especially Johnathen.

"An evolution of human species?" Johnathen questioned, showing a slight worry in his voice.

"Of course. Have you seen Thyra sick at all?" Anthony questioned. Johnathen looked over to his wife, seemingly lost in thought. "No? That's what I thought. Gryphons are immune to more than ninety percent of known pathogens. And what of their strength? Their ability to fly, for God's sakes! Isn't that what humankind has dreamt of since the dawn of time?"

"Are you saying we are eventually a replacement for humankind?" Aadhya added in. The question sat heavy not only on Thyra, but everybody at the table. Anthony sighed and drank from his mug, eyes wandering around the Christmas market garden.

"In a way, yes," Anthony admitted. His playful tone was now more serious as he looked around at the table. His eyes settled heavily on Johnathen and a hint of disgust entered his voice. "Think about it. How long are we destined to last as a species, John?"

Johnathen sat his mug down. "What do you mean?"

Whatever cheerful mood Thyra had felt was now gone, despite the environment that all sat in. All around, gryphons laughed and chirped amongst themselves, but she felt like she was in a different world all together.

"Humans are the disease of this earth," Anthony said plainly. "You know it as well as I do. We create religion, false beliefs, preach about our fellow man, the earth we live in, but human folly knows no bounds. We cut down every tree and consume every animal, not because we need it, but because we want it. Millionaires strive to be billionaires, not because they are hungry, but because they want more."

"But-," Johnathen interrupted.

"But what? It's the way humans are. Are you telling me you're any different?" Anthony asked sternly. "You have everything a person could ever want! Money, a beautiful home, a gorgeous wife, free reign of the city, cars of any kind, and limitless opportunity, but I know you still think about what if."

Anthony sat silent and drained his mug. Thyra could tell by Johnathen's body language that Anthony was somewhat right. It did not matter what he had, he always strived for more. Even earlier that day he had been talking about starting a new law firm.

In a way, Anthony was hitting the nail on the head. There was something about humans that she could never fully understand. No matter their intention, a human always wanted more. They were never truly content, no matter how much they lied to themselves or others.

"You hate humans," Anfang said from the corner of the table. Anthony blinked in surprise and looked over to him. "I know that hate. I once hate humans. They hurt others for nothing. But now I know humans can be good."

Anthony smiled and nodded. "Very good, Anfang. I'm glad you've came around. I was starting to worry if you were lost in hatred, like I once was, but I think you know more than you lead on. Still, you of all beings can't ignore the fact that humans as a whole can't be trusted, even if they are trying to be good. As they say, the road to hell is pathed with good intentions"

"Then what is this all for?" Thyra asked.

Anthony began to laugh, much to everyone's confusion. "This? This is for all gryphon kind!" he exclaimed, motioning to everyone.

He suddenly began to cough loudly and brought out a handkerchief to cover his mouth. Anthony held a finger up until the fit was over with. Thyra looked over to the others, seeing the slight worry in their eyes.

"Let me get you some water," Johnathen said.

"No. I am fine, but thank you for your concern," Anthony said and returned his gaze to Johnathen. "You must have read my logs by now."

Johnathen looked over to the group and all shared the same concerned yet serious expression. He fumbled with the correct way to reply. "Yes, and I can't begin to imagine the emotional struggle you went through with-."

"Stop. The reason why I wanted you to read those files is to know why I'm doing exactly what I'm doing," Anthony said plainly. "I cared for every creature under my watch. I never had physical children of my own, but I feel as if every gryphon created under my watch were my own. Again, another basic need of humankind. We wish to procreate our own species, which speaks to not only our most feral instincts, but gives our sentient brains a purpose."

Anthony sighed and finished his mug. "To have children of our own completes our basic purpose as a species at the most primal level. People feel like they can live forever through their children. But if our species as a whole is set to destroy and consume, then we can't continue."

"So, you just want the human species to die off eventually and have nothing left but gryphons?" Johnathen asked, shocked. "Is that your true intention?"

"If all happens like I think it will, yes," Anthony replied.

Everyone fell silent. Thyra did not know how to feel about this sudden realization that Anthony meant for gryphons to become the main sentient species on earth. She looked to the other gryphons at the table, but all were just as speechless as she was.

"But . . . we are exactly like you," Antonio said. Everyone turned their attention to the once silent Harris hawk. "We create like you do, we learn like you do, we adapt like you do. We are basically human, for better and worse."

Anthony weighed Antonio's words and nodded. "It's true. You learn from us. There are a lot of good aspects of humanity you can duplicate, but I aim to only teach the best," Anthony explained. "I'm sorry if I sounded harsh before. Lately, all I see is the worst in humanity. However, I will say there is a lot of beauty to be learned from us. Humans can be wonderful, creative, passionate, and lively as well as destructive, toxic, and hateful at the same time. I believe your species will come to learn from us and make this world a better place when we are gone."

"Then what does any of this mean?" Thyra asked.

Anthony stifled a laugh and looked around him, motioning to the sky. "What does any of this mean, Thyra? Really. Do you believe in a god? Do you think there is a greater existence to us rather than being good to one another and having equality for all species and genders? Honestly, I think that's all there is."

Anthony swirled his empty mug, seemingly desperate for another drink. Lately, Thyra had noticed Anthony's openness towards not only her, but the group. He seemed to answer any question on their minds and drank a lot more than usual. It seemed he was indulging in self-destructive tendencies, all while sharing his secrets. She wasn't sure if this was just his personality or the stress of his job now that his dreams were so close to being realized. Perhaps his recent actions were the cause of his own dim mortality. Even in the dull colorful lights hanging above them, she could see his cracked aging face.

"I played God," Anthony said. "I created you, and all your friends. I'm a man of science and unfortunately, I don't believe in anything past that. I do recognize that religion is important to those people that need it. And that's fine, so long as it doesn't hurt others in the process." Anthony switched his vices to the half-eaten bag of candied nuts. "Unlike the religious crusades of the eleventh century onwards, but that's beside the point."

"I not understand this God and religion, but I have question," Anfang said. Anthony motioned for him to continue. "I hear people say 'First Class' a lot, what is 'First Class'?"

"You will know soon enough," Joseph interrupted, finally breaking his long silence. Until Anfang spoke up, he had seemed uninterested in their discussion.

Anthony, happily chewing on his candied snack, looked over to Joseph with a raised eyebrow and pointed to the beast. "You mean you haven't told him?"

Joseph stirred and snapped to attention with eyeridges raised high. "Sir, I thought we agreed that-."

"You haven't told him?" Anthony repeated to which Joseph simply shook his head. The old man sighed and stood from the table. "Well, I believe seeing is believing." He gave them an eager smile. "Would you all like to see?"

Chapter 22 New Fang

Johnathen followed Anthony's car as they pulled off the main road. They pulled into an expansive gravel lot and came to a stop outside an old warehouse. As the vehicles' lights turned off, the word seemed to fade to black. Debra exited the driver's side and opened the rear door for Anthony. The short car ride had been mainly quiet, but Thyra knew everyone's heads were filled with questions. Thyra stepped out of the vehicle along with the rest of the band and looked over the seemingly dilapidated building. Off in the distance, she could make out the shadows of nearly-completed structures on the hill slope. The Redtails' new homes.

The abandoned building was vast, but in a state of disrepair. The only signs of life came from a dim light shining through two small broken windows framing the main wooden door. The plain lumber structure looked worn. Rotting boards decorated most of the front and the slopped terracotta roof seemed just moments away from caving in. Anthony led the group through an overgrown path, pushing snow and dead vegetation out of the way as he walked. Thyra could tell the path was semi well-traveled, despite how hidden it was.

Anthony pulled a card out of his pocket and swiped it against the wall next to a solid wood door. A loud thunk echoed and he stepped inside to a brightly lit lobby. The new concrete floor-to-ceiling construction inside vastly conflicted with the outer rotting structure. The area was completely empty except for two marsh kite gryphon guards who were speaking quietly to each other. They looked up from their metal desk and perked their ears. Anfang seemed to recognize them, perhaps from the training classes he went to every day. The guards stopped their conversation and stood to attention as Anthony entered, yet their eyes wandered to the guests that were with him.

"At ease," Anthony said. The two marsh kite gryphons relaxed and readjusted their body armor. They stood on opposite sides of two great metal doors and watched as Anthony swiped his card across another reader. Another loud thunk rang out and the door opened with a gentle push of his hand. Thyra looked up at Johnathen. He seemed just as on edge as she was, yet she was pretty sure they both had a good guess as to what they were about to find.

The group followed Anthony into a room filled with monitors and various lab equipment. There was a red kite gryphon stationed at a wide desk at the far side of the room. At the room's opposing wall was a wide freight elevator door. The red kite gryphon glanced over his wingshoulder as the group walked in and turned to salute them.

"Evening Holger. Everything quiet?" Anthony asked.

"Yes sir. Nothing worth mentioning. They continue to sleep as usual and vitals are all normal," Holger responded, giving the group that accompanied Anthony a wary glance.

Anthony nodded and walked over to one of the medical tables, organizing the various test tubes for a moment. "Very good. Let them in."

Holger seemed reluctant at first, looking at the new faces.

"Let them in," Joseph said more sternly and approached the station desk.

"Yes, Commander Joestar," Holger replied and turned to click away at the keyboard.

With a few short keystrokes, there was a loud clunk and the metal doors began to roll out of the way. A red light above the threshold blinked repeatedly, accompanied by a gentle alarm. Anthony was the first through the doors, and the group followed along. They stood in the elevator together and watched as the first grate door closed, and then the pair of rolling metal doors. Anthony reached over to press the only button on the wall. Another loud clank echoed out as the elevator shifted, then began it's decent.

"What, not enough money in the budget for elevator music?" Rachel chimed in. Aadhya glared down to the kestrel and shoved her gently with a wing.

The elevator stopped. As the main metal door slid open, Thyra could hear the echo of unseen mechanisms reverberating in the great cavernous room beyond, but she could not see but a couple feet inside. As Thyra entered in the gloomy room, she could their footsteps echoing a great distance. Focusing her eyes, could make out the shapes of large cylinders far away in the dark.

"Lights at full," Anthony said.

A moment later, the vibrant glow of overhead fluorescents turned on in series, starting at their side and clicking on bank after bank of lights. Every half second, the room seemed to double in size, then triple, until it was bigger than a gryphball stadium. Thyra's feathers went flat and her beak fell open. Before them were countless rows of gryphons in large cylindrical devices, each one suspended in an unknown liquid. There were wires and tubes going to each sleeping gryphon, hooked to their beaks and around their heads. Every one of them looked to be spitting images of Anfang and Joseph.

"This is Project Soldier," Anthony began. He did not even glance back at the shocked group or wait for them to speak, which was fine. Everyone was too mesmerized to even form a word. "As you all have probably read in my logs, this is what Anfang was meant to be part of." He walked up to the nearest tube and clicked at the touchscreen attached at its base. "When I began the gryphon project, Anfang was chosen to be First Class, the base template for what would eventually become Project Soldier. He was a guinea pig for what was to be."

He paused and turned to Anfang with an apologetic look. "Perhaps that is too harsh. Let's call him a prototype." Anthony turned back to the screen, swiping across it, seeming to look at vitals and other necessary information.

"Once they saw the success of their First Class, the military began to mass produce these soldiers. At first, it was hundreds, and then thousands, and then into the tens of thousands. I received the funding I needed through that project to continue my vision and dream for a race of gryphons, all the while knowing that the United States military was amassing an army of my creations."

Anthony paused and sighed. He looked up at the sleeping clone of Joseph and placed his hand on the glass. "I could bite my tongue for only so long, until the guilt began to eat at me. Finally, I told them I was going to come clean to the public. I thought that was going to be the end of me, dragged off to some unknown military prison to be hidden away until I died, or assassinated on the spot. But it seems they still needed me," Anthony took a deep breath and placed his hands in his pockets. "They offered me my own army of soldiers as an additional buyout and told me to go about my business in secret."

Anthony turned to the group, his green eyes looking upon each of them. "I was scared, upset, and out of options. I took their offer. I had the military build this base here for my future colony plans and left these soldiers here to sleep. After that, I began working on acquiring this land for you, my children. I know it sounds horrible, but I wanted a future for all of gryphon kind. I want you to spread your wings and become a race to be recognized as part of the world." Finally, he grew quiet and stood before them, waiting for someone to speak.

Anfang was the first to speak and his question caught everyone by surprise. "Do they dream?"

"Yes. Brain scans indicate cognitive activity while they are sleeping. Why do you ask?" Anthony questioned.

"They like me," Anfang said. "I remember dreams. Long dreams while asleep like them."

"Precisely. They are like you, Anfang," Anthony said.

Thyra was the next to speak. "Why don't you let them out now? They could live with us and be part of the colony."

"Trust me, I don't like this situation either," Anthony said. "For one, we don't have the infrastructure to suddenly support ten thousand more gryphons tight now. But the more important answer is, though they are much like Anfang, they are not like you."

Thyra seemed puzzled by that response. She looked over to Anfang and Joseph, thinking that they were definitely different physically from other gryphons, but mentally they were relatively the same. "What do you mean? If these soldiers are anything like these two, then they could easily live amongst us."

"But they wouldn't be like them. Not as you know them right now. The initial awoken ones behave no differently than a dog of the military. They act on simple commands, follow their leadership, and are faithful to their owners to a fault. They cannot think for themselves. They don't understand fear, love, kindness, or any of the human emotions. They should have the ability to learn these things depending on their teachers, but to put it frank, they are weapons," Anthony explained.

Thyra felt a pit grow in her stomach. The thought of these gryphons being simple, murderous and violent creatures really ate at her. She shook her head. "All gryphons have good in them."

"They all have a soul," Aadhya spoke up. "Readings of brain activity cannot explain the element of our humanity. Only another gryphon can judge these things."

"And you may be correct, Aadhya," Anthony admitted. "But that leads us back to my first point. It will take direction, dedication, training and resources to properly train them. Emotionally, they are children. Left to their own devices, without orders, they will resort to their basic feral instincts; kill, eat, breed, and survive."

"If I can learn, then they can too," Anfang said sternly.

Anthony nodded in agreement. "I believe that. I really do but look at the destruction you alone caused without the right direction," Anthony pointed out. "It's different now. You have the best support group I could ever ask for, but you are just one. Imagine thousands." He motioned to the endless rows of stasis incubators behind him. "How would we give them all the attention they need?"

Everyone fell quiet. Thyra knew that these questions and perhaps several hundred more had crossed Anthony's highly intelligent mind. She could tell he did not like the situation any more than they did.

"It's just wrong, man," Rachel said earnestly. "It's just not right having these guys all suspended and asleep for forever. Have they even been awake? I know if I was in a coma for forever, I would just want it to end," Rachel rambled. It was one of the most heartfelt expressions Thyra had ever heard her conjure up. "I don't know. Let them out or just kill them already. I mean, how long have they been like this??"

"At least fifteen years," Anthony responded. "But I believe your suggestion is quite irrational. You would rather have me kill them than let them continue to live with the possibility that one day they might be able to live like you do?"

"Yeah, kind of. It's just-." Rachel began to grow angry. Thyra could see the tiny kestrel's feathers stand on end as she took a step forward. "Don't start with your big ass words and shit. I'm talking about fellow gryphons here! How can you know what they are feeling right now? I-."

"Rachel, please calm down," Joseph was the first to interrupt.

She turned towards Joseph and fanned her wings in a threat display, eyes growing wide as she advanced on Joseph. "And why should I?! You've been in on this from the start! And you're basically one of them! You mean to tell me that you don't even feel for your brothers and sisters inside those…those…things?!"

"It's complicated," Joseph stated in a half growl, his own leathery wings unfolding.

"No, it's not! What do you mean! You stupid beast! Why don't you just…"

Suddenly Joseph leaped and pinned the tiny kestrel under his foretalons. The group gasped. Rachel wheezed loudly, causing Thyra's blood to boil.

"Get off of her!" Thyra screeched. Johnathen quickly wrapped his hands around Thyra's shoulders to hold her back.

"Listen carefully," Joseph said and leaned his towering beak over the tiny gryphoness. "You know nothing of my past. You don't know what it means to be me, or what they are." He looked up to all of them and raised his feathers. "What you all speak is nonsense! Listen to Anthony. He brought you here to explain everything, not to be put on trial!"

"I suggest you remove your talons before I remove your head," Antonio stepped forward, challenging the gryphon. Joseph took a deep breath and pulled his talons away, leaving the small gryphoness under him trembling. She struggled to return to her feet and quickly skidded over to hunker under Antonio.

"Make a threat like that again and I'll show you just what kind of animal all these soldiers are," Joseph said.

"And my point has been made," Anthony spoke up. Everyone paused and looked up to the elderly human. "Joseph is one of the awoken and is fiercely dedicated to me."

Joseph's eartufts flattened as he realized his transgressions and went to stand beside Anthony. "Excuse my outburst, sir."

"It's alright," Anthony said, placing a calming hand on the large gryphon's arm. His eyes remained focused on the rest of the group. "This is an example of the problem. Joseph has been nurtured to be who he is today. It's taken many years of domestication and teaching for him to become a reliable gryphon. Yet, despite all that training, his instincts can show through in a split second."

"Sir, if I may," Joseph asked. He sighed and looked to address the band. "What he says is true. I lose my temper more easily than other gryphons. Sometimes my bloodlust is barely containable. I was like Anfang in his earlier years and I've done a lot worse than he ever has. I don't want to go into details, but when I say believe Anthony, that is what I mean. I fear the thought of awaking all my brothers and sisters at once. Without the right leadership and initial direction, it could become a disaster."

"What do you mean by the right initial direction?" Thyra asked as she settled down.

"Not to kill. We were designed to be soldiers, not peacekeepers," Joseph said, his voice uncharacteristically soft. "When I awoke, I was compelled with the strong urge to kill. Without the right direction, I would have murdered everyone in sight. But with a motive, directions, and a very easy set of rules to follow, I was able to put my… talents… to use in a somewhat positive manner."

"We'd need an army of damned therapists," Rachel said, still cowering under Antonio's legs.

Thyra knew what Rachel meant. She could only imagine what someone like Anfang could do without proper motives. She shuddered at the thoughts and took a deep breath. "So, where does that leave us?"

"Exactly where we left off," Anthony replied. "I wanted to put your curiosity to ease and show you everything. Now that you've seen this, we go along like nothing has happened. You all live your life, play gryphball, and thrive as a society. But know that if anything ever happens, you will be protected," Anthony said sternly. "I will protect all of you to the bitter end."

"What of the others on the team?" Johnathen spoke up. "I get the implication you want us to be quiet about all of this."

"If you felt the need to tell others, you would have spread rumors already about your findings on the drives, yet you haven't, have you?" Anthony pointed out.

He was right. They had kept everything they found strictly confidential, besides the new addition of Isabell. Thyra looked over to Anfang, who seemed lost in thought.

"Look. It's been a long night and this week will be very busy. After all, the teams new permanent housing will be done by Friday. I suggest we-." Anthony began.

"What am I to you?" Anfang asked. He was looking down at his scarred talons, thinking out loud.

Anthony readjusted himself and cleared his throat. "Anfang, you…"

"Am I just dog? I stupid beast? Failed experiment?" Anfang asked and looked up, staring directly in his eyes.

Anthony shook his head and approached Anfang. "No, not at all. I regret every decision I made with you and it was the hardest thing I've ever done in my life. Anfang, signing the contract to turn you over to the military hurt me more than anything. When I look at you, I see myself. I see you battered, abused, neglected, and used."

Anthony knelt on one knee before Anfang and Thyra could swear she saw a tear in Anthony's eyes. "It's so much better now. I can't tell you how much I love seeing you in such care and in good health. I never thought I would see you again. Nor did Thyra," He paused to look over to her. Tears now shone on his cheeks.

"I don't want any of my children to go through what you went through. But without your sacrifice, we wouldn't have everything you have seen. A colony of your brethren, your sister, and all the gryphons. I had to make that horrible decision so that all of this could come into reality. I hope some day that you will understand and forgive me."

Anthony held his arms open. Anfang looked to him for a moment and leaned in to press his beak to Anthony's chest. Anthony wrapped his arms around Anfang's broad frame to pull him in close.

"I understand," Anfang said, nearly in tears himself. The group watched as the two shared a tender moment. Anthony backed away and stood up, wiping his eyes with the back of his hands.

"Well, I feel complete. Like a great weight has been lifted off my shoulders," Anthony said.

"I just feel more burdened," Thyra admitted. Anthony frowned slightly and took a deep breath.

"With knowledge comes responsibility, and that carries it's own weight," Anthony said. "And I trust that each one of you will keep this to yourselves. I want you to sleep on this and come to realize this is for your own protection."

Anthony started to walk past the group, heading out towards the entrance. The rest of the group looked at one another, realizing he was done with his explanation. They followed after him.

"Our protection from what, exactly?" Antonio asked cautiously.

Once everyone was in the security and laboratory room, Anthony cleared his throat. "It's not from what, but from whom."

Chapter 23 Welcome Home

The day to see her new home had finally come. Thyra had known about the row of new homes being built on the side of the mountain ever since she had arrived to Greifsburg, but this was her first time seeing them up close. She could have checked up on the progress at any time, as the flight from town was not but a couple minutes, but she hadn't wanted the surprise to be spoiled. The rest of the team had agreed and unanimously decided it was well worth the wait.

It was apparent that the architect and Anthony had put a great deal of thought into the arrangements for their gryphon players. The design of each house was prevalently in the Swiss Chalet style, except with a modern twist. They had large bay windows that overlooked the city below with great rounded wooden patios that jutted out of the bare snow-covered mountain slope like helicopter landing pads.

From afar, the dozen or so houses almost blended into one, giving the illusion of a castle structure. It was breathtaking, to say the least. This would be her new permanent home amongst her new 'family.'

"He could have dropped a little bit more cash to have the road paved," Johnathen complained out loud as he concentrated on the rough terrain ahead. He maneuvered the vehicle as best he could but lacked any sort of off roading

Colony

skill. The SUV hit another rough bump, lurching him from the seat and slammed his head into the carpeted roof. He groaned and rubbed the back of his head. "There's no way my Mustang will make it up this road."

"You're the only one that will be driving up this road anyways," Isabell pointed out. "Anthony probably made this road purposely hard to navigate by a vehicle, so that nosy humans couldn't make it up this road easily. Gives the team members, and you, more privacy."

Isabell sat steady as a rock as the SUV rocked hard to one side and then the other as it climbed the side of the mountain. Thyra nodded with agreement. She was onto something there. She watched out the window as a couple of her teammates landed on one of the multiple platforms and walked inside.

"Well, I guess I'll have to park it somewhere in town, or build a garage down at the bottom of the mountain," Johnathen thought out loud. "I can just drive this up and down when I need to, and-."

"Is that all you can think about right now? I mean look at this!" Rachel interrupted, her foretalons on the plush leather dashboard. She pointed up at the towering houses just a couple hundred feet away. "This is where we are going to live! It's like our own personal castle and I bet that view is going to be amazing!"

Johnathen sighed and slowed down to a crawl to cross a small stream running over the snowy mountain road. "You're right. I should be really thankful for this."

Thyra looked into his rear-view mirror, surprised that he just agreed with Rachel. He caught her eyes and shrugged without so much a witty comment back. Thyra grinned, thankful for Rachel's outburst for once. Now she did not have to hear Johnathen complain about his Mustang and nitpick for another ten minutes.

"I swear you humans are never content," Isabell chuffed.

As they approached, Thyra spotted multiple Mercedes G-Wagons and Range Rovers parked outside a makeshift lot. Humans traveled to and from the vehicles, unloading furniture, decorations, boxes, and other necessary household items. She even spotted a slew of Christmas trees tied down to the roof of one lifted van. Anthony was standing outside on the porch of one house, watching as the men went to work. He turned and waved at them as they approached. Johnathen parked next to a group of other vehicles and everyone got out.

"Good morning!" Anthony said loudly.

"Morning!" they all replied.

The bitter cold wind whipped through Thyra's head feathers as the snow crunched under her booted talons with every step.

Anthony shook hands with Johnathen, grinning widely. To Thyra's unease, she felt something akin to distrust of that man's smile. Her feelings about Anthony had soured a bit since the revelation of his secret gryphon army tucked away under the ground. They had not seen him since that night and Thyra could not help but wonder what else he was hiding from them. He seemed nonchalant about it all, even now. If there was one factor to him that Thyra had to admire, it was his acting.

Anthony motioned to the row of houses that stretched across the mountain face. "So, what do you all think?"

He seemed excited for his gryphon children, as he admittedly should be. She could only imagine how long he had planned and how much he put into these just for the team.

"They are beautiful," Johnathen replied, putting his gloved hands into his pocket. "But it's cold as hell out here."

Anthony laughed. "To be expected! We are now at almost twelve hundred meters above sea level." He turned to head towards one of the house's doors. He opened it and motioned for the small group to step inside. They gladly followed him into the welcoming warmth of the house.

Thyra looked around the open concept living room and kitchen before them. Dark red wood contrasted against the homey cream paint that lined the walls. She took a deep breath of the rich scent of fresh hardwood and the crisp smell of new house. The wall of glass on the far side of the room gave an incredible view of the Austrian landscape beyond. It was simply breathtaking.

"Each house is an exact replica of this one. 280 square meters each, that's close to 3000 sq ft for you all. Three bedrooms. 3 ½ baths. Propane ranges, two wood fireplaces," Anthony continued giving the details as Thyra walked into the kitchen. The area was massive, more than she could ever want, but she was more interested in the gigantic back deck. Anthony noticed. "And of course, the deck. That was my main focus since you all will travel by air."

Thyra opened up the sliding door and stepped outside. There was plenty of room for patio furniture around the half moon deck. At the center, the deck extended out into a rectangle without any railings. The wind whisked through her flight feathers and she walked out towards the edge and looked down. The sheer drop off was hundreds of feet down before leveling out. She could feel the deck swaying ever so slightly.

"Not to worry. I had my best engineers on this. This deck will last for decades," Anthony reassured her as he walked out to stand beside her.

Thyra looked around at the wide-open Austrian mountainside and breathed heavily, taking in the crisp air. The small town of Greifsburg dotted the landscape underneath her. She could see the gryphball stadium populated with trucks and people as well. Her binocular vision could make out the signs of stage building at the center. Probably the stage for the band that would be playing at the new year's festival. Innsbruck seemed way out in the distance, yet it all felt attainable. It was everything she had ever wanted. She felt like she could leap off this platform and fly for days.

Anthony peered over the edge himself, showing no fear of falling despite the hard winds threatening to push him off. "It's beautiful, isn't it," he said calmly as he took in the sight himself.

Thyra looked up to him. His usually bright green eyes had lost their shimmer and life he once had. He seemed to stare out into nothing, despite the magnificent sight before him.

"How does it feel to fly?" he asked.

Thyra opened her beak to respond but had to think about it. Humans had asked her the same question time and time again, but Anthony clearly was not looking for the typical answer.

"It's like nothing else in the world. It's complete freedom. When I'm in the sky, it feels as if everything else falls away. There's nothing that can ground me," she replied, looking out into the distance. Even the chatter from other teammates on their own decks did not distract her. "Flying is the greatest gift anyone could receive." Thyra looked up to him with a thoughtful smile. "Thank you."

He smiled back at her, but his eyes told a different story. He took a deep breath, standing at the edge of the deck. "Thyra, are you afraid of death?"

This question took her by surprise. She looked back at Johnathen, who had remained inside. He was walking around with a group of other gryphons, touring the house. He had always been scared of heights.

Anthony saw her hesitation and rephrased the question. "Are you afraid of dying, what lies beyond, what it means?"

"I... Of course, I am," Thyra managed to reply. It was the kind of hard existential question all sentient beings faced. "I don't even know how long I'm supposed to live. I mean, I'm one of the first gryphons ever made and I don't even know what our natural life spans are supposed to be." She stopped and glanced at Anthony. He was the one that created them, after all. Maybe he had the answer she was looking for all this time. He seemed to know everything. "Anthony, can you answer that question?"

"I don't know," Anthony said with a sigh. He shook his head and Thyra felt a surge of frustration. Even one of the greatest minds in history did not have the answer she sought. "Death is inevitable, and it comes for us all," the old man muttered, standing solid as a rock.

"Why are you . .?" Suddenly, it hit her. He had been exhibiting faint signs of sickness ever since moving here. He was drinking constantly and holding nothing back. He was telling them all his secrets and his desires. He was wrapping everything up. "Anthony, are you dying?"

He was silent for a few long moments. "I've had cancer for decades and I'm losing the fight. I don't have too much longer here," Anthony admitted. "This colony is my final gift to you."

Thyra took a deep breath. Tt seemed her whole world crashed before her. The sun that reflected off the white mountain slopes had lost its beauty in an instant. Up until this moment, she had wondered why he suddenly came forward with this grand plan. He was wrapping everything up for the gryphons in a nicely tied bow.

"All those years of hiding. The secrecy, the planning… All of this," She motioned to the city below them. "Because you want to do one last thing for us?"

"I felt guilty for all the years of silence, but I'm a dead man. I hoped that maybe, just maybe, this would be enough to lift my guilty conscience," Anthony said. He turned weary eyes her way. "I'm come to terms with what will happen, but I'm scared."

The strong, intelligent, and seemingly unshakable image she had cultivated of this man shattered before her. Not all the money, power, and resources in the world mattered. Despite everything, he was as human as everyone else.

"I find reprieve knowing that you will live happily and comfortably with Johnathen and the others." Anthony paused again and looked down at her. He was fighting back tears yet again. "I just wanted to say that I love you, daughter."

Thyra felt herself choke up. She had never had real parents. The only father she known was the one in her dreams, the man that took care of her early life, and here he was, standing with her on the mountainside, dying slowly from the inside. "I…"

The sliding door opened behind them and Rachel rushed out. "Thyra! You have to check out how big the bathtub is!" Thyra closed her eyes and took a deep breath as the small gryphoness yammered on. "It's so big that it's practically a swimming pool for me! I mean, you and John could easily take a bath together if you wanted to!"

Thyra forced a smile and turned around. "That's great! I'll be right in!"

She saw Aadhya and Antonio walk in through the front door. Rachel heard them and rushed to greet them. Thyra waved politely in their direction and turned to look at Anthony. His face was cold as stone, both figuratively and literally. "Anthony, I don't know what else to say besides thank you…"

"And that's all I've ever wanted to hear," Anthony responded. He turned to see the group of gryphons laughing and conversating inside which seemed to spark what little joy he had left in him. "Come now. Today isn't the day for tears. It's Christmas. How about we go inside and get decorated for the party tonight?"

"I would like that."

Thyra absently used her fork to separate the peas from the mashed potatoes and gravy. The pile of honey glazed ham and roasted turkey sat on the opposite side of her plate, untouched. All around her, gryphons chirped and carried on in gleeful conversation at the long table. Everyone was in attendance and seemed to be blissful; Everyone besides herself.

317

The sun had set hours ago. Their house was now furnished with brand new beautiful furniture and embellished with festive decorations. Bright colored lights illuminated an impressively tall live evergreen tree while classical Christmas music played in the background, only adding to her dreadful mood. Humans found the traditional music to be festive, but tonight she loathed it.

The portable wooden tables were stocked full of every delightful dish she could ever ask for, yet nothing looked appetizing. She had not even touched the full glass of red wine in front of her. Thyra glanced up at Anthony every couple of minutes. He seemed to be so carefree as he laughed and talked amongst the others; a completely different person than she had seen mere hours ago.

"Thyra?" Johnathen said, breaking her deep thoughts. He pointed to her full plate. "You've barely eaten anything hun. Is your crop upset?"

"Ah, yeah, a little bit," Thyra replied a little absently. He seemed concerned and rubbed her back. "But it's nothing to worry about," she added with an attempt at a smile.

Johnathen apparently bought her act. He gave her a half drunken grin and nodded. "I'm sure there will be leftovers for days,"

"So, how are you lovebirds settling in!" Jason the golden eagle exclaimed, motioning his full glass of wine over to Rachel and Nathanial. The immediate group of gryphons all joined in laughter as the hothead caracara flushed his nares.

"I don't think it's any of your business!" Nathanial snapped.

Rachel smacked the back of his head with a loud laugh. "It's awesome! There's plenty of space for Nathanial and I to... you know." The little kestrel grinned as her drunken nares flushed, earning a loud laugh from the gryphons.

"I do not allow maternity leave on this team! I need you for this season!" Coach Victor shouted from nearby at the head of the table. Everyone began to screech loudly in amusement but Victor, in his half drunken stupor, tried to remain professional. "So .. you two better wrap that or I swear to..."

"Please!" Aadhya interrupted. Everyone fell silent save for a couple chuckles. "We are at the dinner table. Please remain civil." Everybody piped down immediately.

"Sorry! Sorry. It was my fault," Jason admitted and tilted the wine glass into his beak to finish the rest of the red liquid off.

"Apology accepted," Aadhya replied and sipped from her tea.

Thyra could not help but chuckle at her mother-like attitude towards the whole team. No one dared to challenge her. It was the little reprieve from reality that she needed to enjoy the moment. They had everything they could ever ask for, and with a great gryphball season in front of them. There were questions left unanswered and uncertainty ahead of them, but for the moment, everybody was cheerful and happy. She realized she should enjoy it.

The dessert went around in rounds, passing talon to hand to talon. Everybody dug in, including Thyra, enjoying the sweetness that was offered. For the moment, everything was good. She let herself enjoy the energy of conversation and the joy everybody carried along.

A loud clang erupted from the end of the table after everybody had enjoyed their dessert and all eyes concentrated on Anthony, standing at the end of the table. "Everyone, I just wanted to begin by saying what a delightful meal this has been, and I'd like us to offer a huge round of applause...I mean acclaws to Antonio for spearheading this dinner."

Clapping ensued. Antonio seemed to almost blush as he waved them off, as if all his efforts were nothing. "I had a great group of other chefs to help. I cannot take full credit."

"You are too modest! We know you were head chef!" Anthony exclaimed, earning a laugh from the harris hawk. "Anyway, I really appreciate everyone here tonight. It really means a lot to me. I can't imagine a better family for this celebration. There's been a lot of change in all of our lives, but I like to think it's for the better. We all come from completely different backgrounds. There's gryphons here from every part of the world, and I can't imagine a better team than this year's Redtails.

"But it's not only gryphball that brings us together. I believe you all have become a family," Anthony stated and looked around at the table. "Some have become lovers." He motioned to Rachel and Nathanial, earning a couple laughs. "Some have found a safe space for their relationship." He motioned to Priscilla and Viola. "And some have found family for the first time in their life," he looked to Anfang, Joseph, and Isabell all sitting together.

Anthony took a deep breath and continued, "I see a generation of happy gryphons here, ones that can thrive in this crazy world and continue through life uninhibited by old-fashioned social concepts. I believe that in this new country, you all can be anything that you want to be. So, play for the best seasons and trophies the Redtails can earn, or the relationships you build along the way." Anthony raised his glass. Everybody joined him. "To you, my children."

Colony

There were a couple of confused faces amongst the crowd, but most of them knew exactly what he meant.

"To you," the group said in unison and drank from their glasses. Anthony sat back down and within moments, the conversations picked right back up where they started.

Johnathen leaned in to wrap his arm around Thyra's neck, bringing her closer to his chest. "I've got something for you," he said with a little chuckle.

Thyra perked up and nipped at his cheek before he left the table. Several others followed in his stead, picking up wrapped presents to bring back. Thyra accepted the small, decorated present and held it in her talons. She looked around as others excitedly tore into the wrapping paper, throwing caution to the wind.

Johnathen watched excitedly as she carefully peeled the tape off. "Oh, come on! Just tear into it!"

Thyra worked her sharp talons against the box and tore it open, as instructed. Inside was a gift certificate to Zach's butchery. Thyra stared blankly at the piece of paper and Johnathen began to laugh.

"I know it's nothing much, but Zach had a sale on his gift certificates a couple months back, before, ya know, the fire and all of that terrible shit, so I picked them up. I've had that in my wallet ever since, and it's the only thing I have from home. I thought about throwing it away and just getting something else but I just...I just don't know anymore," Johnathen rubbed the back of his head, attempting an awkward chuckle. "I figured it's a good excuse to go home and visit sometime. Get your favorite cuts of steaks, grill out at Keith's or Saul's place. You know, maybe regain some sense of normalcy and be home for a bit," Johnathen rambled on, watching as Thyra teared up. He frowned and placed his

321

glass down. "Hun, hun what's wrong? I'm sorry it sucks but it's all I could…"

"No, it's perfect," Thyra choked out. "I like the idea of going back to Georgia and having everything normal again. Sometimes I wish we'd never left."

Johnathen wrapped his arms around her and pulled her in close. Only a couple of others noticed it was tears of sadness instead of joy while the rest excitedly opened their presents.

"I know featherbutt. I know, but there's very little left for us there anymore," Johnathen said and rubbed the back of her head. "We have a new life here. We can start all over, just you and me."

Thyra could not respond. She sulked into his chest, trying not to be too loud. She did not know why she was suddenly hysterical. It could be a combination of everything going on, but she had lost herself for just a moment. Johnathen shrugged at the others, really not understanding why she was reacting so hard to it all. He kissed between her eartufts and rubbed the back of her head. "That sound good?"

"Y…Yeah," Thyra said as she regained herself. By then, half of the gryphons were staring at the couple.

Johnathen let out a loud laugh and motioned to the papers, making up a lie on the spot. "We are renewing our vows!" Everybody smiled and clapped together. He leaned in and kissed her cere. "You know I love you more than anything."

Thyra nodded and wiped her tears off on his thick sweater. Aadhya approached to rub her back and offer a comforting smile. Thyra hysterically chuckled and sniffled. "I'm just… I'm so excited for everything."

Aadhya bought into it and nodded back. "Do not fret, I will help you re-write your vows if you wish."

"Congratulations," Anthony interrupted. Thyra looked up at him with confusion and cocked her head. "I would like to be in attendance, if you would have me."

Johnathen cleared his throat and exclaimed, "But of course! Everyone can come! I would love it and I'm sure Thyra would too!" He nudged her gently.

Thyra nodded. "Oh yes. I would love everyone to be there."

The room raised their glasses to them once again and quickly continued onto their own discussions. Thyra looked up at Anthony as he sipped his wine glass. She could tell just from the tone of voice; he knew it was an empty gesture. He would be long gone by then.

Chapter 24 Dark Horse

The energy inside of the stadium was contagious. Thousands of gryphons and humans alike all stood around tall cocktail tables underneath heat lamps, carrying on in joyous conversation. The stage at the center of the field was empty for the moment, save for a big projection screen hanging above it playing music videos of Beast and Man.

Towering speakers pumped out the band's electronic, beat heavy melodies and Thyra could feel every bass hit shake her chest from far away. She looked around at the field, eyes open wide. The crowd recognized the Redtails team walk onto the snow-covered field, and many of them began to clap. Others either did not acknowledge them or did not seem to care.

Johnathen leaned down to yell loudly in Thyra's ear, "Go to our assigned table! I'll go get some drinks!"

Even with him yelling, Thyra could barely make out what he was saying. She nodded and proceeded off to the right side with Aadhya, Rachel. and Antonio in tow. The snow crunched under their paws and talons and gave way to the fake field grass underneath. The other teammates separated to their own tables. Off to the side, where they were seated, the speakers were less overpowering, and she could actually hear others talking.

Rachel started to ramble off, taking her place at the table. "I'm so excited! I've always wanted to see Beast and Man play! They put down some damn hard beats but it's all with real instruments! Not like studio mixed and stuff like that. And Patricia, the nightingale lead singer, can really sing!"

"This music is, how do I put it?" Aadhya searched for words. "It is interesting. Not what I would typically listen to but-."

"Oh, sorry this is like too cool for your old feathers!" Rachel replied with a loud laugh. Aadhya brushed off the comment like it was nothing. Rachel received a playful bump from Antonio.

"It is just the fact that we prefer actual music, not this loud nonsense," Antonio jested.

Rachel huffed and shook her head. She motioned towards the center. "Whatever! Y'all can't handle how badass it is. You'll see for yourself when they get on stage!"

"Then I hope to be positively overwhelmed by their artistic ability," Antonio jested once again, earning a chuckle from Aadhya.

"I'm sorry if it's not the Spanish guitar bullshit mariachi band that you're looking for!" Rachel replied with a laugh to herself. Antonio frowned.

"Ok, that was low!" Thyra interrupted.

Rachel flattened her ears. "Yeah, yeah sorry!"

Johnathen approached the table with a handful of drinks and placed them down on the table. "Ok! So I just got glühwein for everyone because it's warm and delicious and gets you messed up pretty quick." He laughed and passed around the steaming mugs of spiced hot wine. He stood under the heat lamp and shivered before letting out a loud sigh. "I'm glad they have these lamps, or I would be miserable."

"We will get used to it," Thyra said and sipped from the hot mug. She trilled as the tasty beverage hit her tongue and warmed her crop.

"Oh yeah says you. I don't have feathers and fur covering my whole body!" Johnathen complained and then motioned to Aadhya. "I mean look at Addy! She just has a light jacket on!"

Aadhya shrugged her wingshoulders and sipped from the mug. "It is not my fault you are a pussy." Everybody stopped and turned to her, clearly shocked by the comment. The normally reserved and kind bearded vulture gave them a smug grin in response.

"Daaaaaaamn Addy!" Rachel yelled. The group joined together in laughter.

"I believe I am allowed to talk the bullshit every now and then, yes?" Aadhya asked.

"Absolutely. And it means a lot more coming from you," Thyra chuckled and slapped a wing playfully against Johnathen's back, giving him a pointed look. "So, shut up and enjoy the moment!"

"Ok, I deserved that," Johnathen admitted and drank from his glass.

Thyra turned to watch the entrance of the field as more people and gryphons continued to pour into the stadium grounds. Joseph and Anfang spearheaded the security checks, watching each guest closely as they entered through a metal detector. It was pleasant to see Anfang taking his role as security so seriously. It gave him direction and purpose, something he needed. The beast turned around to look at her occasionally, as if he were constantly keeping tabs on her in particular. Instead of a constant fear of dread that he may cause to her and others around them, she now felt safe with him around. He had grown in such a short time.

Coach Victor approached their table with Jason beside him and placed their glasses down on the table. Johnathen was the first one to address them.

"Victor! Jason, how are you two doing?" he asked.

"Very well! This celebration is something that we all need before our season begins. After tonight, it's going to be two-a-days and hard training!" Victor said pointing at all the gryphons at the table sternly before letting out a little chuckle. Thyra could see his nares were already flushed from drinking.

"I am ready, Coach," Antonio responded. "After all, we have to start this new season strong! The European Gryphball League is not ready for the Georgia Redtails."

"That's the spirit. We may not be in Georgia anymore, but home is where we make it," Victor said with a laugh and looked to Jason. The golden eagle smiled and nodded his beak.

"And I know we can count on everyone here to take home the First League trophy," Jason said. "I think we are going to surprise these gryphons and show them what some backwoods Georgia team can do!" He held his glass out for a toast.

Everyone at the table joined in and clanked their mugs together. "To us!"

"To the Redtails!" everyone joined in in unison and drank.

Victor looked over to Johnathen next and cleared his throat. "So, with your powerful wife bringing home the bacon now, what are you going to do?"

Alex Bizzell

Johnathen rubbed the back of his head and nervously laughed. Thyra could tell the question had weighed on him for a while now. "Well! I've had some opportunities to start up a law firm in town. I think the gryphons could always use some sort of legal representation but it's going to take a while to get my license and read up on everything," he began. "I mean there's a lot of gray areas as far as gryphon rights are concerned, not to mention a whole new country inside the European union. The logistics behind it are…"

"I don't need the whole story," Victor interrupted. "I'm not going to begin to act like I understand what you do. I'm a gryphball coach and that's all I understand." The coach drank from his mug again. He shivered gently underneath his thick coat and moved closer to the heat source. "But I can guarantee that your wife and the rest of the gryphons will be safe and successful under my watch."

"I really appreciate that," Johnathen replied. Victor looked over to Thyra with a smile. As much of a hard-ass as he was, Victor always cared for his teammates. He looked at them as family and she appreciated that more than anything in the world.

Thyra glanced over Victor's shoulders to see Anthony walking onto the stage. Half of the audience slowly silenced as they saw him approach the mic.

"Good evening, Greifsburg!" Anthony shouted. By now, everybody in attendance was silent. "Never in my wildest dreams would I have believed I'd see this big of a turnout for our very first New Year's celebration! We have gryphons and humans from all over the world tonight, and I cannot thank you all enough for being here. Tonight, is not only a celebration of what has happened, but of what is yet to come. I believe many gryphons have found their permanent home here."

The elderly man gripped the mic tightly and looked around the crowded stadium grounds. "We come from all walks of life, backgrounds, religions, species, but we are united with one cause. We all want a better life for all species. We want unity, peace, and wellbeing."

The speech was unexpectedly heartfelt and serious, especially during the party atmosphere this night portrayed, but it was obvious he meant it. He locked eyes with Thyra, as if his speech was meant for her. "And I believe that this country can thrive with the help of everyone else. Humans and gryphons can live together in harmony. I believe this is just the beginning of a fruitful relationship between us all."

"But enough about all that! I know everyone is here to see Beast and Man. Am I right?!" Anthony shouted excitedly, much to the crowd's delight. Everyone joined together in excited yells and claps.

Anthony held one fist in the air, pumping the crowd up again. It was odd seeing a stern scientist trying to hype up a crowd. Thyra could not imagine what he was going through at that time, knowing he was a dying man. Yet, he stood before them all with such contagious life and vigor.

"I don't think you all are excited enough! I said, are you here to see Beast and Man, or not?" he yelled again. The crowd erupted loudly in cheers which shook the entire stadium grounds. Anthony turned towards the end of the stage and motioned with an open palm. "I think they are ready! What do you think, Patricia?"

A pale white gryphoness walked on stage wearing a thick red coat. She waved a plain brown wing to the crowd. The people erupted again with louder cheers as she took the center stage. She was no bigger than Rachel and Anthony had to lean down to hand the mic over to her.

"Wow! Look at this crowd!" the band's lead singer exclaimed. "I can't tell you how excited we are to play for the country of Greifsburg tonight!" The other band members walked up on stage, a cockatoo gryphon and two darker skinned humans. The cheers slowly died down as they all listened to what she had to say.

"I never thought I would see a city, let alone a whole country of gryphons in my lifetime," Patricia said in her Northern Yankee accent. "It's incredible to see you all thriving so well in this beautiful country and we feel honored to be in this new gryphball stadium tonight." She checked over her shoulder as the members of the band readied their instruments. "And without further ado, we are Beast and Man, and I hope you enjoy our set list tonight!"

Some roadies appeared on the stage, handing the band members their equipment and checking their sound set up as the audience cheered. Within a short couple seconds, the drummer put his sticks together to give them a beat, and then the music began. The heavy electronic tempo set the tone as the drummer played along, and the human's electric guitar pulled the melody all together.

Thyra did not think it was the best music she had heard, but as she watched Rachel and other gryphons in the crowd beginning to jam with the music, she understood why it was wildly popular. Then the singer opened her beak and Thyra had to admit that Patricia did have the most beautiful voice she had heard before. There was nothing like the melodies a songbird could sing, but you give that skill to a gryphoness and they are unmatched. She watched Johnathen dance and groove a bit to the music as well. Lights dazzled the arena in a multitude of colors while the big screen showed mesmerizing images. As the first song ended, the crowd erupted into applause once again.

Colony

Rachel leaned over and yelled excitedly. "See! I told you!"

Thyra chuckled. "It's not bad at all! I was expecting nothing but noise, but the real instruments and the electronics work together."

Rachel ruffled her crest up happily and looked over to Aadhya, waiting for her comment. She simply shrugged her wingshoulders and held a feathered foretalon out. "It is not my style, but I can see how others enjoy it."

Rachel opened her beak to say something, but the next set started with a loud bass blast that rattled the mugs on the table. Rachel thought it best to leave it be and let herself enjoy the music.

Johnathen left several times to get drinks for everybody, and even brought a couple of delicious snacks. With every new song, Thyra began to like it more and more. She could not tell if it was just the energy in the stadium as humans and gryphons danced with one another, or just the alcohol, but she was enjoying herself nonetheless.

Aadhya even began to dance with Antonio. Rachel could not help herself from grabbing a couple sneaky videos and pictures of them two together, and that's when Antonio really let his dancing skills be shown. The group had never seen a gryphon move the way he did, as if he glided along the ground in a show of fanning wings and feathers.

When Antonio noticed Rachel grabbing pictures, he grew slightly embarrassed and half-heartedly chased Rachel around to get the smart phone away from her. The group laughed under the loud music.

Thyra looked around the stadium. For the moment, everything else faded away. The cares and stresses from everyday life did not exist at this time. Everyone seemed lively and carefree, living in the now. She understood why this high energy music meant so much to others. The upbeat tempo made it feel like she could take on anything and reinvigorated her.

The setlist came to an end and the tired nightingale came to the center of the stage. "I hope everybody has enjoyed the music so far!" Patricia shouted out. Everybody erupted into cheers once again. "And as we approach the new year, I'm going to hand the stage over to President Clearwater once again!"

Anthony walked up on stage. He smiled and waved to the crowd, taking the mic from her politely. "What a night!" he began. "We have just minutes until the new year, and I wanted to take this time to send out this successful year on a positive note."

Thyra frowned. She could read him better than most. Maybe he was only tired, but something ate at her. Despite the positive words, the energy he portrayed hours ago was gone. He seemed distraught, lost and worried.

"As most of you all know, I began work on this country years ago, hoping that it would become the beautiful city that it is today. We have all worked hard to accomplish our goals and overcome every obstacle set before us. And I believe that there is no force in heaven or hell that can stop us from becoming everything we should be," Anthony paused for applause, taking a deep breath. He seemed nervous, almost like he was waiting for something. "And by we, I mean all of gryphon kind. You have more potential than any human could have, and I want to remind you all of that."

This invoked a less excited round of clapping and whispers moved among the crowd. It was a weird comment, to say the least. As Anthony looked around the crowd and caught Thyra's eyes once again, she began to worry more.

Even from afar, she could see how afraid he was, but for what, she did not know. He cleared his throat and looked down at his watch. "I started this colony as a safe haven for gryphon kind, but this is just the beginning. I wish to see humans and gryphons live amongst one another in the future, but-." He paused again. "But I'm afraid that some will not let that happen."

"Thyra, what the hell is he doing? He's really killing the vibe!" Rachel whispered. She waved the small gryphoness off and Antonio took Rachel into a wing to hold her close, almost to shut her up. She struggled against him and tried to get away.

"Just let the man talk," Antonio whispered and held her tight. She gave up and huffed.

Anthony checked the clock again and swallowed, which only made Thyra more nervous. She turned to see Anfang and Joseph standing together with a whole slew of uniformed guard gryphons. Anfang did not appear to be be worried but Joseph, on the other hand, seemed just as concerned as Thyra was.

"I hope this year can be a real eye opener for all living beings. The gryphon species are here to stay, and they belong to this world just as much as any human." Anthony finished just as the gigantic counter on the screen started ticking down the seconds to midnight. The old man seemed to hold back his tears as the mic in his hand shook. "We will live together in harmony! Let's begin this new year with a fresh start." Anthony said, and began to yell out the numbers.

The crowd shrugged off the awkward feeling and began to chant with him, counting down. Spirits lifted ever so slightly as the thirty second mark came, then the twenty, but Anthony stopped repeating the numbers. He stood at the center of the stage, locking eyes with Thyra. She saw him mouth "I love you," as the clock struck ten seconds.

Nine.

Eight.

Seven.

A loud shockwave echoed in the stadium and Anthony's face crumpled, his head encircled by a halo of red mist. Thyra's heart skipped a beat as everything froze in place. The arena was silent for what seemed like minutes, but it happened in an instant.

Screams brought her back to reality as Anthony's lifeless corpse hit the ground hard in a spreading pool of his own blood.

As the timer hit zero and the scheduled fireworks set off, a round of gunfire erupted behind them.

Chapter 25 Mister Blue Sky

The fireworks illuminated the stadium in multicolored flashes of spectacular light. It was intended to captivate the audience, but instead of the awe-inspiring spectacle that was intended, pure chaos reigned. Humans and gryphons screamed in varying tones, running amok on the stadium grounds. Several of them tripped over bodies that lay on the ground.

The band scattered as parts of the instruments and equipment sprayed in the air. The nightingale gryphoness collapsed on stage next to Anthony in a heap of her own blood. The once bright screen displaying happy New Year suddenly went dark as a round of stray bullets struck its screen.

Thyra could hardly breathe. Her vision blurred as confusion and pure dread filled her mind. The ringing in her eartufts stung as gunfire continued throughout the stadium. She could not pinpoint how many weapons were being fired, or where they came from. Thyra felt herself being tackled to the ground as Johnathen shielded her from harm. He wrapped his arms tightly around his wife with the strength of a python. She gasped for air, and the slow motion scene she was witnessing started to become more real.

Gryphons all around were taking to the air to flee. Thyra watched with horror as several of them fell from the sky in a heap of crimson-stained feathers. The gunfire ever so slightly slowed and she heard German shouting over the panicked screams of the audience. She turned just enough to witness Anfang and other security forces tearing their talons into humans clad with body armor-. There were four, no, five groups of humans around the back half of the stadium. The assailants fired on the trained gryphons and several of them went down but Anfang and Joseph continued their advance.

Another round of fireworks lit up the sky in a dazzle of colors, startling Thyra again. Johnathen's weight still pressed her to the ground. He was saying something undecipherable, but soothing. She took deep breaths, realizing that the worst was over. The attackers were no longer focused on the crowd, now concerned with their own threats as the gryphon guard advanced.

Anfang and Joseph worked in perfect unison, dispatching the nearest threats to them. Every quick slash from their talons earned a vibrant spray of dark purple blood, accented by the bright flare of the fireworks.

Thyra turned her head and saw Rachel clinging to Antonio. The Kestrel was covered with blood, her huge eyes filled with tears as she clutched her bleeding friend tightly. Thyra's heart skipped a beat. She struggled under Johnathen's grip, attempting to escape him to check on her friends, but he remained steadfast.

"Stay down!" he demanded.

"It's Antonio! I think he's hurt!" Thyra cried out and struggled again.

Johnathen stubbornly refused to let go. She frantically looking for the other threats, but they were no were to be found as the gunfire died down. The remaining assailants continued to fire on the gryphon guard in a series of three round bursts, but she could tell their numbers were diminishing. Within a minute, the gunfire all but ceased as the remaining attackers fled.

Johnathen lifted his head and surveyed the scene, allowing Thyra just enough room to break his grasp. She quickly crawled over to Rachel's sobbing form and turned Antonio over. Intense dread filled her heart once more as she saw her friend clutching his stomach, his chest heaving as he struggled for air. Thyra's eyes filled with tears as she quickly took of her jacket and applied it directly to his gunshot wound.

"Antonio, Antonio, it's ok," she lied desperately, trying to convince them both. The harris hawk's frightened brown eyes looked up into hers and a talon found her arm to grip it firmly.

"Thyra, is Rachel okay?" Antonio asked between labored breaths. She looked over to the kestrel, who was soaked with Antonio's blood. She was struggling to stand, but appeared uninjured. Thyra choked and attempted to speak but lost her words. She quickly nodded her head.

Anthony smiled slightly as his grip around her arm slowly faded. "Thyra, please, I want..."

His voice slowly trailed off into unintelligible whispers. Thyra watched as his eyes slowly dulled and drifted off into unconsciousness. She held her breath, hoping that he would speak once again, but she knew he never would. Thyra gasped, folding in on herself and placed her beak against Antonio's still warm chest.

Thyra wept. Her screams of anguish echoed in the stadium along with those of multiple others. The occasional gunfire still rang out but it fell on deaf ears. Her world was dark and gray. She clutched her friend's body tightly, shaking uncontrollably until a large white wing wrapped around her.

Thyra looked up through blurred vision to see Aadhya standing next to her. The bearded vulture looked down upon her. No words were shared but Aadhya's kind red and yellow eyes told all. Johnathen knelt down next to the group and tucked Thyra's head into his chest.

Rachel collapsed next to them, breathing heavily, her eyes wide with disbelief. "Antonio, Antonio, please wake up," the shell-shocked kestrel said quietly and shook his body with her tiny foretalons. Tears fell off the edge of her beak as she grasped his jacket. "Antonio please!"

"He's dead!" Thyra said, her voice filled with anguish. What pain and fear she felt were replaced with pure anger. Rachel looked up at her friend in disbelief, eartufts folded back against her head.

"I…" Thyra attempted before another round of gunfire from behind interrupted her train of thought. She turned to see another gryphon stumble and fall to the ground before the feet of a body-armored human.

Something animalistic rose inside her. Everything else faded away into nothingness, until all that remained was the instinct to kill. She screeched and leapt from the ground. Aadhya, Rachel, and Johnathen cried out in alarm, but the protests of them fell on deaf ears as Thyra took to the skies, her eyes set on the target.

Thyra rose overhead, then folded her wings in and dove on the human. The individual noticed her attack all too late. Thyra hit the person's upper body with full force and felt the sickening crack of bones under her talons. The armored human slammed into one of the stadiums seats with Thyra on top. Thyra screeched and moved her talons to their throat, squeezing tightly. The knife-like appendages sunk deep into soft flesh without much resistance, and hot purple fluid poured around her talons.

The human let out gurgling cries, clutching weakly at their throat. Thyra growled ferally, slashing repeatedly as the body twitched and squirmed underneath her until finally all motor function ceased.

Thyra looked into the human's eyes and hooked a talon underneath the ski mask to reveal the horrified features of a teenage girl. Shocked, Thyra removed her talons from the girl's throat and looked down at the damage she just done. She just killed a human, a young one. The awfulness of the situation threatened to swallow her up. She panicked, her head spinning with anger, fear, and revulsion.

She barely noticed the guard gryphon that the human had shot standing to his feet once again, coughing and holding his chest. "Thank you," he said heavily.

But she could not receive any kind of thanks. She stepped back from the body, watching the white snow around it quickly dye red with its blood. Thyra looked down at her gory talons, dripping with the human's life in horror. All consciousness left her mind as she was lost in her most feral instinct. She leapt from the stadium grounds in a flurry of wing beats and fled.

"God damn it! Status!" Joseph yelled at his radio a second time. Several seconds went by before he received an answer.

"The stadium is contained! All threats neutralized!" the radio blared, the gryphon's voice frazzled. "But, um, there's multiple friendlies down! I don't know man! Finn and Elias are in bad shape! We need help immediately!"

The radio clicked. Joseph cursed under his breath. "This wasn't supposed to happen." He clicked the radio attached to his shoulder. "Check the perimeter. Are there any enemies fleeing?"

Joseph dropped the clip of his sidearm before feeding another magazine in, then chambered a round and holstered his sidearm on his chest rig. The radio clicked, and then went silent for a second. Joseph looked over to Anfang and ruffled his feathers in frustration at the delay.

"Affirmative. There is a vehicle in motion exiting northwest of stadium," a second, slightly calmer voice on the radio blared out.

Anfang growled low in his chest and looked over the horror show of the stadium.

His eartuft perked as he frantically searched for Thyra with his eyes. He saw Johnathen and her other friends, but she was missing. "Where is she?"

Joseph looked up at Anfang, eyes dead as night. He ignored the beast's concern for the moment and clicked the radio button. "Pursue out of sight," he commanded.

"Where is she?" Anfang said again, worry rising in his voice.

Joseph took a deep breath and started to survey the horrendous scene before him. "I don't know, but we have to focus on containing the threat."

Screams and cries of pain filled the arena. Countless humans and gryphons alike lay dead in the snow. The living surrounded the dead, heaped over bodies in a grotesque symphony of howling cries. Anfang finally understood what life meant to them.

As the fireworks ended, the front stage lighting turned back on, casting a new light on the carnage. Anfang could tell Joseph's heart felt for them, but he could not share the same emotion. He did not know what true anguish was, but he could see in Joseph's eyes that the commander felt defeated and lost.

A thought occurred to him. "What you mean by not supposed to happen?" Anfang questioned.

Joseph shook his head and turned away from the morbid scene. "Take to the skies and pursue that fleeing vehicle. We need answers," he commanded.

Anfang frowned. He had not yet adapted to the social concepts of what death meant to civilized people and how it took its toll on them, but he knew enough to see that the commander was either in shock or avoiding his questions completely.

When Anfang did not obey immediately, Joseph shouted. "Anfang! Take to the skies and pursue that vehicle!"

Anfang bit back the urge to growl. "Yes sir."

The beast ascended into the skies with a quick downward stroke of his large leathery wings. The cries of the others quickly disappeared as the bitter wind whipped around his jacketed form. He breathed heavily, watching the vapor quickly disappear as he gained enough altitude to fly away from the stadium. He saw multiple red lights flashing around the stadium as additional ambulances arrived. It would not be enough. The small country was not prepared for a tragedy like this.

Anfang's eyes caught the faint glimpse of a second gryphon in air, and another firework lit off to reflect the

Greifsburg police badge on its shoulder. Anfang quickly followed, his wings pumping hard against the wind gusts. He caught up with the other gryphon. It was a goshawk gryphon he had seen around the training grounds from time to time. Anfang could not remember his name.

The gryphon followed the van from high above with Anfang next to him. "Anfang, sir! I can't tell you how glad I am to see you!"

It was odd to be welcomed, even in a situation like this. He realized, for all his faults, he was a symbol of strength to the young cadets, but he did not know how to process that.

"Thank you," Is all Anfang could muster for a response. He looked down at the van swerving all over the snowy roads, accelerating down the streets towards the exit of town. "What do we do?"

The gryphon seemed lost, as he was expecting commands himself. "Well, um, I'm not sure." He flapped his wings hard, keeping up with Anfang. "Commander Joestar said to pursue out of sight. After that, I don't know."

Anfang snarled out loud and steadied out his wings to descend. "I say attack!"

Anfang did not look up to see the other gryphon's look, but he followed steadfast behind him. Anfang descended until he could almost touch the rooftop of the fleeing van and held his breath. He did not know if it would work, but he was going to attempt to run the vehicle off the road. After all, he knew he was stronger than most, and maybe a shove in the right direction would send the van off the road.

Anfang banked hard right, matching the speed and altitude of the automobile. He came up beside it and looked into the window, seeing the shocked faces of the humans inside. He then turned sharp left, his wing folded in, and collided with the hunk of metal.

The window shattered and the door crumpled in with the force of his body. The van fishtailed right, and then left again before spinning out. Anfang managed not to tumble to the ground, but righted himself and flicked his wings out to brake hard, landing on the ground with a run. He watched the van spin into the side of a snowy ditch with a loud crunch of machinery and metal. The airbags inside deployed, sending an audible bang that echoed in Anfang's eartuft.

The fellow gryphon guard landed next to him and drew his weapon with shaky talons, aiming it towards the vehicle. Anfang stepped in front of him and opened his wings slightly to approach the disfigured vehicle, cautiously watching.

The driver side door opened, and a human spilled out of the vehicle before collapsing on the ground. Anfang rushed over and pinned the human under his talons before surveying the scene inside. The other humans inside were either unconscious for the moment, or dead, he could not tell.

He turned his attention to the human under his large foretalons. "Speak!" He yelled. It gasped for air and laughed hysterically before saying something in a language he could not understand. Anfang grew angry and flipped the human over onto its back with ease. He stood over it with a talon to its throat and leaned his beak down. "I said speak!"

A male voice came from the human as it replied in English this time. "About what? The job is done!" The human laughed again and suddenly reached for his sidearm attached to his hip. Anfang quickly grabbed the male's wrist and broke it with ease, earning a sharp cry.

"What job is done?" Anfang questioned. His partner gryphon swept the car with sidearm in talon, containing the scene. The human simply laughed again and fell limp, looking up at the gruesome creature.

"Fuck you and all gryphon kind," the human said with a groan before rolling his head off to the side, unconscious. Anfang growled loudly, thinking about breaking the human's neck then and there, but they needed him for answers.

The goshawk took a step back and keyed in the radio. "Commander Joestar. The enemy vehicle is, um, down? It crashed,"

The radio was silent for minute and then clicked to life. "Location?" Asked Joseph's voice.

"Um, A108 leading towards the border, I think," he responded.

"Detain all suspects and await further instructions," Joseph commanded calmly.

Anfang could only imagine what he was dealing with at the moment. The fellow gryphon began to pull the humans out of the van and bind their arms with zip ties from his pack. Anfang quickly followed, helping to drag the people out and detaining them until everyone was lying on the cold snow in a line.

When they were done, Anfang noticed that his gryphon companion was trembling. Anfang cleared his throat. "What is your name?"

"It's Holger, sir," the goshawk responded, his voice quivering.

Anfang nodded and surveyed the scene. All was quiet for the moment, save for the distant sirens far away at the stadium. He still could not process the full reality of it all,

Colony

but he could tell Holger was in shock. Anfang tried to think of the proper thing to say. "Are you married?" He had been told to try asking common phrases like that with others to draw conversation.

Holger seemed slightly shocked but gulped and nodded. "Um, yeah. Her name's Tania. She's a human . . . I know it's a little unconventional, but I really love her, and she really loves me." Holger looked down at the row of unconscious terrorists. "I know gryphons are few and we really need to marry and reproduce with our own kind but, I just," he paused and looked up into Anfang's sharp green eyes. "I really love her. You know what that's like?"

Anfang thought about the question for a minute. It was not unheard of for gryphons to bond with humans, thanks to Thyra and Johnathen. But love? It was a complicated social construct to him, but he knew he had feelings for Thyra. He deduced that feeling was what love felt like. It was perplexing in its own nature, but he had finally figured out what it meant to others.

Anfang nodded. "I do."

Holger checked his gear and sat down on the snow-covered bank, taking a deep breath. "Well, I'm glad you understand."

The gryphon looked up at the stars overhead. Anfang found himself following Isaac's gaze and felt instantly calm. At the far edges of the city, the light pollution was all but absent and the true beauty of space showed brilliantly.

"Anfang, I know you're like, one of the firsts. A true combat gryphon . . . What does that feel like?"

The question weighed more heavily on Anfang than he expected. He hadn't thought about it before. How

345

different it would be to be a regular gryphon. "I am the first, but I not know how it feel. I simply am."

Joseph's voice crackled over the radio. "Anfang, there is a patrol car on the way to detain the suspects."

"Uh, copy," Anfang replied in a scripted voice. Over the months, Joseph had explained the ins and outs of basic radio communication and he was glad to be somewhat trained in the language at the moment.

"So, what do we do now?" Holger asked. "There's like, a lot of people and gryphons dead. We don't know what the hell happened."

Anfang shook his head and readjusted his leathery wings. "For now, we wait."

Chapter 26 Road To Nowhere

When Thyra awoke, the soft crashing of waves against the shoreline echoed in her eartufts. She lifted her head to find herself lying on a sandy beach. The sun was setting beyond the horizon of ocean before her. A cold, salty breeze ruffled her head feathers and caused Thyra to shiver.

Seagulls swept across the freezing waves, searching for their food. She heard cars on the outskirts pass by.She had no idea where she was, but everything was quiet and peaceful. Something about that was alarming. She dug her talons into the cold sand and took a deep breath as cognition slowly returned to her. She had no recollection of how she had arrived. An animalistic instinct had taken over and she had flown south until reaching this place.

She brought a talonfull of cold sand out in front of her, and slowly released it, watching the grains blow away in the strong breeze. Her talons were still encrusted with brownish red blood. The reality of what had happened slowly came back to her and she buckled in on herself. Thyra wept, hanging her head above the ground, watching the tears fall onto the soft beach sand.

"Thyra," A soft voice said behind her. Thyra spun to see Aadhya standing a short distance away from her. "Are you ok?"

Thyra shook her head and was immediately greeted with a body of feathers and soft down jacket. Aadhya held her friend tightly in a cocoon of warm comfort. Foretalons and wings pulled her tightly against the bearded vulture. Thyra realized that Aadhya must have been extremely patient, following her all this way, and waiting in the background for her to come back to reality. Thyra sobbed loudly into the comfort of her friend, letting her emotions go as Aadhya remained steadfast.

"What happened?" Thyra finally asked through gasps and tears.

"You fled after you killed one of the shooters," Aadhya responded simply. "I observed you flying away from the stadium, and I chased after you." She watched as Thyra cried out again and leaned in harder. "Thyra, it is perfectly natural to do what you did. I understand."

She saw it again and again in her minds eye. Flashes of colored light, blood, gryphons screaming as they fell from the sky, people running amok, and the cold stare of the young girl's dead eyes. A very small piece of her wanted to believe it was all just a wild dream, but she knew it was all too real. "Antonio . . . He's really dead, isn't he?"

"Yes. He's gone," Aadhya said in a low voice and pulled her back in tightly, fighting back her own tears. "I am glad you are alright. I do not know what I would do if I lost you too."

"Thank you, Addy," Thyra managed to muster out in between heavy gasps of breath. She closed her eyes and took a deep breath of the comforting nutmeg scent from Aadhya's feathers. Finally, she broke away from Aadhya's hug to gaze over the ocean once again.

The setting sun reflected a burnt orange glow over the dark blue water. The white caps of the waves crashed against the beach again and again. "I don't know what to do now," Thyra said.

"I do not know either," Aadhya admitted and sat down next to her friend. They both seemed lost at the moment.

Thyra wiped her eyes on a sleeve and sniffled, forcing herself to calm down. The sea itself was vast and unforgiving, but something about its strength captivated her. She felt the icy cold water brush across her bare foretalons.

"What do you think is happening now?" Thyra questioned.

Aadhya stared out at the setting sun and shook her head. "I would assume the responders are dealing with the dead, as grim as that sounds, it must be done. The citizens must feel dread, hurt, anger, and most of all, confusion." Aadhya paused in contemplation and after a moment of silence, she took a deep breath. "You need to contact home. Your husband, amongst others, are deeply worried for you."

"I know, I just…" Thyra shivered and closed her eyes again, watching the memories replay in her brain time and time again. "I don't know how to deal with the reality of it all. I don't want to go back yet."

The ever-patient bearded vulture wrapped a large white wing around Thyra. "But you must. Despite how you feel right now, you are a light of hope for many."

Thyra leaned into the warm confines of her embrace, but the comment confused her. "What do you mean by that? I'm just another gryphon. I'm nothing special." She said, knowing deep down that Aadhya was onto something, but still denying it.

"Sometimes you are more modest than I. Do you not realize what you have accomplished in your life?" Aadhya shook her head and looked down at the smaller gryphoness. "Your marriage very publicly defined that love knows no bounds, no matter the species, gender, or nationality. It gave confidence to even I, years ago."

Thyra was puzzled by the idea that her actions apparently had taken affect to a lot of gryphons, including Aadhya herself. "What do you mean, Addy? Were you in love?"

The bearded vulture smiled once again and looked across the amber ocean. "Yes. There was this gryphoness, Kita, who I met in my first years of playing Gryphball. She was an Egyptian vulture. Strong. Beautiful. Kind. And had such poise to her. It started out with mutual friendship. As the weeks went by, we found our relationship growing into something...more."

Addy's eyes seemed to glaze over as she stared off into the distance, recollecting her memories. "I never felt anything like I did when I was around Kita. Her smile warmed my heart. Her spirit soothed mine. She completed me like no other had. The other Gryphons on the team saw our relationship blossom, but they disapproved. They ridiculed us, despised us, and eventually we were fired from the team." Aadhya stopped and sighed.

"You were fired because of her?" Thyra said.

"It is difficult for me to admit this to you. I was not truthful about my reasons for coming to America and I have not told others of this. But I want you to know that Kita and I found confidence in our relationship from reading about you and Johnathen." Aadhya looked directly into Thyra's eyes. "See? You have been a symbol of inspiration more than you realize."

Thyra did not know how to respond. She was shocked, in more ways than one. She had always suspected Aadhya's orientation, but it was the first for her to admit it. On top of that, she was dealing with the death of hundreds weighing heavy on her heart, along with one of her best friends. She was sitting on a cold desolate beach far from her new home, with a worried husband and friends back at home. Yet, Aadhya was there pouring her heart out to her.

Aadhya gave her an encouraging smile. "We believe in you. Remain strong. Be our symbol of light to continue, please."

Thyra nodded, but there was still one question heavy on her mind. "What, what happened to Kita?"

Aadhya shook her head and tucked her wings back to her sides against the down jacket. "I do not know. I was banished from my hometown, and found refuge in Georgia. I have not seen her since." She pulled out her cell phone, checking the time. "Enough about that. We must find somewhere to rest. I do not want you flying in the shape you are in again," she commanded and turned her head to look at another passing car on the street behind them.

Thyra pulled out her phone as well and tried to call Johnathen, but for some reason, both her and Aadhya's phones could not get signal. She figured that their carrier could not get signal in whatever country they were in.

Aadhya and Thyra rose onto all fours. The temperature was dropping quickly as the sun set and Thyra could feel it through her thin sweater. She remembered leaving the jacket behind, using it in an attempt to stop Antonio's bleeding. She shivered once more and closed her eyes, trying not to lose herself again in the memory of his dying eyes.

"Come. I believe I saw a restaurant not far from here on the flight in," Aadhya said and began to walk away from the darkening shoreline.

The mention of the restaurant made Thyra's crop growl with hunger. She realized it had almost been a full day since she had eaten, even if it had been a blur.

Aadhya lifted into the air and Thyra followed close in tow. Immediately, she felt the strains in her wings. Every flight muscle complained with each stroke of her wings. Any question of returning that night left her mind as they descended on a single isolated building by the shoreline.

They entered the quaint restaurant and the human guests turned to watch the gryphons make their place at a table. A young female waitress approached the table with a smile and handed them leather-bound menus.

"Benvenuti ad Alleia! Posso iniziare con un aperitivo e un drink?" the woman said.

Thyra blinked, not knowing a lick of Italian.

Aadhya put the menu down for a moment before responding. "Assolutamente. avremo un carpaccio di manzo per iniziare e una bottiglia di vino rosso. Inoltre, possiamo usare il tuo telefono?"

The waitress smiled and said a quick response before heading off to the bar.

"Just how many languages are you fluent in?" Thyra asked.

"I only speak Indian and English fluently. My Italian is barely passable," Aadhya replied.

Within a minute, the waitress was back with two glasses of wine, and a common household wireless phone. She placed them on the table before them and took her leave.

Aadhya motioned to the phone and took her glass. "You should call Johnathen."

Thyra took a deep breath and pulled her cellphone out, looking up his new number. She dialed it into the headset and waited before hitting the call button. Her beak quivered with hesitation. There had been a lot going on in the past twenty four hours, and she did not know how to begin.

"Start with an I love you," Aadhya instructed.

Thyra nodded and hit send. She put the device up to her eartuft and fought back tears as it clicked on. "John. It's me... Yeah... I know I'm sorry... I love you... I'm sorry to keep you worrying I... Yeah, I don't know what happened I just fled... I had no control... Me neither but yes, I'm ok. Aadhya is here too... Yeah she's a good friend... I think we are somewhere in Italy... I have no clue but it's getting dark and I'm surprisingly sore... No, we are going to stay the night...Yeah, we are going to eat and find a place to rest. Are Rachel and the others ok?..." Thyra choked up, desperately trying to keep it together. "I know... ok...Ok I love you too." Thyra hung up the phone and rubbed her eyes with her foretalons before downing the red wine before her.

"Easy. You have not eaten in some time," Aadhya warned and read over the menu quickly.

"It'll help numb the pain. Besides, I think getting too drunk is the least of my problems right now," Thyra responded sharply.

Aadhya frowned and put down the menu. "These burdens are not yours to carry alone."

She was right. Thyra felt like she was the one responsible for everything that had happened, and it was only her world in jeopardy. The reality hurt everyone just as much as it hurt her. It was an eye opener. She could see the pain in

Aadhya's eyes, but she carried it like someone that had experienced such tragedy before.

"Hai deciso cosa vorresti mangiare?" came a sudden voice from beside them as the waitress returned.

"Portami la carbanara e il pollo Alfredo per lei," Aadhya replied before promptly handing their menus back to the server. The server left just as quickly as she had come, and they were alone except for the prying eyes of the other customers.

Thyra wondered why everyone was looking at them oddly. Surely there were some gryphons in whatever town they ended up in. Her eyes drifted up to a television and her heart skipped a beat. She saw Debra in full view of the camera in front of a podium, giving a speech. The volume was muted and the subtitles were in Italian.

"Aadhya, look!" Thyra exclaimed and pointed towards the television hanging above the bar. "What is she saying?"

"I will attempt to translate," Aadhya responded and started reading the subtitles. "Travesty... heavy hearts...Mayor assassination... Greifsburg is weeping... Terrorism and..." Aadhya was struggling.

Thyra stood up and rushed to the bar, drawing the already suspicious attention of the room towards her directly. "Turn it up! Please!" She begged the shocked bar tender. The heavily set mustached man quickly grabbed a remote and turned up the volume.

"...and the gathered information leads to a suspected attack by a local terrorism group, name unknown. Twenty individuals made the attack and we currently have four in our possession. The other sixteen are dead. We will not rest until we conclude who is behind the attack. Founder Anthony

Clearwater is dead as are the band members of Beast and Man. As of now, the total count is 194 humans dead, 145 injured, 323 gryphons dead, and 221 injured," Debra stopped and took a deep breath. "We will retaliate, and justice will be served. That is all."

Debra turned away from the podium as the press erupted into yelling questions. The camera switched back to an Italian news host and all was lost on Thyra's eartufts.

The same fury rose up inside Thyra that she had felt inside the stadium. Every feather stood on end. She felt herself consumed by pure anger and hatred. There were hundreds of gryphons dead, and it was at the hands of humans.

Thyra turned her eyes on every human in the restaurant. She felt an impulse to lash out against their kind. After all, their race was responsible for every hardship she had in her life, the cause of death for her best friend and her only true father.

"Thyra," Aadhya warned in a low tone, watching her friend quickly loose herself again. The small restaurant seemed to share the same fear as they watched the red tail with wide eyes.

"Thyra, sit," Aadhya commanded harshly. Thyra huffed through her nares and quickly approached the table.

"We need to leave now! We need to go up there and…"

"And do what, exactly?" Aadhya growled under her breath. She gripped the wine glass on the verge of shattering it. "I said sit!" Aadhya commanded again.

Thyra had never heard her use that tone with anyone, not even in the confrontation with Matthew. Thyra promptly sat in the seat, staring into the bearded vulture's fierce red and yellow eyes.

"Do you not think I am pissed as well?" Aadhya began in a low tone, leaning her head closer to Thyra's "Do you not think I have felt the urge to kill every human in sight? Rise up and avenge our fallen brothers and sisters? Act on pure instinct?" She paused for effect and took a deep breath. "It might feel good. Just ask Anfang. I want to fly in to be everyone's savior. That is who I am. But we cannot do anything right now. Calm yourself this instant."

It took the perfectly calm and sane Aadhya to finally express herself before Thyra was brought back down to reality. She turned to face the many frightened faces of the guests, many of which were gathering their jackets and leaving.

"We are hundreds of miles from home, tired, and starving, all thanks to your impromptu reactions. Now, we must regain what sanity we have left, fill our crops, and find shelter. Do you understand?" Aadhya asked, raising a cautious eye ridge. Thyra did not know who to fear more at this point, the unknown threat, or the wrath of her friend.

Thyra sat back in her seat and swallowed hard with a nod.

"Good." Aadhya grabbed her wine glass and quickly emptied it into her beak, yet another first Thyra had witnessed. Aadhya breathed heavily and sat back in her seat.

"Excuse," the frightened waitress said as she stood next to the table, holding a large tray of food. "I have pasta alfredo?"

Aadhya immediately put on her polite mask and motioned to Thyra with a single talon. "That would be hers. And please bring us some garlic bread."

Chapter 27 Sleeping At The Wheel

Thyra let out a deep sigh as Johnathen rubbed his hand over her tussled crest feathers. She lounged on their new couch with his one arm wrapped tightly around her and his other hand caressing her head. She knew she should be happy in his arms again in their immaculate new house filled with everything she could ever ask for, but a heavy dread hung over her heart. She could tell Johnathen shared the same emotion as he was staring blankly at the enormous flat screen television hanging above the fireplace.

Aadhya and Thyra had awoken the previous morning and flown for a full day back to their homesteads. Johnathen had greeted her with open arms and hadn't chastised her, but offered her nothing but support. She had tossed and turned in their bed together that whole night, not caching a wink of sleep.

Thyra felt a heavy pressure behind her eyes, yet still she could not rest. However, the ease of the new home and her husband next to her managed to keep her somewhat sane for the time being.

One frustration was that every time she tried to bring up what had happened, Johnathen quickly silenced her and tried to comfort her. Thyra realized he was having just as hard of a time accepting the grim reality of the situation as she was. For the moment, they relished in the comfort between them, although it was sure to be short-lived. Sooner or later, they would come to face the music.

Johnathen's stomach growled loudly, causing Thyra's eartufts to perk up. She lifted her head from his shoulder, earning an awkward chuckle. "Well, at least one thing remains constant. Always hungry," Johnathen said, trying to lighten the mood. "I could sure use some good schnitzel or pizza."

"Antonio made the best schnitzel I've ever tasted," Thyra replied with a smile, and then her voice grew grim. "I'll never taste it again. Or hear his positive voice. Or see him bring the team to victory..." She trailed off, fighting back tears.

Johnathen brought her head into his chest, and tried to comfort her once again. "I know hun, I know. There's nothing we can do."

"What about his funeral?" Thyra asked, sniffling once again.

"I don't know yet. None of us do. There's a lot of people, both gryphons and humans dead. They are still trying to figure it all out. Greifsburg's infrastructure isn't set up to..."

"I just want them to pay." Thyra clicked her beak and squeezed her talons together until they shook. "I want all of them to pay."

Johnathen placed a hand on top of her foretalons and gripped it. "We will find whoever is responsible and bring them to justice."

"I want blood for blood," Thyra replied and looked up at Johnathen to see that her husband seemed shocked by her response. It was unlike her to be violent.

"Hun, I'm sure we will do everything necessary, but an eye for an eye leaves the whole world bli…"

"Don't spout that shit at me!" Thyra quickly sat up and huffed through her nares, hackle feathers rising. She leapt from the couch and paced back and forth on the floor, like a lion locked in a cage. "I'm tired of waiting for evil people to get 'fair' trials. It's all weighed in humanity's favor. Hell, I don't know if we have proper rights in this European union! I want to see the responsible party hang!"

Johnathen tried to remain calm in his seat, watching as Thyra's talons scraped against the fresh hard wood floor. "We can't just go out and…"

"Yeah we can! Just like they did! Just like all the humans back home did! I'm tired of all you creatures just walking over us like we are animals!" Thyra yelled and stopped in front of Johnathen.

Her husband frowned and furrowed his brow. "I don't appreciate you taking this out on humanity as a whole. Not all of us are bad. You're married to one, to begin with, second…"

"Oh yeah? Not all humans are bad? Well, why the hell did I move halfway across the world to get away from them just to experience the same sort of resentment and discrimination as I did with The Gathering back home?" Thyra asked loudly. "And not even that, it's worse! Hundreds of gryphons died that night!" Johnathen did not have a response. "It seems like no matter where I go, humans will be humans! Disgusting, hateful, intolerant creatures!"

A knock came out the door, throwing off Thyra's line of thought. She looked at the door and huffed through her nares, turning away to stand in front of one of the gigantic floor-to-ceiling windows.

Johnathen sighed and stood up to go answer the door. Thyra heard conversation on the far side of the room, and recognized the voices belonged to Rachel and Aadhya. She took a deep breath to calm herself and turned to see the small kestrel carrying a couple thin boxes on her back like a pack mule.

"Hey girl. Um… I know everything like, sucks, but I brought your favorite pizza from that little place you really like," Rachel said somewhat meekly, her tone vastly different from her usual attitude. She then walked into the kitchen with Aadhya.

When Thyra did not reply immediately, Johnathen answered. "We really appreciate it. We were starving." He looked over to his wife with an encouraging smile. "Weren't we, hun?"

"Yeah," Thyra replied absently, not even attempting a smile of her own. She walked over to the kitchen as Aadhya took the boxes off Rachel's back and placed them on the island table.

Rachel stood on the tips of her hind toes and opened one of the boxes. She grinned and perked her eartufts. "Tomato and bacon thin crust with butter base. Just how you like it, Thyra. Oh! And plenty of parmesan too." She reached into her jacket pocket and pulled out heaps of packets to lay on the table.

"You know me too well," Thyra said absently and poured a healthy amount of the fake parmesan on a couple slices.

Johnathen went to the fridge and pulled out beers to pass around. Thyra bit into the still warm pie and swallowed it quickly. Usually she savored the flavor, but the meal tasted like nothing in her mouth. She ate the slice in silence.

Aadhya shared an occasional glance with Thyra as they all stood absently around the island table, barely acknowledging one another as they ate.

"Thyra," Aadhya broke the silence. Thyra looked up at the bearded vulture and the tension between them could be felt throughout the room. They had flown together for almost a full day without a word to each other and had not spoken since retreating to their homesteads. "I apologize for my outburst at the restaurant. I…"

"It's ok. I needed it," Thyra quickly responded.

The others were confused, as they had not shared any information about their time in Italy. Rachel seemed like she desperately wanted to press for details, but remained quiet for once. The rest of the meal went by without a single word, besides the occasional head nod as the group pretended to enjoy their pizza. Johnathen put away the leftovers in the fridge while the other gryphons gathered around the living room with beers clutched in talons.

"So, what happens now?" Rachel finally asked. She was good at bringing difficult questions to light.

"I don't know," Thyra responded. "I guess we just… continue." She paused and drank from her can. "It's all we can really do. Just exist."

"Sometimes it is ok to simply be," Aadhya responded. She looked out the window and then to the other gryphonesses. "We all need time to recover and find ourselves. We are here together, and for the moment, that is all that matters."

Another knock came at the door, interrupting everybody. They all suspected it was another teammate, or perhaps one of the Greifsburg guards. Johnathen was closest to the door and promptly opened it.

Debra stood at the threshold, holding a package under her arm and a blank expression. Thyra's heart skipped a beat as she saw the human step in and take off her snow covered boots.

"What are you doing here?" Thyra questioned first. Debra looked at the group with an absent gaze. The dark circles under her eyes and unkempt hair indicated she had not slept in days.

"Anthony left this on his desk with a note that said to give this to you immediately upon his death," Debra said and presented an envelope to Thyra.

The indication that this was sitting on his desk waiting to be delivered answered many questions she had about Anthony's odd behavior the night it all went down. He had thought something like this might happen.

She took the envelope and quickly opened it up. The others looked on with curiosity as she pulled out a single unlabeled USB stick. She held it in her foretalons and observed it. The stick seemed to be nothing special, though there was a blinking transmitter attached to the end.

"Here, I'll put it in the computer," Johnathen said and reached out his hand. Thyra somewhat reluctantly handed it over. Johnathen switched the input of the television over to his desktop and plugged the USB in.

"Out of everything you have to deal with right now, you needed to hand deliver this?" Thyra asked Debra.

Debra nodded and collapsed on the couch, clearly exhausted. "Yes. I would have brought it sooner if not for the press constantly surrounding my home. I was given clear instructions to bring it to you personally as soon as I was able to."

The indication that it had to be hand delivered by his vice president was enough to tell her the importance of the file locked inside the USB drive.

Johnathen took a couple steps back from his monitor. "Well, there is just one file. It's a video. Are you ready?" Everybody took their slightly comfortable places around the television and nodded. Johnathan hit the play button.

The scene began to play before them. It began with a wide view of Anthony's office. He was sitting patiently at his desk on the far right, and then the door to the left of the screen opened.

Debra opened the door to his sparsely decorated office and let herself in. "I hope I'm not interrupting anything,"

Anthony shook his head, turning his full attention to the short blond female before him. "Not at all. Just catching up on some local news. You know my door is always open." He motioned for her to take a seat. She closed the door behind her and sat down in the plush seat in front of his desk. Anthony leaned forward, folding his hands on the desk. "How did it go?"

"It's done," Debra said sternly, not looking away from Anthony's green eyes. "I just want to go on record that I don't agree with this."

Anthony nodded and took a deep breath. "I know you don't. You've expressed that several times, but I don't see another way."

"No other way?" Debra blurted. "You can just live the rest of your life out here! You can be with us and instruct us as this nation grows. I don't know if I..."

363

Anthony held up a hand. "Debra, I know between you, Joseph, and the others running this country that it will be left in good hands. I believe in you all, or I wouldn't be doing this." He leaned across to extend a hand to her. She had to choke back tears as she placed her hand in his. "I don't want to die in a hospital bed. I don't want my gryphons watching me fade away into a sickly old man who can't even feed himself anymore."

"But I thought the drugs were working, I thought..." Debra trailed off. Anthony squeezed her hand tighter and shook his head.

"They were, but the cancer is spreading faster than it ever has. I know my time is short. I thought I had cured the cancer with gryphon DNA, and I have extended my life decades past the original doctors' deadline, but not even the greatest minds and tech can stop death altogether," Anthony released her hand and sat back in his large leather chair. He looked up at a picture of himself with Thyra on the wall. "I have come to terms with my mortality. And this way, it will mean something. My death will bring the nation together, fortify them, strengthen them, and lead the way towards future expansion."

"But it will also bring violence and rage. I don't know how to mold that negative energy into something beneficial for gryphon kind," Debra expressed.

Anthony gave her a pitying look. "You will figure it out. I know it won't be easy. There will be war, blood spilled on all sides, very tricky politics, and several other unforeseen consequences. But I have no doubt that, in the end, the gryphons will have a large thriving country to call their own. A space safe from the threats of humanity and somewhere they can call home for generations to come," Anthony assured her. When Debra looked away, he frowned and leaned forward again. "Debra, if I wasn't absolutely sure we would win in the end, I wouldn't be doing this. But it's very apparent to everyone that this small track of land is not substantial enough and will never be enough."

"Then why don't you negotiate more! We can expand through proper means, we can…" Debra pleaded.

"You know as well as I do that it's not possible. You've been with me since this country's very inception. You know how much I had to sacrifice and how much effort it took to get this established. This small foothold is all I could do. This is all anyone could ever do for the gryphons." He sighed. "I gave everything for what we have now. The least I can do is give what little life I have left for the future of this country. For the future of my children."

"So, what do we do now?" Debra asked dully, trying to accept the reality of his situation.

Anthony shrugged his shoulders. "We live every day like it's our last. It's almost December and that means Christmas markets, celebrations, watching my daughter's home being completed, the accomplished gryphball stadium, and reveling in my final New Year's party." He gave her a pointed look. "It means that for now, you do your best not to think about my plans, okay? This is the final time we speak of this. Let's enjoy this last month together."

Anthony stretched before leaning back and opening his desk drawer. He withdrew a cigar box and raised the lid with a slow creek. Inside, there were two cigars left. He brought one to his nose and took in a deep breath of the rich whiskey tobacco aroma.

"Sir, if I may," Debra began.

Anthony chuckled and sliced the end off of his cigar carefully. "If it's about smoking being bad for my health, then you know how redundant that sounds. I basically signed my death certificate today."

Debra shook her head as Anthony pulled out a matchbox and struck a match, puffing on the fat cigar. He took his time, charring the edges until the office filled up with a thick plume of smoke.

"It's not that. It's that I question the morality of your decision," Debra said.

Anthony puffed on the cigar and sat back in his chair. He let the light buzz fill his head as he exhaled, tasting the subtle notes of oak on his tongue.

He thought about Debra's statement for a moment and stared off into the distance. "'The ends justify the means.' It's a quote as old as time, yet it's one of those morally gray truths we all have to face. What I plan to do is not inherently 'evil' as some would say. I believe the definition of evil is bringing others down to your level instead of helping others up. I believe what we are doing here is bringing them up," Anthony responded. "And some would say the road to hell is paved with good intentions, but I would have to believe in hell first to make that true." He puffed on his cigar again as the air grew thicker in his cramped office.

Debra stood and walked over to a window, opening the blinds and cracking it open. "And you are at peace knowing that once you're gone, there will be blood? Gryphons will die. Humans will die," she said, staring out the window across the snow covered hills.

"There isn't another way. I've calculated the different scenarios hundreds of times, trying to find an alternate plan. The reality of the situation is gryphon kind is at a huge disadvantage from the start. The dice are weighted against

their favor. No amount of fair man's game and honest work will allow them to grow as a species. If fighting doesn't start now, it's next decade, or the decade after that," Anthony argued.

He watched Debra take her place in the seat once again, rubbing her eyes. "Humankind has not advanced with mere good intentions and negotiations. Do you think America itself was established with humble roots and morally honest practices?" Anthony asked. Debra shook her head. "No. America was founded by lies, false treaties, empty promises, blood, and by developing significantly stronger weapons than its enemies."

"We only have Project Soldier and a handful of trained gryphons. Do you think that's enough to go up against the EU army?" Debra questioned, worry in her voice.

"We won't be facing the entire EU army. The cards are laid out for our fight be a repercussion of an act of terrorism against this country. The general public will be sympathetic of our, I mean your position, there will be UN court cases after that, and everything will weigh out in your favor. I promise you," Anthony said firmly. He took Debra's silence as a positive and ashed his cigar into the tray placed at the center of his desk.

"How do you think Thyra and Anfang will react?" Debra questioned.

"I'm trying to mold them into what I think they will be. If things go as expected, they will be angry and upset as the rest, Thyra maybe even more so, but I don't want to cause more harm than necessary. She will hate humans just as the rest of them will, but I don't think it will lead to her divorcing Johnathen. I don't want that. But as long as her anger and hatred is directed well, she will be fine," Anthony responded.

"As for Anfang?" He paused and exhaled, sending another plume of smoke into the air. "He will do what he does best. Kill."

The video feed cut promptly to the image of Anthony sitting directly before a camera. Everyone continued to hold their breath. Thyra briefly glanced over to Debra, seeing the shock and embarrassment on her face. She clearly had not known this video had been recorded.

"Thyra and others, when you are watching this, I will be gone," Anthony began. The scene was recorded from his personal camera on his computer. She could see the bookshelf from his office in the background, and even spotted a personal framed photo of her, Anfang, and Anthony all together. It was the same photo she had seen in the hidden labs.

"I'm sure you all are hurt, confused, and lost," Anthony stated with a heavy heart. *"And I hope that everyone you loved survived the attack, but if they didn't, know that their sacrifice was needed, and just."*

Thyra could not agree. She grew angrier by the second, but had no time to react as the video continued.

"The assault on the stadium that you have undoubtedly been through was prompted by myself, but don't pity the attackers. It took little to ignite the powder keg. There were individuals in the surrounding government that wished Greifsburg to not exist. They hated the idea that gryphons would populate a once thriving Austrian community, and were already conspiring against the city upon its inception. A little money and some suggestions in the right places was all it took for the avalanche to begin." Anthony paused and moved a couple of papers around.

Thyra held her breath as the rest of them stared
blankly at the television in disbelief.

*"As you saw in that video, the way I died was my
decision. It was a controlled travesty, so to speak, and I
entrust you amongst the others will keep this under wraps."*
Anthony paused again and rubbed his eyes. *"It was not an
easy decision, and the aftermath will be hard, but the
outcome will be beneficial for gryphon generations to come. I
hope the terrorists did not run amuck with their body count,
but I fear they might. To the rest of the world, this tragedy
will mean that our need for expansion will be justified,"*
Anthony said firmly, looking directly at the camera. He
checked the time on his wrist watched and sighed. *"I'm
running out of time. Once this video finishes, the file will
erase itself, and the sleeping soldier class will awaken with
very specific instructions."*

Anthony took a deep breath. *"War will come. They
will do what they are designed to do. They will invade, kill,
contain, and occupy to the best of their ability. But once
these soldier gryphons complete their tasks . . . I'm not quite
sure what their actions will be after that."* Anthony stopped
and chuckled in a dark manner.

*"Honestly, it's not my problem any more. It's been
my problem for decades, but now I'm handing off this heavy
torch to you all. I wanted you all to know about my plans
now, just as Debra does. She's going to need all the help she
can get fixing the mess after the dust settles. But, in the end,
you will see why this very difficult decision had to be
reached."*

He sat back in his leather seat and stared at the ceiling
for a moment. *"What I'm saying is, good luck."* Anthony
leaned forward and reached for his mouse. *"And never*

forget, Thyra, I love you, and I'm doing this for all gryphon kind. Anthony Clearwater, signing out."

The video went dark and Johnathen's computer sparked loudly several times. All the LED lights went dark inside the case, indicating the desktop was fried.

"You knew about this, Debra?" Johnathen asked, gritting his teeth. He stared over at the frightened women.

"I…I had no clue it would turn into the massacre that it did! I swear!" Debra defended herself as tears filled her eyes.

"But you knew there would be a body count! And you said nothing!" Johnathen yelled, standing from the couch.

Suddenly, the ground underneath the house shook. It felt like a miniature earthquake.

"What the hell is happening?" Rachel screeched and leapt off the couch.

"I don't know!" Thyra responded, standing steadfast on the wood flooring.

Within a minute, the earthquake stopped, and the house was filled with echoed screeching. The group all looked at one another and rushed to the windows, glancing out to see a dark mob of flurrying bodies rushing out of a single exit at the base of the mountain.

The group watched as hundreds of Anfang-like gryphons took to the skies and circled the area, casting a dark shadow on the town below them. Thyra's heart sunk deep in her chest as she realized that Anthony's commands were already a reality.

"Thyra, what's going to happen?" Rachel asked desperately.

The feral gryphons circled around the town, growing exponentially in numbers as the seconds ticked by. Thyra watched them organize, and then take off all together in a single direction against the sunset.

"War."

Made in the USA
Middletown, DE
04 January 2021